Also by ROBERT CONROY

RED INFERNO: 1945

RED INFERNO: 1945

A Novel

ROBERT CONROY

BALLANTINE BOOKS TRADE PAPERBACKS

NEW YORK

A Ballantine Books Trade Paperback Original

Copyright © 2010 by Robert Conroy

Published in the United States by Ballantine Books, an imprint of The Random House Publishing Group, a division of Random House, Inc., New York.

BALLANTINE and colophon are registered trademarks of Random House, Inc.

LIBRARY OF CONGRESS CATALOGING-IN-PUBLICATION DATA

Conroy, Robert (Joseph Robert)
Red inferno: 1945: a novel / Robert Conroy.
p. cm.
"A retelling of what might have happened had America done what Churchill, Patton, and others had wanted: ordered the Allied armies to move toward Berlin in an effort to keep Stalin from establishing rule over much of Europe. In *Red Inferno: 1945,* this act causes the Russians to turn on their allies, the U.S., causing a chaotic new phase of ruthless warfare."
ISBN 978-0-345-50606-1
1. World War, 1939–1945—Fiction. 2. United States—Foreign relations—Soviet Union—Fiction. 3. Soviet Union—Foreign relations—United States—Fiction. I. Title.
PS3553.O51986R43 2010   813'.54—dc22   2009050830

Printed in the United States of America

www.ballantinebooks.com

4 6 8 9 7 5

Book design by Barbara Bachman

INTRODUCTION

In April 1945, advance elements of the U.S. Army reached the Elbe River, a mere sixty miles from Berlin, and some units actually crossed it. As far as they could tell, there was nothing of substance between them and the capital of the Third Reich. The Germans had largely pulled back and were concentrating on defending Berlin from the Russians, who were massing on the Oder River to the city's east.

In London, Churchill wished to prevent the Soviet Union from becoming dominant in Europe and urged the Allies to go on to Berlin. Montgomery concurred. In the American military, Patton and his Third Army strained at the leash, while Simpson made plans for his Ninth Army to attack Berlin by way of Potsdam. The plans were bucked up to Bradley, who sent them to Eisenhower, while the Americans on the Elbe prepared to move forward.

In the Kremlin, Stalin was very concerned. In March of 1945, he had decided that "the Allies were trying to beat the Red Army to Berlin." Weeks later, he scolded Marshals Zhukov and Koniev: "Well now, who is going to take Berlin? Will we or the Allies?"

WE WILL NEVER know what might have been Stalin's reaction had Eisenhower and Truman agreed to Simpson's plan to "enlarge the Elbe River bridgehead to include Potsdam." Henry Kissinger described Stalin as a monster who had slaughtered millions by this time, and one who was a supreme and implacable realist. Yet he was also frightened of the specter of a Soviet Union surrounded by non-Communist countries. He made no distinction between the fascists and the capitalists. They were all his enemies. Further, Stalin knew about the atomic bomb and feared that the Allies would use it to contain and defeat the Communist revolution.

For these reasons, Stalin was reneging on the agreements made at Yalta, which included freedom for those nations "liberated" by the Soviets and who weren't part of the Axis.

Stalin may have had one nervous breakdown due to the 1940 Nazi invasion of the Soviet Union, and may have been on the verge of a second at the time the Allies were contemplating a move on to Berlin. So what would an unstable Stalin have done if confronted by an American advance on Berlin?

All of the preceding is history. Eisenhower did not give Simpson permission to move toward Potsdam. But what if the American armies actually had attempted to enter Berlin? Instead of the fretful peace that presaged the Cold War, there is the strong probability that Stalin would have unleashed something like an "Operation Red Inferno" against the Allies in the spring of 1945.

THE UNITS INVOLVED at Potsdam are all fictitious, as are all the characters assigned to them. To the best of my knowledge, there were no such units active in World War II.

RED INFERNO: 1945

CHAPTER 1

The hastily gathered flotilla of small motor launches plowed through the calm water of the Elbe River as their outboards churned toward the rapidly closing enemy-held ground ahead. The helmeted men inside the collection of small boats hunched down, as if willing themselves to be invisible and, thus, out of harm's way.

This was when soldiers were the most vulnerable, and the tightly packed men in each of the dozen assorted craft knew that a hit anywhere would impact on something soft, meaty, and human. In a perverse and illogical way, the American soldiers hoped they would be opposed only by rifles and machine guns. Anything, they thought, but the damn German 88 mm antitank guns that could instantly turn their frail craft into flaming coffins.

But where were the Germans? The April morning was clear and the GIs knew the little boats must stand out vividly to enemy eyes that must be watching them. Yet the only sound they heard was the roar of the straining motors and the splash of the waves only inches below the freeboard. The launches were overcrowded, with almost twenty stuffed into some of them. The men themselves were strangely silent. This was water. Their environment was land. Afloat, they felt useless. On land you could dig a hole and hide, or even run, but what the hell did you do on water?

Soldiers would look up and glance forward, trying to pick out the places where terror would emerge but saw nothing frightening. The German countryside was green and friendly, like something from a postcard. Where could there be terror? At this crossing point, the Elbe was less than a quarter mile of blue-green water. Yet it might as well have been the English Channel for the fear it caused.

"Lieutenant, get your head down," yelled Sergeant Jack Logan. "Please," he amended, belatedly conscious of the difference in their ranks and that he shouldn't show up any officer, even a brand-new replacement like Second Lieutenant David Singer.

"I wanna see, Sarge. I wanna be the first Jewish officer east of the Elbe and maybe the first in Berlin."

The young sergeant chuckled and a few of the other men nervously joined in. Sergeant Logan was big for an infantryman, nearly six feet tall, stocky and muscular, and with a shock of red hair that was kept out of view by his helmet. He had open, even features, and some, particularly his mom, described him as having a "friendly" face, whatever the hell that meant. He certainly wasn't friendly with a rifle in his hands. Logan contrasted sharply with the shorter young officer's pale skin and thin blond hair. Lieutenant Singer would be bald before he was forty.

Logan liked young Lieutenant David Singer. He had arrived only a couple of days earlier and was replacing another young lieutenant who'd gotten badly wounded. It was hard to realize that he, the old man of the platoon, was only a year older than the lieutenant's twenty-three years. War had such a wonderful way of aging its participants.

"Can this thing go faster?" came a lament from the rear of the launch. Logan thought the voice was Crawford's, but he couldn't tell.

Lieutenant Singer responded. "If you want, you can get out and push."

This was greeted with a few more nervous giggles and an offer to paddle with helmets. The jokes were stupid, but they broke the tension. Anything to hide the fact that they could be dead in an instant.

The water shallowed and the boat slowed, finally crunching up on the mud embankments. The men hurled themselves from their unwelcome craft and ran up the low embankment, fanning out like the veterans they were.

There was no need for either Singer or Logan to give any orders, and the two men prudently concentrated on staying out of everyone's way. To his left and right the other craft disgorged their human cargoes as well. In a matter of moments, almost half of D Company was safely across and forming a defensive perimeter.

The commandeered boats began their return to the west bank of the Elbe and would return again and again with more and more soldiers. On the far shore, engineers were assembling a pontoon bridge.

Singer fidgeted with his rifle. "Sergeant Logan."

"What, sir?"

"Where are the Germans?"

Logan took off his helmet and wiped his head quickly before replacing it. He had this unreasonable fear that his red hair could be seen from quite a distance and, therefore, made a great aiming point. When he didn't have a helmet on, he made certain he wore a cap. Regulations said a soldier had to wear headgear when outdoors, although a lot of men ignored the rule. Not Logan. He always wore something on his head.

Lead elements of the 54th Infantry Division were across the Elbe River and, if the reports were true, there was nothing but green grass and woodland between them and Berlin and, just maybe, an end to the war.

"Doesn't look like they mind us being here, now do they sir?"

This was totally unlike a crossing of the river a couple of days earlier when elements of the 2nd Armored Division had run into stiff resistance at Magdeburg, and had returned to the western shore before crossing a second time and establishing a beachhead. On the other hand, the 83rd Infantry at Barby had crossed some lead elements unopposed, just like this.

Logan squatted on the ground and Singer plopped down beside him. Logan was the platoon sergeant, and to the woefully inexperienced Singer he was not only friendly, but knowledgeable and willing to share that hard-learned knowledge. Young lieutenants were sometimes ignored by the veterans. Lieutenants had to earn the respect of their men.

Singer grinned sheepishly. "I can't say I'm disappointed. Some others might be lusting for their first time in combat, but it wouldn't bother me if we postponed it for a very long time. Like until I was ninety-seven."

Logan chuckled. "Count me in on that."

He looked about and satisfied himself that his men were in proper position. He then took out his entrenching tool and began to dig yet another hole in the sacred land of the Third Reich. They had safely crossed the Elbe and, if his knowledge of European geography was not too far off, were only about sixty miles from Berlin. He had heard the rumors that they would go on toward the German capital, but he'd also heard rumors that they would be held back so the Russkies could have a little revenge on the Nazis.

With a little luck, Logan thought, he and his men could stay here forever and the Germans would continue to ignore them. With a little more luck the war would be over in a few days or a few weeks at most, and then he could begin to worry about stuff that was really important, like going home, finishing school, getting a job, and getting laid. Not necessarily in that order.

Logan also knew that someone killed on the last day of a war was as dead as someone killed on the first. As the war seemed to draw to its inevitable conclusion, there was a concerted effort on the part of his men to avoid becoming that last man. They weren't cowards or failing to do their duty, it was just that no one wanted to die, especially now. The war was almost over and they would be going home soon— unless they had to fight the Japs, and that would really be for shit. But no, he thought, concentrate on staying alive and getting home, and let the future take care of itself. The hell with heroes, was the watchword. Don't die in Germany. Not now.

Logan glanced behind him to where another load of soldiers was about to land as the small craft continued their shuttle. Soon they would be too strong a force to dislodge except by a major attack, and the Germans seemed to have too little left for that to occur. By the end of the day the engineers would have at least one pontoon bridge across the river, and some armor would have been brought over, and maybe artillery too if the Germans did decide to show up.

In a little while, they would also have to contend with the swarms of refugees who clogged every road. They seemed to emerge from every rock and would be drawn to the new bridge like flies to garbage in their haste to get away from the advancing Russians. The human refuse was pathetic, but they could not spend time with them. They had a war to end.

Like a dog, Logan sniffed the air. There was no smell of smoke and death. American artillery chose that moment to open up. Shells shrieked overhead and hit something a few miles away. They waited for return fire, but nothing happened. It was weird. Where the hell were the Germans!

• • •

HARRY TRUMAN PACED angrily around his desk in the Oval Office which, until recently, belonged to his late predecessor. He needed fresh air and a drink, some bourbon and water, light on the water. Real light on the water. He was being lied to and condescended to and it galled him all to hell.

At least he was making some headway with his so-called key advisers. They were Roosevelt's men and were only gradually coming to the reality that their loyalty was to the office of the president and not a dead man. Truman was a small man physically, but a terrier when it came to temperament. He was always being underestimated since, unlike some of the dandies from the State Department and the graduates of West Point and Annapolis, he'd never been to college. They didn't know all the time he'd spent reading and learning, acquiring a superb but informal education.

He'd also been annoyed that secrets, such as the atomic bomb and the Yalta agreements, had been kept from him, but that was the way FDR operated.

Damn it to hell, he thought. He was so poorly prepared for his new job that he wanted to curse, which he did frequently and colorfully, much to the consternation of some of FDR's people, especially those from the State Department.

Most galling to him was the fact that the Soviet Union's Josef Stalin, America's erstwhile ally, was lying through his damned Communist teeth. He had agreed to free elections in those areas his armies would conquer that were not part of Hitler's Axis. Instead, Stalin was gobbling up countries like a child taking candy at Easter and seemed to be daring Truman to do something about it. Free elections were not about to happen in Poland or anywhere else.

Stalin apparently thought Truman was weak, inexperienced, and ineffective. Inexperienced, Truman admitted, but by damn, he was not weak and would not be ineffective.

Berlin was the final straw. Stalin had said he would not attack Berlin and now he was approaching the German capital with a massive army. The Yalta agreements called for Germany to be divided into four zones—American, Russian, French, and British—and that Russia could advance west of Berlin to the Elbe River. The agreements also said that Berlin would be divided among the four powers.

But with Stalin lying about everything, would he share Berlin once he took it? Stalin could not be permitted to keep what Americans had rightfully earned with their blood. American soldiers were across the Elbe, although in small numbers, and some of his advisers were urging him to send them on to Berlin to show that America would not be pushed around.

But that could also mean a confrontation with the Red Army. Damn.

"Mr. President?"

"Yes, General Marshall?" The army's highest-ranking and most respected officer was one of the few who'd shown him total respect from the outset.

"Have you made a decision?"

Truman took a deep breath. First choice was to stop at the Elbe, as the agreements called for and Eisenhower wanted. Second choice was to rush full bore to Berlin and damn the consequences.

However, a third alternative had been proposed, and Truman liked it. He would send a small force, maybe two divisions, in the direction of Berlin to signal America's intent to take and keep what she was entitled to. Two divisions should not threaten Stalin and, if they ran into heavy German resistance or the Red Army, they could either stop or pull back.

Stalin was testing him. He would not fail the test.

"Yes, General, I have made up my mind. Send two divisions toward Berlin."

CHAPTER 2

As Steve Burke entered his small Georgetown apartment, he devoutly wished the evening had been more of a success. While he had taken the lovely and amazingly sensuous Natalie Holt out to dinner and a movie, and while there was the implied promise that he might be able to do it again, there were no tangible results for his efforts. Of course, an old Laurel and Hardy comedy was not exactly his first choice for a movie that would lead to a night of sexual adventure, but it had been her idea and he had acquiesced. And here it was, not even midnight, and he was at home, once again alone with his thoughts and books.

He flipped his brimmed cap on the couch and took off his short Eisenhower jacket. In a city of uniforms, he knew he looked nothing like an officer in the army. Burke was over six feet tall, but so thin he almost looked frail, and his hair was thin as well. Indeed, the only thing thick on him were the lenses of his glasses. No, he did not look like a warrior. He knew he looked—and felt—more like an Ichabod Crane type of college professor dressed up in a uniform for a costume party.

And whoever started the rumor that any male, single or not, would be gobbled up by the hordes of female secretaries and clerks who vastly outnumbered the men in Washington must have been joking. Burke was very single, and since coming to Washington his social life had been far less than spectacular. As to any sexual life, well, he might as well have been in a monastery.

Yet Natalie Holt, a staffer of some sort in the State Department, had agreed to go out with him. He had first seen her at a party at the Russian embassy and watched from a discreet distance as a small horde of real military and diplomatic types had fawned and fussed over her. And why not? She was tall, dark-haired, lithe, intelligent, wide-eyed, lovely, educated, and doubtless unattainable.

He had managed an introduction and struck up a brief conversation. That one talk led to a longer one and, in ensuing weeks, a number of casual dutch treat lunches that she seemed to enjoy. Her apparent pleasure made him ecstatic. He realized he had a crush on her. They had found common ground in their mutual expertise on Russia, and he was delighted to realize that someone as lovely as she could be so intelligent and educated.

The lunches were followed by an offer to take her out on a real date, which, to Steve's astonishment, she accepted. So why the hell did she want to see a Laurel and Hardy film? Because, she had answered, it made her happy and these times were so gloomy that she sometimes needed something silly to lift her spirits. Silly like going out with him, he wondered, and banished the idea. He was slipping off his tie when the phone rang.

"Lieutenant Colonel Burke," he answered, still uncomfortable with the title the army had conferred on him. A mature woman's voice asked if he could confirm that he was indeed the Lieutenant Colonel Steven Burke of the Russian Section of the War Plans department, and he assured her he was. She then informed him that General Marshall would like to see him immediately.

"Which General Marshall would that be?" he asked innocently. There were a lot of generals in Washington, D.C.

There was the sound of gentle, middle-aged feminine laughter. "Colonel, you are being summoned by the chief of staff."

He flipped a mental coin. Either the caller was telling the truth or someone was playing a joke on him. He felt it was the latter. He was about to make a snide comment when the woman continued. "Let me reiterate; you are the Lieutenant Colonel Burke who is a Russian expert on the War Plans staff, are you not?"

"Yes."

"Well, there are a number of Colonel Burkes around as well as, just perhaps, more than one General Marshall, and I so wanted to make certain I had the right one too." The caller had teased him gently, but he still felt his face flush. "Yes, Colonel, the General Marshall who is chief of staff of the U.S. Army does wish to see you, and right now. Does that pose a problem?"

"No, ma'am," he said weakly.

"Fine. A staff car will be around for you in fifteen minutes." With that, the woman hung up.

Fifteen minutes, Burke thought. If it's a gag, I can go along with it for fifteen minutes, but I'll be damned if I'll wait up all night.

The car arrived in ten.

BURKE STOOD AT attention but squirmed inwardly as General Marshall eyed him coldly. Despite being in the War Plans department and working in the Pentagon, Burke had never before met the man, although he had seen him on a number of occasions. Marshall was aloof, austere, correct, and had a reputation, perhaps undeserved, for personal coldness.

"Relax and sit down, Colonel."

Burke did sit as he was told, although it was difficult to relax in the presence of the four-star general who gave directions to both Eisenhower and, when possible, to MacArthur, who thought himself superior to everyone. He had been driven directly to Marshall's office at the Pentagon and an aide had whisked him immediately into the general's presence. He still had no idea why he was there in the spartan office.

"Colonel, you are purported to be an expert on Russia. Why?"

The bluntness of the question startled Burke, but he recovered. "Sir, prior to enlisting, I was a professor of Russian history at Notre Dame. The subject has always fascinated me, particularly the upheavals of the revolution and after."

"How did you get into War Plans?"

"After Pearl Harbor, I thought I should enlist. Since the army doesn't want thirty-six-year-old privates and I was too old for normal officer training, I was turned down. Fortunately, a friend of mine knew Eisenhower and submitted a résumé. The general thought the War Plans group should have someone with my background on the staff, and I was appointed." He flushed slightly. "I was given the immediate rank of captain, and as the war effort grew, I was promoted to major and, most recently of course, to lieutenant colonel."

"Are you comfortable with that, Colonel?"

"Not really, General. I like to think I'm doing a good job, but I keep telling myself I'm a college professor in a costume. I'm not a professional soldier. Sir, I am no more a soldier then I am a Martian, and I sometimes feel uncomfortable when people confuse me with anyone who has actually served his country and been in combat."

Marshall's expression softened. "And you doubtless don't want to be a professional soldier for the rest of your life, or actually see combat, either. Yet you're an expert on the Russian military?"

"Sir, I have to amend that. I have memorized all the names, weapons, statistics, and organizations that I could get my hands on, but no, I am not an expert on the Russian army. There are others who are far more qualified than I am in that area. My area of expertise is in Russian culture, the current Russian mentality, and how they got that way. The history of Russia, sir, is one of tumult and torment, and they are a people who behave quite differently from us.

"Sir, I was told that military intelligence can rather easily tell of a country's capabilities, but gauging its intent to use those capabilities is quite another matter, and that's where my so-called expertise comes in. Just because a nation possesses an army does not necessarily indicate it will use it."

"Have you studied Stalin?" Marshall asked softly.

"Yes, sir. As extensively as is possible."

"Ever met him? Ever been to Russia?"

"No to both questions, General. I hope to rectify that after the war."

"Colonel, my staff tells me you are rather unique and somewhat unpopular because of opinions you hold regarding our erstwhile ally, Russia, and its leader. Would you please give me your opinion regarding Stalin's state of mind."

Wow, Burke thought. Where the hell is this going? "General, in my opinion Stalin is certifiably insane. He is a cruel and calculating mass murderer. If he were in this country, he would be locked up in an insane asylum, hanged for his crimes, or be some gangland boss in Chicago."

Marshall almost smiled. "Colonel, a few months ago, our political leaders met and carved up postwar Europe. Now it looks like the man FDR used to refer to as Uncle Joe may be taking a larger piece of the pie then he's entitled to. Does that surprise you?"

"Absolutely not, sir. That would be consistent with his behavior."

Marshall nodded. "It now appears that he might not let us have our share of Berlin. Along with that, he's taking over countries that rightly belong to their inhabitants. In order to forestall this, I have been ordered to send a military force to Berlin to try and enter that city. As a rationale, we are telling Stalin that we are doing it to continue pressure on the Germans, thus preventing them from swinging their armies around to take on the advancing Russian armies. However, there is concern that Stalin will see this as a provocative attempt on our part to take credit for ending the war, credit that he believes is rightfully his. In your opinion, what do you think he would perceive and how would he react?"

Burke paled. He swallowed and composed himself. "Sir, I said the man is mad and a criminal and I stand by that, which means he is impossible to predict logically. Among other things, he is paranoid, and yes, he might just see it as a power grab on our part. As to how he might react, good God, sir, the man is normally very patient and calculating, but, on rare occasions, has appeared to act irrationally. What will he do? I have no idea."

"Guess," Marshall said firmly.

Burke took a deep breath and thought, what the hell. "He's a bully and if confronted could easily back down and wait for an opportunity to try again. I rather think that would make everyone happy." Marshall did not respond, but seemed to nod almost imperceptibly. "If he doesn't back down, he could use his massive army to swat our force like flies."

"Which, Colonel?" Marshall insisted. "I want your opinion."

Burke tried not to stammer. "He operates from a position of strength. He cannot afford to show weakness. I think he'll use force to expel us from Berlin. God help those poor soldiers."

Marshall rose and did not appear to notice it when a thoroughly stunned Burke remained seated. "Colonel, thank you for your help. You will be driven back to your apartment. Be in my office at eight in the morning."

"BERLIN," WHOOPED PFC Tommy Crawford, a gangly kid from Georgia. "We goin' to Berlin!"

Sitting on the ground, Sergeant Jack Logan could only shake his head in wonderment. Where the hell did some of the kids think they were going? To the circus? Crawford was a scarcely literate nineteen-year-old from some squalid little place south of Atlanta and, until a few months ago, had never been more then ten miles from his home. Now he had been to New York, London, Paris, and maybe was on his way to Berlin on his government-paid world tour. Logan still didn't think Crawford realized all these cities were in Europe. Maybe he didn't realize what Europe was?

"Sergeant?"

"Yeah, Lieutenant?" To Logan, Singer looked shaken and pale.

"Tell me about combat."

Logan looked at the line of tanks forming to head out, and the trucks that would carry the infantry. The Sherman tanks looked strong and dangerous, but the cloth-sided trucks appeared horribly vulnerable. Even the Shermans' strength was somewhat illusory. The stubby little 75 mm guns they carried just weren't strong enough to knock out the newest and biggest kraut tanks, and their thin armor and high silhouettes made them easy victims.

"What do you mean, sir?"

"You've been in combat, haven't you? What's it like? How do you react?"

Logan patted the ground. "Have a seat, sir." When Singer made himself comfortable, he continued. "Lieutenant, the first time I was in so-called combat it was a few months ago and a mortar shell landed a couple of hundred yards away, and we all fell flat and hugged the ground for as long as we could. We'd still be lying there if someone hadn't told us it was safe to get up. Y'know, I have no idea where the shell came from or if it was even German and not one of our own.

"The second time, there was a report of a sniper in a grove in front of us and the entire platoon fired twenty or thirty rounds each into the trees. I don't know if we hit the sniper, if there ever was one, but we scared the hell out of a bunch of trees and it felt damn good to be firing back."

"You mean you've never seen a German in all this time?" Singer was incredulous.

"Sure I have. Dead ones and prisoners. But have I ever had the privilege of confronting one who was coming at me with bayonet fixed or aiming up a shot at me? No. Maybe I did see a few of them. Sometimes you see motion in the night where there isn't supposed to be any, or you see shapes running like hell in the distance, but you can't be certain whether they are krauts or civilians or, in the case of nighttime, just a case of the jitters."

"You're not a big help, Sergeant. Captain Dimitri said you were supposed to advise me." Singer's grin was shaky.

"Sorry, Lieutenant."

Logan hadn't told him the whole truth. He would have to learn for himself about bowel-emptying fear and the horror of seeing a friend blown to little red pieces. There were some things you had to live for yourself and could not describe for others. Sergeant Logan, D Company, and the entire division had been in Europe since January 1945, a mere four months. At least they had missed out on the big German attack in the Ardennes, but they and he had been involved in a number of minor skirmishes that could be as deadly as one of those major and climactic battles historians were going to discuss for generations.

Singer laughed quietly. "Captain Dimitri told me to stick with you because you were such a combat veteran."

Captain Dimitri chose that moment to stop by and squatted on the ground next to them. Singer remembered not to stand up and snap to attention like so many new men did. Dimitri, like most experienced officers, did not like actions that drew unnecessary attention to them in a combat zone. Dimitri also carried a rifle instead of the .45 automatic he was entitled to, again so he wouldn't stand out to a sniper. Snipers loved shooting officers.

"What's so funny?" Dimitri asked. "You people haven't decided that this monumental adventure we are about to depart on is a joke, now, have you?"

Before Lieutenant Singer could form a reply, Logan answered. "No, sir, we haven't gotten that far. We were just discussing why I am qualified as a combat instructor. But now that you mention it, this does have all the earmarks of a fiasco."

Dimitri half smiled. "Better a fiasco than a tragedy. But why, Sergeant Logan?"

"Captain, because we're sending one long column up one thin road toward Berlin. It can be blocked or ambushed at any place or at any time. Didn't the British get their asses all chewed up trying to do something similar near Arnhem a while ago? Worse, it looks like someone got armor and mounted infantry all mixed up together, although at least the lead infantry are in half-tracks, which will provide some protection against small arms if they're shot at. Unfortunately, the rest of us have to ride in trucks, and canvas sides won't stop a peashooter. Frankly, sir, I'd rather walk."

"Can't," said Dimitri. "We wouldn't be able to keep up with the high-speed convoy that will soon be racing down those excellent German roads toward Berlin."

Both Logan and Singer caught the note of sarcasm in the captain's voice. Nobody was going to race. The move forward would be slow and cautious. "At least," Singer said, "we won't be in the lead group, where the action will likely take place."

Captain Dimitri rose to leave and shouldered his carbine. "Tell him, Sergeant Logan," he said as he walked on.

"Tell me what?" Singer asked as the captain departed. He had the terrible feeling that the captain and the sergeant, who went back a ways together, were laughing at him. Somehow, he didn't really mind it. They were the experienced soldiers and not he, and, despite Logan's protestations, the sergeant was a solid and respected soldier.

"Sir," said Logan, "if you were a German unit setting up an ambush, which would you prefer to attack, the heavily armored and protected head of the column, or those soft, fat, and dumb trucks?"

Singer shook his head sadly. "You go for the trucks. Then the head of the column would have to hold up and wait until things got sorted out. Damn. Maybe we should volunteer for point. I promised my wife's parents that I'd keep her as a JAP, and I'd like a chance to keep that promise."

"What's a JAP?" Logan asked, feeling that Singer was teasing him.

Singer grinned. "Jewish American Princess. And I do think it'd be best to be the lead dog."

"That's right," said Logan. "And if they do set up a roadblock to delay the point of the column, then the rest of us will have to stop and wait for it to be cleared. *Sitting ducks* is the phrase I think fits best."

"Shit. Well, intelligence says the Germans are gone."

"Lieutenant," laughed Logan, "with all respects to the fine men in G-2, I will believe that when pigs fly."

Singer was puzzled. "Sergeant Logan, how come you're not an officer? You are certainly intelligent enough, and I understand you do have a couple years of college."

Logan shrugged. "At one time I thought I was going to be an officer. I tested out okay and put in the papers for Officer Candidate
School down at Fort Benning, but we all got shipped out before anything could happen. My tough luck, I guess. At any rate, I can't complain. I got my three stripes fast enough and, now that I'm a platoon
sergeant, I think they owe me one more."

Singer got up and left, saying he was going to write a quick note to
his wife before they moved out, and Logan wondered what kind of
woman he'd married. Lieutenant Singer was short and a little plump.
Logan wondered if his wife was short and plump as well. He shook his
head. No way he should start fantasizing about his lieutenant's unseen
bride. He stood and shook the dirt off the seat of his pants. Time to
get his squad together and make sure the new lieutenant didn't get lost
on the way to Berlin.

Logan guessed he was flattered that it was he who was assigned
as Singer's babysitter until the man got the necessary experience.
First Sergeant Krenski was just as happy to have the virgin Lieutenant Singer out of the way until he learned the lay of the land and
could actually begin leading.

Logan looked again at the line of tanks now moving slowly down
the road preparatory to jumping off for Berlin. The tanks, even with
their high silhouettes and stubby guns, still looked strong and powerful. So how come he had this feeling of foreboding?

THE SMALL ROOM in the Kremlin was brightly lit by the sun streaming through the high glass windows, which had been built in the days
before electricity. The glare caused Josef Stalin to blink as he entered.
The other two men ignored the premier's momentary discomfort as
he moved behind the desk and seated himself. Stalin, who was quite
short, liked to be seated when in the company of others. The first of
the two men was the bespectacled Vyacheslav Mikhailovich Molotov,
who at age fifty-five held the official title of Commissar for Foreign Affairs, although he fulfilled whatever duties Stalin assigned him.

The second man was Lavrentii Pavlovich Beria, the squinty-eyed
and reptilian chief of state security, the dreaded NKVD. He held the
rank of marshal. Beria's army consisted of border guards and, most im-

portant, those men whose duty was to hold the regular army commanders responsible for their loyalty. Virtually at will or whim, they could shoot deserters or execute officers for failure to accomplish tasks. It hardly mattered whether the tasks were achievable. The NKVD considered failure as treason. Along with enjoying torturing people, rumor also had it that Beria was fond of small children.

Molotov and Beria waited impassively while Stalin stripped the tobacco from a couple of cigarettes, tamped the shreds into the bowl of an old pipe he habitually used, and lighted it. Each of the two men knew his place. They were Stalin's key advisers, but not trusted ones. Stalin trusted no one. Each knew that one misstep could result in his own personal destruction. They both knew what screaming horrors were in store for those who found themselves the targets of Stalin's wrath, and whose lives ended in the basement of the NKVD's Lubyanka prison. Even Beria, who administered the Lubyanka, knew he was only a word away from dying there.

Stalin blew out a cloud of noxious smoke. "You've read this man Truman's message. What do you think?"

Molotov knew he had to speak first. "Incredible," he said, and Beria nodded.

"Comrade Molotov, I expected more of a response."

Molotov found himself sweating and knew it wasn't the heat. "It is as if it were Churchill speaking and not Truman. With Roosevelt dead, there appears to be a degree of confusion in the White House." Again, Beria nodded.

"Comrade Molotov, do you know Truman?"

"I met him briefly, but I do not know him well at all. Few do. As you know, he came from nowhere, a political nothing."

It was not quite a lie. Molotov had racked his brain and been unable to recall meeting Truman at any time, but concluded that it was prudent to say he must have met the former senator from Missouri who was, until very recently, the almost anonymous vice president of the United States.

Stalin relit his pipe. "Yet I am expected to believe this nonsense? That, in the name of our sacred and fraternal alliance against the Hitlerites, the Americans are going to send two full divisions into Berlin as a favor to us? I suspect the treacherous hand of Churchill in this American action. He has coerced the Americans into taking Berlin from the rear and robbing us of our glory in being the ones to take it from the Hitlerites. I suspect that the American divisions will not only try to liberate Berlin, but will also attempt to liberate Hitler and his coterie of lackeys, and use them for their own purposes. Hitler has tried for so very long to split the alliance and sue for a separate peace, and now it appears he has succeeded."

"But why, Comrade Stalin?" Beria asked. Only his eyes betrayed any sense of nervousness.

Stalin stared at him coldly. "Because Churchill hates us almost as much as he hates the Nazis, perhaps even more. Now that Germany is defeated, he feels he can move to stop us from becoming too powerful, and he has convinced this Truman thing to go along. Do you doubt me?"

"No," they answered in unison.

"It is utter arrogance. We will not let them rob us of our rightful vengeance. It will be stopped."

Stalin rose and looked out the window onto the sunny but empty courtyard. "I will contact Marshals Zhukov and Koniev to discuss the final drive on Berlin. We have waited years for this moment and we will not be denied. We will be the ones to take Berlin and destroy the Hitlerite nest, not the Americans. We will not let them liberate a thing. The Americans will be stopped before Berlin, whatever the consequences and regardless of the lies they give as their intentions."

Stalin glanced at the clock on the wall. It was midafternoon. "In a few hours, we will commence the greatest bombardment the world has ever seen. Then more then two and a half million men will assault Berlin and drive toward the Elbe. I will inform both Zhukov and Koniev that they are to expedite the pincers movement behind Berlin and seal off the rear approaches to Berlin."

Molotov, normally impassive, paled. "But, Comrade Stalin, what if the Americans are already in Berlin or within the pincers?"

Stalin smiled tightly. "Then so be it. The Americans will squeal very loudly and learn a lesson."

"WHAT IS THE comrade tank commander staring at this fine night, this most wonderful of evenings, which signals the end of the Nazi empire?"

Commander Sergei Suslov climbed down from the dark turret of the T34 tank and stretched his tired muscles like a cat.

"Comrade driver," he said with a tired grin to his slightly insane crewman Ivan Latsis, "I was staring at Germany across the lovely Oder River and wondering how much longer they can possibly hold out against our armies."

They glanced across the clearly visible river where hundreds of flashes of light on the heights overlooking them showed where shells were impacting with horrible regularity. Each man had to speak clearly, as the noise level was deafening. Suslov wondered how it could be endured.

"They are not responding to our barrage," Latsis said.

If that was the case, Suslov could not blame them. His company, his brigade, were part of the largest army the world had ever seen. It had more men, tanks, guns, and planes than could have ever been dreamed of only a few years prior, and had been accumulating and gathering its strength along the Oder for what would surely be the final assault on Berlin, only thirty miles away.

Suslov said, "They have very likely withdrawn from their fortifications, which we are so intently bombarding, and will not return to them until the advance units start to cross the Oder. Only then will they respond to our invitation to do battle."

The Germans on the hills had an excellent view of the Russian preparations, but had chosen not to waste ammunition on them or to give away the location of their few remaining heavy guns. Suslov could not complain about that decision on their part, nor could he complain about the fact that he and his armored brigade would not be part of the first wave. Instead, they would follow once a bridgehead had been secured and would be part of the breakout.

Latsis was constantly brooding, his face looking particularly dour in the flickering lights of the distant explosions. "I hear a rumor that we won't be allowed to attack Berlin, that the honor will fall to others."

Suslov shrugged and tried not to see the hate on the other man's face. "It would be an honor I could do without. Tanks are meant to fight in the open, not in streets. I had all the city fighting I could ever want at Stalingrad."

Latsis agreed reluctantly. The name of Stalingrad was both sacred and evocative of slaughter on a mass scale. Suslov had taken another tank and crew through the battle, been wounded, and returned to duty as this tank's new commander a few months earlier.

"Even so," Latsis insisted, "I would like the opportunity to destroy a portion of the city and the people inside it."

"I know," Suslov said gently.

Latsis had told them several times what had happened to his village when the Nazis took it. It was not just that the people had been killed, but how they had died. *Slaughtered* was the better word, although even that was inadequate to describe the rape and torture that had preceded death in so many cases. Latsis was obsessed with the fact that both his mother and his sister had been gang-raped and mutilated by a bunch of Nazis, and left to die. He had found through the handful of survivors that his thirteen-year-old sister had lived in screaming agony for a few days after, but that his mother had died almost immediately.

Suslov slapped Latsis on the shoulder in an attempt to break his driver's dark mood. "Don't worry, there's more of Germany than just one city. You'll have your opportunity to make them squeal."

Latsis grunted and moved away, leaving Suslov to wonder just what was in store for those Germans in Berlin. There were hundreds of thousands of Russians with stories just as horrible as the one Latsis told. As for himself, he had no love for the Nazis, nor hatred either. He just wanted them dead so he could go home. That is, if there was a home for him anywhere in this mutilated world.

CHAPTER 3

Major General Walter Bedell Smith, "Beetle" to his friends, was a short and belligerent man who some compared to a bulldog with a bad attitude. As chief of staff to Dwight David Eisenhower, he served at Ike's pleasure and frequently did the tough and dirty jobs that preserved his boss's benevolent and affable reputation. His input was received and respected. That included this afternoon's meeting between Omar Bradley, who commanded the huge Twelfth Army Group, and Eisenhower, who commanded all the Allied military forces in Europe except the Russians.

"Shut the door, Beetle." Smith did as Ike asked.

Eisenhower was grim as he paced the floor of his office. "Brad, what do you think?" Ike asked.

"I don't like it one bit." Bradley was tall and lean. He was rarely seen smiling in public. Despite this, he was considered a friendly man, and was delighted when soldiers started calling him the "GI's General."

Ike nodded. "Good, so what have you done about it?"

Bradley walked to the map. "I've given Simpson orders that he is to do as much as is humanly possible to avoid casualties and unexpected contact with either the Germans or the Reds. The 17th Armored and 54th Infantry divisions have crossed the Elbe above Magdeburg and, unlike the previous crossing, have met almost no resistance. Unless you object, they will be the force that moves on Berlin. They will pick up the autobahn and follow it toward Berlin. However, just south and west of Potsdam, the autobahn branches, with one route going to the Spandau district, which is on the outskirts. We will take the Spandau route and not charge into the heart of the battle for the city."

Ike nodded and lit a cigarette. For the last year he had been chain-smoking. "Good."

Bradley continued. "That will put us in Berlin proper, but a long ways from where Hitler is hiding and where the Reds will be making their main assault. The river, the Havel, will help separate us from that battle and any accidental involvement."

"Are they up to strength?" Beetle asked.

"The 17th Armored is a new division with very little combat experience, and is pretty well up to snuff as far as men and equipment go, but the 54th has been in action since January and has been worn down a bit, but it's still in good shape. I'm sending Chris Miller from my staff to command. He's a good, solid man who won't make any mistakes and who won't go off like a cowboy."

Ike liked Bradley's thinking. It would satisfy the political need to be in Berlin without actually being in the dangerous heart of the city. Hopefully, the Reds would understand the American army was not going to interfere with their vengeance.

Smith stared at the map and smiled. "Gatow?"

This time the corners of Bradley's mouth did rise in satisfaction. Gatow, along with Tempelhof, was one of the two major airports serving Berlin, and it was in the Spandau district, right along the line of American advance.

"Well," Bradley said. "I couldn't see us not having an airport to use if we actually got there. Tempelhof's on the other side of town and the Russians will own it soon enough, but Gatow could easily be ours."

"Brad, what if our boys can't advance? The Germans could slow them fairly easily."

"Ike, my orders to Simpson and to Miller and those boys are very simple. They go to Spandau safely or not at all. This is not a suicide mission and they are not, under any circumstances, to do anything foolish. If German resistance is too great, they are to stop and dig in. If it looks like they are going to get overwhelmed by the Germans, they are to cut bait and run back to the Elbe as fast as their legs will carry them."

Smith shook his head. "Truman might not like that."

"Screw Truman," said Ike, and Bradley laughed. Eisenhower's carefully nurtured image as a fresh-faced country boy was not quite correct. Decades of military service had taught him to swear fluently.

Bradley teased. "Ike, you'd better not let the boys from *Life* magazine hear you talk like that."

Ike grinned the now famous cheerful smile. "Fuck *Life*."

•   •   •

THE RIPPING SCREECH and clang of bullets hitting metal jarred them from their trancelike state in the truck to one of total animal alert. "Out!" screamed Logan. "Out, out, out!"

The horrifying noise continued, only now it was joined with the sounds of men screaming and crying out in fear and pain. The soldiers in the truck needed no urging as they tumbled to the ground and rolled or crawled to any fold in the earth that might provide some cover from the bullets. As the German machine guns continued, there was still more screaming.

Where the hell was the firing coming from? Logan thought. A Sherman about a hundred yards ahead responded with its own machine gun and Logan saw the tracers arc toward a farmhouse on a low hill a quarter mile away and splatter on its stone walls. In a second, the Sherman's main gun fired and a section of the house blew away, followed by other pieces of the building as additional tank guns found the target. The machine guns inside responded with a quick burst and then fell silent as the building disintegrated into a pile of burning rubble.

Logan rolled over to where Singer lay staring wide-eyed at the house, or what was left of it. "Hey, Lieutenant, so how'd you like your first taste of battle?" Despite the apparent casualness of the question, Logan was shaking from the suddenness of the attack.

"Jesus, Logan. I was just looking at that particular house when I saw the krauts open fire from a window. God, it was so sudden!"

And so violent, Logan thought.

"And how the hell did they get inside our patrols?" Singer asked, his hands shaking too.

"Not difficult at all for a couple of Nazi fanatics who want to commit suicide. Our patrols can't be everywhere, so they probably just hid in a basement or a closet until our men passed by."

Logan checked his men and found them all unhurt except for a couple who complained about being trampled in the mad rush to get out of the truck. They were still alive and there was nervous joking about it. Logan looked forward a couple of trucks and grabbed Singer's arm.

"Come on."

Unceremoniously, he pulled the lieutenant to the truck that had recently passed them on the other side of the divided road. It had borne the brunt of the raking fire by the gunner in the house, and a half-dozen bodies lay sprawled about it, horribly torn and bleeding profusely. Medics had separated the dead and dying from those who might live, and were attempting to stop the blood that seemed to flow like thick red water from fire hydrants.

Singer paled at the sight and the stench of the smelly gore, which was already darkening and beginning to congeal. "It's awful, Logan," he said and tried not to gag.

"I know, Lieutenant, that's why I wanted you to see it. That's what could happen if you fuck up when you're in charge. In this case, no one did anything wrong and certainly these guys did nothing to deserve to be shot to pieces like this. Hell, it could have been us as easily as them."

Logan turned toward the now totally destroyed building. The actions of those few Nazi soldiers had slowed the entire column.

Dimitri's loud voice penetrated their thoughts. "Singer, Logan, take some men up there and check it out."

They gathered the platoon and moved up the hill, weapons at the ready. The farmhouse had been flattened and was smoking, but death could still be hiding in the ruins. They fanned out and approached it from three sides. Once close, it appeared that nothing was alive in the rubble. A charred body stuck grotesquely out of the ruins, but that was it. A blackened arm slowly moved. Someone yelled that it was still alive. A couple of men fired at the body, blowing it to bits. Satisfied, they turned and returned to the stalled column.

Attacks had happened before, but never so close. Always it was a distant chattering of machine-gun fire from up ahead or way behind, or maybe the threat of mines in the road. But never anything like this. Never right beside them. Along the way they had passed a couple of burned-out buildings and a destroyed truck, but everything human had been picked up before they arrived.

Logan shook his head grimly. "Y'know what's worse, Lieutenant. I'm damn glad these guys weren't from D Company. I don't feel guilty about it. It's like them being from another unit makes it easier to deal with."

Singer understood. "Yeah, like they're not even in our army and this really didn't happen."

They returned to their own truck and the men gathered about it. "Like I said, Lieutenant, now what do you think of combat?"

"It's shit, Sergeant Logan, really, truly shit."

Logan nodded. "Now will someone tell me just what the hell we're doing here? Everybody says we're going to fall back to the Elbe when the krauts surrender, so why did our guys have to get killed and wounded when they should have been safe and happy on the other side of that damn river? Whose idea was this?" he said angrily. "Who the hell is trying to prove a point with Stalin?"

Singer nodded. Captain Dimitri had read a letter from a general named Miller in which he spelled out the goals and objectives of what he referred to as Miller Force. It didn't make anybody happier. The war was almost over and they were sticking their necks out. It wasn't fair.

ELISABETH WOLF LURCHED, seemingly drunkenly, as she forced her aching and weary legs to move. Walking more than a couple of hundred feet was something she'd been unable to do for several weeks, and the inactivity had made her soft. The lack of proper food—or any food at all, for that matter—had made her weak, and her young and once nimble joints were racked with pain. Her head pounded from pain as she and her young nephew Pauli followed the bearded and one-legged man who was going to save them. Save them from what? she wondered as her eyes tried to focus. From the Russians, she remembered. From death.

If only she knew his name, Elisabeth thought dizzily. She had been brought up to believe in God, and she wondered if the one-legged man was a saint or an angel. Maybe he was the Archangel Michael? A few feet away, the man hobbled along on his crutch, crippled in body but leading them through strength and force of will.

Behind her, she heard the rumble and thunder of the battle for the city of Berlin, the center of Nazi Germany. For several days, the artillery had been incessant and the bombing had been a nonstop drumming that shook the earth and caused buildings to disintegrate on top of their occupants, burying and crushing the people inside. It would seem a miracle if anyone was alive. Yet there were many people still hiding in their basements and shelters while others, like Pauli and herself, attempted to flee westward from the burning city.

A sharper noise intruded as something large exploded in the distance. She resisted the urge to turn around and gaze at the billowing black clouds that sometimes blotted out the sun. In her confusion, she thought she would be like Lot's wife and be turned into a pillar of salt for her sin of inquisitiveness.

There were about fifty refugees. They stopped and she looked up ahead to see what the cause was. It was another roadblock, and the jackals from Himmler's SS were searching for deserters. The slack body of a young man hung from a telephone pole, and she tried in vain to keep a wide-eyed Pauli from seeing it. The corpse's eyes were open and his purple tongue stuck out.

A golden-haired and well-fed SS officer in his late twenties, clad in a shockingly clean black uniform, walked through the little crowd and sniffed at them in dissatisfaction. There were no deserters here. Only the old, the lame, a few women, and a couple of children. He stood in front of Elisabeth and stared, and she looked back at him although her eyes continued to have a hard time focusing. In her condition she was physically thin and shapeless and was wearing the clothing of a small man. She also probably looked quite mad.

"And what is this," the officer sneered. "Male or female?"

A couple of soldiers snickered, and the officer ran his hand down the outside of her shirt, searching for breasts. Once she had had a nice petite figure. Now she was a shapeless stick.

"I can't tell," the SS man pronounced to his men in mock confusion. He laughed at his own joke and his men laughed along. Then he jammed his hand down Elisabeth's slacks and grabbed her crotch so hard that she yelped in pain and shock. "Female!" the officer proclaimed triumphantly. "But so wasted she isn't worth fucking." He waved to the one-legged man who was glaring at him. "Cripple, get these people out of here. Heil Hitler!"

Elisabeth stood transfixed by the brutal actions of the SS officer until the one-legged man limped up to her. Steadying himself with his crutch, he patted her cheek with his hand. She was almost in shock from the incident.

"It's all right, little girl. It is all a bad dream that will soon be ending." He looked at her sunken cheeks and pale skin. "When did you last eat?" he asked.

"She feeds me," Pauli chirped with the innocence of his six years.

"Ah," the man said, understanding. The girl had been giving her scant supply of food to the boy. "What is your name?" he commanded her, and Elisabeth told him.

"Good," he said. "I am Wolfgang von Schumann. Once I commanded a brigade of tanks. Now I shepherd this little flock. Do you understand me?" Elisabeth nodded dreamily. She was almost out of energy and the world was starting to revolve. Von Schumann continued. "In a few minutes, I am going to call a halt for the night. We will distribute what food we have. I will see that the boy has his share and you will eat yours and not give it away. Do you understand? If you love this boy, you will help yourself stay alive for him."

Elisabeth blinked and started to cry. "Yes," she whimpered. She saw that von Schumann was about the same age as her late father, maybe fifty. He had a stern face, but his eyes were sad, not cruel.

Von Schumann gestured for a couple of women to help Elisabeth, who was about to collapse. "Perhaps we can even find some extra food to help you regain your strength."

As the women led Elisabeth and Pauli away, motion in the distance caught von Schumann's eye. A line of military vehicles, including tanks, was driving on the autobahn a couple of miles away. His military experience and his excellent eyesight told him the tanks were not Panzers and the silhouette was not that of a Russian T34. It was too high. He sucked in his breath. Was it possible they were American Shermans? From this distance, he couldn't be certain. But what if they were? God in heaven, what would happen now? The Russian army was on both sides and behind his group. In front of him was the once lovely city of Potsdam. When the two forces did link up, he wanted to be on the American side.

He felt a tug at his sleeve. "Sir, what's wrong with Aunt Lis?"

Von Schumann sighed. The girl had fainted and was being half carried, half dragged into a building by the women who had been holding her up. She was young and presumably healthy. Some food, rest, and water would help immeasurably. He remembered that the boy's name was Pauli.

"Pauli, I'm sure all she needs is a little rest and some food."

"Was I bad for eating her food?" the boy asked.

Von Schumann laughed at the innocence of children. It felt good to laugh. "No, Pauli, your Aunt Lis was very good for sharing it with you."

CHAPTER 4

Harry Truman finished reading his briefing papers and put his wire-rimmed glasses on the desk. He was exhausted, but no more so than the man in front of him.

"General Marshall, what about our boys and Berlin?"

"Mr. President, they are still making progress, although it is much slower than we had hoped."

"They're not taking heavy casualties, are they? I don't want that. Certainly not at this stage." Truman had been having second thoughts about the decision to send soldiers toward Berlin. The realization that he was solely responsible for whatever befell those men was a heavy one.

"Actually no, sir. While there have been some casualties, the rate has been quite light. They are simply moving slowly and cautiously, checking for mines and possible ambushes. Also, the roads and bridges have been pounded by the Air Corps, so there's quite a bit of maintenance to perform as they move out. They are just about ready to move into the suburbs of Berlin."

Truman snorted. He hated the term *light casualties.* To him it was an oxymoron. Casualties were light unless, of course, you were one of them, in which case casualties just became heavy. He'd seen casualties firsthand as an artillery officer in World War I and hated the thought of causing them, light or not. He thought it was a good thing that America's new president was actually a combat veteran who understood the human cost. Too many presidents, FDR included, had never seen real combat.

"At which point," Truman said, "if I read these maps correctly, they will be very close to the northern arm of the Russian army."

"Correct."

Truman put his glasses back on and stared at his secretary of state, Ed Stettinius. "Ed, what about Stalin? Has he responded yet to our note?"

"Not yet, sir."

Truman scowled. "I certainly hope the man has received it and has given his generals notice of our intentions."

Stettinius almost looked affronted. "Sir, I handed it to Ambassador Gromyko myself. We also directed several other copies through the Swiss and the Swedes. He has it, sir. Stalin is just being his usual mysterious self."

Marshall thought that Stalin was a little more devious than mysterious but held his tongue. Stalin's intentions would become evident soon enough. He hoped to God that Colonel Burke's assessment of Stalin's aggressive intentions would prove wrong.

THE SOVIET EMBASSY was housed in a large, old, and grim building on 16th Street in Washington, and the party was in full and rowdy swing when Steve Burke arrived with Natalie Holt on his arm. He noticed with amusement the number of Marxist-Leninists who were goggle-eyed at the sight of Natalie's off-the-shoulder green silk dress, which showed both a wonderful shoulder and the hint of well-rounded cleavage. Due to the cloth shortages that decreed shorter hemlines, it also showed a surprising amount of extremely lovely leg. He couldn't decide whether he liked their overt attention or was jealous. And why would he be jealous in the first place? It wasn't like he and Natalie were engaged or anything. He decided he was acting like an adolescent.

"Natalie, I think they would like to coexist peacefully with you."

"How charming," she said, smiling affably, not at all put off by the stares. With her looks, he thought it was doubtless something she had gotten used to. "But they can't have me, and it's all their fault for eliminating the aristocracy. Now they have nothing to strive for."

Invitations to the Soviet reception had not been difficult to get. Several had been left with the Russian section of the War Plans department and it would not have surprised Burke if he saw some of his colleagues bellying up to the very large and crowded open bar.

The party's ostensible purpose was to commemorate both the arrival of a new cultural attaché, who was doubtless a spy, and to celebrate what everyone was referring to as the Allies' mutual final push on Berlin. When Berlin was finally taken, it was said, Hitler would be displayed in a cage in the Kremlin where he could spend the rest of his days sitting in his own shit. Would serve the bastard right, was the consensus, and Burke agreed.

Burke suspected that the real reason for the party was the fear that the war would be over and many of the Russian staffers sent home to their socialist paradises before all the booze in North America could be consumed. Tonight, the Reds were making a valiant effort to solve this horrendous problem. It was only nine in the evening and several Russians, civilian and military, were staggering about in advanced states of drunkenness.

Natalie squeezed his arm tightly as they navigated through the crowded hall and toward the buffet table. They each took a glass of champagne—decadent French, of course—and a plate of hors d'oeuvres.

Steve pushed a shrimp into his mouth. "Do the peasants eat this well in Minsk and Pinsk, I wonder?"

"Of course they do, Steven. Have you forgotten it's a workers' paradise? These are merely their leftovers shipped over to make us capitalist swine envious. I just can't believe someone ate all the caviar already."

"Ah," he said and turned as a scuffle broke out across the room. He was beginning to have second thoughts about whether he should have asked her to accompany him as he heard the sound of glass breaking. His presence at the party was more or less a command from General Marshall's office, because Marshall wanted several Russian experts to mingle and try to read what the Reds were doing and thinking. In particular, the higher-ups wanted to know of any stray thoughts or comments regarding the two divisions called Miller Force now en route to Berlin. This had been reported by various overzealous American newspapers as an attempt for the Americans to get there first and take the city. General Marshall was upset by this interpretation and had urged the State Department to further reassure the Russians that this was not the intent.

Burke's immediate impression was that the effort to gather information was an utter waste of time. There were no major players from either government present this evening. No Gromyko, and nobody from the upper levels of the American or other Allied governments to set the tone and go through the elaborate dance of conveying messages via statecraft. Both the hosts and the guests were mid-level officials from a number of countries who were taking advantage of a free feed and the challenges of an inexhaustible supply of liquor.

"This is amazing," Natalie said. "They're behaving like there's no tomorrow. Of course, if they're sent back to the Soviet Union, they could be right."

In the distance a small musical group began playing something that could scarcely be heard above the din and was barely identifiable as music.

A Russian officer whose name Burke scarcely remembered lurched drunkenly in his direction.

"Burke!" he said. The Russian's breath was an alcoholic stench, and Steve recoiled while Natalie turned her head and laughed. "War almost over. We kill fucking Hitler, no?"

"Colonel Korzov, your English is improving remarkably." Korzov rewarded Burke with a huge hug and lurched away, but not before trying to peer down the front of Natalie's dress. He looked much like a three-legged bear.

"You've charmed him," Natalie said, continuing to laugh. Burke decided he was glad he had brought her, although he would now have to have his uniform cleaned. Korzov had spilled a drink on his pants and there were food stains on the front of his Eisenhower jacket as well.

"Everybody loves me," he said and then froze. There was something wrong with his jacket. Carefully, he patted his chest and confirmed what his mind had told him. There was something inside his jacket. Korzov had slipped him what felt like a sheet of paper.

"Steven, is something the matter?" Natalie looked worried at the sudden change in his behavior.

He leaned down and whispered in her ear. She nodded understanding. "Excuse me, please," he said loudly. "I have to go to the restroom. I don't think I should have had that shrimp."

He had said that last part for anyone who might have been listening, although common sense told him that it wasn't necessary and no one could possibly be eavesdropping on them in the din.

The men's john was almost empty and he had no problem finding a stall. Deciding to play the role to the hilt, he closed the door, dropped

his pants, and seated himself on the fairly clean commode before re-
trieving the document. The paper was a folded sheet of loose-leaf on
which a message had been written by hand and in Russian. He
scowled and tried to read it. The penmanship was crude and not at all
like the scholarly works he was used to perusing.

The words came slowly and, as he translated them in his mind,
shocked him and filled him with dread. He read them a second time,
and then a third before he was satisfied that he had made no mistake.
With shaking hands, he folded the paper again and stuck it in his pants
pocket. Now he felt the enormity of what he knew and the preposter-
ousness of his own situation. If there was a more vulnerable position
for a human being than enthroned on a toilet, he couldn't think of
one. Yet here he was in the men's room of the Soviet embassy with his
pants literally down around his ankles and a message from a traitor in
his pocket. The NKVD could burst in and kill him without his lifting a
finger or his pants.

Fearing the tramp of footsteps, he flushed the toilet, straightened
his clothing, and stepped quickly out into the hall. Natalie was speaking with several Russians and they were not pleased to see him return.
When she took his arm again, the Soviets grudgingly departed toward
the bar.

"Are you all right?"

"No. It's my stomach," he lied, again speaking for any unseen lis-
teners. "I think we should leave immediately."

She blinked and nodded understanding, and they stepped out into
the cool of the night. "I've got to contact Marshall," he said, and her
eyes widened.

"The chief of staff? Now? My God, Steve, what was in that
message?"

They had found his car and he opened the door for her. He deferred
answering until they were well under way. "The Reds," he finally told
her, "are mad as hell that we are sending those two divisions toward
Berlin and are going to attack them at first contact."

They drove in silence in the direction of the Potomac River and Arlington. Steve concentrated on his driving while Natalie sat stunned.
Finally, after several glances in the rearview of his '36 Buick, Steve nervously broached a concern.

"Natalie, I think we're being followed." It was a line out of a dumb movie and he felt foolish for saying it, but the lights of the same car had been behind him for some time. Natalie turned and looked behind her.

"Turn right on Constitution," she commanded. It would take them past the White House and toward the river. The Soviet embassy was only a few blocks from the White House. Ironically, they had driven around the White House on their way toward Constitution Avenue. He obeyed and saw the mystery car turn as well.

"Okay," she said. "Keep going in this direction until you hit the road that leads to the Memorial Bridge and the cemetery."

Steve did as instructed and watched as the car kept pace with them. "Natalie, could someone have seen Korzov give me the message?" The answer did not have to be spoken. If he was being followed then someone had indeed seen it pass. It also meant they were in danger. Whoever was following them had no real idea where he was headed. However, they would figure it out in a couple of minutes.

They made the bridge and crossed over into Arlington. There the road split. Turn right and they would be in a civilian area. Turn left and they would be headed toward Fort Myer and the newly constructed Pentagon. It would be a clear signal of intent to whoever was following them. He turned left.

The car followed and seemed to speed up. "Hang on," Steve yelled. Hang on to what? he thought inanely as he jammed the accelerator to the floor and felt the big car's surge of power.

The other vehicle continued to gain. For what seemed an eternity, the chase went on. Now he could see the lighted gate to Fort Myer and two guards, probably armed. He urged the Buick forward and leaned on the horn. In the mirror he saw a couple of winking lights and realized to his horror that they were being shot at. Something clanged. The car had been hit.

As the car careened wildly toward the gate, Steve saw the first two guards drawing pistols and two more men with rifles appearing from the shadows. He waited until the last second and slammed on the brakes. The mystery car did an abrupt and high-speed U-turn and sped away.

An MP with a .45 automatic drawn and aimed at them approached cautiously. He lowered the weapon only slightly when he saw Burke's rank. "Sir, just what is going on?"

"Get the officer of the guard," Burke ordered.

A second MP took up station on the other side of the car. "He's on his way, Colonel."

A few moments later, a very young lieutenant arrived and seemed stunned when Burke told him to contact General Marshall immediately.

DESPITE THE MP lieutenant's understandable reluctance to call the general at that late hour, they finally did make telephone contact with someone at Marshall's residence, and Burke insisted that it was extremely important that a lowly lieutenant colonel see the chief of staff immediately.

Marshall received them in his library and in uniform. The short drive from the gate had given the man a chance to dress.

Marshall glanced at Natalie and seemed to glare briefly at the stains on Burke's uniform. Whatever Burke had, he clearly thought it both too important to wait for morning and to change into a clean uniform.

"All right, Colonel, what do you have for me?"

Burke quickly explained about the party and how Korzov had delivered the message. He handed the folded paper to Marshall, who looked at it briefly while Burke gave a summary translation and then put it aside.

"Burke, you are certain this says what you think it does?"

"I am, but please have the translation confirmed by others."

Natalie interrupted. "I've read it as well and I agree with Steve's interpretation."

If Marshall thought it strange that she, a civilian and a female, had been allowed to see such an important document, he didn't show it. "You have a Russian background?" the general finally asked her.

"I was born there," she answered. "My parents were minor nobility and what are now referred to as White Russians. Those of us who survived the revolution and the wars left in the 1920s and made it to the United States. My first language was Russian and I am now employed at the State Department."

Marshall nodded. "What do you think of Stalin?" he asked her.

"He is a thief and a murderer." She said this with a venom that caused Marshall to blink. "He had several members of my family, including my father and sister, executed for the crime of being born."

Marshall turned to Burke. "This Korzov, is he reliable?"

"General, I have no idea. I've spoken to him a couple of times, but never anything like this. Until tonight, I really wasn't certain he knew I existed. I have no idea why he chose to give me the message. On the other hand, I know of no reason for him to lie about something like this. What does he have to gain?"

"A bullet to the back of the head," said Natalie. "If he's lucky."

Marshall rose and Burke knew he was being dismissed. "I don't know why he selected you either, although perhaps out of desperation. Why he did it doesn't matter if the information is correct. The point is, you were chosen and now I've got to do something about it. You did the right thing by coming here right away, even though—" he smiled briefly—"you'd ordinarily fail inspection. Because of the attack on you, you will both stay on the post until we are certain that you are safe."

Back in the car and heading toward her temporary quarters in Fort Myer, Natalie rested her head on the back of the car seat and turned toward Burke. They both were exhausted by the events of the night.

"Two divisions," she said. "The papers are full of terms like that and have been since this damn war started. And that's what you've been talking about, but what on earth are two divisions? How many men are we talking about? How many lives are involved in this potential tragedy?"

"Maybe thirty thousand, all told."

Natalie paled. "So many? If the Reds attack, it will not just be a slap by Stalin, will it? If he does attack them there will be a great many dead and wounded, won't there?"

He agreed grudgingly. How could he say otherwise?

Natalie persisted. "Then we'll be at war with Russia, won't we?"

He saw a tear roll down her cheek. He put his arm around her shoulder, and she rested her head alongside his. "Yes, Natalie, by this time tomorrow we could be at war with the Soviet Union."

CHAPTER 5

The meeting in the Oval Office convened just before dawn. Truman looked alert and fresh while Stettinius and Stimson looked tired and disheveled. Marshall, of course, looked impeccable although working hard to hide his fatigue. The previous night had been long. Burke, standing behind the general, had managed to find a clean uniform and looked reasonably presentable.

Truman looked around, glared, and began. "All right, who is this source and just how good is he? I find it rather incredible that what General Marshall describes as a mid-level functionary at the Soviet embassy would even have access to such inflammatory information as this. I also find it dubious that any other Russian in the United States would have it either."

If Marshall was insulted by the implied rebuke, he didn't show it. "The question's a plausible one, Mr. President, and I've been trying to find that out as well. First, I would prefer not to divulge the Russian's name. The more who know it, the more likely the fact of his treason will get back to his masters. That's not to imply that anyone in this room can't be trusted, but I believe his name is irrelevant. He is, however, one of a number of field-grade Russian officers stationed at the embassy. I have been able to confirm that he has, in the past, provided our intelligence people with little nuggets of information that would indicate he is not in love with his Communist leaders."

"For money?" asked Truman.

"Yes."

The president grabbed on to that line of thought. "Then the man could be doing this totally for reward. He could be lying through his teeth and there's nothing we could do about it once he's been paid."

Marshall answered. "He knows the rules. He hasn't been paid for this, and won't be unless it is proven correct. He also hasn't asked for anything." Truman grudgingly nodded his appreciation of the fact.

"Yet," said Truman, "he contacted your people and this colonel of yours was unexpectedly given the message. How did this come to pass?"

Burke was standing along the wall and felt a number of eyes on him. Some of the most important men in the United States were looking at him. He tried to appear stoic. He made it a point to memorize everyone and everything in the room along with what was being said. He could hardly wait to tell Natalie.

Marshall thought briefly of the grief that so often comes to the best-laid plans of men. "Sir, I found out that the Russian had contacted one of our intelligence people by telephone, probably a pay phone, and said he had information to give. In response, the Russian was told that an officer he knew would be at the embassy reception that night, and that the Russian should pass on whatever he had to that officer. At that time we had no idea of the contents of the message, or any indication from our source that it was so explosive. Our Russian played his cards very close."

Truman laughed harshly, shook his head in disbelief, and glanced at Burke. "So when this Colonel Burke showed up, he was presumed to be the contact since your source knew him slightly."

"Correct," said Marshall. "The American officer originally designated to be the contact was delayed by car trouble. I have commended Colonel Burke for coming directly to me."

The general added that the Russians had chased Burke and tried to kill him. Truman smiled tightly and looked at Burke with new respect.

Marshall continued. "Had Colonel Burke attempted to go through channels, it could have been many, many hours before I received it."

If at all, he did not bother to add. Someone in the chain of command might have decided it was too preposterous to believe.

"But why?" Truman persisted. "How would this Russian creature even know of these plans and, again, why would anyone in their embassy be aware?"

Marshall answered. "It is just possible that they would, sir. Ambassador Gromyko is still in town and would have been advised that this attack on our force was going to occur, if for no other reason than to save him the confusion and embarrassment of being confronted by us after the attack took place. In hindsight I think it is significant that no senior Soviet embassy people were at that reception. They were probably lying low and out of sight just so they couldn't give anything away."

Truman turned to Marshall. "Then what have you done, General, to save our boys if this ungodly threat is true?"

Again, Marshall ignored any implications of insult. Truman's bluntness was already well known. He thought of reminding Truman that the men were in this pickle because the president had ordered it. The look of concern on Truman's face told everyone that the president already knew it.

"Sir, I have contacted General Eisenhower by phone and given him a previously agreed-upon code to cover this contingency. He will be contacting Bradley and Simpson and they will be taking the appropriate precautions. That is, those that can be taken under the circumstances. Regardless of what we do, we can only minimize the effect of any Russian attack. Sir, those boys are really out on their own."

"General, what do you mean by 'appropriate,' and why didn't you spell things out for Ike?"

"Sir, specific decisions should be made by the man at the scene, and that is Eisenhower. As to appropriate, I must remind you that we have not yet been attacked and no one has come forth to verify absolutely that this message is real. And, even if it is, there is nothing to stop the Reds from calling off their dogs at the last moment. General Eisenhower will order the column to halt, form into a defensive posture, which itself might forestall a Red attack, and we will do nothing to precipitate combat with them. If the Russians want to start a war, it is imperative that they are indeed the aggressors and not us."

Truman seemed mollified. "You are right, of course. I just don't want another Pearl Harbor."

Nor did Marshall. He still churned inside whenever he thought of the time lost in warning the Pacific Fleet a little less than four years ago.

"Then what are their real intentions?" Truman asked the room, dismay evident on his face. "Do they really want war with us?" He stared at Burke. "You're the one who got the message, and Marshall seems to be impressed with you. What are your thoughts, Colonel?

Burke was having difficulty breathing. The atmosphere had just gotten rarefied. "Presuming the warning is true, sir, an attack will be their version of a shot across the bow, a potentially very bloody and stern message, if you will, that we are to stay away. Very simply, sir, a paranoid Stalin does not believe our communications with them. He believes his own fears, and what's being printed in some of our newspapers about the motives behind our drive on Berlin supports that."

American and British newspapers had cheered the thought of American troops heading toward Berlin and getting there ahead of the Russians. One had even suggested that Hitler be held as a prisoner at Sing Sing.

Truman nodded sadly and cupped his chin in his hands. The enormity of his decision to send troops was weighing heavily. "But we cannot let our boys be slaughtered. If attacked they will fight back and we will try to save them, won't we, General?"

Marshall's face was set even more firmly then usual. "Yes, sir," he said slowly.

MAJOR GENERAL CHRISTOPHER J. Miller sucked on his pipe and exhaled a small cloud of smoke from his dwindling supply of Virginia tobacco. It was this virtually continuous act that had given him his nickname of "Puff" early on in his military career. He had hated it, as he felt it made him seem soft. Now it no longer bothered him, and anyone who dealt with him knew that while he was polite, considerate, and even gracious, he was far from soft. He had to admit, though, that the additional pounds he had recently added to his five-foot-six-inch frame were also making him look just a little puffy.

Miller tapped his pipe against the heel of his boot and knocked out a clot of ashes as he watched a column of vehicles arrange themselves along the highway a few yards away. They were no longer advancing.

Now, only a few miles from their goal of Berlin, General Miller was not a very happy man as he contemplated the two messages he'd received. The first was an administrative one. The move on Berlin had been thrown together so quickly that there had been no time to name it. The two divisions had each belonged to two different corps and their being together was a marriage of military necessity. Thus, instead of creating a new corps, they had initially named the group

Miller Force and now it was confirmed. It was unusual for a group that size to be named after an individual, but it indicated the temporary nature of the situation.

Miller supposed he should have been flattered. For an intoxicating moment, he had allowed himself to visualize the headline "Miller Force Takes Berlin." For a career that had been undistinguished for almost thirty years since his graduation from Texas A&M, it would have been a crowning achievement and a fitting end. At the war's beginning, he had been an overage major with little hope of promotion. For a moment he allowed his imagination to run wild and he visualized another headline: "Miller Captures Hitler." Damn it all, his family would have been so proud.

Then he got the second message.

It had come moments later and directly from Omar Bradley, bypassing Simpson. It said the Russians might attack him and he should circle the wagons and prepare to fight a defensive battle. But how the hell did he do that? The two divisions were strung out for a score or more miles and were vulnerable at a number of places. He was prepared for an attempt by the Germans to cut the column, but Russian military capabilities were far different and much stronger than the collapsing Germans. Additionally, the message said he should not start anything. If the Russians wanted a fight, they were going to be allowed to get in the first punch. It didn't seem fair, but he had his orders.

Miller heard a buzzing sound overhead and saw yet another Russian airplane flying parallel to the column. It was a Stormovik, a heavily armored tank killer designed for ground support. He couldn't fire at it since it hadn't done anything yet. Nobody had. It was simply watching. So too were American planes, and they had reported heavy concentrations of Soviet armor moving toward him. What the Air Corps couldn't tell him was their intentions.

What the air force also couldn't promise him was continuous cover. The speed of the American advance meant that airstrips were well behind the lead tanks of Miller Force. Without drop tanks, American planes would not be able to linger long over his men. He was beginning to feel naked and he didn't like it at all.

Puff Miller had done what he could. He had ordered the column to halt and ordered each of his units to assume whatever defensive formation was logical under the strung-out circumstances. It seemed likely that any defensive alignments were going to be highly fragmented and rarely more than company or battalion strength, if that.

Miller turned to his radio operator. "Did anyone make contact with Colonel Brentwood?" The radioman, busy with his dials and switches, nodded affirmative.

Brentwood had the point of the column. His tanks and vehicles were closer to Berlin than anyone else, and that concerned Miller. Actually, Brentwood concerned Miller. He was a fire-breather who thought Patton was the new messiah and attack was the only way to wage war. Even though he had yet seen little or no combat, Brentwood was consumed with the urge to be the first American in Berlin and had volunteered for the point position. Miller had acquiesced and now wondered if he hadn't made a mistake.

Miller had heard the jokes that Brentwood wanted to run for Congress after the war. Under other circumstances, Brentwood would have been an ideal leader for the column. Now, however, things had changed. Yesterday they needed someone with a little daring. Today they needed utmost caution, and that was not Colonel Thomas Brentwood. However, his unit now led Miller Force and his tanks were rumbling toward Berlin.

"Son, does he understand he is to stop immediately?"

"Yes, sir. He was given your order in clear terms."

"I assume you did not actually speak to him."

"No, sir, but I did spell it out in no uncertain terms to his radio operator."

Miller wasn't confident. "Son, get him on the line directly."

A few moments later, the radio operator said he couldn't make contact, and Miller felt a chill going up his spine.

Miller nodded and walked a few steps away from his command vehicle. To his rear was the river, the Havel. To his right was the small, ruined, and nearly abandoned city of Potsdam. To his front he could see the rolling clouds of smoke in the distance that marked the dying of the Third Reich in Berlin. He wondered which curl of smoke might be Hitler. Serve the bastard right if he toasted, Miller thought.

In front of him was the autobahn and it was choked with American trucks and tanks. Groups of civilians, refugees from Berlin, trudged slowly on the grass alongside the road. All they wanted to do was get away from the war. Miller wondered what they would do if they knew they might be moving right back into it.

He looked up again. A couple more Stormoviks had appeared above the column. Why did they remind him of vultures gathering over a kill? Would they recognize the change in the American stance? If they did, would it make a bit of difference?

And what the hell was Brentwood doing?

TONY "THE TOAD" Totelli was nervous. One of the advantages of being in the command tank with the ambitious Colonel Brentwood was the fact that he could overhear all the communications that the colonel sent and received. Tony had heard the order to halt and then heard Brentwood mutter and swear that it was the stupidest piece-of-shit order he had ever received. Brentwood said they were within spitting distance of Berlin. Hell, for all Tony knew they might actually be in the damned city.

Certainly, they were on the outskirts of the German capital. The wooded and semi-built-up nature of the area was changing and there were more and more buildings and homes. Also, he could see an open area that the colonel had assured himself was the beginning of Gatow Airport.

"Sir, do you want me to stop?" Tony asked hopefully.

"Not yet," the colonel muttered. Tony could barely hear him over the rumble of the Sherman's engine. He sighed and kept the tank slowly moving forward. Tony was a good driver and that was one of the reasons the colonel had selected him. While Tony's squat and dark physical appearance accounted for his nickname, his short size made him ideal for a tank with a full colonel jammed in along with additional communications equipment on top of its normal crew. Tony just didn't take up much room.

Tony wished he was back home in New Jersey, where the vehicles he had driven were expensive cars. Unfortunately, those cars always belonged to someone else, and the owners had objected to Tony's taking them and selling them, which was why he found himself in the army four years ago at the age of eighteen. The judge had given him a choice: enlist or go to jail. To compound Tony's problem, Pearl Harbor had occurred while he was finishing basic training. Over the years,

Tony had seen the good and the bad of army life, and it seemed to him that this little foray of Brentwood's seemed downright silly, even dangerous, under the circumstances.

In Tony's opinion, the colonel was disobeying orders from higher up. He had heard Brentwood explain on the radio, to some captain in the group, that all he was going to do was make sure the area was safe before halting, but everyone knew that was just an excuse for continuing on. Orders or not, Brentwood was going into Berlin if only a few feet, and he'd take his chances on getting his ass chewed later. In another of Tony's opinions, Brentwood doubtless thought that a shot at glory would far outweigh any risk of disciplinary action. Brentwood wanted to run for Congress after the war, and being the first American in Berlin would be a good way to start. There had been no further radio contact for several minutes and Tony had the damndest feeling that Brentwood had disabled the radio.

Tony was driving with the hatch open and his head and shoulders outside. This gave him an excellent view forward, although he could not see the eleven other tanks behind or the twenty lightly armored half-tracks that, full of infantry, followed the tanks. The area had been quiet and he was not particularly concerned about snipers.

"Hey, Toad." It was Ernie the gunner. "What do you see?"

"Eva Braun dancing naked and calling out for you to fuck her," Tony responded. If Ernie wanted to see what was in front, all he had to do was open the turret hatch and look. Fortunately for Tony, Brentwood usually ignored such idle banter between his crew. Brentwood was not totally stupid and knew it helped keep them sane.

The tank moved around a charred building, and there was a great deal of open space before it. In the distance, Tony could see a number of shapes and he stopped the tank abruptly, causing everyone to lurch forward and swear. "Tanks!" he yelled.

"Jesus," Brentwood said. "How many do you make, Corporal?"

Tony started counting and also started shaking. "I see thirty but there may be more coming through the dust."

"Where the hell did the Germans get them?" Brentwood muttered. There was a degree of silence as the rest of the column had halted behind Tony's lead tank.

"Sir," Tony said, an unsettling fear filling him. "They aren't German. Those are Russians. That silhouette belongs to a T34."

"Bullshit," the colonel said. "The Reds can't be this far west. Those are German Panthers, not T34s. They just look a lot alike."

Tony admitted that possibility. Their silhouettes were very similar from a distance. A spotter plane radioed that a large number of tanks was headed toward them, but didn't specify nationality.

Brentwood prudently ordered them to take up defensive positions. What had started out as a public relations stunt now had the potential to be a disaster.

Tony was shaking. This had all the earmarks of a bloody mistake. "Sir, I still think those are Commies."

Brentwood was puzzled. The dust kicked up by the approaching tanks obscured any insignia. "We can't take chances. They have to be German. We'll treat them as if they are the enemy."

And even if they are, we're in deep shit, Tony thought. Even though many of the American Sherman tanks had been improved with a higher-velocity main gun, they still didn't stand a chance against a Panther. Or a T34 for that matter.

The unknown tanks were in range. Tony saw a flash of light. Was it gunfire? Were the other tanks shooting at them?

"Goddamn Germans are shooting at us," Brentwood yelled.

"I still think they're Russians, Colonel," Tony said.

"Then why the hell are they shooting at us and why the hell are you arguing with me?"

Tony winced. He had gone too far. Now there would be no reasoning with the colonel.

"Open fire," Brentwood ordered, and a dozen American guns blasted. At long range, only a couple of enemy tanks were hit and they weren't damaged.

At that moment, the spotter plane's pilot confirmed that the tanks were Russians and might be shooting at a German position. Brentwood paled and Tony declined to say I told you so.

Brentwood grabbed him by the shoulder. "Toad, get the hell out there with a flag while I contact division."

Though reluctant to leave the relative security of the tank's armored womb, Tony clambered out onto the ground and pulled out the bag that contained a good-sized American flag and a collapsible pole. Many of these had been distributed so they could identify themselves visually should the need arise. Tony thought the need was now absolutely imperative and scrambled to connect it to the pole. He looked around and saw crewmen from a number of American tanks and half-tracks doing the same thing. There was a decent breeze and the flags unfurled themselves so that even a blind Russian could see them.

The Russian tanks continued to close on them and he could now see they had infantry trotting alongside. He counted more than the thirty tanks he first saw and many more were still coming into view, and they were definitely within range. Why hadn't they shot at them? Were they concerned about killing Americans? Christ, he hoped so.

Suddenly, the Russian tanks opened fire. Dozens of guns barked, their sound barely preceding the stunning concussion of their shells impacting around him.

Tony clambered onto the hull as the tank began to back up. He could hear Brentwood screaming into the radio that he was being at-tacked by Russians. Tony was just about to climb down the hatch into his tank when the shock of a near miss threw him to the ground and rolled him away from his Sherman. He tried to rise again, but his tank took a hit. It lifted off the ground, then settled with a crash. For a mo-ment he thought he was dead. He wasn't, but his tank had been killed. It was burning furiously and the intense heat drove him back. The tur-ret hatch opened and a living torch tried to crawl out. Tony watched in horror as the blackened, burning thing with no face moved a little, twitched, and stopped halfway out. Tony thought it was Ernie, but he couldn't be sure. Asshole Brentwood was doubtless still cooking inside the tank.

He gagged from the sight and the stench of burning flesh. He crawled farther away from the Sherman and then looked around. A half-dozen other American tanks were also in flames, as were a couple of half-tracks. The sound of ammunition exploding inside the Sher-mans told him he was ungodly fortunate to be alive. The remainder of the American vehicles were running away from the one-sided battle as quickly as they could. He looked at the rapidly closing Reds and didn't see any of their tanks on fire or stopped.

There were some other Americans lying on the ground around him. Most of them were quite still and only a couple were moving their arms or trying to rise. Tony checked himself and realized that he was basically unhurt. Bruises and cuts didn't count in a disaster like this.

He looked at the Russian tanks. They were advancing faster toward him than he could ever think of running. They were outstripping their own infantry, which was rapidly being left behind. He whimpered without realizing it and settled himself to wait for whatever the Russians might do.

The sound of airplane engines from behind him caused him to look up quickly as a pair of American P-47 fighter-bombers roared only a few feet overhead. Their machine guns chewed through the Russian infantry but did no harm to the tanks. The fighters banked sharply and began strafing the rear of the Russian tanks and firing their five-inch rockets. This time the Russian tanks suffered. Less heavily armored in the top and rear, several of them took hits and exploded.

"Kill the bastards!" Tony yelled.

In a moment, however, the two planes were out of rockets and ammunition. He watched sadly as they flew off, leaving the field to the Russians. For a second time, he sat and waited for the inevitable, knowing full well that the Reds would be pissed at the aerial attack and would likely take it out on potential prisoners.

Thus, he watched incredulously as the Russian column veered away from the killing ground and turned off on a mission of its own. He stood up and unconsciously dusted himself off. He was alive. Damned alone, but alive. Find a weapon, he told himself, and get the hell out of here. And oh yeah, just who the hell was the enemy, the Germans or the Russians?

He found an M1 Garand on a body from a half-track and took it along with a couple of clips of ammunition. He looked at the wounded. Only a couple were still alive and he didn't think they would last long. Maybe the Reds would find them and care for them. There sure as hell wasn't anything he could do.

He swore and half sobbed in frustration as he walked quickly away. Damn Brentwood and his run for glory, and damn the Russians.

CHAPTER 6

The first hint of an attack was the screaming sound of airplane engines and the chatter of machine guns as a wave of Russian fighters flew low over them, strafing them.

"Those are Russian Stormoviks," yelled Singer as they hunched in their hastily dug foxholes.

In his own hole a few feet away, Logan didn't give a shit what type of planes they were, just so long as they didn't shoot him.

Unimpeded by any opposition, the Red planes made pass after pass, hitting tanks and mangling other vehicles. Some attempt was made to shoot at them with machine guns and other small arms, but with no apparent effect. He watched incredulously as a stream of machine-gun bullets bounced off the armored belly of one low-flying Russian plane. The Russians had flying tanks, he thought.

Logan slowly realized he was fairly safe in his burrow. The planes were destroying vehicles, not looking for red-haired platoon sergeants. Even so, the air was alive with a hot rain of flying debris and metal fragments that could kill as quickly as a well-aimed bullet. He fought the urge to continue looking around and tucked his head down so that his steel pot protected it. He cupped his balls with his hands and wished he had another helmet for them as well. A lot of guys protected their testicles with their helmets, instead of their skulls. A helluva choice to make, he thought.

Jack could hear the screams and moans of the wounded. An explosion sent another shower of debris onto him and he heard an animal-like shriek that was almost in his ear. Doubtless one of his men, but which one? And where the hell were the American planes? Thank God they'd had enough warning time to dig in at least a little bit. Had the enemy planes caught them on the road and in their trucks, the slaughter would have been unimaginable. As it was, it would be bad enough.

As suddenly as they had arrived, the Red planes were gone, their ammunition spent. Logan jumped out of his hole and started to check his men when the cry of "medic" came from only a few feet away. He recognized Crawford's voice and ran to where the young PFC was cradling a bloody Lieutenant Singer.

"Aw, Christ," Logan said as he saw the mangled ruin of Singer's left arm. Bloody bones and muscle were visible, and they were connected to his upper arm and shoulder by only a few threads of flesh and gray muscle. Singer's face was pale and he appeared to be unconscious. With Crawford's help, Logan attached a tourniquet and tried to make Singer as comfortable as possible. He covered him with a blanket to prevent shock until he could get a medic or take him to a hospital tent. If there were any hospitals, he thought.

Having done what he could, Logan checked the rest of his men and found only one other slightly wounded. Fearful of leaving his comrades, that soldier refused to go to the rear. Logan didn't have time to argue and left him with his buddies.

The road was littered with damaged and burning vehicles of all types, and many were surrounded by the fragmentary and smoking remains of their crews.

Logan was vomiting on the ground when Captain Dimitri found him. Dimitri's face was one of controlled fury. "Where the hell is Singer?"

"Badly wounded, Captain. I think he's gonna lose his arm."

"Goddamnit."

"Captain, how bad off are we?"

Dimitri shook his head. He was having difficulty comprehending the magnitude of what had just occurred. "Looks like a half dozen killed in the company and maybe twice that many wounded. It's bad, but it could have been a lot worse. Do you hear the big guns?"

Logan hadn't. Concentrating entirely on his own problems, he had been unaware of the crash and rumble of artillery fire that was coming from the west of their position back toward the Elbe.

"Those poor bastards down there," Dimitri said, "are really getting clobbered. Battalion says they are being hit by waves of armor. At least we've been spared that." Dimitri smiled wryly. "Thank God for small favors."

Captain Dimitri told Logan where he could find some help for Singer and departed to continue checking on the rest of his company. What the hell is going on? Logan thought. Just a little while ago we were all planning on going home. Now the Russians have attacked. Do we have a whole new war? Against Russia? He had heard of the size and ferocity of the Russian military and had no urge to test the truth of the stories.

Logan and the rest of his platoon stayed in their positions for a couple of hours until they saw the familiar form of Captain Dimitri again approaching. He could tell from the look on the captain's face that they would be moving and there would be new holes to dig.

"Logan," Dimitri snapped. "You're in charge, at least for the time being. Take a couple of men and a jeep down the road and see what's happened to our armor and if the Russians are coming."

"I sure as hell hope they aren't, Captain," he said, and Dimitri grunted.

Twenty minutes later, Logan's slowly moving jeep found what appeared to be the point of the column. Ruined and burning tanks and half-tracks littered the field along with a number of bodies. There was no sign of the Russians. A small blessing, Logan thought. They were out there, and he wondered if Red Army scouts were watching him and his jeep and wondering if they should kill him. Now I know how someone who's paranoid feels, he thought.

They got out and walked around, checking to make sure that no American was still alive. None were. There were too many dead to take back in the jeep. Jack hated to leave them, but had no choice.

"Sarge, I think we should go," said Crawford.

Logan concurred. They were well ahead of their column and the only people to their front would be Russians. They'd stayed long enough and were pushing their luck. A burst of machine-gun fire chewed up the ground near them, punctuating their thoughts.

"Agreed. Let's get the hell out of here."

There was no more firing from the unseen Russian gun. Maybe the Reds were taunting them. What the hell was happening? Goddamnit, Logan snarled silently. They were supposed to be going home soon.

• • • •

WOLFGANG VON SCHUMANN watched incredulously as the attack on the Americans took place about a mile away from where he and his flock huddled along the riverbank. It was incredible, like watching a pageant unfolding. The Russians and the Americans were fighting each other. He recalled an officer in an SS unit a long time ago saying that Hitler believed the Anglo-American-Russian alliance against the Third Reich was so fragile that it would shatter into brawling fragments before the Allies could destroy Germany.

Had Hitler been right? If so, what did this mean for Germany? For that matter, von Schumann wondered, was Hitler still alive to appreciate the situation? For what the führer had done to his beloved Germany, von Schumann fervently wished death for Hitler. Whatever approval he had once felt for the führer and the Nazi regime had disappeared in the snows of Stalingrad and the refuse dump where overworked surgeons had cut off and thrown away his gangrenous leg.

He looked again at the people who had chosen to follow him out of the city. They were uniformly filthy, ragged, thin, and terrified. He looked to where he could see the young woman, Elisabeth, and the boy. The boy looked intrigued by everything that was going on around him, while the girl looked a little better than earlier. Amazing what some broth, a small piece of bread, and the realization that you are not alone can do for a person's health and sense of well-being.

She saw him watching her and ventured a shy smile. Von Schumann nodded at her and smiled back. She was young enough to be his daughter and pretty enough with her un-German black hair. The thought of his daughter sent a stab of pain through him. Where was she? Where was his wife, Hilda? He knew it would be a long time, if ever, before he would be able to find out. The last letter from them had been more than a year ago and it said they were heading for Hamburg. Hamburg had been destroyed by bombs and fire. Had they been consumed as well?

Elisabeth watched as von Schumann turned and hobbled away. For the first time in weeks she was not afraid. Instead of lurking and skulking in the cellars and tunnels of her apartment complex in Berlin, she was out in the air and actually doing something. Better, she had found people who would help her and Pauli survive this horror. Her gums didn't hurt as much, nor did her joints. The women in the group had adopted the two of them, and a number of food scraps easily became a meal. For the first time since leaving Berlin she felt that she might just survive and that both she and Pauli might have a future.

Pauli stared at the departing von Schumann. "Is he our new papa?"

For the first time in weeks, Elisabeth laughed, causing others to turn and glance at her in case she had gone mad. "No, Pauli. He is not our new papa. He is a friend, a very good friend."

Pauli nodded solemnly and prepared to digest that piece of information. He dug a piece of stale bread from his pocket and began chewing on it.

But what in God's name was von Schumann talking about? The ever-present sounds of battle meant nothing to her. She'd presumed that the Germans were fighting the Russians. But had he said that the Americans and the Russians were fighting each other? Even though the Russians were animals, they were on the same side as the Americans. If they were indeed fighting each other, what did that mean to her feelings of safety?

Foreboding returned. "I think we might have gone from the frying pan into the fire," she said.

Pauli looked puzzled. "Is somebody frying something?"

MORE THAN FIFTY people were jammed in the smoke-filled conference room in the West Wing of the White House, filling it well beyond capacity. When Steve Burke arrived along with General Marshall and a number of other army officers, Truman was already there. To his surprise, Marshall formally introduced Burke to Truman and reminded the president that he was the man who had received the message from the Russian.

"I didn't have a chance to tell you before, Colonel, but it was a good job," Truman said tersely and shook his hand. "Your quick actions may have saved a lot of our boys' lives."

Burke had found out a little earlier that he was being put in for a commendation, perhaps even a medal, for his actions that night. While pleased, he was a little embarrassed. All he had done was blunder into the event with Korzov, who, he had later been informed, had suddenly taken "ill" and was on his way back to the Soviet Union before the fighting started. The poor bastard's treachery had likely been found out and he would be lucky to get a bullet in the head.

If Truman was upset by Marshall's late arrival he gave no sign. He gestured people to their seats, and the truly important people along with Marshall sat at the main table along with Truman. Aides like Burke arrayed themselves behind their principals in inverse order according to rank. As junior in the army delegation, Burke found a plain wooden chair along the wall beside a navy commander who smiled politely. They kept their silence and would do so until called upon for information by their leaders. It was highly unlikely they would address the group.

Truman called the meeting to order. His face showed strain and anger. "General Marshall, please give us all an update on the military situation."

Marshall pondered a sheaf of notes. Much of the information had been received only a few moments before he had left the Pentagon for the White House, and updates were still being called in by telephone.

"Mr. President, much of my report is going to be incomplete and dealing in generalities. Too much has happened too quickly for specifics and details. First, Miller Force was ambushed at two major points by large Soviet forces. The point of the column, a fairly small armored group of ours, was attacked by an overwhelming tank force. It took heavy casualties and was forced to retreat."

Secretary of State Stettinius interrupted. "I have spoken with Ambassador Gromyko, and he says the Americans violated their space by entering Berlin, and that the Americans opened fire first on the Russians, and, therefore, that the Russian response was purely defensive."

Marshall's eyes turned sad. "According to reports from the handful of survivors, that may be correct. There is evidence that Colonel Brentwood's force was still moving forward after being ordered to halt, and that it fired first in the mistaken belief that the approaching tanks were German and had shot at them. We now believe the Reds were shooting at another target."

"Aw, Jesus," Admiral King said.

Marshall continued. "For whatever it's worth, Brentwood was killed in the fight, so we'll never know his version of what happened."

Otherwise, Marshall thought grimly, the overly ambitious SOB would be looking at a court-martial. Marshall had the nagging thought that Brentwood's exceeding his orders had given the Reds an excuse to attack. If, of course, they had needed the excuse.

Truman nodded. "But he had been ordered to halt."

Marshall grimaced slightly. "Yes, sir, he had. Why he continued on, even for a little bit, we may never know." The general shuffled through his notes.

"The second Russian attack was a truly massive one and it hit the column approximately half of the way down its length from the point where Brentwood was attacked. It also occurred at almost the same time, which makes the Russian claim that we started it utter nonsense. I believe both attacks were planned.

"Reports are sketchy, but they indicate hundreds of Russian tanks took part along with coordinated infantry, air, and artillery support. They struck the column where it was weakest, as the greater portion of Miller's armor and infantry strength was, logically, at the front of the column. What remained at the rear was more in the way of a rear guard, including administrative and follow-up units. In a way that was a blessing since much of Miller's armor and artillery are still intact. Miller is attempting to establish a defensive perimeter in the city of Potsdam."

"What about casualties?" Truman asked softly. The look in his face said that he really didn't want to know, but had to. All the casualties would be his responsibility. He had ordered the advance beyond the Elbe. He wanted to be sick. How could this have occurred?

"Sir," Marshall replied, "once again specifics are unknown. General Miller has reported that he has three hundred dead inside the perimeter and at least that many wounded. He has, altogether, about ten to fifteen thousand men fit and remaining in his command."

Truman bolted from his chair. "But he had thirty thousand men!"

Marshall nodded sadly. "Yes, sir, he did. When the Red armor hit the rear third of the column it severed it and apparently rolled it up toward the Elbe. While many, perhaps most, of those men are still alive, we have to consider them missing in action and very likely to become prisoners of the Russians. There is very little chance that many will make it back to the Elbe."

Truman's face was pale. "Fifteen to twenty thousand casualties? I can't believe it," he said, sitting down slowly. Truman's mind was in turmoil. His bold gesture to stand up to Stalin's lies and belligerence had resulted in a catastrophe that was all his fault. There was a sign on his desk. It said "The Buck Stops Here." God, he wished it had passed him over.

Secretary of State Stettinius again interrupted. "Consistent with his first statement, Ambassador Gromyko has stated that the American column opened fire on Russian tanks that were passing the Americans on their way to assume their rightful place on the Elbe."

Marshall's face flushed red. "He's a liar. It took planning and effort to have those Soviet units in position to attack as they did."

Truman had regained control of himself. "We know that, General. Tell me, was the battle all that one-sided?"

"Fairly so, but not totally. Our fighters did knock out some of the Russian tanks at the point of our column, and our armor and artillery acquitted themselves well, at least until they were overwhelmed. That and other fighters flying cover for the column did take on and shoot down a number of their planes without loss to our own. Altogether, we estimate that we killed about fifty of their tanks and a dozen planes, along with an unknown number of their infantry. I wouldn't be surprised if the Russians suffered at least a thousand casualties overall."

"War," murmured Stettinius in disbelief. "We have another world war on our hands."

"I sincerely hope not," said Marshall. "We have got to end this quickly before the situation does expand into a full-scale conflict. Despite this terrible provocation, we do not want to take on Russia in a land war." He turned to Truman. "But if it should come to that, sir, we cannot fight the Russians and the Germans at the same time. We are now involved in a two-front war, with the Nazis and Japan. If we add a third front with Russia, we will most surely lose."

There were gasps from throughout the room. Marshall had hinted, and none too subtly, at the need for a separate peace with Germany, or even Japan, should the need arise. It was unthinkable. Or was it?

"Amen," Truman said slowly, barely controlling his rising anger at the thought of peace with the Nazis or the damned Japs. "But we have suffered so many dead and wounded and, if you are correct, General, they have taken thousands of our boys prisoner. They will be hostages in any negotiations to resolve this. It may not be so easy to avoid a war. Which"—he sighed—"brings me to another point. What is the current status? Is there still fighting?"

There was a short pause while an aide whispered to Marshall.

"Sir," Marshall responded, "apparently things are fairly quiet. As I said, General Miller is establishing a perimeter in and around the city of Potsdam and is digging in. With the Havel River at his back and lakes to his flanks, he is in a fairly strong position and should be able to defend himself, at least for a while. Despite fueling problems we are flying air cover over the perimeter and the Russian planes are staying away. The Russian ground forces have pulled back as well. It looks like the beginning of a waiting game."

Which, Truman thought, is better than a shooting game. "How long can Miller's boys stay there?"

"We are air-dropping supplies to them now. If the Reds don't do anything rash, they could remain in Potsdam for quite some time. If they do renew the assault, it would depend entirely on the strength of the attacking forces. As it appears right now, the bulk of the Russian armies around Berlin are either closing in on Hitler's Chancellery, where he may already be dead, or have bypassed Potsdam and are heading for the Elbe. The future will be determined by what the Russians do when they reach the Elbe."

Truman gasped at the implication. "Are you intimating that they might not stop there? Our boys are already along that river. It would mean outright war and no way of turning back from it!"

Marshall agreed. "Ike is beginning to prepare for that contingency."

Truman sagged. Events were so terribly out of his control. The nation was reeling from news accounts of the "incident." Censorship was in effect, but it had proven impossible to stifle word of the battle; too many people had been involved. He would have to meet with congressional leaders to get their advice, which he didn't want, since congressmen were always running for reelection. In his opinion, Congress was as useful as tits on a boar. As a former senator, he saw the irony of his thoughts, but a committee of several hundred could not run a war. Also, he would soon have to deal with Churchill, who had openly urged the Allies to move to Berlin.

The meeting broke up and Burke left with Marshall's entourage. There would be a number of late nights while they tried to fathom Russia's intentions. At best, the Russians would hold American prisoners and the soldiers in Potsdam as hostages for concessions to the Yalta agreements, which many Americans felt were already skewed in Russia's favor.

At worst? Burke's mind boggled at the enormity of it. At worst, another world war was about to start and with a whole new cast of characters. His return to the faculty of Notre Dame could become a distant fantasy. On campus, he was safe from the problems of the world. Now he knew there wasn't safety anywhere. Like it or not, he had become a part of the action, and he found that he liked it. Someday he'd go back to South Bend and spend fall afternoons watching jocks try to kill each other playing football, but not for a long while.

He desperately wanted to talk with Natalie, but she had been busy at the State Department doing essentially what he was doing for War Plans and General Marshall.

No matter what time he got free, he would call her.

MARSHAL ZHUKOV DID not look pleased at having been pulled from his army group headquarters for consultations with Stalin in Moscow. Prudently, he did not say anything. If Josef Stalin wanted to speak to him, then so be it.

Stalin entered the room and went through the familiar ritual of lighting his battered pipe. He sucked deeply and released a cloud of smoke. "Is Hitler dead?"

Zhukov was unperturbed by the question. "He may well be, Comrade Stalin, but we haven't yet received proof. Our army is within sight of both the Reichstag and the Chancellery. Dead or alive, he will be rooted from his cave in a very short while. The Third Reich now consists of a few blocks in the center of Berlin."

"And, Marshal Zhukov, what of the American force that reached so near to Berlin?"

"Pinned down in Potsdam, Comrade Stalin. We have, at last count, taken several thousand American prisoners and more will surely fall into our hands as our soldiers round up their strays, who are wandering about in total confusion."

Stalin nodded, pleased. Thousands of hostages, he thought. The Americans were so sensitive regarding the lives of their soldiers. When the time came they would do anything to get them back. "What are you doing about the American perimeter at Potsdam?"

"At the moment, very little," Zhukov replied. "I have a reinforced second-echelon infantry corps under Major General Bazarian watching them and blocking any attempt at withdrawal toward the Elbe. The main part of my army is concentrating on finishing the task in Berlin and on reaching the Elbe. The Americans in Potsdam can wait. They will be there when we want them."

The Russian army was so huge that the name of General Bazarian did not ring a bell with Stalin. Obviously, the man was Armenian. Second echelon meant that Bazarian's troops were shit.

"Good," said Stalin. "All is in order. Instruct this Bazarian that the Americans are to be let alone for the time being. Now, however, I have a change in plans for you, Marshal Zhukov. Very simply, I wish our armies to move westward across the Elbe, crush the Americans, and put an end to their presence in Europe."

Zhukov could not hide his astonishment at the blunt and unexpected order. "Comrade Stalin, I am honored. When shall this assault commence?"

Stalin leaned forward grimly. "Immediately."

Zhukov was further taken aback. "Comrade Stalin, our armies have been fighting heavily and are exhausted. Our supply lines are stretched, and we still have the remaining German armies to destroy. Please let us finish the Germans and then prepare for a proper assault against the Americans. A week for the Germans and another two or three weeks in preparation—"

"Immediately," snapped Stalin. "Ignore the Germans. They are finished. When we have bagged Hitler, the remaining German armies will disappear into the mist. Your advance units will be reaching the Elbe within hours, if they have not done so already, and major units will be in place in a couple of days. I will give you forty-eight hours from that time to regroup and resupply. You will then cross the Elbe and attack the Americans."

Zhukov paled, but he knew better than to argue. His armies were exhausted, had suffered heavy casualties, were short of ammunition, and their tanks and trucks desperately needed maintenance. Food was not a serious problem. They could simply take from the Germans, and nobody would care if they starved as a result. However, a T34 could not move without diesel nor could it shoot without ammunition. Still, he would carry out his orders.

Stalin stood and paced the room. "I understand your concerns, comrade, but the disarray of our forces will be more than matched by the confusion and panic within the American and British armies. The capitalists are weak. They will crumble under your onslaught."

"Yes, Comrade Stalin."

"Excellent. Now for the command arrangements. My day as overall commander is done. General Zhukov, you will assume control of the entire western front."

Zhukov blinked in surprise and Stalin continued. "You are doubtless wondering why the sense of urgency. I know you have heard the rumors that the Allies will send their armies home or to Japan once the war against the Hitlerites is over, and, if true, the rest of Germany could be ours for the taking anytime we wished. Is this not correct?" Zhukov nodded like a student listening to a particularly stern lecturer.

Stalin folded his hands on the desk in front of him. "I can only say that there are forces and events emerging that could change everything. The opportunity for success is now. If we wait, the opportunity will surely be lost."

After Zhukov left, Stalin was alone in his office. He pulled the one-page intelligence summary from the center drawer of his desk and read it for the tenth time. Events at a place called Alamogordo in New Mexico were at a critical stage, but success was more than probable. Indeed, it was highly likely. Stalin chuckled slightly when he recalled how he had told Zhukov of "forces emerging." If only his generals had any idea of what was emerging from that base in New Mexico.

CHAPTER 7

All in all, Major General Christopher Miller was not displeased by what he saw when he toured the defensive perimeter in his jeep. Getting out and checking things was a lot better than staying in the old German imperial barracks and staring at maps. It was also good for the men to see that at least one general had survived the ambush. His aide, Captain Roy Leland, hadn't been thrilled, as there had been sporadic sniper fire from either the Russians or die-hard Nazis in the area, but he had been overruled.

"Not bad," Miller said, "not bad at all."

The soldiers within the perimeter had been reorganized where necessary and now had coherent chains of command. They had spent their time digging furiously in anticipation of further assaults, and the perimeter now bristled with bunkers and trenches. Miller could wish for more barbed wire and a greater number of tank traps, but they would come in time. If, he thought ruefully, the fucking Commies gave him some time. They had been quiet for a while but that was no guarantee the solitude would continue.

An area near the river had been cleared and an almost continuous stream of C-47s flew overhead and parachuted supplies in low-level drops. It had taken a couple of tries, but they had stopped dropping their loads in the river. Again, the Reds had made no effort to stop the resupply efforts. It was puzzling. It was as if they didn't care.

Miller voiced his thoughts to his aide. "Roy, why the hell are the Russians so quiet? I mean, they jumped us, chewed the shit out of us, and now are leaving us alone? It doesn't make sense."

Leland, who was the soul of discretion and very used to being a sounding board for Miller's thoughts, shrugged. "In the grand scheme of things, sir, I just don't think we are all that important to them anymore."

Miller nodded. "That's what I feel, too. Battling us served a purpose and now that purpose is over. We can't advance and we can't retreat. All we can do is sit here and wait for them to do something. In the meantime, we just grow old."

"Well, sir, we will be prepared for them this time."

"Yep," Miller said without qualifying the response. He knew that he was vastly outnumbered by the Russians. If they should decide to turn against him in all their fury, his newly built defenses would be overrun in little time. He understood that he and his men were pawns in a larger game being played out in Moscow and Washington. It was a frustrating and helpless feeling.

"General Miller?"

They wheeled at the sound of the new and accented voice. With both men deep in their thoughts, a German civilian had managed to walk right up to them. Or limp up, as the man was on a crutch and had only one leg. The jeep's driver reached for his carbine and Leland pulled his pistol. The civilian balanced himself on his crutch and held out his hands.

"Gentlemen, I have no weapons."

"Then what the hell do you want?" snapped Leland.

"My name is Wolfgang von Schumann and I would like to talk to the general. I have several questions and some few suggestions in which I might be of assistance to you."

"Where'd you lose the leg?" Miller asked. From his bearing, he had deduced that the man was likely a German officer.

"Stalingrad."

"You're a Nazi?" Miller continued.

"Yes. At least I was."

Miller laughed grimly and Leland joined in. "Jesus Christ," said Miller, "I knew there had to be at least one of you in Germany. Everybody we talk to says that they never were Nazis although all of their neighbors were. At least you're somewhat of an honest man. Now, what were your questions?"

Wolfgang gestured behind him, where a number of disheveled civilians were gathered, watching him talk to the American general.

"Somehow, General Miller, I have become the leader of several hundred refugees, with more gathering by me each day. I help them collect and distribute food and clothing, and try to ensure that they have shelter until they can somehow find their way to their homes. I might add that not all the refugees are Germans. Some are forced laborers, while others are slave laborers from other countries who have been freed as a result of the upheavals around us. I even have a number of Jews who were in concentration camps and have managed to escape in the chaos."

"Great," Miller said. "I am sincerely glad that someone is taking care of them. Now, what was your question?"

"Since we are in your area of control and unable to leave, we will shortly be without resources. When that time comes, I have a simple question—will you feed us?"

Miller blinked. "Shit. What would happen if I asked you to leave?" he asked, thinking of the additional strain the growing number of refugees would put on his limited resources. And there had to be many more than the few hundred von Schumann was referring to.

Von Schumann gestured with his hands. "It would be the same as shooting us. In fact, shooting us would be a great favor. The Russians would kill every one of us, every man, woman, and child, regardless of age. The men might die quickly, but the women's deaths would be lingering and horrible. And God only knows what they would do to the children."

Miller was not surprised. He had been hearing stories of unbelievable atrocities committed by the Russians as reprisal for the barbarities inflicted upon their people by the Nazis. He had no love for the Germans, but neither did he want to be responsible for the deaths of civilians. Not directly, at least.

"All right," he said grudgingly, "your people can stay and I will do my best to get you enough food and medical supplies. But your people get theirs after my boys go first."

Even as he said it, Miller knew it was an empty statement. He had already seen GIs giving food to hungry German children, and the inevitable bartering system would start up shortly. He would have to issue a nonfraternization order and hope his troops paid at least some attention to it. A realist, he knew they probably wouldn't.

"You said you had suggestions, von Schumann?"

"General, I believe a number of my civilians have skills that you can use during your unintended stay here in Potsdam. For instance, did you take any prisoners during the battle?"

Miller looked at Leland. "Half a dozen," Leland responded, thinking angrily of the thousands of missing Americans.

"Have you interrogated them?"

"No," Leland responded.

"And why not?"

"Because," Leland snapped, "we don't have a single fucking soul who speaks Russian. A couple of the Russian prisoners are too badly hurt to talk, but the others just sit there and smile at us and eat our food."

Von Schumann smiled. "I know of several displaced workers in my flock who are from the Soviet Union. Russian is their native tongue and they have learned out of necessity to speak German. They will translate Russian to German and we have several people who speak English."

Miller's mind raced. He would dearly love to know what orders the few Russians he held had been given prior to the attack. The answers to that sort of question might end all that bullshit about the attack being a mistake.

"I'll take your translators," Miller said, "if they speak English as well as you do. Where did you learn it?"

Von Schumann laughed, something he hadn't done much of lately. "Thank you, General, but in Europe it is virtually essential that an educated person be conversant in at least one language other than one's own. I also speak French and can get by in Spanish."

Miller cringed inwardly. The kraut was right. Everyone spoke more than one language in Europe. He sometimes considered himself barely adequate in English.

"General," von Schumann continued, "I have a number of other people who can serve as medical assistants, cooks, laborers, and such to free your people from some of those tasks. I have been watching your soldiers dig trenches. Wouldn't you like to have some of my people digging for you and earning their food?"

Von Schumann was offering a trade, and it was an easy decision to make. Food for labor while his men did the important work of preparing for battle. "Okay," said Miller, surprising himself by holding out his hand to von Schumann. It just seemed the right thing to do. "You're on."

Miller hopped in the front seat of the jeep and gestured for von Schumann to get in behind him. "Von Schumann, when you were a Nazi up at Stalingrad, just what did you do there?"

"I commanded a Panzer unit. A brigade of tanks."

"Against the Russians?" It was a foolish question, Miller realized. Who else would have been there?

"Certainly."

"Von Schumann, I think we should have a long talk fairly shortly."

ELISABETH HAD GOOD days and bad days. Until earlier, she thought her life was getting better. Her body no longer ached very much and she was able to think clearly at least most of the time. Survival no longer seemed laughably impossible.

Lis had been fortunate. She had been spared much of the horrors of the siege of Berlin. She had lived in her late parents' apartment on the outskirts and had to endure only a little of the bombing and, more recently, the incessant shelling from Red Army artillery had passed her by. Of course she'd gone to the air-raid shelter on many occasions, but most of the bombs had not fallen near her home. Several times, she'd looked skyward and seen the shapes of the hosts of bombers flying overhead. She understood the routine—the Americans bombed during the day and the British at night. Like everyone in Berlin, it was clearly evident that the city was defenseless. The Luftwaffe was nonexistent. She'd known some young men who'd been pilots and wondered if they still lived. Likely not, she thought.

On the radio, Propaganda Minister Joseph Goebbels told his shrinking world that the Allied bombers weren't enough to frighten the German people. Well, Lis thought, they were certainly enough to frighten her. Even at a distance, the shock waves could be felt and the clouds and fire and smoke were clearly visible. Berlin was a city in agony and she could feel the pain.

She recalled seeing a painting of what an artist thought was Hell and concluded that the people in the center of Berlin were living there.

When an occasional bomb did land near her home, she immediately went to the site to help as much as she could. She was far from alone in that effort as her neighbors all pitched in to help out. Sometimes, however, it was futile, as the mangled bodies of the dead were pulled from the debris, or the screaming maimed and injured were loaded into improvised ambulances and driven to overcrowded and understaffed hospitals that also lacked even rudimentary supplies.

She'd considered herself lucky until the food began to run out. She'd joined others in picking through garbage and in the ruins of bombed-out buildings looking for something to put in her stomach. She'd eaten things that were half-rotten and sometimes defied identification. But first, she knew her responsibility was to feed Pauli. He got the best parts of what she scrounged.

To the best of her knowledge, he was the only living relative that she had in Germany. She'd seen women of all ages, from the very young to the very old, prostituting themselves for food. There were hoarders in Berlin who took advantage of them and there were some soldiers who always seemed to have rations to trade. She thought she would rather die than stoop to that. A quiet voice told her that she might rather do anything than die.

Von Schumann had saved her and she felt she was on the way to recovery. When he said he'd seen American tanks approaching them, everyone had been elated. But the Russians and the Americans had fought and the Yanks had been driven off. All her hopes had been dashed. The barbarians, the Russians, had defeated the Americans. She'd watched with growing dismay as long columns of American soldiers made their way into Potsdam. Von Schumann said that the Americans had been defeated but not destroyed. He'd explained that they had brought their wounded and their equipment, withdrawing into Potsdam in what he referred to as "good order."

She understood when she saw them immediately begin to dig in. They were calm and determined, and she continued to watch as the day wore on. Her emotions were like a roller coaster. The Americans were real soldiers, not the old men and boys the German army was reduced to conscripting. Perhaps there was some hope.

"A penny for your thoughts," von Schumann said as he sat down beside her.

She smiled. "I think they're worth more than that. How are your conversations with the American general going?"

"Miller will feed us what he can and protect us as well as he is able. We will work for our keep. You might be of use doing some translating for them."

"Good. It will help pass the time." Pauli had found a couple of young friends and was playing in a basement.

Von Schumann smiled knowingly. "Would it be better than watching well-muscled young men doing heavy labor? You're a year or two older than my daughter, but you and she are so very similar."

Lis actually giggled and missed the look of sadness on his face. She'd been staring at one heavily muscled young man in a T-shirt who had a shock of short-cut red hair. He was clearly in charge of a group and she thought he must be a sergeant. He was about fifty yards away and she could hear laughter. Were the Americans so confident they could laugh in the middle of a war that had turned bad for them?

Suddenly, a screeching sound filled the air. "Get down!" yelled von Schumann. "Everyone down!"

Lis hurled herself to the ground and all around others did as well. A second later, explosions ripped through the area, shocking and deafening her. They seemed to go on forever. They didn't, of course. In a moment, they were over.

Lis stared at von Schumann. "What in God's name was that?"

"It's a multiple-rocket launcher called a Katyusha by the Soviets and a Stalin Organ by us. I heard it many, many times when I had two legs and was fighting them."

She picked herself up, wondering when the rocket assault would begin again. Von Schumann answered her unspoken question. "Unless they have a lot of them, they take a while to reload. Also, they aren't very accurate. I don't think this volley caused many casualties. However, they do make a horrible noise and terrify inexperienced soldiers."

"And civilians," she said.

With that, she looked to where the red-haired soldier had been working. It didn't look like any of the Yanks in the area had been hit, and a couple were coming out of their foxholes and trenches. They were looking around and laughing nervously. There. She saw him and was relieved. She laughed at herself for worrying about someone she didn't even know.

She smiled to herself. "I think I should go and see how Pauli is doing."

·   ·   ·

AFTER NEARLY TWO solid days of sleepless work, Steven Burke was finally allowed time to go back to his apartment and get some rest. There was real concern on the part of the higher-ups that some of the staff were being worked to exhaustion. However, instead of returning to his home, he called Natalie and she told him to come right over to her place, that she wanted to sit down and talk with him. When she said that, he wasn't so tired anymore.

Natalie lived in an extremely large apartment in a Victorian-style building. Because of Burke's position in the Pentagon, he was not really affected by gas rationing and wasn't concerned about the extra driving, although his head was bobbing drowsily by the time he arrived.

She grabbed his arm and pulled him inside. "You look awful," she said with a smile that softened it. "Have you slept in that uniform?"

"If I did, I wasn't aware of it. I'm not certain I've slept at all in a long time." He checked his watch and suddenly realized it was eight in the evening and not in the morning. He had lost that much track of time.

Natalie made them some strong, hot tea, and as he sipped the scalding brew he could feel a minimal amount of life returning to him.

"Can you talk about what you've been up to?" she asked. Each knew the other was cleared for sensitive information. "I'm certain you've been trying to figure out what the Russians will do next."

Burke savored the tea, enjoying its warmth. "That is precisely what we talked about, but with no definitive conclusions. Some think the crisis is over, although it will take a lot of work to resolve it, while others think it is just beginning. I fall into that latter group. I don't think it's over by a long shot. I think there's the strong possibility that a lot more blood will be spilled before we're done."

Natalie nodded, shaking her long dark hair. "I agree with you. God knows where we will be a year from now. Perhaps this will result in the downfall of the Communists. I hate them," she concluded with a sudden vehemence that surprised Steve. "Do you know why?"

"Yes," he said softly. "They killed your father and others in your family and took your property."

"But do you know how they died? Of course not. But I will remember it forever. My father's name was Nikolai Siminov. I changed mine to Holt when my mother remarried and my new father—a wonderful, loving man who cared for us until he died a couple of years ago—adopted me. One day, a couple of years after the Revolution, the Bolshevik secret police came for innocent Nikolai Siminov, and dragged him outside screaming. They kicked and punched him while my mother and I watched through a window. When that bored them, they threw him in a car and came back in and raped my mother while I hid in a closet listening to it all. Then, days later and just when we thought we'd never see him again, they dumped him on the doorstep of the house we were sharing with a couple of dozen others like ourselves."

Natalie paused, and Steve saw it was difficult for her. Her hands were shaking and her eyes were tearing up. "You don't have to do this to yourself," he said gently. He reached over and took her hand.

She ignored him. "My mother dragged him inside. No one else would help her and I was too small. He was a ruined man and I barely recognized him. All the bones in his face were broken. His teeth had been pulled out and there were burns and cuts all over his body. His fingernails had been ripped out and a couple of his fingers were infected stumps. Years later, my mother told me they had used red-hot pliers on his testicles. He was alive but almost totally mad with pain and fear. My mother treated him for a couple more weeks until the secret police, what is now the NKVD, came again. It seems he was released because of a bureaucratic mistake. They took him outside the building and shot him in the back of the head." She shook slightly. "They left him there."

She laughed bitterly. "For all I know, his body may still be lying on the pavement. My mother and I began running at that moment and didn't stop until we reached America. Along the way, my mother sold herself for food, for shelter, and finally, for passage to America. Yes, I love the Communists," she said, her voice a snarl.

She put down her tea and pulled out a cigarette, which Steve lit for her. It was unusual, as she rarely smoked. "I'm sorry," Steve said. "The words are totally inadequate, but I mean them."

Natalie touched his cheek with her hand. "I know that you do and I thank you. That story belongs to the past, and we have the present and the future to deal with. Now, what else do you know?"

Glad to have the topic changed, he continued on. "Well, there's a chance I'll be with a group going over to France to see Ike and help brief the bigwigs. That would be interesting."

"How exciting for you!" It was the normal Natalie speaking and it sounded wonderful.

"Yeah. It's hard to believe everything that's happened to me in the last couple of weeks. Marshall knows who I am, Truman spoke to me, some dumb Russian passed me a message, and some dumber ones tried to shoot at me. That reminds me, did you hear the rumor that Korzov was sent back to the USSR?"

"It's true," she said grimly, "and I wouldn't want to be in his shoes when they get their hands on him in Moscow. They are not gentle with traitors. What they did to my father will only be his beginning. Korzov's masters told the State Department he was 'ill' and they shipped him out before we could do anything about it."

Steve felt bad for Korzov, but he must have known the risks. "What about the rest of the Russians? Have they left too?"

"No," she answered. "While they have been confined to their embassy, none have been expelled. Nor are they likely to be, even if the problem becomes more serious. Thinking at State is that we need them here so we can talk more or less directly to Moscow, and somehow negotiate an end to this mess. If we send their personnel home, they will retaliate by expelling ours in Moscow, and then we will be reduced to communicating through either the Swedes or the Swiss. Frankly, we don't trust either country all that much. They have their own agendas."

They talked a while longer as the night grew later. As darkness fell, the effects of the tea wore off and the urge to sleep almost overwhelmed Steve.

"I think I'd better leave," he said, unsuccessfully stifling a yawn.

"Do I bore you?" Natalie quizzed him impishly. "Put your feet up on the couch and rest for a bit. Take a short nap. If you don't, I'm afraid you'll fall asleep while you're driving and get into an accident."

"Good thought. Wake me in an hour," Steve said sleepily as he complied with her command.

When he woke, it was to the smell of coffee and the streaming of sunlight through the window. "What the hell," he said and sat up, only to become aware that he was in his GI skivvies and covered by a thin blanket.

Natalie entered the room. She was wearing a robe and her hair hung down across her shoulders. She looked lovely. Better, she held out a steaming cup of coffee. "Has Lazarus returned?" she teased.

He flushed and took the coffee. It was both real and excellent. "Did you steal my uniform?"

"It was not a difficult achievement. You were sleeping so soundly I probably could have shaved your head and painted your body green without your noticing. I cleaned your uniform with a sponge and pressed it with an iron. You may put it on after you shower."

On top of the coffee, the thought of a shower was an outstanding idea. But then he realized something. "Natalie, I've been here all night. What will your neighbors think?"

"Thank you, brave soldier, for being worried about my reputation, but, even if someone did see you, I don't particularly care. In case you haven't noticed, I am not a child and my life is my own."

He mulled that over and had a second cup of coffee along with some toast that had been lathered with margarine. Coffee she could get, but not butter.

She gave him a robe. "In case you're curious, it belonged to an old and very dear friend of mine. He was killed in a battle in the Pacific. Midway. Now go take your shower. Leave your filthy underwear outside the door and I'll clean them as well."

"You don't have to do this," Steve said.

"I know." Natalie smiled.

The shower was a luxury and he wallowed in it. After drying, he put the robe on again, absurdly conscious that he had nothing on underneath.

In the living room, Natalie was still in her own robe. "My, my, don't you look refreshed."

He laughed. "I do feel like a new man."

"When do you have to report back?"

"Not until tomorrow. General Marshall and the war will just have to go on without me."

"I'm glad," she said, moving so that she stood directly in front of him. Barefoot, she came a little taller than his shoulder. She reached out and caressed his cheek with her hand. "You really are a gentle, sensitive, intelligent man, Steven Burke, and you're all mine until tomorrow."

The touch of her finger on his face was electric and he felt himself immediately aroused. She slid her slender body up to him and kissed him softly on the lips, gently pressing her belly and hips against him.

"Now it's your turn to kiss me," she said, and he complied. He tried to keep his kiss as soft as hers was, but he was having difficulty breathing. The two of them pressed tightly against each other while she responded and their kisses grew more fervent.

They separated and he became aware that his robe had parted and was open. Natalie looked down and smiled. Then she slid hers off her shoulders, and let it fall on the floor, standing naked before him. He gasped at her beauty. She had firm, full breasts, a slightly curved but still fairly flat belly, gently rounded hips, and the legs of a dancer. Natalie walked behind him and slid his robe down his back. Hand in hand they went into her room, where they fell on her bed and made love with a degree of pent-up urgency that shocked him.

As they lay beside each other, temporarily sated, she ran her finger down his chest and smiled. "Steven, you are so skinny. Doesn't anyone feed you?"

He chuckled quietly. "And you, Natalie, are so lovely." He could scarcely imagine this was actually happening to him. Natalie Holt was the most beautiful woman in the world. "I'm afraid I'm going to wake up and you'll be gone."

Natalie rolled over on his chest so that she was looking directly at him. "Don't worry about it. You're not going anyplace and neither am I." She laid her head on his chest. "Did anyone tell you I was cursed?"

"No," he answered, puzzled.

"Yes. Ever since I was twelve, I became aware of the effect I had on men. I could look in a mirror and see that I was what men think of as beautiful. Unfortunately, I also had a brain and that was my curse. Men—and women too—thought of me as a lovely ornament, only to be looked at, and not as an intellect to be taken seriously. I had to do twice as well in school and often I was accused of cheating or trading sex for a good grade. Very few people could accept the fact that I could succeed on my own."

She raised her head again and looked at him in wonder, almost shyly. "Everyone wanted to touch my breasts and not my mind, while you, dear Steven, wanted to do both. First, however, you did actually touch my mind by respecting my thoughts and opinions, and doing it so sincerely and so gently. That's when I started to fall in love with you."

She stopped talking and began to caress his manhood while kissing his chest. He felt himself stiffen again and, this time, didn't care if the world knew.

"Steven," she purred, "you are one in a million and I've waited a long time for someone like you." She guided him back on top of her and into her, wrapping her legs tightly about him. She smiled, biting her lower lip. He was aware of a bead of sweat on her forehead as she moved her hips in response to his thrusts. She took a deep breath.

"Do you love me, Steven?"

"Yes," he gasped.

"Now that I've found you, I have no intention of letting you go. When you go to Europe you will always remember who is waiting here for you, won't you?"

"Yes," Steve answered as their bodies moved in primal tune with each other. "Yes, yes, yes, yes!"

TONY THE TOAD squatted alone in the living room of a little house outside the Spandau district of Berlin. He didn't count the two corpses upstairs in the main bedroom. They didn't stink too badly yet. For a little while, he had been puzzled, since they didn't show any signs of wounds. Then it dawned on him—they had taken poison. They'd either been Nazi bigwigs who couldn't deal with the fall of Hitler and the Third Reich, or they were ordinary Germans who saw themselves dying in agony at the hand of the Russians.

Either way, he didn't give a shit. They had died and left him with a house that wasn't too badly damaged, and a storage room full of food they had probably hoarded while other loyal Germans went hungry. Fuck 'em, he thought. They probably deserved to die. Even if they didn't, it didn't make a helluva lot of difference.

Tony shifted his rifle to a more comfortable position and again looked out the window for a sign of the returning American army. As usual he saw nothing, only the lengthening of shadows that preceded the coming night. There was no sign of the Russians, either, which somewhat cheered him.

Count your blessings, he told himself. He was alive and unhurt. He was also safe and had a roof over his head. There was several weeks' worth of food in the basement, maybe more, and he had a rifle with some ammunition. It could have been a lot worse.

Tony stiffened as he heard a noise. It was a soft and gentle scratching. A cat? Possibly. A dog? He didn't think so. He quietly slipped off the safety on his weapon.

The sound of a window opening in the next room sent a chill down his spine. Should he run? Should he fight? If intruders were inside, they were probably outside the house as well, and, besides, where could he run to? He hunched over and walked to the doorway, took a deep breath, and lunged in, his rifle at the ready.

A small, thin, ragged man sat on the floor while another dangled awkwardly from the window, his head and chest inside the room and the remainder of his body still outside. They were both dirty and emaciated, and his first impression was that of human rodents. They were wearing what he immediately realized was some kind of prison uniform. The second man slid onto the floor and they both raised their hands stiffly in surrender and glared at him and his rifle in feral anger. Tony had never seen humans who looked so much like tortured animals.

For what seemed an eternity they stared at each other. Finally, the first man inside muttered something at him that Tony didn't understand but thought was German. The man then followed in what Tony took to be French. Perplexed, Tony asked if either man spoke English.

The man who had just come through the window responded, showing a mouth full of rotten teeth as he looked down the barrel of the menacing rifle. "I do," he said with a heavy accent that Tony didn't recognize.

They seemed to relax slightly, although they never took their sunken eyes off Tony's weapon. Apparently, English-speaking people were not their enemy. "Now," asked Tony, "who the hell are you and what are you doing here."

The English-speaker responded, talking hesitantly, as if he was trying to recall the words. "We are refugees. The Nazis forced us to leave our homes and work for the Germans in their factories. We are both from Poland. As is apparent, I speak English somewhat while my friend speaks it only a little. My name is Vaslov and his is Anton. Are you British?"

"American," Tony answered, and they both looked incredulous, fear immediately disappearing.

"The Americans are here?" Vaslov asked, disbelief evident in his voice.

"We were," Tony said ruefully, and explained that the Russians had ambushed the column. The information appeared to stun the two Poles.

Vaslov spoke solemnly. "If the Russians and you Yanks are fighting, this war could last a very long time and make our lives very, very dangerous."

Tony hadn't thought about the time factor. For some reason he'd felt his ordeal would be a short one. Now he had to rethink his position. "Are you Communists?" he asked.

"No," they answered quickly. Vaslov explained that they feared the Russians as much as they feared the Germans, as both had taken turns devouring their country. "Either will kill us," he said. "They are both beasts. One of the reasons the Germans imprisoned us was because we were part of the democracy movement. The Russians would not be gentler. They hate and fear the intelligentsia."

Vaslov curled his lips. "What's that smell?" When Tony explained about the bodies upstairs, both Vaslov and Anton smiled grimly. "Good. When it is real bad, no one will come in here. If we can stand it, we can remain here in some safety."

Tony thought about it and agreed. "Hell, we can always go out and find some more corpses if we have to, to sweeten the joint."

The two former slave workers chuckled at the macabre thought of dead Germans protecting them from discovery by the Russians. Cautiously, they talked through the afternoon. They decided they were in a fairly strong position. They had a weapon and they had food, although it would now have to be split three ways. They had a house and it would serve as a place to hide. They would stay there until they were either rescued or they thought it might be safe to try and head west from Berlin.

Tony asked, "What do you suggest we do while we are waiting?"

"Well," said Vaslov. "I would suggest we kill Nazis, although I think they are fast disappearing. It seems that the new enemy is Russia. Would you like to kill them?"

Tony the Toad smiled. He thought about Ernie and his buddies burning to death while trying to get out of the Sherman. Brentwood had died as well. He'd been an asshole, but he didn't deserve to bake. Killing Russians would be dangerous and they must not be so reckless as to invite discovery, but he thought they might be able to hurt the Commies and get some small measure of revenge.

Yes, he would indeed like to kill Russians.

CHAPTER 8

Outside, the spring sun was bright and warm. This made the air inside the squad bunker stifling and hot, a foretaste of what the summer would bring.

First Sergeant Stan Krenski hunched down and entered the bunker through the low and small entrance in the rear. An angular and rawboned man, he was not as tall as he sometimes appeared, and was only slightly taller than Logan.

"Jesus, it stinks in here," Krenski said in mock dismay. "Doesn't anybody shower anymore?"

Logan looked blandly at the others. He knew they were all pigs. "Why, I bathed just a little while ago. How about you guys?" The remainder of the squad assured Krenski that they had not only bathed but generously doused themselves with cologne in the last hour. It was a running gag. They all were filthy and stank to high heaven.

Krenski laughed and wiped his own dirty, sweaty brow. "Nice job," he said admiringly as he looked around. The bunker was roofed with metal beams over which there were thick layers of sandbags and earth. The walls were similarly constructed and firing slits faced in all directions in case someone infiltrated behind them. Much of the material for this and the many other fortifications had been liberated from the nearby buildings. There was additional joking that the American army had done more damage to Potsdam than the American air force.

"Thanks," said Logan. "Now, for God's sake, Sarge, don't tell us we've got to move someplace else. A helluva lot of work went into making this pleasure palace the beautiful creation that it is."

Krenski took off his helmet and wiped his forehead. "Nope. I came to tell you that the captain wishes to see you, Sergeant Logan, and right away. I'll stay here and admire how you put this place together while you and him talk."

Logan grabbed his helmet and rifle and left the bunker for the short walk to the captain's headquarters. Shit, he thought as he stepped outside, what the hell did Captain Dimitri want? Was he still pissed off because Lieutenant Singer got hit? Hell, that wasn't his fault. Wasn't anybody's, really. Dimitri, who was usually around all the time, had been conspicuous by his absence for the last day or so. What did that mean?

Logan ducked his head as he entered Dimitri's command bunker and took off his helmet.

Captain Dimitri was seated behind a makeshift desk made of planks. He did not look up from his papers. "Singer lost his arm, you know."

Damn, thought Logan, he is pissed. "I'm not surprised, sir, it was pretty well gone when we got him to the aid station. I didn't think anything short of a miracle was going to save it, and I haven't seen many miracles lately."

Finally, Dimitri looked up. Logan saw sadness in his face, but not anger. "Singer could have been a good officer. Now he gets to go home the first time we figure out how to get people out of here."

"I liked him," Logan said sincerely. "You're right. He wanted to learn and to do the right thing."

Logan felt a little guilty that he had not had an opportunity to visit Singer in the hospital. He made a mental note to rectify the problem. While the last few days had consisted of a lot of work, there still had been some free time during which he could have gone.

Dimitri nodded. "Sit down." Logan pulled up a crate and complied. "But that's not why I called for you. By the way, you stink and look like shit. Starting tomorrow we will be offering showers on a rotation basis and, with luck, you'll be getting one about every week or so. The engineers have figured out a way to pump, strain, and somewhat purify the water from the river so we can bathe in it, but for Christ's sake, tell your men not to swallow it or cook with it. That damn river is still stuffed full of corpses."

"Yes, sir."

Logan knew all about boiling the water for drinking and cooking, and had seen the swollen and rotting bodies of people and animals float slowly by. The news about showers would definitely cheer up his platoon. Maybe they could even do laundry. Maybe they could even get real food instead of rations. He never thought he would long for the dubious pleasures of a mess hall, but he did now.

Dimitri started speaking again, ending Logan's thoughts. "For the second time in two months, your damned platoon needs an officer, and it's highly unlikely we are going to get one from outside. I made a proposal and it went all the way up and everyone concurs. Congratulations, Jack, you are now an officer and a gentleman."

Logan was stunned. "You've got to be joking, sir."

Dimitri grinned. "I never joke. You know that." He reached into his pocket and pulled out the gold bars of a second lieutenant. "Here, these used to be mine. Just don't go wearing them until we get our asses out of this place. Snipers are attracted to shiny things."

Logan took them, his mind awhirl. "But what about Sergeant Krenski. He's the most senior NCO in the company."

"Don't worry about Krenski, Sergeant—I mean Lieutenant Logan—I've taken care of him."

"Captain, I don't understand. With all of Krenski's experience, he'd be a great officer."

"Disagree, Jack. He's a great NCO. He'd be a shitty officer. He's not officer material."

Logan was puzzled. "Can I ask why? What you said almost sounds elitist, and I know you're not that way." Dimitri had commented several times on the fact that his parents were poor immigrants from Greece and how hard they had worked to achieve what they felt was success.

Dimitri chuckled. "I'm disappointed in you, Jack. You've been working with the man for months and you really don't know a thing about him. Tell me, what's the first thing he does when he gets a written order?"

"Uh, he usually fumbles for his reading glasses, which he can never find. He lost them a while ago, so he gives the papers to someone else to read for him." Logan paused as the truth dawned. "Oh shit, he can't read, can he?"

"Bingo," said the captain. "Krenski's thirty years old and has been in the army since he lied his way in at sixteen. He can read a little, very damn little, but he's pretty much illiterate. That, my new lieutenant, is why he will not take over the platoon. In case you're curious, he came to me when he thought I might promote him and told me his story. Bottom line, the man was terrified we'd make him an officer. He'll be delighted that you got it instead, and he can stay as my senior NCO."

Logan chuckled. "I'll keep his secret."

"Good, now let's walk over to your platoon so I can formally introduce you in case they think you're lying about the promotion."

When the two men entered Logan's bunker, they were surprised to find the entire platoon assembled.

"I took the liberty, Captain," said a grinning Sergeant Krenski. "We're gonna have a little party to celebrate, if you don't mind, sir. Some of the guys, uh, managed to find and liberate some schnapps that might have otherwise fallen into the wrong hands. It would be an awful thing to have abused."

IN HIS HEADQUARTERS, Major General Miller listened to the reports in icy fury. The Russians had begun shelling their positions. The barrage wasn't all that heavy, but the unofficial truce was obviously over.

"Sir," said Leland, "the artillery wants to fire back."

"At what?" snapped Miller. "Do we know precisely where those shells are coming from?"

As he said that, a heavy one landed a hundred yards from where they were dug in and shook dirt from the roof. Miller was puzzled. Yes, the Reds were firing at them, but the effort seemed to be directed at nothing in particular. It was just a number of pieces of artillery lobbing shells into the perimeter without any direction or purpose at all. It didn't make sense.

Captain Leland dusted himself off. "No, sir, we don't really know where their batteries are. We can do some guessing and start shooting back, but God knows if we'll hit anything."

"Then hold fire," Miller said. "No point in wasting ammunition and giving away the location of our own guns." That, he thought wryly, presumed the Commies hadn't already figured that out.

The situation was frustrating as well as puzzling. Despite the barrage, he really didn't feel that his defenses were in any danger. Lookouts could see no troops or tanks moving up for an assault. It was as if a bunch of drunks had taken control of the Russian artillery and were having a good time.

"Any report on casualties?" Miller asked, and he was assured that all units were reporting nothing in the way of killed and only a few wounded. Of course, they all were dug in and hunkered down and only a direct hit would cause damage. He was told that a number of civilians had been killed and wounded, and he regretted not pushing them harder to dig their own shelters. The one-legged German, von Schumann, and his people were probably okay. Miller recognized the kraut as a survivor.

After a while, the firing ceased. "Now what the hell was that all about?" Miller wondered out loud.

"General," called a sergeant with a radio headset over his ears. "We're getting something from Ninth Army. Looks like the Nazis have just announced that Hitler is dead, committed suicide in his bunker in Berlin, and that some guy whose name sounds like Donuts is now in charge of Krautland."

"Doenitz," corrected Miller, stifling a smile. "He's an admiral in their navy."

Good God, he thought, could the shelling have been nothing more than a bunch of drunken Russians celebrating? The Commies might have gotten the news first, and God knew they had so much more reason to celebrate Hitler's death. What did it mean for their situation in Potsdam? With Hitler out of the way, did it mean an end to the war with Germany? But did it mean the start of a new one with Russia?

General Miller checked the calendar on the wall and noted the date. It was April 30, 1945. What on earth was going to happen now?

Miller put on his helmet and stepped outside with a puzzled Captain Leland close behind. He decided he needed a dose of reality so he walked over to a nearby squad bunker and ducked in.

"Ten-hut!" Leland ordered.

"Carry on," Miller said. This was more like a normal army. However, it was definitely against regulations for enlisted men and officers to be drinking together. Damn, it was something else he would have to ignore.

"Gentlemen," Miller said, "I have just heard that one Sergeant Logan has been promoted to lieutenant. I've also heard that Hitler is dead and I don't know which is more important. If the rumor is true it's great news. However, if Logan's been promoted, then this army is doomed and we should all plan to surrender right now."

There was stunned silence followed by hoots of laughter. "Congratulations, Lieutenant," Miller said, and the two men shook hands. "The lieutenant and I go back a ways. When I first got to England, Mr. Logan was a mere corporal and got dragooned into driving for me. I knew he was officer material the first time he got behind the wheel and we nearly ran into an oncoming truck."

"Sir, it wasn't my fault," Logan answered with a smile. The schnapps was very relaxing. Hitler was dead and he'd been promoted. Not a bad day at all. "Nobody told me those crazy Brits drove on the wrong side of the road."

"Yes, but after two weeks you still hadn't figured it out and you damn near got me killed a half-dozen times more. And besides, they think we're the ones who are nuts for driving on the right."

Miller eyed a half-full bottle of schnapps standing proudly on an empty ammo carton. Sergeant Krenski tentatively handed him a glass. Miller poured a decent portion and held up the glass. "Good luck, Lieutenant."

"Thank you, sir."

"And good luck to your men. They're going to need it."

Again, more good-natured hoots. Miller knew it was time to leave. He'd had his fun, and generals have a way of suffocating parties. If anyone asked whether he'd seen officers and enlisted men drinking together, he'd simply say that he'd seen them drinking separately but in the same room. Sometimes regulations are meant to be ignored.

He and Leland stepped outside into the bright sunlight. Logan followed them. "Who got the dollar?" Miller asked.

"The first sergeant, sir," said Logan. Traditionally, the first person who salutes a brand-new second lieutenant got a dollar from him. "But I think he cheated."

Miller laughed and walked away. Logan took in his new domain, which consisted of three bunkers in a couple of ruined buildings. It was not a magnificent kingdom. "Officer and a gentleman" had a nice ring to it, but what it really meant was additional responsibility and more work. Instead of a squad, he had a platoon of more than thirty men. He had to admit, though, he wasn't displeased. He'd been chafing under the realization that he was capable of being more than an enlisted man, even a sergeant. A damn shame it had to come as a result of Singer's destroyed arm.

A group of refugees was working at clearing the area of debris. He spotted the dark-haired girl he'd seen several times earlier. He'd never met her, but almost felt like he should apologize. She was so small and thin he'd first thought she was a child. He'd seen her a couple of times since then and realized she was a young woman, and not bad-looking at all.

She hung around a lot with that von Schumann character, and Logan wondered if she spoke English. It would be nice to talk to a young woman again. Hell, he laughed, it'd be nice even if she didn't speak English.

ASSISTANT SECRETARY OF State Dean Acheson was shown almost immediately into the drab and spartan office of the Soviet ambassador, Andrei Gromyko. As always, the grim and unsmiling Russian dispensed with formalities and went to the heart of the matter. If Gromyko was upset that it was the lower-ranking Acheson and not Secretary of State Stettinius who had come in response to his summons, he made no comment. And if he was surprised that Natalie Holt followed Acheson, he again showed nothing, merely nodded as terse introductions were made.

The reasons for Natalie's presence were twofold. First, she could translate if necessary, and second, Acheson and others wanted to gauge the Russian's reaction on seeing her after Soviet goons had tried to kill her and Burke.

"My government is most upset," Gromyko began.

"As is mine," responded Acheson, interrupting the Russian. His instructions were to not play games. He was to be polite, but very firm. He had requested Natalie's presence as a means of possibly discomfiting Gromyko. Although the Russian stared at her, it didn't seem to be working.

"The attack of the American army upon the peace-loving Soviet liberators of Europe was unprovoked and showed a side of the capitalist states that we suspected but could not prove."

Acheson was annoyed by the lie but dared not show it. "Your information is incorrect. We specifically told you our small force was coming to assist you, when and what direction it would take, and all this was done to avoid any kind of tragic incident like what just occurred.

Your troops in the field should have been well briefed, but weren't. Unless, of course, the attack was intentional."

Gromyko sat stonily. He didn't even blink.

Acheson continued as Natalie sat, transfixed, by the dialogue. "And, as to the question of who attacked whom, it is now irrelevant. Soldiers on both sides were killed and wounded, and taken prisoner, and that includes some Russian soldiers from your 47th Army. They confirm that they were ordered to attack our positions. We also hold you responsible for the casualties caused by Russian soldiers, doubtless drunk, who indiscriminately fired artillery at our positions, particularly in Potsdam, in celebration of the death of Hitler."

"No troops of ours fired on yours. We are too disciplined. More than likely the drunks wore American uniforms." Gromyko sneered. He leaned forward and glared, and Natalie could almost feel the heat of his anger. "Now, let us get to matters that are truly important. We hold over five thousand of your men as prisoners and are gathering more each day like a farmer gathers wheat. Your soldiers are uninspired and fearful, as well they should be."

Gromyko leaned back in his chair. "I will not argue with you as to which army fired first. It does not matter, as you have doubtless been told lies by your Eisenhower, who wishes to cover for his mistakes.

"As to any of our Soviet soldiers in your hands spreading such filth as you stated, it is apparent that they are either lying to gain advantage or were tortured. However, whatever transpired to start the fighting is done and cannot be undone. Now we must discuss what happens next and what price you will pay for your country's insolence."

Acheson stiffened. Now it comes, he thought.

"The Soviet Union will both release the men we have taken as prisoners and permit the force in Potsdam to depart upon your agreeing to the following conditions: First, you will not attempt any further offensive actions against the Soviet army."

Acheson mentally concurred. There were no plans to do any such thing, anyhow. "I presume you will permit us to continue our supply efforts and provide us with a list of those Americans being held prisoner."

"Certainly. The second condition is that you will disavow any rights to Berlin, which our brave socialist comrades have taken and hold by right of conquest. Further, the zones of occupation that were to have been divided among the United States, Great Britain, and, at your insistence, France, shall now be limited to the Rhineland and the area just to the northwest of Switzerland. You will not occupy any of Austria."

The fifty-two-year-old Acheson was stunned, and Natalie was hard-pressed to keep her emotions in check. She spoke for the first time. "That, Ambassador Gromyko, is not what was agreed to at Yalta."

Gromyko shrugged, as if dismissing the query of a small and not particularly bright child. "Women should not be involved in these sorts of discussions."

Despite his pious-sounding statement, he had been undressing Natalie with his eyes. She was used to this sort of treatment and simply glared at him. Gromyko represented all that she hated. People like him had destroyed her family.

Natalie responded angrily. "I am involved because your people tried to kill me."

Gromyko was unmoved. "You and your lover, Colonel Burke, had something that belonged to us. It was considered quite important at the time. However, there was no attempt on your life. You imagined it. My men may have gotten overzealous in an attempt to halt you and recover our property, but they have been chastised, and, after all, nothing came of it. Colonel Korzov has returned to Moscow for reassignment following his indiscretion. Regardless, neither you nor Colonel Burke are of any interest to us. You may do whatever you wish without any paranoid fears. Neither you, nor Burke, nor your mother are of any interest to us."

Natalie tried not to gasp. Korzov reassigned? Probably to a grave. And how the devil did he know about her mother?

"Secretary Acheson and Miss Holt, the Yalta agreement no longer applies; in fact, it no longer exists. When you attacked the Russian army you repudiated it. You should be fortunate that the Soviet Union, which has suffered twenty million dead at the hands of the Hitlerites, is permitting you any voice whatsoever in the future of Germany. I agree with Premier Stalin and Comrade Molotov that our terms are most generous."

"Ambassador," Acheson persisted, "that sort of settlement would be unacceptable to the American people. It would be as if all our efforts in Europe were for nothing. We too paid a debt in blood and cannot simply walk away from it."

Gromyko stared at the ceiling. It was as if further discussion of a closed topic bored him. "What the American people think is of absolutely no concern. You should be more strict with them. As is Comrade Stalin, for instance, with those who do not see his vision for a united peoples' Europe."

"I am well aware how your government treats those who disagree with it," Natalie said acidly. "I would not think it something to be proud of."

The comment appeared to amuse Gromyko. "Your opinions are of no concern to me, Miss Holt. I am well aware that your parents were traitors to the Soviet Union."

The comment stunned her. How did Gromyko know so much about her background? Or were there Soviet sympathizers in the State Department who would leak that sort of information? Perhaps some State Department employees were being blackmailed. She might have been vulnerable if her mother's past hadn't already become common knowledge within State. But what about others? The FBI was already checking. What would they find?

Gromyko turned to Acheson. "If you were implying that acceptance of our most generous terms will cost Mr. Truman his office, then I am utterly unsympathetic. Having permitted this insanity to occur, it is likely that he is incompetent and should go. We can deal with his replacement as readily as we do him, and our terms will not change."

Gromyko rose, signaling an end to the short meeting. "Please convey my regards to Mr. Stettinius and Mr. Truman, and inform them of our terms. Also please inform them that we expect a favorable response in a very short time. We cannot permit the remnants of that annoying Miller Force to remain very long where they are. It is only our innate generosity that has allowed us to permit your planes to drop food and medical supplies to them without interference. Good day, Mr. Acheson, Miss Holt."

CAPTAIN MACK WALTERS truly liked piloting the military version of the Piper Cub. Unlike most pilots who lusted after the chance to fly fighters, or, second choice, bombers, the thirty-year-old Walters was quite happy flying low and slow scouting missions. He was a good pilot, but knew his limitations. In a dogfight, his lack of lightning re-flexes would surely get him killed, and he really was terrified at the thought of hauling around a B-17. He was firmly convinced that air-craft that large were not intended to fly. Besides, he would have had to share the plane with others, while his current little craft was usually his and his alone, even though there was room for one more person. This left him plenty of time for reflection and contemplation.

He did not think about the unique hazards of his job, that flying a slow, unarmed plane over enemy territory would have struck some people as utter insanity. Mack enjoyed it. He liked to joke that every-one from Texas was just a little crazy anyhow, and damn few people argued with him.

Beneath him, golden sunlight reflected off the Elbe. U.S. forces were on the western side of it and the Russians on the east. His assign-ment was simple—to see if he could figure out what the Russians were up to as they settled in on their side of the river after the debacle that had cost so many lives.

Top brass was clearly disconcerted by the numbers of Russian troops and tanks massing along the river. Just because they were there, however, didn't mean they had intentions of doing anything but gather and wait. But wait for what?

Walters took a deep breath and turned his tiny plane eastward, flew across the river, and over the Russian area. After a moment, he exhaled loudly when it seemed that he was unnoticed. More than likely, they had seen him but thought he was too insignificant to bother with.

He climbed higher to get a better view of the unfolding panorama. "Hot Dog to Bun," he said, cringing at the call sign his demented com-manding officer had thought up. "Hot Dog to Bun. Come in, Bun."

A tinny voice responded over the plane's radio. "This is Bun. What do you see, Captain?"

"I see hundreds of tanks, about the same number of trucks and other vehicles, along with many, many infantry units. A lot more than I can count. It looks like still more are coming down the pike too."

"Hot Dog, are they still parked?" the voice asked. Mack said they were. Bun sounded disappointed. "Okay, see if you can spot anything unusual."

Walters signed off without sharing the opinion that the whole thing was fucking unusual. He was about to turn back to the Allied side of the Elbe when a strange shadow caught his eye. Something was camouflaged, and that something was rather extensive.

He dropped lower, until he was scarcely a couple hundred feet off the ground. "Shit," he muttered in disbelief at the sight below. He got his camera and began taking pictures. He was so engrossed he didn't see the tracers streaming toward him from the ground as he flew over his subject.

The shells hit his tiny plane and, fortunately for him, went through its thin exterior and on into the sky. Walters began to bank and juke the plane frantically to shake off the Russian gunners as he headed in the direction of the Elbe and safety.

The plane suddenly bucked hard and he knew it had taken a bad hit. He tried to shift in his seat and a shaft of almost unendurable pain raced from his leg to his brain, and he nearly blacked out. He looked down and saw raw red meat just above his left knee. One of the machine-gun shells had gone through his leg and exited through the roof of the cabin, where he could now see blue sky.

His body began to shake and his vision started to blur. He was going into shock and losing blood fast. He called Bun and told them what had happened and that he would try to set down on the west side of the Elbe. He explained what he had seen and that corroboration was in the camera. Bun, voice tense with real concern, wished him luck.

Suddenly, there was silence. The engine had cut out. He tried to restart it, but it refused. Mack looked down and saw he was across the river and theoretically safe. Now all he had to do was land the damn thing. There. He saw a field. Even better, there were a couple of jeeps not too far away. As he dropped to the ground, he saw people running to them and driving toward where he would land. Help was coming and he knew he would need it fast.

The plane touched the uneven ground, skipped along, and finally came to a bumpy, jolting stop that made him scream from the pain of his shattered leg as the Piper hit every lump and furrow. Then there was silence and a feeling of deep peace settled over him. Mack Walters was delighted. As his world faded, his last living thought was how strange it was that his leg had stopped bleeding and he didn't hurt anymore.

• • •

HARRY TRUMAN WAS outraged and felt betrayed. He glowered at the handful of people in the Oval Office.

"Would someone tell me just how the hell the *Chicago Tribune* gets away with printing national secrets? I knew that the *Tribune*'s publisher, McCormick, hated Roosevelt, but why has he transferred that nastiness to me?"

"Because we're Democrats," muttered Attorney General Francis Biddle. "Colonel Robert McCormick hated FDR with an intensity that bordered on the pathological. As Roosevelt's successor, you are the logical beneficiary of his wrath. To McCormick, anything that smacks of the New Deal is evil. As the *Tribune*'s publisher, he can print pretty well anything he wishes if he isn't afraid of the consequences."

"Can we deny it?" Truman asked. "We still have a number of things we've either lied about or withheld from the public for the good of the war effort."

General Marshall answered, "I don't see how."

The original press releases had referred only to a tragic misunderstanding that had caused "some casualties" and that steps were under way to ensure that the situation did not repeat itself. It was true, but terribly incomplete. Somehow, the *Tribune* had gotten hold of the full story of the battle and had printed it. Now the uproar was sweeping the United States and Congress was raging for an answer.

"The *Tribune* says there are more than ten thousand casualties," Biddle said. "That can't be correct. Aren't most of them just missing?"

Marshall patiently instructed him that soldiers who were missing in action were counted as casualties, and that many were Russian prisoners. Gromyko had said five thousand, and no one could dispute him. "Dear God," moaned Biddle.

Truman laughed bitterly. He didn't like Biddle. The man was a weakling and some said he was totally dominated by the FBI director, J. Edgar Hoover. What the devil had FDR been thinking when he appointed the man? When the situation got settled, one of his first changes would be to name a new attorney general.

Marshall appeared deep in thought. He was still mulling over the flash message he had gotten from Ike's headquarters. The implications were ominous, but he was not ready to share them with the others in the room.

"Sir," Marshall finally said, "like everyone else gathered here, I have no idea which way the Russians will jump. It is indeed possible that the apparent victory over Germany will result in everything they wish, but I somehow doubt it. As Mr. Stettinius reported on Acheson's meeting this morning with Gromyko, I think they will hang on to our boys in Potsdam as well as those in their prison camps and try to wring concessions out of us. Worst possible alternative is that they will launch an all-out attack across the Elbe that will result in a full-scale war."

"If the Reds do come, is Ike prepared for it?" Truman asked.

"As much as anyone can be with so little time to actually do anything. However, if the Russians do attack, I am confident the results will not be as one-sided as the attack on Miller Force."

Truman shook his head. "Gromyko has told us what they want in return for our boys. It is totally unacceptable, practically absurd. Berlin cannot be handed to them entirely. That would leave us very little control of Germany, and then only at the sufferance of Russia. Acheson thinks there's a small possibility Gromyko's comments might have been a starting point for real talks, but I am not so certain."

The president stood and looked out the window behind his desk. "War with Russia?" he said, thinking aloud. "God help us."

CHAPTER 9

*S*talin seated himself. The building in which they were meeting was in the devastated German city of Kustrin and had been badly damaged. Light streamed through the shattered roof and dust was everywhere. He ignored it.

"Proceed," directed Stalin.

Zhukov took a pointer and walked to the map. "We have developed a plan for the defeat of the Allies that will be both decisive and as swift as we can possibly make it. As a result, there will be very little subtlety in our attack. We will hit them, bleed them, and push them back. We have titled the plan 'Red Inferno.' "

"Good," said Stalin.

"Nor, as you have wished, will there be any delay. Our forces are simply gathering their breath and not doing anything major in the way of resupply and reinforcing. Because of that, we are confident the attack will be totally unexpected."

Stalin again agreed, and Zhukov felt his confidence growing.

"Comrade Stalin, our strategy is very simple. The main thrust will be against General Bradley's army group. It will be attacked with overwhelming force and driven back to the Rhine. Koniev's army will protect our southern flank and Rokossovsky's will protect the north. Both those armies and others will be stripped to support the main attack, which will be led by General Chuikov and myself. Even reduced, however, Rokossovsky and Koniev will still be able to apply pressure against the American and British units confronting them."

Zhukov pointed to a city on the map. "Even as we drive to the Rhine, we must plan to go on. Antwerp is the key. Militarily, Hitler was right when he started that assault in the Ardennes last December, the one the Americans refer to as the Battle of the Bulge. Take Antwerp, and the American advantage in supplies and ammunition will cease to exist. Take Antwerp from them, and the channel ports and Marseilles in the south will not be able to supply their armies in the manner they need to fight. Comrade Stalin, we take Antwerp and the Allies are through."

Stalin's eyes glowed with fervor as he thought of the possibilities success would bring. "What will the Allies be doing to stop us while we are driving on Antwerp?" he asked.

"Comrade Stalin, they will try to reinforce their armies from Italy, but we will choke that off by air attacks. Even if they do succeed to a point, Koniev will seal them off and prevent them from being a factor in the thrust toward Antwerp. They will also seek to prevent us from maintaining a steady stream of supplies through their own air power, which is much greater then that of the Nazis. The one who wins the supply war will win the shooting war."

"What about Potsdam, Comrade Zhukov?"

Zhukov shrugged. "As I stated the last time we met, the Americans inside are of no consequence and can stay there and rot. I have General Bazarian and a reinforced corps of second-echelon soldiers keeping tabs on them, and he is free to do as he wishes so long as it does not interfere with our main purpose. His primary orders are to ensure that Miller Force does not get loose in our rear, or try to cut the autobahn, which we will be using for supplies."

"How long will this campaign, this Red Inferno, take, Comrade Zhukov?"

Zhukov was reluctant to make a prediction. There were too many variables. However, he knew that an impatient Stalin wanted a schedule.

"Three to six months, comrade. In six months at the latest, we will be on the Rhine and in Antwerp. At that point we can either dictate peace or keep going into France." Zhukov chuckled. "I have never seen Paris," he joked.

Stalin too smiled at the thought. He would have preferred that Zhukov had predicted a quicker victory. So much could occur in six months. Yet he knew his armies were tired and that the Americans would likely fight bitterly to prevent being expelled.

"When will it begin?"

"Tonight, Comrade Stalin," said Zhukov, enjoying the look of pleased surprise on the other man's face.

THE LARGE, DRAB tent suited the mood of the men all too well. The flap opened and Major General Francis "Freddie" de Guingand entered, smiling affably at the handful of confreres at SHAEF's field headquarters near Reims, France. De Guingand was liked and respected by the Americans. His boss, Field Marshal Bernard Montgomery, was not.

"Where the hell is Monty?" snapped Beetle Smith.

"He could not make it," sighed de Guingand. "The suddenness of the meeting conflicted with other plans. I believe he is in London, meeting with Sir Alan Brooke. Therefore, you have the honor and high pleasure of dealing with me."

"Bullshit." Beetle Smith chuckled. "But probably just as well. At least you understand English."

"Freddie," injected Ike, "we are trying to decide just what the Russians are up to. This afternoon we received a piece of information that could be of enormous significance."

Bradley interrupted. Ike did not mind. "Aerial reconnaissance photos. The pilot died getting them."

"Which," Smith added, "does not necessarily mean the objects he photographed are going to be used as he thought. He may have died a hero, but he still could be wrong."

De Guingand reached for the small pile of glossies and perused them. "My, my. It does look like bridging equipment and small boats. Where on earth were these things when the pictures were taken?"

"Only a couple of miles east of the Elbe and in the middle of a huge tank park," Bradley answered. "These were the only things that were camouflaged. Everything else—tanks, guns, trucks, men—was all in plain sight, but the bridging equipment and the boats were hidden. The pilot of the scout plane saw them and was shot down for his pains. He died after making a crash landing on our side of the Elbe."

"So," said Freddie, helping himself to a sandwich, "the question becomes, Why did the Russians bring the equipment to the Elbe. Was it a mistake? Just the normal baggage of an army on the move? Or"—he paused, unintentionally dramatic—"are they intending to cross? And another thought. If there is one place where they are hidden, mightn't there be a number of others?"

"Exactly," said Bradley. "We think they are going to try and pull another sneak attack, just like what they did to Miller, only this time much, much bigger. We have other recon planes out trying to confirm this. It would mean an all-out war, and not just the mess at Potsdam." His normally gloomy face was more downcast than usual.

De Guingand said solemnly, "That equipment is intended to be used."

Ike stood and paced nervously. "I agree too. Freddie, ever since the incident with Miller, we've been making contingency plans that would cover just such an eventuality as a full war with Russia. We have to let them fire the first shot, but then we must be united, and that means you must convince Montgomery to cooperate fully and without question." A thought struck him. "Good God, what do we do about the Germans? Do we continue to fight them as well?"

No one had an answer.

SECOND LIEUTENANT BILLY Tolliver desperately wished that he was back at home in the sleepy backwater town of Opelika, Alabama, instead of hiding by the Elbe River, above the German town of Magdeburg. It was night and he was on the east-facing front of a low hill, scarcely a mound, that gave him a decent view of the river, which was only about a half mile away. It was not a pleasant sight. The entire world about him was going up in flame and fury as hundreds of big Russian guns pounded the area behind him with their shells.

If it hadn't been for the fact that two of the three men he'd brought with him were now dead, he would have found humor in that all the Russians were doing with their barrage was to churn up the dirt and make it easier for the German farmers to plant their crops. He and the annoying PFC Holmes were likely the only Americans alive in the area, and Holmes's radio was their only direct link to the outside world. Holmes was annoying because he thought he knew everything and spoke with a nasal New England accent.

Holmes had burrowed himself deep in a foxhole as Tolliver watched while the Russians completed the bridging of the Elbe with methodical and ominous efficiency. Soon the first bridge would be complete and the second, only a few yards downstream, would follow in a matter of minutes. Both spans were swarming with people connecting pontoons and bridge segments. In the moonlight, he could also see what appeared to be a long line of T34 tanks waiting patiently for the bridges to be done so they could rumble across.

Without fanfare and almost without Tolliver realizing it, the first bridge was finished. Then the second. "Holmes, tell them people back at battalion that tanks are starting to cross."

He thought about telling them that he was going to leave in about thirty seconds, but decided not to mention it. He was afraid he might be ordered to stay and fight to the last man, which he did not think was a good idea.

An explosion shook both bridges as a bomb landed between them, causing a geyser of water to lift high in the air. "What the hell," Tolliver yelled gleefully. Then he saw the faint shadow of a passing plane in the dark sky. He briefly caught a faint silhouette and thought it was a P-47 Thunderbolt.

An excited Holmes appeared beside him. "Holy shit, sir, we're hitting back." Russian antiaircraft tracer fire punctuated the statement. It didn't appear that they were shooting at anything in particular. Nor were they hitting anything.

"Yeah," said Tolliver. "Hey, don't those things usually fly around in pairs?"

As Tolliver made the comment, the second Thunderbolt roared low overhead and dropped its bomb load. This time, it was close enough for the blast to separate the upstream bridge from its mooring. While they watched, fascinated, the bridge swung until it collided with its downstream brother. The jolt separated more sections and dumped a couple of tanks, along with about a score of men, into the water, where they disappeared.

Both men whooped as the planes returned again to strafe the Russian side of the river. Then they became aware of a new sound in the air—Russian planes had belatedly arrived to protect the vulnerable crossing site. In horror, they watched as one of the P-47s lost a wing and cartwheeled into the ground while the other flew away, its bombs and bullets expended.

"Holmes," said Tolliver, "this has just gotten bigger than all of us. You think you can find where you hid that jeep yesterday?"

"Not a doubt in my military mind, sir."

"Good," said Tolliver. "We've seen more than enough Russian fire-power. Let's get the fuck out of here."

NEWS OF THE Russian crossing of the Elbe sent everyone in the Pots-dam perimeter to their battle stations in the middle of the night. Dis-cipline was good, and only a few shots were fired at shadows and stray animals. When the dawn came, so too did relief. There was no sign of the Russian army. Patrols and listening posts reported that nearby Red tanks had not moved. This was quickly confirmed by scout planes that braved the battles going on around the Elbe to provide Potsdam with the needed information regarding nearby Soviet locations.

Thus, by midmorning life in Potsdam had returned to a semblance of normality. The soldiers were told to stand down and get some rest, and food was prepared. For Jack Logan, it meant that he could finally visit the hospital where Lieutenant Singer was convalescing.

On arrival, Logan was appalled by the number of wounded in the makeshift hospital in the palace of Sanssouci, once used by the Kaiser. He really hadn't known what to expect and he thought he had been steeled for the worst. But he had not been prepared for the sight of hundreds of men lying in rows of beds amid remnants of baroque splendor. Many of the wounded were heavily bandaged, and many were also moaning and crying in pain. It was the sounds of pain that got him, along with the smell of antiseptic and the primal scent of fear. The sounds were a low chorus of agony while medics and doc-tors moved among them. It was hard to believe that the battle that had caused the majority of the wounds had been days ago.

With good directions from a harried medic, he found Singer. The once plump lieutenant was a sallow-cheeked parody of himself. Logan tried not to stare at the heavily bandaged shoulder and short stump, which was all that remained of Singer's left arm.

With some effort, Singer greeted him. "Good to see you, Jack, and congratulations. You'll make a great officer. Even better than me."

Logan smiled. "I see news travels fast around here."

"Captain Dimitri came by and told me yesterday. Besides," he chided, "your stripes have been removed from your sleeve and, unless I've gone blind as well, that's a dark bar on your helmet."

"Well, thanks again. Now how the hell are you doing, Lieutenant?"

"My name's David. You can call me that since we are all brother officers and allegedly gentlemen. I'd like that, Jack."

"I would too," said Logan and found he meant it. "Now, how the hell are you, David?"

Singer fought back a tear but gave in to a grimace from the pain. "About as well as a one-armed Jewish lieutenant could be. It hurts, Jack, and not just the physical part. They give me morphine and other stuff so that I can deal with that. It hurts inside me, inside my mind. I don't want to be a cripple, someone kids stare at on the street. I don't want Marsha to be married to a cripple, either. And don't give me that bullshit about what great artificial arms they make nowadays or I'll get one and give you the finger with it."

Logan agreed that bullshit wouldn't do. Instead, he said sadly, "Dave, when this is over there are going to be a lot of people without arms and legs in America. You won't stand out from the crowd that much at all. Can you walk yet?"

"No, but the medics think I should try real soon."

"Well, when you can, David," he said with more firmness than he intended, "why don't you walk your ass down these aisles and see people who really are crippled. Yeah, you've been hurt, but you can still see, hear, talk, walk, and even pick things up with your remaining hand. Like your own food, for instance. And I'll bet you can even get a hard-on if you worked at it."

Singer was silent for a moment. "Are you telling me I'm feeling sorry for myself?"

"Not really. You've gotten a really shitty wound, and there's no kidding about it. But it could have been worse, lots worse." Maybe, Logan thought, the worse one would be his own. After all this time, he'd barely been scratched.

Singer sighed and seemed to relax slightly. "You're right, I guess. I can hear people crying and moaning all day, and sometimes I do it too."

"Were you gonna make the army a career?"

"Hell, no. I'm not that stupid."

"Aw shit, Dave, don't tell me you were gonna be a surgeon."

Singer managed a grin. "A paperhanger, and fuck you too, Lieutenant Logan. Actually, I'm going to be an accountant, and I guess I can juggle books with one hand. And that reminds me, along with everything else I got that still works, there's one little thing that Marsha was very, very fond of, and you're right, it checked in this morning, loud and clear."

Logan rolled his eyes. There was a picture of plump, blond, and pretty Marsha Singer on his bedstand. "Can't imagine what that might be. And don't you Jewish types have most of it cut off at an early age?"

Singer laughed. "That's because there's so much that, if we didn't, you Gentiles would feel deprived. Now, what's this crap going around about the Russians?"

"They did it again, David. The bastards have crossed the Elbe and are taking on Bradley's army. Happened last night. That's why I can stay only a little while. Everyone's tensed up about the possibility of the Reds attacking here."

"Gawd," said Singer. "What a mess. I hate to be greedy, but you're telling me it could be a long time before anyone's evacuated from here, either."

"Looks that way."

They talked for a few more minutes until Singer said he was tired and wanted to sleep. Logan left, after promising to return when he could. It was a promise he intended to keep.

The way from the hospital back to the platoon went by the old barracks and other buildings and bunkers used as General Miller's headquarters.

As he passed, a slight, dark-haired girl emerged from a doorway. Instinctively, he nodded and said, "Good morning."

"It is indeed," she said softly. "I just hope it stays that way."

"You speak English," he blurted, realizing immediately that it was one of the truly dumb comments he'd ever made.

The girl smiled at his gaffe, and he realized she was the girl he'd noticed before and that she was indeed older than he'd first thought, perhaps in her late teens or early twenties. She was also fairly short, which somewhat accounted for his originally thinking she was a child, only a couple of inches over five feet. She was thin, and dressed in very poorly fitting man's pants, shirt, and jacket. She did, however, have large, expressive eyes, and had bestowed a wide smile on him.

"I'm sorry," he said. "I'm usually not that foolish in the face of the obvious."

"Goodness, Lieutenant, I would hope not." She softened the rebuke with her smile. "Before you ask, I learned to speak English in Canada, where my father was a member of the German diplomatic corps, and now that skill is being put to use by my translating for refugees and German prisoners. My mother was Canadian and I have dual citizenship, for whatever that is worth in this terrible war. Now that you Americans are fighting the Russians, there is a belief that we may soon be on the same side."

Logan thought that one over. Allied with the krauts? Incredible. He realized that they had been walking alongside each other and that he wanted to see her again. "My name is Jack Logan."

"Elisabeth Wolf," she responded.

He didn't see a wedding ring and she hadn't said frau or fraulein. "I hate to ask, but are you alone here?"

"I have my nephew, Pauli. He is six, and to the best of my knowledge we are all that is left of the German side of my family. We still have a number of relatives in Canada, near Toronto."

"I'm sorry," he said. "It must be rough for you."

Elisabeth's eyes clouded. "We lived very near Berlin, where it was a good deal more than rough, and someday you may find out about it. It's amazing that we are, for the moment, in an oasis of relative peace. Something tells me it won't last, particularly since the Russians have once again attacked your soldiers, but we must enjoy each moment of tranquillity that we are given. But I thank you for your sorrow about my family. Many Americans aren't yet ready to accept the fact that we Germans have suffered enormous pain as well from a war that many of us never wanted. Tell me, Lieutenant Logan, have you lost friends and loved ones in this terrible war?"

He mulled that one over. "Friends, yes, but not loved ones. Someone said love is not for the military."

He often wondered about that. Sometimes the pain he had felt on the death of a fellow soldier had been so bad and so wrenching that he and others had blocked out forming relationships with new people. This was horribly unfair to the replacements who were alone and terrified, and this attitude only reinforced their fears. He had intentionally, but incorrectly, trivialized what combat was like in that long-ago discussion with Singer.

"This is where I get off." She grinned, and he realized that they had walked to the refugee encampment. He had also walked about a half mile out of his way.

"How often do you translate for the almighty generals?"

"I'm on call. They contact me when they have something. Otherwise I am here, helping out as best I can. Why?"

"Perhaps I could stop by. We could talk again. I could bring some food, perhaps."

She frowned. "Please do not misunderstand me, Lieutenant, but I am not certain that bringing food is a good idea. Some of the women are trading their bodies for food and cigarettes, and that I will not do. If that is what you have in mind, do not even think of coming back to see me."

"No. Not at all," he stammered truthfully. While he knew of guys who were ignoring the rules and taking advantage of German women who were sometimes very willing to make the trade, it genuinely hadn't occurred to him that she might be that type. He was shocked at his unintended implication. "I was only thinking of food to help out."

He dared not say she really looked like she could do with a couple of good meals.

"If you bring food for me, I will not accept it. Because I help out with your officers, I do get some additional rations. A little while ago I was quite hungry and sick, but that is no longer the case."

"Consider the food forgotten."

"On the other hand," Elisabeth smiled gently, "my nephew is only six and he is very sad."

"Does he speak English too?"

"Yes, fairly well."

"Gotcha," said Logan. He turned and walked away briskly while Elisabeth smiled at his large, retreating back. Americans, she thought, were so very much like large toys.

Pauli saw her and got up from where he was sitting. He walked over and hugged her tightly. Every time she had to leave him he was afraid she wouldn't come back. Could she blame him, with all that he had endured? She hugged him tightly in return and drew comfort from the presence of his small body. Pauli was all she had as well.

CHAPTER 10

*T*he rumbling sound of the diesel engines of a score of Russian tanks made attempts at normal conversation a difficult task. Sergei Suslov wondered precisely where in Germany he and his men were and what was happening to the rest of the world. All he was certain of was that he was a couple of miles west of the Elbe, and that they were fighting the Yanks instead of the Nazis.

The crossing of the Elbe had been uneventful for him, although he had seen a handful of burned-out T34 hulks and the remains of a shattered pontoon bridge that told him earlier crossings had not been as peaceful as his had been.

The ground he was driving on was fairly level and he could see the silhouette of a number of buildings and a church steeple ahead. Word had earlier come down that there were Americans in the village. This had resulted in a nighttime attack that had been a disaster.

The battalion had gone forward in improper order with the infantry well behind the tanks instead of alongside for mutual protection. When the lead tanks had gotten to the buildings, they were assailed by antitank weapons, machine-gun fire, and bazookas. American bazookas, he'd been told, would not penetrate the armor of a T34. But that referred to the front armor, and the damned Yanks had waited until the tanks passed by and fired into their more vulnerable rear. In the confusion, a half-dozen T34s had been destroyed and a hundred belatedly arriving infantry were killed or wounded before the order to withdraw had been given.

Now they were going to go into the damned village the way they should have. Artillery had pounded it and Stormovik fighter-bombers had sought out targets, although rumor had it there were no American tanks in the village for the Soviet planes, whose specialty was killing enemy armor. Even more important to Suslov's personal safety, Russian soldiers were trotting alongside his tank. No more would American infantry get behind him.

"Any targets?" yelled his gunner, Pavel Martynov. The previous night's slaughter had shaken him. It had shaken all of them. Now they knew the Yanks would fight and fight well.

"I'll let you know, comrade gunner, when you can shoot your big gun." Suslov spoke gently, almost teasingly. He didn't want the boy panicking.

"Fuck this shit," snapped Ivan Latsis as he maneuvered the iron monster around an obstruction, grazing a brick wall and causing a metallic screech as the tank bulled along. "I want to kill the fucking Germans, not the fucking Americans."

Everybody has an opinion, thought Suslov, just as they have an asshole. Only the loader was silent. Sasha Popov rarely spoke. He was half Asian and seemed to resent being with Russians. Or maybe he was NKVD? There were a number of them in all units to spy on the troops and ensure loyalty. Who the hell knew nowadays?

Of course Suslov wondered why they were fighting the Americans today when yesterday's sworn enemy was the Germans and the Americans were their allies. It was a question he kept to himself, as one never doubted the orders from on high. The speech from the political officer, which said that the Americans had betrayed some damned agreement and had sworn to overthrow the People's Revolution, seemed to ring just a little hollow. How could yesterday's ally be today's enemy? However, one does not argue with a commissar.

The tank rocked over a ruined wall and lurched into a debris-filled street. Suslov had closed the hatch, and he squinted through the tiny slit that gave him an inadequate view of the world. He couldn't see very much, but it was safer that way. A tank commander had been shot through the eye by an American sniper last night while looking brave at the top of his tank. The hell with bravery, Suslov thought.

His radio crackled, ordering him to halt. He waited, and the word came that the infantry had completed their sweep through the village and it was abandoned. Suslov considered himself fortunate to have a radio. So many of the Russian tanks didn't. He had heard that all the American tanks did, but he found that hard to believe. He had also been told that American tanks were more comfortable and thought that ludicrous. Whoever heard of a comfortable tank?

Suslov opened his hatch and stuck his head and shoulders out. The fresh air was a delightful alternative to the diesel-and-sweat stench-filled air of the tank. Latsis had stuck his head out as well.

"Hey, Sergei," yelled Latsis. "Look at that."

Suslov followed where Latsis was pointing. He saw a couple of dead bodies and realized that the bloody lumps were Americans. He had never seen Americans close up before and wanted to get out and take a look at them. Of course, he wouldn't dare.

A nearby explosion shook the tank. "Where the hell did that come from!" he screamed and prepared to duck down into the relative safety of the tank.

"Planes," yelled Latsis.

Suslov gazed skyward. While they had been fighting their personal battle on the ground, another one had been going on high in the skies above them. In amazement, he watched the swirl of planes dancing and darting among one another, the contrails painting delicate white lines in the sky. He saw a plane get hit and blow up, while another seemed to lose interest in life and started to dive toward the ground. Perhaps that was the explosion he'd felt—a crashing plane.

Still another explosion shook him even harder and almost knocked him down into the turret. As he closed the hatch, he felt stones clattering onto his vehicle. This was followed by more pulsating explosions, and he knew they could not all be crashing planes. The Yank planes had broken through and were bombing his position.

"What do we do now?" asked Martynov. He was almost in tears. The Red Army, Martynov knew, never had much to fear from the Luftwaffe. The German air force had been pretty much wiped out as an effective weapon by the time Martynov had been given a tank to drive. Suslov, however, did remember the early days of the war when the German planes wreaked havoc on the Russian tank formations.

Now they had a new enemy, one with its own powerful air arm, and the Russian tanks were once again vulnerable from the air.

What the devil should we do? Suslov thought. If we stay in the village we'll get bombed. If we retreat without authorization, we'll be back in the open field and be even better targets. And, oh yes, the fucking commissar would scream at them for being cowards and possibly have them shot or, at best, sent to a penal battalion where death was just as certain. He decided to advance.

Before they could move, another bomb exploded close by and caused the tank to rock violently. Latsis cried out in pain as his body bounced off the inside hull of the tank. Suslov had hit his head, and he touched his forehead. There was a little blood, but it was not much of a wound and not his first. He ruefully thought it would not be his last.

Finally, word came. They would retreat, not advance. Perhaps they could make bombing difficult for the Americans if they were on the move. Suslov also realized they were giving up the shitty little village that had cost them so much already.

Shortly after he managed to pull his tank out, the bombing ceased. Either the Americans had been chased off or they had run out of bombs. While Martynov praised the Soviet fighter planes for saving them, Suslov quietly thought it was likely a lack of bombs and bullets that had caused the Americans to depart.

He opened his hatch and climbed out to the top of his turret. Without appearing obvious, he counted the remaining T34s in the battalion. Fourteen. Yesterday there had been twenty-six. Maybe a couple were only stuck in the village or had minor damage that could be repaired fairly quickly, but certainly not all of them. They had lost six in that nightmare last night and six more from the bombings. He watched as a wounded man was helped out of the tank next to him and realized that even some of those tanks that had survived had men who'd been hurt.

And what if this was happening elsewhere? The Yanks had used cunning and skill in their mauling of his battalion. It had been like that in the early days against the Germans before they ran out of people and weapons and had to draft old men and young boys. Now it looked like the Red Army would have to do it all over again to the Americans and defeat another powerful new enemy.

Suslov looked at Martynov, who had finally stopped his sobbing, and began to wonder. Was Russia up to it? Was he up to it? After Stalingrad, how many lives did he have left?

• • •

THE ATMOSPHERE FOR the meeting in the Executive Wing conference room was even more tense than usual. President Harry Truman did nothing to alleviate it when he strode in, grim-faced and angry.

"All right, people, let's begin," he ordered.

Attorney General Biddle had asked to speak first. "Sir, Director Hoover wishes to know, in light of the Russian attack, whether the FBI should commence interning Russian nationals and nationalized citizens who emigrated from Russia, along with known Communist sympathizers?"

Steven Burke, sitting against the wall behind Marshall, was stunned. Biddle was talking about people like Natalie Holt.

Truman was puzzled. "I can see picking up Russian nationals, but why bother American citizens who came from there? We didn't do that to naturalized Germans, did we? And are we really that concerned about some idiot left-wingers?"

"Sir," Biddle persisted stiffly, "the director is very concerned about the number of Russians working in the State Department who, while they are American citizens, could be sympathetic to the current regime and possibly even agents for the Soviet government."

Assistant Secretary of State Acheson responded. "Mr. Biddle, while I will gladly acknowledge the presence in State of persons born in what is now the Soviet Union, I will also say that their loyalty to us is without question. One only has to look at the circumstances under which they fled Russia and how they arrived here to know the depths of their hatred for the current government in Moscow. These people were deprived of property, livelihood, dignity, and the lives of many of their loved ones. I would also add, from personal knowledge, that many so-called Russian nationals who are not yet citizens are fugitives from the Bolsheviks who have never asked for American citizenship because they hope and pray daily for the overthrow of Stalin's government. When that happens they will return to their homeland. I would tread lightly with them as well."

Burke smiled to himself. Natalie had told him of their meeting with Gromyko, and Acheson was at least in part referring to her.

Truman turned to Biddle. "I agree. Tell Mr. Hoover that he can and should investigate as he sees appropriate. But I do not want anyone jailed or deprived of liberties without due process and without proof that they are acting on behalf of the Soviet government. Mere opinions, beliefs, and personal stupidity will not suffice. I trust that will be satisfactory."

Biddle nodded reluctantly.

"Good," said Truman, glad to have that matter disposed of, at least for a while.

In Truman's unspoken opinion, Hoover was a stubborn prick and would come back to it first chance he got. "Now, what did Mr. Gromyko tell you this morning, Mr. Acheson?"

Acheson grimaced. "For those who are not aware, I once again met with Ambassador Gromyko to protest the Russian advance across the Elbe. Gromyko blandly handed me a line of pap that said the Russians were acting totally defensively and in reaction to our attack on their forces in Berlin. He said their troops are merely defending themselves."

"That is absurd," snapped Truman, and the others murmured agreement.

"Sir, Gromyko is a liar," said Acheson.

Truman grinned slightly. "Well, that certainly simplifies things. Now, General Marshall, please tell us how that war is going."

It was Burke's cue. He stood and uncovered a large map on an easel. The familiar blue arrows that had been denoting American advances into the heart of the Reich were now countered by a number of red ones.

"Gentlemen," Marshall began, "as I mentioned, the Russians have crossed the Elbe at a number of places and have attacked us at some points south of that as well. There have been a number of battles and we have both taken and given casualties. We do not have even rough estimates, but they are not likely to be light. Since we had some notice of the possibility of attack, General Eisenhower decided he would not confront the Russians directly at the Elbe or elsewhere they were gathered in force. Instead, he pulled his troops a few miles back and has begun a fighting withdrawal to the west."

"Why?" snapped Truman. A pugnacious man, any form of retreat was anathema to him.

"Sir, he intends to wear them out and bleed them until their advantage in numbers is eliminated, or at least reduced. He is also aware that it will take some time for their army to cross the Elbe and organize itself in force. However, when done, they will vastly outnumber us on the ground."

"And our navy's useless for this war, isn't it?" Truman asked.

"Absolutely," said Marshall, "except to ensure that supplies reach Europe safely. The news does not get better. The Russian air force is estimated at between fifteen and twenty thousand planes, most of them Yak fighters and Stormovik tank-killing fighter-bombers, although they also have several thousand P-39 Airocobras and Douglas A-20 Havocs that we gave them as war supplies. Ike is reporting some very large air battles currently going on over the armies.

"Further, the Russians have a very real advantage over us in the area of armor. The T34 tank, which they have in the thousands, is simply the best tank in existence today. The Russians also have large numbers of artillery and like to use them for mass destruction."

"Sweet Jesus, General," Truman murmured. "What can we do to help Ike?"

"Two things, sir. First, in the short term we have to realize that we have no further army to send him. We have a couple of divisions forming in England and some troops in training that we can scrape together and send, but we will have to win or lose with essentially what we currently have in Europe. I have reviewed possibilities with Admiral King, and there is nothing in the Pacific we can send to Europe in the near future.

"There are, however, two very important things that must be done. First, every available plane and pilot, both fighters and bombers, must be sent to the European theater, even if that means stripping carriers and land bases that are currently operating against Japan, or taking men and planes from training units in the States. For us to win, we must first control the skies. When that happens, we will be able to attack their massed armor and artillery and destroy it. But they have thousands of planes and, while our planes and our pilots are definitely better, it will take us a long time to win as things currently stand."

"General," said Truman, "you said two things?"

"Yes, sir. The German question must be resolved. We cannot fight both the Russians and the Germans at the same time and place. We must settle a peace with the Doenitz government."

Truman was aghast. "Peace with the Nazis?"

Acheson took over, and Burke realized this had been planned. He would have an interesting conversation this evening with Natalie.

"Sir," said Acheson, "there is a great deal of merit to what the general says. At some point in the not-too-distant future, we will indeed make peace with Germany and a German nation will be resurrected. What the general wants, and I agree, is that this process be expedited so that we can at least identify our enemy."

"What about the idea of unconditional surrender?" asked Truman. "We and our allies swore we would never negotiate and that Germany would have to surrender without any conditions."

"I think," Acheson said drily, "the Russian attack on our army has eliminated any obligation we might have had to not enter into a separate peace with Germany. Sir, I propose we explore the possibility of an immediate truce with Germany, and I believe we can have an agreement in principle on a real armistice within a few days."

"How?" asked Truman. He was beginning to realize he'd been euchred.

Acheson smiled. "We have been in indirect contact with representatives of Doenitz's government. He is sending Albert Speer to London. When he arrives, both he and Churchill will fly to the United States for discussions."

"I despise the thought of a peace with the Nazis." Truman shook his head, and then, having made up his mind, glared defiantly about the room. "But to paraphrase Churchill, if we must deal with the devil in order to win this war, then deal with him we shall."

TONY THE TOAD was a little disconcerted by the fact that Anton and Vaslov had brought in two more refugees. Both were emaciated men who wore prison rags and a yellow star that identified them as Jews. Now there were five people in the small house and things were starting to get out of his control.

For one thing, the stench was unbearable. They had finally gotten rid of the corpses upstairs by dragging them out in the night and leaving them in a nearby street. There were so many bodies around that a couple more would doubtless go unnoticed. As long as the stench lingered, there was no need to find fresh corpses. Their real problem was the lack of water for bathing and for elimination of body waste; very simply, the toilets were overflowing with feces.

Strangely, there was no real problem with food. They had gotten extremely skillful at rifling abandoned houses and finding small hoards left behind by owners who had either fled or been killed in the bombings.

"Anton," Tony said, "we gotta get out of here."

The Pole nodded. Both Polish refugees' English had improved significantly as a result of the constant contact with Tony, and Anton was the acknowledged leader of the others. "But where can we go? East leads to my home, but it also leads to Russia. West will take us to where the fighting is, and your army, but it would be a dangerous journey."

Tony agreed in silence. Anton and the other Pole also spoke Russian and had been able to snoop around, and they had found out about the heavy fighting to the west.

Tony asked. "You wanna go back to Poland?"

Anton shrugged. "Not while the Russians are there, and I don't think they'll be leaving soon. If I know the Russians, they will never leave Poland."

"Well, that leaves us exactly two other choices. One, we can stay here in the city and continue to hide out, or, two, we can very carefully head west and find the American lines. Somehow, I think as a soldier that's what I am expected to do."

They thought it over. Berlin was now a Russian city. The SS troopers who had manned the roadblocks had disappeared. The SS had been responsible for the hundreds of corpses hanging by their necks from telephone poles and wearing the signs that said "Deserter," or "Enemy of the Reich." Some of the bodies looked too old or too young to have been deserters or anyone's enemies. But then, it was common knowledge that the SS just liked to kill and had gone into a murderous frenzy in the last moments of the Reich.

The Russians were beginning to set up an administration in Berlin. That would mean police, and Tony and Anton both knew their little band would ultimately be discovered.

Anton smiled grimly. "Sometimes choices are made for us, aren't they? We must leave here. We shall travel as refugees. Certainly, that is not far from the truth."

"Yeah. We go west and try to find my guys. Y'know, I'm gonna need some different clothes. I can't be a refugee if I'm wearing an American uniform."

"Don't worry," said Anton, "we will have no trouble finding clothing for you." He brightened. "Perhaps we will, as we work our way west, find some opportunities to cause inconvenience to the damned Russians?"

Tony reached into his shirt and squeezed a bug, probably a louse, that was crawling along his chest, looking for a home. "Y'know, a while ago and regardless of what I said, I really didn't think that screwing with the Russians was the smart thing to do. Now I'm beginning to change my mind."

CHAPTER 11

The furnace room in the basement of Moscow's Lubyanka prison was unbearably hot. It was a warm spring day, and normally the furnaces would not have been working too hard. But today, the grimy and dour men who kept them burning had them at full blast.

More than the heat affected the thirty or so men jammed into the small room. Almost all of them were senior army officers and they were in full and heavy uniforms. Many were pale and sweating profusely. Most felt terror and were fighting waves of fear and nausea. They knew what happened in the basement of the Lubyanka. They had been ordered there for a command performance in the price of disloyalty.

A door opened and the NKVD head, Lavrentii Beria, entered silently. He stood off to the side and looked directly at no one. One of the officers started to whimper and was quickly silenced by a companion. If Beria noticed, he gave no sign. He could have been his own statue.

The screeching sound of an iron-wheeled cart dragging on the cement floor was heard. The officers looked in the direction of the wide double doors that led to a hallway where the worst or most important prisoners were kept.

The door opened and two NKVD officers pushed in a hospital-type gurney on which a man was strapped. They stopped in front of Beria and the assembled officers, and unstrapped the man, who began moaning loudly. As he was pulled to a standing position, he screamed from the pain of having to use joints and limbs that had been pulled apart and broken.

In fascinated horror, the officers stared at the man. He was vaguely familiar to some, but so distorted as to be a caricature of himself. His nose was flattened and there was a dark hole where one eye had been. The man howled in pain, and they could see where the teeth that hadn't been pulled out had been broken off into stumps. They wondered what other physical horrors his shapeless prison garb hid. They also wondered what he had told his interrogators, who were so obviously through with him, and whether it could come back to threaten them.

"Korzov," came the hissed whisper of recognition from the rear. Now they knew the rumors were true. Korzov was the army officer who had betrayed his country while in the United States. Exactly what he had done, they didn't know. Rumors had said only that he had betrayed a major secret to the Americans. Collectively, they shuddered. Beria did not move and, like a reptilian predator, did not seem to be aware of the heat or the collective scent of fear.

Korzov looked about the room with his one eye. It looked like he was trying to focus on the rows of faces to figure out what was going on, and what new agony was in store for him.

The two NKVD men set up a chute that led to one of the furnaces while two furnace operators watched in detachment. They had seen all this before. At a nod from one of the NKVD men, one of the operators opened the furnace doors, and a wave of additional heat surged across the room while the white-hot flames made a roaring sound that buried the collective moan of thirty horrified and terrorized men.

Puzzled, Korzov turned his head in the direction of the unaccustomed warmth. His nights had been damp and bitter cold. He saw the flames but his mind did not register any particular significance.

The NKVD men grabbed him and wrapped his arms and legs in straps so he could not move, only wriggle like a worm trapped on a hook. Then they roughly put him on the chute, feet facing the open furnace. When he was set, they lifted the chute, but steadied Korzov, so he could see the furnace and the flames within.

Now it registered. Korzov's screams of fear seemed to come from the bowels of hell. Some of the most hardened officers began to tremble. Korzov tried to thrash, disregarding the agony of his broken arms and legs in his effort to flee his fate.

It was no use. If there was a signal from Beria, no one saw it, but as if on cue, the two NKVD men released Korzov, who began a slow, screaming slide down the chute.

His legs entered first and his clothing flared, then his torso, and then his head and contorted face. For an instant he held that position. He was visible in the flames as a dancing, writhing specter until finally collapsing and disappearing as the furnace men closed the door on the ghastly show.

There was silence. Beria walked from the room, a hint of a smile flickering on his face. The lesson had been delivered.

AFTER KNOCKING SEVERAL times, Steve Burke tried the door to Natalie's apartment and found it unlocked. Surprised, he entered. Natalie was seated on a chair in her living room, looking out her window.

"Are you all right?" he said, approaching her quietly.

She turned and smiled wanly. "I've had better days."

He knelt before her and took her hand. "Anything you care to share?"

"Yes, but make me a martini first." He obeyed, and she saluted him before taking her first sip. "Here's to new wars."

Steve was puzzled. What on earth could have happened? Could she have heard he actually was going to Europe as part of Marshall's entourage? That was why he had dropped by, to inform her. He didn't know how she would take the information. Would the fact of his leaving upset her or would she be proud of him?

Natalie put her glass down. "The FBI was around today. They see Communists and other undesirables everywhere."

He was incredulous. "You?"

"No, at least not seriously. They did question me to reconfirm what they already knew about my past life in Russia and my citizenship. I don't think I am considered a subversive. But they may label my mother as an undesirable and deport her. God only knows where they would send her. Certainly not to Russia."

"What on earth for?"

Natalie laughed harshly. "Because she was too frank a few years ago when applying for American citizenship. Remember when I told you she sold herself for food and passage to the United States? Well, a few years ago some sanctimonious fool at immigration labeled her a prostitute and rejected her application for citizenship. I knew she had been turned down, but never wondered why. Stupid me. Today they came and informed her that the combination of Russian citizenship and a record as an admitted whore was too much for the puritans in our government and would she mind leaving the country. It didn't matter that she'd married an American who, unfortunately, died and isn't around to defend her. My stepfather certainly never thought of her as a whore and he knew full well how she got to America. I've spent most of the day trying to straighten out that mess."

"Any success?"

She took a deep breath and swallowed the rest of her drink. He took the glass and started to mix another. "I think so. Unfortunately, we won't know for several weeks. Not everyone who works for the government is an idiot—just most of them." The irony that both of them were on the government payroll did not escape them.

"That's awful," he said, handing her the drink and taking a seat across from her. Steve had never met her mother but Natalie had told him a great deal about her. It wasn't fair that someone who had suffered so much should be called upon to suffer again.

"And things are terrible at work," she continued. "Once again the iron hand of J. Edgar Hoover and his FBI stormtroopers is at work. They are going through our personnel files and talking to anyone who ever belonged to a left-wing organization, even though some of those so-called memberships might have occurred years or even a decade or more ago, and at a time when the Russian Revolution was thought of as a part of the liberation of oppressed peoples."

Or even more recently, Steve thought, since, up until a little while ago, the Soviet Union and the man Roosevelt referred to as "Uncle Joe" were our allies. He knew of the activities of the FBI, but he was not aware they were so extensive or so oppressive. On the other hand, it made sense to him that State would be so heavily investigated. They were the first line of contact with other governments and privy to so many federal secrets.

"What is happening to the ones they suspect?"

"Nothing officially," she answered. "Apparently they are under orders not to arrest anyone without real proof, but they are making life miserable for people who are now under dark clouds of suspicion. Some zealous, perhaps fearful, administrators have placed a few people on administrative leaves of absence until they are cleared. A couple of people have had the misfortune of being both homosexual and leftist, and they are in real trouble. It's sad. You are legally innocent, but still guilty of something until they prove otherwise."

With that off her chest, she smiled warmly at him. "Now, what caused you to come rushing over here and burst through the door I was so distressed that I foolishly forgot to lock?"

"Well, General Marshall is going to Europe to meet with all the big shots and he is taking some of his staff. He decided he needed some people who knew about the Soviet Union and Joe Stalin in particular, so I, as I suspected might happen, am going along."

Her eyes misted over. "I know you're thrilled, but I will worry about you. I've already lost one man to war and I don't want to lose a second one."

"Don't worry. I can't imagine General Marshall getting anywhere near the front lines. More likely, we'll be holed up in some fancy hotel in London or Paris, roughing it with the elite."

"Don't count on it," she said. "Things have a strange way of working out just like we don't expect. The gentleman whose robe you wore that first night was a navy pilot, and, like all pilots, he thought he was immortal. He flew a torpedo plane off Midway Island and was shot down. So were all the torpedo planes. I heard through the grapevine that it was because they were lousy, slow planes and the Japs had fast and good ones. You may have no intention of getting caught up in the war, but events have a way of controlling us, don't they?"

"True," he said. "In real life, I should be at Notre Dame grading papers from students who don't even know how to even spell *Communist*. Instead, I'm going to Europe and may meet heads of state and other people who are making history and not teaching it. In a way, it doesn't make sense. Here I am jumping up and down like a little kid going on an adventure, and I am actually going into a war area where thousands of people are getting killed and wounded each day."

"Like you said, it doesn't make sense, but then, it doesn't have to. When do you go?"

"Later tonight. I've packed and my bags are in the car."

Her eyes twinkled. "And you presumed to come here and impress me with your departing-warrior routine? You probably thought you could dazzle me out of my clothes and I would drag you off to my bed and let you work your evil way with me? Is that what you had in mind?"

He grinned. "Frankly, yes."

Natalie stood and swallowed the rest of her drink. "Well, my fear-less scholar-warrior, I would have been horribly angry if you had thought otherwise." She took his hand and pulled him to a standing position. "You are going to remember the next few hours for the rest of your life." Which, she thought with a trace of sadness, I hope is a very, very long one.

"GRETEL, LET ME see your baby."

Elisabeth Wolf framed the request as gently as possible. The tor-mented wraith in front of her clutched the lifeless bundle to her bosom and looked about in terror. The woman was about Lis's age but looked decades older.

"It's all right," Elisabeth soothed. As Logan watched, she continued to gentle the frightened young woman. Finally, the woman started to sob. After a moment, she handed the bundle to Elisabeth with a shy smile and started to walk away.

"Where's she going?" Jack asked.

"Back to the others. She's finally accepted the fact that the baby is dead."

"And she can walk away from it?"

Elisabeth opened the cloth wrappings and looked on the bluish and distorted face of the dead infant. "It isn't hers."

"What?"

Elisabeth covered the tiny face. "I heard her story from one of her friends. She found it a few days ago. I guess the real mother had been killed. Gretel hoped that her having a baby to care for would keep the Russians from hurting her. It didn't work."

"Oh God." Logan had been hearing more and more stories of the unspeakable atrocities the Russians were inflicting on the German women in revenge for the equally barbaric treatment of Russian women by the Nazis.

"Oh God is right. She was probably raped many times in the last couple of weeks. Sometimes more than once by the same man, but more likely she was just passed around or periodically singled out. Every Russian knows at least two German words, *frau komm*. When a

Russian calls you like that you have no choice but to comply if you have any hope of living through it. Gretel was once fairly attractive. I think she's younger than I am."

"How did the baby die?"

Elisabeth looked again at the lifeless bundle in her arms. "According to one of the other women who came in with her, some Russian pig stomped on it and killed it because it started crying while he was having his way with Gretel."

To Logan, who thought he was inured to horror, the story was a nightmare. "What now?" he managed to ask. He wondered how Elisabeth could deal with these things so calmly.

"I will take the child to the cemetery. Von Schumann has people who will bury it. As to the woman, perhaps she will begin to heal. Perhaps not, though. She is on the verge of total madness. The only thing that can heal people like her will be peace, and that isn't likely to happen anytime soon, is it?"

It was only a short walk to the cemetery, and they left the body with two older women who accepted it without comment. It seemed to Logan that it was so perfunctory it was like mailing a package. Except a package had an address on it. No one had any idea what the child's name had been. There were a number of fresh graves, and he wondered how many of them contained unidentified bodies.

Then they walked to where Elisabeth and Pauli lived with the other refugees. Pauli was on his hands and knees, solemnly examining the shiny object before him. It was a top, and Pauli was figuring out how to spin it. He was having difficulties, and it occurred to Logan that the boy didn't really know how to play. Jack thought he would work to rectify that. There were only a few boys Pauli's age in Potsdam, and most were as confused as he.

Elisabeth smiled. Logan thought he saw the hint of a tear in her eye. "Thank you for the toy. I almost forget when he last had a chance to be a little boy."

Logan shrugged and grinned. It hadn't been all that easy rummaging through the abandoned and looted buildings until he found something he thought a child Pauli's age would like. Now he thought the effort had been well worth it. If Elisabeth was happy then he was ecstatic.

"Yeah, he does seem to be having fun."

"And it's the first time he's let me go without jumping all over me when I return. That is a very good sign that someday he too can live a normal life when we get out of this."

If, Jack thought, not when. *If* we ever get out of this stinking mess. All signs indicated that the American army was being pushed farther and farther to the west and away from them. So far there had been no effort on the part of the Russians to overrun Potsdam. Apparently taking the city was something they felt they could do at any time they wished. It was one thing to be an optimist, but he preferred realism, and realism said their stay in Potsdam could be tragically, violently short. It was a thought that nagged him, but what could he do about it?

He checked his watch. "I've got to go. Captain Dimitri wants to meet with his officers in a little while. Would it be all right if I stopped by again? I might not be able to find any more toys, though."

Elisabeth laughed. For a big, bright officer, he could be so dense. "Well then, you will have to be his toy. But yes, you may come back and visit. I would like that. When Pauli goes to bed, perhaps you and I can simply sit and talk."

"Now would you take some food if I brought it?"

He had brought some "extra" rations for Pauli and the boy had gobbled them down. Despite her protestations that she was receiving enough, he had seen her eyes widen at the sight of what he and his men thought of as tasteless and undesirable C rations, which included meat, instant coffee, lemonade powder, a chocolate bar, hard candy, toilet paper, chewing gum, crackers or canned bread, and cigarettes. Pauli, of course, did not get any cigarettes or coffee. K rations, which were intended to be eaten without being cooked, were even worse, but the boy had no qualms about eating them either.

"I will think about it," she said softly, then brightened. "Perhaps we can have dinner together."

CHAPTER 12

Major General Mikhail Bazarian was livid with rage, his lean and handsome face contorted and tears of anger being squeezed out of his eyes. In impotent fury he watched as the American artillery shells chewed up the column of Soviet armored vehicles that had strayed too close to a portion of his lines confronting the Americans in Potsdam. He had warned their fool of a commanding officer that the Americans could see them, and now they were paying the price.

The Soviet tanks had marched down the autobahn as if on parade. They had given no thought to the Yanks who were in Potsdam, only a few miles away. Just because the Americans had been quiet for so long did not mean they would remain dormant forever. The sight of the column of Soviet tanks had been too much of a temptation, and the American shelling had started almost as soon as the Russian vehicles were within range.

"Damnit!" he snarled, and a handful of officers nearby moved farther away from the tall and elegantly uniformed general. Another T34 was hit and tumbled off the roadway. A half mile away, at least a score of vehicles were burning and the remainder of the column was scattered in every direction in an attempt to find safety from the scourging artillery.

"I warned that stupid fucker," he raged, "but would he listen to me? No! He was a fucking Russian and all I am is a stupid fucking Armenian. I hope the fucking Russian asshole has been blown to hell!"

A gasp from behind him reminded him that such criticisms were frowned upon, could even be fatal.

Bazarian pounded the table in his spartan office. It wasn't fair. He was a good general, but what help had the Soviet high command given him? None. He had three divisions of second-rate infantry and one brigade of armor to contain the Americans. Worse, his tanks were not first-line. Most of them were light, old, and obsolete.

It would be enough to contain the Americans, he had been told. Bazarian's orders were to prevent the Yanks from breaking out and rejoining their main army. Now, as the front lines moved farther west, it was less and less likely that any breakout would even be attempted.

Bazarian was in a backwater and the war was moving away from him. He was only a major general when he deserved to be a lieutenant general. If he were Russian and not Armenian he would have had the higher rank. He would also be commanding better-quality troops and would be in the front lines against the Yanks, instead of this military sewer.

Only rarely did a non-Russian achieve any real status in the new people's government. It sometimes discouraged him that such prejudices still existed, but he presumed that it would take time for them to disappear. The Russians of Moscow and Leningrad neither liked nor trusted people whose skin was swarthier or whose hair was darker, or who thought and spoke differently because they were from different cultures.

He seethed. It wasn't fair. He had always supported the people's revolution and had devoted his life to the success of communism. He had even turned in relatives for practicing Christianity in secret. Religion was the opiate of the people and the enemy of the state, particularly the forms of Christianity and Islam that were practiced in the southern republics of the USSR. These religions were not docile, not like the tame Orthodox faith that had failed the tsars. Instead, the religions in and around his homeland of Armenia fomented rebellion and had to be stopped.

Another barrage landed, chewing up the ground around the destroyed column, hurling more metal and bodies into the air. There would be hell to pay for this defeat, and he knew who would be blamed. He would. His guns were returning fire and shelling the Potsdam perimeter, but he knew their effect was minimal. For one thing, he really didn't know just where in the perimeter the American guns were situated. For another, he could logically presume they were well dug in and impervious to anything but a direct hit.

Nor could he continue firing for very long. He simply didn't have the ammunition. Stavka, the military headquarters in Moscow, apparently didn't think he needed much ammunition to hold the Americans at Potsdam. Nor were many of his weapons very good. A familiar shriek told him that his Katyushas were firing their multiple rockets at Potsdam, and that would have been good but for the fact that they were small 3.2-inch rockets mounted on an old Studebaker chassis. They might as well have been firecrackers. Stavka wouldn't give him some of the 11.8-inch rockets that could really do some damage. Nor did he have any of the marvelous T34 tanks that were now burning in front of him. Instead, he had the older models that were now almost relics.

Chuikov would rip his ass and possibly relieve him of command. It wouldn't matter that he had warned that drunken asshole Russian colonel in charge of the tanks that he was straying too close to the Americans. No, it would only matter that he, an Armenian, had let a Russian armored column be destroyed.

Bazarian had to do something and do it quickly in order to save his career, and possibly his life. He turned to an orderly and told him to get his division commanders and his armored brigade commander to his headquarters for a council of war. The Americans had lived in solitude and luxury for long enough. He would attack them and make them pay. No more pinpricks like a Katyusha rocket barrage, or a few artillery shells. No, he would launch an attack. It would take a few days to move and gather and position his men, particularly the brigade he had on the other side of the Havel, but it could be done. Then the Americans would pay.

A FEW MILES away, the American general Chris Miller absently sucked on his empty pipe. He was out of tobacco. He continued to receive reports of the damage his howitzers were inflicting on the Russian column. He hadn't wanted to open fire on the Russian tanks, but quickly decided he had no choice. A radio message had told him that the air force was up to its ass in alligators and could not attack the column. He could not let it go by unscathed and cause American deaths in the future. It was also good for morale to strike back and cause such heavy damage.

"Cease firing," he ordered.

The major of artillery was puzzled. "But, sir, the Reds are still firing back at us."

"I know, but they're not hitting anything. Besides, we don't exactly have a lifetime supply of ammunition in here, now do we?"

Chagrined, the major agreed and relayed the order. The airdrops had been continuing, but now on an irregular, almost sporadic basis.

Miller sighed and wished someone had thought to airdrop some tobacco. He hated poking among the enlisted men who smoked pipes and borrowing it, but he would and they would cheerfully lend it. He had a lot to think about and he needed the peace of mind the smoke from a pipe gave him.

"Leland."

"Yes, sir," the captain answered.

"Tell that kraut, von Schumann, that I want to talk with him."

WOLFGANG VON SCHUMANN saw Elisabeth and the little boy strolling in the sunshine. She had told him of her concerns that Pauli would never be able to get over his fear of the noise the guns made. Who could? he had answered. She said she wondered if he would quiver and shake every time a thunderstorm rumbled. She had said, harshly, would there ever be a time when they could marvel at the sound of nature and not of the guns of man?

Von Schumann was limping by in the company of an American officer when he saw her. "What are you thinking of, little girl, a hot meal or your American officer?"

Elisabeth smiled and stuck out her tongue at him, making von Schumann laugh. He knew that the girl—he had a hard time thinking of her as a young woman—would have been incapable of such an impudent act in response to his teasing only a short while earlier. As to the American officer, he had been by only moments before to see whether she was safe from the Soviet barrage, and then literally ran back to his unit. Von Schumann had caught the look on both their faces on learning they were all right. He had seen them together several other times and sometimes envied them their youth, their innocence, and, God willing, their future.

"Amazing. All that shelling and they accomplished so little?" said von Schumann.

Leland agreed. "In most cases, all they did was rearrange some earlier ruins and knock down some empty buildings. Casualties were extremely light."

Unless you happened to be one of those casualties, von Schumann always thought on hearing the phrase.

On arrival at headquarters, he was ushered immediately into Miller's office. As in prior instances, there were no other American officers present. This helped Miller continue the fiction that he was not receiving any official help from a German.

Miller gestured von Schumann to a seat. "Using your artificial leg today, I see."

Von Schumann grinned. "The crutch was a shameless cry for sympathy. It didn't work."

"I'm not surprised. No one considers you helpless. You don't know where there's any pipe tobacco, do you?" As leader of the civilian population, von Schumann had made a number of interesting contacts and had turned up some surprising creature-comfort articles.

"Not offhand, but I'll look into it."

"Good. Now what do you think of what just happened? What was this Bazarian creature trying to prove?"

Leland had informed von Schumann of the destruction of the Russian tank column. The former German colonel paused before responding. "I think you have made a mortal enemy of the man who commands the Russians. Not that you had a choice, of course. You had to bombard those tanks. To have done otherwise would have been a betrayal of your oath as an officer."

"So what will he do? Attack us?"

Von Schumann nodded. "He doesn't have a choice. You have disgraced him, and the punishment for disgrace in the Soviet Union is loss of command at best, and he could be shot." Von Schumann stretched out his artificial leg. He still had difficulty sitting comfortably. "But you do have some advantages."

Miller smiled. That was why he had invited the German. It was common knowledge that some of his people were skillful at questioning new arrivals. They had also ferreted out a couple of attempts by the Russian commander to infiltrate his own people into the Potsdam area. The Russians had been imprisoned, while the German turncoats had quietly disappeared, likely facedown into the Havel and now floating downstream.

"Herr Oberst," Miller said, using von Schumann's rank in the Wehrmacht. It was equivalent to colonel. "Please tell me of those advantages."

The German responded, speaking in a slow voice. "You know you are confronted by at least three rifle divisions. These are very ordinary units, perhaps even less so. At full strength they would each have just under ten thousand men. I think we can assume that the war has worn them down and that they are not quite at full strength. More important, they are not Russians. They are a mixed lot from the southern part of the Soviet Union and are commanded by an Armenian, Bazarian. This means they are neither as well trained nor as well equipped as an equivalent Russian unit would be. You should also know that they are likely the shit soldiers who have been plundering and defiling Germany. The Russians are tough men, but many of those from non-Russian areas of the Soviet empire are barbarians and animals. Sometimes the Russians refer to those types of soldiers as 'black-asses.' It is equivalent to your referring to a Negro as a nigger."

Miller didn't quite agree with that comparison but said nothing. He toyed with his pipe. "What about their tanks, their artillery?"

Von Schumann chuckled. "They have more tanks than you, but many of theirs are the older, lighter models, and not the T34s or larger Stalins we have learned to fear. As to artillery, they have a number of 122-millimeter guns and you have 105s and a handful of 155s; it's almost a trade-off. They have larger-caliber mortars, but the overall advantage belongs to you since you are on the defensive—at least until they bring in reinforcements and assuming you don't throw away your advantages. They may be shit soldiers, but they can kill very nicely if you let them. If led properly, they may just fight like the animals they are. Like I said, this Russian force surrounding you is second echelon. Their general may or may not be."

Miller digested the information. He had the remnants of one armored division in Potsdam, not even a third of its strength. Far too many had been destroyed or were missing after the initial onslaught.

Von Schumann continued. "You've had a major problem sending

out patrols, since few of your men speak Russian or, for that matter, German. With your permission, I will send out some of my men to find out the exact locations of their artillery and their tanks. To date I have been only passively acquiring information from refugees."

Miller was not displeased at the thought of Germans actively spying for the Americans. "Who will you send? Most of your people are either women or old men."

Von Schumann's answer was tinged with bitterness. He knew what had happened to so many of the women in his flock. "We certainly won't send the women. Those pigs would fuck them and then cut their throats, regardless of their age or condition. No, I'll send old and crippled men like myself. One can hope they will not be considered a threat by the Russians."

Miller cleared his throat. His own attempts at longer-range patrolling had gotten nowhere and had cost him needless casualties. If von Schumann could provide the information he needed, then he could be well situated to resist the Russian attack.

"I appreciate this."

"Thank you, General, but I am not doing it out of any sense of devotion to the American cause. I see cooperating with you as the lesser of two evils. Indeed, there is no comparison."

"Even so, you could have stood aside. Many of your people have done just that."

"Then they are fools, General Miller. Besides, I have my reasons. Do you wish to know them?"

Miller thought he knew the answer. "Go ahead."

"I believe there is a good chance that you will ultimately win. In any case, for me it is the only chance I would have to continue my life. Should that victory occur, I wish your government to know that I assisted you so that I will not be impeded in my efforts to find my wife and daughter."

Miller thought about his wife and two sons back home in Oklahoma. The boys were grown and both were in the service. He understood totally. He always got a laugh by saying he wanted to go home and play with his children's mother. His wife was a delightful and passionate woman he loved dearly, and his children were the joy of his life. He couldn't imagine the agony von Schumann must be feeling.

"I can't promise anything, but I will do what I can."

"I understand. There is another reason for helping you, General Miller. We are both fighting the Russians. If you believe in the saying that the enemy of my enemy is my friend, then we will soon be allies in fact, and not just in principle."

Miller laughed. "Stranger things than that have happened, Herr Oberst. Nothing could possibly surprise me anymore."

THE SEVERAL C-47s that carried General Marshall and his entourage had to make fueling stops on the way to Europe. Thus, a fatigued Steve Burke found that the air force base outside Reykjavik, Iceland, was a desolate and forlorn place, and surprisingly cold for the time of year.

From recently acquired experience, Burke knew it would take a couple of hours to refuel the planes and possibly change pilots for the next leg, which would take them to London. There they would spend a few days before going on to France. As he walked about the area aimlessly, a young captain came running up to him.

"Colonel Burke, General Marshall wishes to see you."

Unlike that time in what seemed to be the distant past, he raised no foolish questions, only nodded and let the captain lead him.

Marshall had been in the first plane and had taken over the base commander's office. He was seated behind a desk and had just finished a quick meal.

"Sit down, Colonel," Marshall ordered as he pushed away his tray. "I need information from you."

"Yes, sir."

"I want you to tell me everything you know about Josef Stalin."

When Burke's face registered surprise, Marshall clarified the order. "Now, Colonel, I know what you're thinking, that I doubtless already know a good deal about the man, and you're quite right. But since I already know what I know, I want to know what additional information you might know. Understand?"

"Yes, sir."

"Besides, we've got more than an hour to kill and I've pumped everybody else on the flight. Now, you've said you never met Stalin, so how do you know him?"

For a moment, Burke was flustered. Had the general forgotten their first conversation? Then he realized that Marshall was not upset, and perhaps was even gently teasing him in an attempt to increase his store of knowledge.

"Well, sir, since I do speak and read the language, I was able to go over his writings, his speeches, and even listen to recordings of his voice. His speeches are quite dull and he speaks in a monotone, by the way. In that regard, he is quite unlike Hitler, who was so bombastic and emotional."

"What about Trotsky? Did you ever meet him?"

Now Burke was on firmer ground. "Yes, sir, I spoke with him on several occasions when he was in Mexico. Ironically, I was supposed to meet with him a few days after he was murdered by Stalin's thugs back in 1940." He saw he now had Marshall's attention. "Trotsky was quite interesting. He really expected to take over Russia upon Lenin's death. Like so many people, he totally underestimated Josef Stalin."

"Haven't we all," Marshall said.

"General, Stalin is not a Russian. He is from the republic of Georgia, which is in the Caucasus Mountains and in the southern part of the Soviet Union. He was raised in a Russian Orthodox environment and even attended a seminary for a while. He may have thought of studying for the priesthood. Some apologists for him see this as a sign of impending or latent Christianity. I don't. I see it as a need to be involved in some sort of belief, and he has chosen communism as his one true faith. Or perhaps it chose him.

"Sir, those Communists who ultimately took over from the tsar and the moderates in the revolution considered themselves world revolutionaries. They were so naïve that they thought the world would turn their way and reject capitalism in a matter of months or, at worst, a couple of years. All they really needed was for the message to get out. For that reason, the first Communist leaders, like Lenin and Trotsky and even Stalin, were unwilling and unprepared to enter into agreements with foreign states they thought would shortly cease to exist. They thought nation-states would go the way of the dodo in their new workers' world, and that the result would be a totally stateless worldwide society."

Marshall chuckled. "It must be quite unsettling for them to see us all still here."

"It is, but the point is very significant. The true believers, and this includes Stalin, see no difference whatsoever between the democracies and the totalitarian states like Germany. If you are not a Communist, then you are a capitalist and must be the enemy. They will enter into agreements of necessity and convenience when they have to, or it's to their advantage, and repudiate them when they wish; thus, it was no surprise to me when the Russians signed that pact with the Nazis, and it is, somewhat in hindsight, no surprise that they have attacked us. They saw a chance for gain and they have taken it."

"And again, we have underestimated Stalin."

"Yes, sir. He became Lenin's successor not because Lenin wanted him but because he was the most ruthless and determined of all the potential candidates to emerge after Lenin's death. He will wait years for an opportunity and then take it without any care for the consequences. Do you recall what he did to the kulaks?"

"I believe they were farmers who opposed him."

"In Russian," Burke said, "the word *kulak* means 'tight fisted.' They were fairly prosperous farmers and other property owners and the poorer peasants were jealous of them. He simply burned their crops, sealed off their lands, and let them all starve to death. There were at least a couple of million of them and now they are all gone. Dead. It's almost like the way Hitler murdered the Jews. He uses his army the same way. He purged it of most of its officers a few years ago and did the same thing with his political rivals. He had almost all of them killed."

Marshall shook his head. "Of course I knew of the purges, but had not realized their scope or impact. What you are inferring is that he is willing to totally use up his army against us if it means victory for him and communism."

"Yes, sir. A man like Stalin would think that another army can be built out of simply growing a fresh crop of children. He might consider their lives like a farmer considers wheat. Something to be planted and then harvested when needed.

"Sir, Stalin is quiet and meticulous. He did not even have an official title until a little while ago. The war has forced him to come out of the shadows and into the light, and I'm not certain he's comfortable with that."

"Interesting. Why?"

"Well, sir, he might have had a nervous breakdown when Hitler invaded in 1940. He'd had plenty of warnings regarding Hitler's intentions, but chose to ignore them. Despite the fact that he doubtless planned on betraying Hitler at some future date of his choosing, he could not cope with someone else betraying him first. I believe the war with Germany was even more devastating to Russia and Stalin's plans than we have estimated. Because of this, I believe he now has several fixations that are all based on previous utterances. First, he believes that he must have secure borders for his country, and that means a large buffer zone which includes Poland, Hungary, Czechoslovakia, and other countries. Second, he must eliminate Germany as a major power, preferably through absorbing Germany's population and resources.

"And finally, he sees an opportunity to export the Communist revolution, which is most dear to him. Yes, he is a dictator and a murderer, but he is also a devout Marxist and feels that communism and capitalism cannot coexist peacefully on this planet."

Marshall nodded thoughtfully. "Good assessment, Colonel. Much of it I already knew, but you brought up some very good points."

Steve basked in the compliment. "Thank you, sir, but there is one thing that puzzles me and that is the fact of the timing."

"And timing is everything, is it not?"

It was obvious that the general was in a very good mood, so Burke decided to continue. "General, it is common knowledge that we would be pulling the bulk of our forces out of Europe as soon as possible for the invasion of Japan. So why didn't he wait until they were gone and we were bogged down fighting in the Pacific? Further, why didn't he wait until we had won that war as well and had disbanded our armed forces? In a year or two we wouldn't have much in the way of a military force anywhere to stand in the way of the Reds if they decided to suddenly take over Europe. So, again, why now? What advantage does Stalin perceive in attacking now? Unless the events of this war have pushed him over the psychological edge, there is no reason for him to attack right now instead of later."

Steve paused. Marshall was looking at him very intently.

Burke swallowed and continued. Was he treading on sacred ground? "Sir, it's almost as if Stalin is aware of or believes that something is going to happen that would wipe out any Russian advantage; that he has discovered some dark secret that has made him make the calculated decision that it is in his, and the revolution's, best interest to make war now and not later. For some reason," Steve added softly as Marshall's eyes bore into him, "he must feel that Russia will be weaker in the near future, and not stronger."

Marshall's face was impassive and his eyes hooded. Steve became aware that he had touched a nerve. There was a hidden reason for the Russian attack, and he realized that Marshall knew precisely what it was.

In a moment, Marshall relaxed and graciously thanked him for his analysis, and then dismissed him. On the way back to the C-47, Steve wondered just what the hell was going on. Was it anything Natalie could shed light on when he got back to Washington? He had to know.

ELISABETH WALKED SLOWLY and carefully into Captain Leland's office. He didn't like Germans and didn't know what to make of her. Yes, she was a refugee and, yes, she was only half German, but the half that was German had supported Hitler, at least for a while, and that clearly bothered Leland.

Perhaps he was just confused, she thought. She knew she certainly was. In a short while she would be meeting Jack Logan and they would have a quiet few minutes together. Perhaps Leland was jealous of the two of them? He didn't wear a wedding ring but that meant nothing. Many men didn't have one and others removed it while in the army. Something about getting hurt, although she wondered how Leland would ever get hurt. He was General Miller's aide, not a combat soldier.

Leland smiled stiffly. "Good afternoon, Miss Wolf. I have something I'd like for you to look at."

And good afternoon to you too, she said and smiled sweetly. He handed her a sheet of paper. The message had been poorly typed and then run off on a mimeograph machine. On the upper left-hand corner was a poorly drawn star and a hammer and sickle. The Communists are at work, she thought as she read it.

"Very predictable," she said and handed it back. "The writer is obviously a German and a Communist and wants us all to surrender to the Russians so we can live in a socialist paradise instead of under capitalism."

"About what I thought," Leland said. "We've found a number of copies. And now the big question—any idea who in your group might be doing this?"

The question surprised her. "Captain, there are close to two thousand refugees here in Potsdam. I don't even know most of their names, much less their political persuasions. There was a time before Hitler came to power when German communism was rather strong, but not anymore. Hitler sent all he could find to the camps."

"Then this might be a German Communist who escaped from a camp?"

Lis nodded. She heard Jack talking to someone in the background. "That's a very good point," she said, and Leland smiled briefly. "Hitler jailed Communists along with homosexuals, criminals, and just about everyone who disagreed with him. I will talk to von Schumann and we will ask some questions. We may also find out that the author is very young. The writing is so naïvely done."

"I have to ask you something, Miss Wolf. You just said Hitler jailed those who disagreed with him. May I assume that you and your family did not disagree with him?"

"Captain, I will tell you the same thing I've told others, including Jack Logan. In the beginning, we all thought Hitler was our savior and, yes, we all joined the Nazi Party. Then when the wars and the deaths began, we had second thoughts. My father was demoted from his position within the diplomatic service because of his reservations, but he never crossed the line where the Gestapo noticed him. In a way, we weren't brave enough."

The answer seemed to satisfy Leland. "My sister married a Jewish immigrant from Poland who came over in the early thirties. He is terrified that all his family have been slaughtered in Auschwitz. He's heard nothing about them, and my sister says it's driving him nuts."

"I'm afraid I can only offer sympathy. However, I do have a question for you. How did your family react to your sister marrying a Jew?"

"Touché, Miss Wolf," Leland said with a wan smile. "My mother said she'd almost rather my sister had married a Negro than a Jew."

"Or how about an Irishman?" asked Logan as he entered the room.

For the first time, Leland smiled genuinely. "An Irishman would be worse. You two have a nice dinner."

Jack took Lis's arm and led her outside. The walked a few blocks to where he could see the bunker he used as his headquarters and have a view of the Havel. Finally, the river was worth looking at, as the flow of bodies seemed to have stopped.

"Would your ladyship like me to open your rations?" he asked.

They each had a twelve-ounce can of something that claimed to be beef along with a soggy mass that purported to be potatoes. Originally, C rations were not intended for long-term use, but people in a siege could not be choosy. With plane drops diminishing, it was understood that all rations would have to last a long time and they would soon be sharing cans and not eating one all by themselves. When that time came, Jack hoped he'd be able to sneak something to Lis and Pauli.

"Outstanding," Lis said as she wiped her mouth with her hand. The food in her can had disappeared, while Jack's was about a third full.

"You're joking."

She punched him lightly on the arm. "I was talking about the company. The food was truly awful, but at least it is filling and somewhat nourishing. A few weeks ago I would have killed for something like that. I just hope I never have to feel that way again."

Jack took a deep breath. "No guarantees, are there? What worries me is that all this must come to an end sooner or later."

"And that, dear Jack, would be both wonderful and awful, perhaps even horrible. My fear is that the Russians would win and we would all die. My other fear is that your Americans will win and we will be separated." She laughed bitterly. "I don't see any way this interlude can have a happy ending."

"I know. If we're relieved, I'll still be in the army and have to go wherever my unit is sent, while you'll be left here as a refugee. In theory, at least, you'd be safe. It just scares the hell out of me picturing you and Pauli wandering all over Germany looking for a place to live and something to eat."

"Jack, do you want us to meet after this is over?"

"Good God, yes."

"Then you've made up my mind for me. When this war does end, I will contact Canadian authorities and use my dual citizenship to get Pauli and me out of Germany."

Jack took a deep breath. It was a glimmer of hope. He reached into his pocket and pulled out a small notepad and began writing. "Do you know where Port Huron is in Michigan?"

"I think so."

"Good. This is my address and my parents' names and our phone number. When you get out, notify them and they will help you."

She squeezed next to him and put her head on his shoulder. She took a deep breath as he put his arm around her. For the moment, she felt secure and content. She had a goal. Canada.

"Jack, when was the last time you kissed a girl?"

He grinned. "Ages. I've forgotten how."

"Liar," she said, laughing, and promptly proved that neither he nor she had forgotten a thing.

CHAPTER 13

As the prime minister entered the Oval Office, Harry Truman's first impression of Winston Churchill was one of mild surprise that the man whose force of will had helped sustain Britain was so darned short. The second impression, and a very negative one, was that Churchill looked so very old. With a jolt, he realized that the bulldog of Britain was seventy-one, an age when most men should have retired and be writing their memoirs. Worse, Churchill showed every year. His wartime service as Britain's leader had taken a serious physical toll. At sixty-one, Truman knew he not only looked much younger but acted much sprier.

Truman shuddered. How would he look in a few years as president? Would the combined weight of the office and continuing aging drag him down too? Well, he thought wryly, nothing like starting a new war to set the tone of a new administration to help him find out.

Churchill broke the brief silence. "Mr. President, it is indeed an honor to meet you. The late president has spoken well of you."

Like hell, Truman thought. He sincerely doubted that FDR had ever mentioned him. "I am honored to meet you too, sir. He spoke of you often when we discussed world matters."

Churchill laughed at the polite lies. They shook hands and took seats along a wall where they were separated by a small table. No one else was present for this brief meeting.

Truman began. "First I should inform you that Mr. Speer has been taken to the Executive Office Building across the street. When we are finished speaking, we can go and hear what he has to say."

"Very good."

"Now, Prime Minister, let me be most frank. Obviously, I am not in the least bit happy with what has transpired with Stalin, and I am concerned by rumors that you are not displeased that we are in this new war."

"I did not want this war either, Mr. President," Churchill said sadly. "I merely urged firmness when dealing with Stalin. I did not for one minute expect such an irrational onslaught. Kindly recall that my British soldiers are bleeding and dying as well as yours."

Churchill smiled bleakly. "I merely wanted the Russian bear caged. I wished Stalin to know that the democracies had strength and a willingness to let him go no further. There was nothing we could do about the countries he'd already seized, but we could not let him impose his will on Germany or the rest of Europe.

"Mr. President, despite the fact that the British empire is far-flung, England itself is a small island that could be vulnerable to aggressor nations should we let it. Unlike the United States, whose moats are oceans, England's moat is only twenty or thirty miles wide, not thousands. In these days of bombers and missiles, safety is virtually nonexistent. I might add, sir, that your moat is shrinking as well, and that your traditional emphasis on isolation may no longer be appropriate. Ergo, we allied ourselves with others, sometimes distastefully, to maintain our security."

"Did it matter," Truman asked, "what the policies were of the nations you were allied with and against?"

"Not at all," he replied candidly. "My predecessors at Downing Street and I have always had one goal in common, and that was the preservation of the empire as a sovereign, powerful, and prosperous nation. I once implied that I would seek an alliance with the devil if I thought it would help England and I meant it."

Truman grinned. "Are you comparing the United States with Satan?"

Churchill chuckled and continued. "France and Italy are hopeless and impoverished both militarily and morally, while Spain and Portugal are inconsequential. Therefore, a resurgent Germany is our only hope for stability in Europe in the face of Communist Russia. If the Russian bear is allowed to swallow Eastern Europe and now Germany, it will be strong enough to reach out with a mighty paw and smash the British empire."

"I see your point," Truman said grimly.

Churchill rose awkwardly. His joints were stiff and he was still fatigued from his trip. "The war with Russia is indeed a tragedy. However, it may have been inevitable. It is at least occurring at a time when our nations are strong, not weak." He dramatically checked a pocket watch. "Do we not have a German waiting to see us?"

"We do."

"Then, Mr. President, shall we not hear what he has to say?"

BILLY TOLLIVER TOOK a moment to take stock of his situation. He and his platoon were settled in an unnamed village about ten miles west of the Elbe, and a narrow road ran through it that ultimately went to the very old city of Brunswick. The village was of fairly new construction and bland, with no front lawns. The road ran almost right up to the sterile houses and buildings.

They had fallen back from a village much like it yesterday and would doubtless find a village just like this one a few hundred yards up the road when the Russian pressure became too much to bear. Bear, he thought and smiled, bear the Russian bear. Or should they shave it and bare the bear?

"Something funny, Lieutenant?" Holmes looked confused. Was his platoon leader losing it?

"A private thought, Corporal. Nothing important."

The recently promoted Holmes shrugged but did not look impressed. Tolliver sometimes thought that Holmes did not have the respect for an officer that an enlisted man really ought to, and seemed to be sneering at him in his New England accent.

Worse, Holmes was a Jew, and Tolliver hadn't had much experience with Jews. There were very few of them in and around Opelika and none that he knew of at the Citadel, where he'd gotten his degree, and the only ones he could think of ran stores or pawnshops in Montgomery or Mobile. Like many people, he hadn't given much thought to what the Nazis were doing and still wasn't certain he believed all that stuff about mass murders. Still, he'd seen a couple of camps and was beginning to change his mind.

Tolliver did some quick calculating just to make sure he hadn't forgotten something important in his troop's dispositions. He had three squads, which, including himself and Holmes, totaled only twenty-four men. With that he was to stop, or at least delay, whatever the Russians were going to send down the damn road and through the damn village. The rest of the company had similar assignments, as did the battalion, the regiment, and the division. So did the whole damn army, for that matter, he realized. Slow or stop the Russians was their only goal.

At least this particular village wasn't in ruins like so many of them. Germany, he decided, was a study in contrasts. While so much of the land had been reduced to rubble only a few feet high, there were other areas that, inexplicably, had been untouched by the physical presence of war. Of course, with the Russians due at any time, there was little likelihood of that continuing for this particular neat and tidy collection of brick and concrete houses and stores.

They were in a *gasthaus,* a tavern, whose location gave his platoon good fields of fire down the main road from the east, as well as a secondary road that he would consider a tempting way to enter the village if he were the Russian commander. He also had men with machine guns, BARs, and bazookas in homes flanking the *gasthaus.*

The *gasthaus* had also given his platoon something they hadn't had in a very long time, a couple of steins of beer apiece. To their astonishment, they had found a perfectly good cask of suds in the cellar that Tolliver had carefully portioned out to his crew. The local krauts, he decided, would never miss it, and if someone complained, fuck 'em. His men deserved it. Even Holmes had seemed appreciative of the gesture.

"Second squad hears tanks." It was Holmes on his radio.

"Can they see anything?"

"No, sir, and it only sounds like a couple."

Yeah, Tolliver thought, only a couple. When this war with Russia first started, he had thirty-five men in his platoon. He had seen how much damage just a couple of Russian tanks could do.

"Can we get artillery or air support?"

Holmes shook his head. "Air is tied up. We'll be getting artillery support in about ten minutes when they finish with other targets."

Wonderful, Tolliver thought. In ten minutes, they could all be dead or speaking Russian.

"Here they come!"

Tolliver had no idea who yelled. It hardly mattered. He saw a wave of humanity, he guessed company-strength, surge into view. Behind them came a pair of T34s. As he watched, his company's mortars started landing in the Russian infantry, flinging several soldiers into the air. His platoon's machine guns and BARs opened up, cutting more holes in the advancing infantry. It didn't stop them, and the two tanks opened fire with their own machine guns as the Americans revealed themselves.

"Duck," Tolliver screamed automatically as the lead tank fired its main gun. A second later, the top floor of the building to his right disintegrated in a billowing cloud of dust and smoke that obscured his view. The second tank fired and smashed another building.

As planned, Tolliver's men fired some more rounds at the advancing infantry and retreated a few houses down the road. Cautiously, the tanks started to enter the village. Built-up areas would be death traps for tanks if they weren't careful, and these tankers looked cautious indeed.

Supported by their infantry, the Russians grew bolder and moved forward to about fifty yards from Tolliver's new position. Tolliver's gunners fired, cutting down a dozen infantry, causing the remaining Russians to dive for the cover of nearby houses.

"No!"

Tolliver yelled to no avail as he saw one of his men with a bazooka run out in front of the lead tank and fire. As he knew it would, the bazooka round bounced harmlessly off the front armor of the Russian tank as its machine gun opened up and, with an insane chatter, cut the soldier into bloody halves. Tolliver couldn't tell who it was. Probably one of the newer guys. The older ones knew better than to try something like that.

The tank rumbled on and squashed the dead American soldier. They would have to abandon the village under close fire from the Russian armor. It was the worst possible situation. Then he saw movement on the roof of a building to his left front. Another American with a bazooka, but this time firing downward. He saw the round hit behind the turret, and a moment later smoke and flames belched from the vents and openings of the lead tank as its ammo started to cook off inside. No one got out. The road was blocked by the wrecked tank, and they had a moment's respite.

"Holmes, any idea where the rest of the Reds are?"

"Glad you asked, sir. We are being flanked. I suggest we phone mother and tell her we're leaving."

Tolliver was about to snap at Holmes for his damn Yankee insolence, but thought it could wait for a better time. "Tell Company we're pulling out." Russian infantrymen were peering from behind the burning tank and firing randomly at the American positions.

"Sir," said Holmes. "I've got artillery. They want coordinates."

Tolliver grinned wolfishly. "Give them ours and tell them to wait five minutes."

Holmes paled and relayed the information. In a barely controlled panic, the platoon gathered its wounded and ran down the road, taking advantage of every wall and shrub to conceal themselves from the Russian soldiers who were now advancing into the village from both sides. Finally, they made it to their previously designated rendezvous point, just as they had done at the last several villages they'd abandoned. Tolliver checked his watch. It had taken seven minutes.

Tolliver looked at Holmes, who shrugged. "I told artillery to wait ten. Five seemed a little close."

Maybe I won't court-martial him, Tolliver thought, just have him flogged and then skinned alive. He counted heads. There were only eighteen left and two of them were wounded.

Just as he finished his tally, the first artillery round hit the village, followed by a dozen more that caused flames and sent concussions that they could feel. In seconds, the neat little German village no longer existed except as smoking rubble. Nor for that matter did the remaining Red tank and the rest of the company of Russian infantry.

"Who the hell's winning this war, Lieutenant?" asked Holmes. He was gasping under the weight of his radio. "And why the hell are we even fighting it? I want to kill the Germans who are killing my people. I really don't give a shit about the Russians."

"Shut up," snapped Tolliver.

He hated it when Holmes asked questions he couldn't answer. But the man had a point. Who the hell was winning and why was it started in the first place? It was, he thought, nothing but a big snafu. No, a fubar—Fucked Up Beyond All Recognition. They were hurting the Reds, but there were always more Soviet soldiers, while reinforcements and replacements for his platoon were nonexistent.

Tolliver understood that modern war consisted of a large number of small skirmishes like the one he'd just fought, and not a grand epic battle like Gettysburg. His great-granddaddy had fought for the Confederacy and lost a foot at Gettysburg. Before his memory failed him, Grampa had told him a hundred times of long rows of Union soldiers in dirty blue uniforms confronting long rows of Confederates in dirty gray or butternut. He'd described battles where thousands of men could be seen shooting and falling. Now, Tolliver couldn't even see the platoon next to him.

So, if a hundred skirmishes were fought and the United States won more than fifty of them, then they were winning the war, weren't they? Fewer than fifty and they were losing. So what had just happened? He'd mauled a Russian company, but lost the village. Had it been a win, loss, or draw?

He was too tired to care.

"Holmes, you figure it out, and when you do, let me know."

IF ALBERT SPEER was awed by the presence of the two men who headed the coalition against his beloved Germany, he did not show it. An architect by education, he had risen in the ranks of the Nazi hierarchy to a ministerial rank that made him virtual czar of the production of all goods in the Third Reich.

That he was good-looking and articulate hadn't hurt him either. Speer was forty years old, and his last official title had been Minister of Armaments and Munitions. He had been in complete charge of Germany's war-making capabilities.

Truman did not shake his hand, only gestured him coldly to a seat in the room they were using. Translators were present to be used if necessary, but Speer's English was up to the task.

"Mr. President, on behalf of my government, I wish to have an armistice between our three nations."

"What about France and Russia?" Truman asked, tight-lipped. He had never seen a high-ranking Nazi before and was uncertain as to how to act. He decided on controlled belligerency.

Speer blinked. Unused to diplomacy, he had forgotten about the importance of France to the Western Allies. "Your correction is noted.

We wish peace between Germany and the western allies of Britain, France, and the United States. Even though the Third Reich is defeated, it should be obvious that we have no desire to surrender to Russia. Nor should you wish us to do so. Surely your policies of unconditional surrender and no separate peace no longer apply under the current circumstances."

Truman said nothing, merely stared at him, which encouraged Speer to continue. "As evidence of our good faith, Admiral Doenitz, as successor to the late Adolf Hitler, has offered the following without reservation or the need for you to reciprocate.

"First, we will release all Allied prisoners we now hold, although that is no longer a large number. Your troops have overrun most of our POW camps. We will expedite the transfer, although some prisoners are wounded and will require special handling. Additionally, any soldiers who have wandered into our area or airmen who are shot down as a result of your new war with Russia and make it to our lines will be returned to you."

Truman thought it was a good start but kept a poker face.

Speer continued. "We will signal all U-boats at sea to surface and surrender. This will occur at noon tomorrow London time, which, I trust, is sufficient time for you to notify your ships that the boats are surrendering. Second, we will be handing over to the British, under Montgomery, the cities of Emden and Wilhelmshaven."

Truman almost snorted. The U-boats had been ineffective for some time and the cities named had been under virtual British control for a number of days. He was aware that the Germans in the north of Germany as well as in Italy had been quietly and individually negotiating the surrender of various units as the war wound down. He had seen reports that indicated a significant level of cooperation between the advancing British and the retreating Germans in order to avoid needless casualties. He could not blame them.

"You can do better," Truman snapped, causing both Churchill and Speer to look startled.

Speer recovered quickly. "We will further direct the garrisons of Dunkirk, Lorient, St. Nazaire, and the Channel Islands to surrender immediately. That will free up one more of your divisions. The 66th, I believe."

The president knew that freeing one division, particularly one that he knew had not yet seen battle, was a drop in the bucket, but it was a start.

"Good," said Truman. "Now just what do you want out of this?"

The bluntness of the question made Churchill smile. It did not faze Speer. "Mr. President, my government is anxious that Germany not be overrun by the Russians and enslaved by her."

"Some say it would be what you deserved." Truman looked like he was beginning to enjoy himself.

"My country, sir, is trying now to free itself from the shackles of Nazism. Germany has a right to exist, just like every other nation. The fact that we made a major mistake and allowed a madman to reign should not condemn a people to extermination or the living hell of perpetual slavery."

Neither Truman nor Churchill was surprised by Speer's calling Hitler a madman. Late in the war, Speer had become totally disillusioned with Hitler, had blocked his orders to burn Germany to the ground, and had even contemplated assassinating Hitler, but the opportunity had not arisen.

"Yet," Truman persisted, "both you and Doenitz were Nazis. In point of fact, wasn't your Admiral Doenitz one of the few ranking navy officers to embrace Hitler thoroughly?"

"It is sad but true," Speer answered. "I too will have to answer for my actions in employing millions of slave laborers to help run the industry of the Reich. I felt it was unavoidable and essential at the time and, I will not lie, I might do it again under the same circumstances.

"As to Admiral Doenitz, he did become an ardent Nazi and, like so many others, myself included, firmly believed that Hitler was the savior of a downtrodden Germany, and, also like so many, turned a blind eye to the man's faults and the atrocities that have been committed in his name.

"Should you accept our offer of surrender, Great Britain and the United States will not have to worry about the German army and air force during this war with Russia. At worst, the German units will be interned after surrender. At best?" He smiled and shrugged.

Finally, Churchill spoke. "Can you speak for all Germans, Herr Speer? Isn't there a rival to Admiral Doenitz?"

Speer's answer was confident, and Truman had the feeling that at least this part of the conversation had been rehearsed. After all, hadn't Churchill and Speer arrived together?

"Rivals? Hardly. The only senior members of the old regime who might still be a factor are Himmler, Goering, and Bormann. Himmler is with Doenitz but under arrest, and Goering is wandering about Germany, apparently alone, while Bormann is either hiding in some Berlin cellar or already dead. No, gentlemen, there are no rivals to the admiral."

"What about war crimes, Mr. Speer?" Truman asked. "Haven't you just admitted your own culpability in that area?"

"Yes," Speer responded, "and I am personally willing to take the consequences for those actions when the time is appropriate. Regarding other so-called war criminals, however, I am aware that any peace between us will doubtless result in the lesser criminals going free to be judged only by God. The major criminals, such as those SS and Gestapo men and women who murdered people and ran the death camps, can still be caught and prosecuted."

Truman nodded. Unfortunately, there was a sad kind of logic to what Speer was saying. Germany had to be removed as an enemy. Even though she and her armies were largely in Allied hands, there still remained the potential for disaster if even the remnants of German armies remained on the loose to fight whomever they wished.

Truman realized he really didn't have much choice. It was time to make a deal with the devil and it was apparent that Churchill had already come to that conclusion.

"All right," Truman said. "I assume you have the power to act on Doenitz's behalf; therefore, you will radio him that we have an agreement in principle and that the German armies still in the field are to lay down their arms to us and the British. I would also like some indication as to whether or not the German people will actively support the Allies, especially regarding information and resistance from behind the Soviet lines."

Speer nodded and made a note.

"On the other hand," Truman continued, "I do not think it appropriate for you to even think of German soldiers fighting alongside Americans and British at this time. The German armies must surrender and become prisoners, not allies."

"Sir," Speer said, "my admiral is currently at Flensburg on the Danish border, with most of what remains of the German army, perhaps a half million men. I propose that these units remain in the area north of the Kiel Canal and south of Denmark to preserve the polite fiction that we are still an independent nation. We would also serve as a buffer between the Russians and the Danes should the British be forced to retreat beyond Hamburg, which, I must say, seems quite likely."

Truman could scarcely believe what he was hearing. The Germans were willing to protect Denmark? What had his world come to?

Speer continued. "However, if you wish us to form a buffer, we will require food. Simply put, both the German army and the Danes are starving. Will you get us food?"

"That sounds reasonable," Truman heard himself say. "And if you are overrun and have to leave this Flensburg place, we can establish a government in exile somewhere, perhaps"—he grinned evilly at Churchill—"in London." Churchill's jaw dropped at the thought.

"Excellent," said Speer with the touch of a smile.

"And now we lie down with the devil," Truman murmured, and Churchill nodded. "Tell me, do you have any thoughts on defeating the Soviets?"

Speer smiled. "Why yes, I do."

TONY THE TOAD saw the Russian a scant second before the Russian saw him. It was enough. It was almost dark, and the Russian soldier had turned the corner of the building and was almost upon Tony. Sensing the recognition of danger on the other man's face, Tony pulled his wide-bladed knife from its sheath on his belt and rammed it deep into the Russian's throat, causing the man's head to snap back at a ridiculous angle. The dying man gurgled, clutched the air a couple of times, and fell backward, leaving the sticky knife in Tony's hand.

There was a sharp intake of breath behind him. It was Vaslov. "Mother of God, what have you done?"

Tony wiped the knife on some leaves. "Killed a fucking Commie, what the hell's it look like? And what the hell was I supposed to have done? He was close enough to kiss me, for Christ's sake."

Despite his brave words, Tony was shaking so badly he could hardly sheathe the knife. This Russian was the first man he had ever killed close up. Any others had occurred while firing a tank's machine gun, and the effect was often unknown. This was too personal and he wanted to vomit from the stink of the blood that was beginning to co-agulate at his feet.

Vaslov looked closely at the dead Russian's throat. "What a nasty wound. You are good, Tony. And thank God you didn't use your rifle, the sound might have attracted too much attention."

Tony took a deep breath and got some control of himself. Had he gone for his Garand, he would be dead. "Thanks. Now don't you think we should get the hell out of here? This asshole surely had friends who are gonna miss him."

Vaslov smiled. "Very likely." He gestured to a couple of the others, who came and saw the sight and nodded appreciatively at Tony's hand-iwork. Counting Tony, there were now ten in the growing little group. One of them picked up the Russian's submachine gun and his pistol, along with spare ammunition.

"Help me remove his clothes," Vaslov asked.

"What the hell for?" Tony snarled. "I ain't undressing no corpse."

"Tony," Vaslov chuckled, "perhaps this uniform, which might just fit one of us, could prove useful. See this symbol on his collar?" Tony looked and nodded. It was a vertical sword within an oval wreath. In the fading light he thought the background might have been blue with a red trim.

"Yeah. Kinda pretty."

Vaslov chuckled. "Better than pretty, Tony, this man was an officer in the NKVD, the Russian secret police. Someone wearing this uni-form is likely to be treated as a god by an ordinary Russian officer. He could go anyplace and do almost anything. He would be an object of fear. This could be most useful to us."

Tony understood. "Okay, but we got a lotta blood to clean off, though, before he could go to any party."

Vaslov gestured, and several pairs of hands rapidly stripped the body, which soon lay shockingly pale and naked. There were a num-ber of ponds nearby, and they selected one and, after tying and weigh-ing down the body, slid it quietly under the water.

"There," smiled Vaslov, "in a few days no one will recognize him, not even his mother. If he had one."

Tony agreed. Even if the man was noted as missing, they had seen and avoided a lot of people who might also be missing from some army or other. And if the man's body was later found, it would soon be bloated and unidentifiable.

"So," Tony said, "we can now be a Russian secret police officer anytime we wish. But do we have anyone who speaks enough Russian?"

Vaslov almost purred. "Remember, I speak it fluently. It will be a joy to use it to help in their destruction."

CHAPTER 14

It began with a thundering and ground-shaking artillery barrage. First the Russian guns commenced pounding those targets they could see, and then those whose existence they suspected from the maps of the area and the few overflights that American aircraft and antiaircraft guns had permitted. Russian gunners had decided there were only so many places to hide supply dumps, truck parks, and the like within the confines of the Potsdam perimeter.

Elisabeth and Pauli joined the others in the basement of an old stone church, and settled in beneath the vaulted ceilings of the crypt to wait out the storm of fire and steel. Elisabeth tried to compare the shelling with what she had endured in and around Berlin and found she could not. Each was equally horrifying, and her mind made it difficult to draw from its hiding places the memories of prior terrors. In a way, she found that fact comforting for it meant that, whatever befell her, she would endure it.

Presuming, that is, she and Pauli actually lived through whatever was going to transpire. She looked about the crowd of people, steadily growing more and more silent and nervous as the shelling continued. She felt she could actually smell the fear. Where was von Schumann? She had not seen him in a while.

HALF A MILE away, von Schumann ducked instinctively as a shell landed near General Miller's headquarters. Miller chuckled wryly. "I thought you were a veteran of this sort of thing."

"A veteran never forgets to duck," von Schumann answered. He, Miller, Leland, and a number of others were well protected in a reinforced bunker. To his knowledge, the Soviets did not have anything that could penetrate the steel beams that formed its roof. It was possible, he supposed, that a shell could ricochet around the right-angled entrance and find its way in, but he doubted that as well.

Leland put down a telephone. "General, our artillery wants to respond."

"Are they being hit?"

"No, sir. A lot of near misses, but they're pretty well protected."

"Then let them wait. Everybody keep remembering that we still don't have all that much ammunition to throw around." Miller paused and tapped his pipe on a table. "Any response from the air force?"

Leland shook his head.

Miller understood but didn't have to like it. The big air battles and the army's major needs were west of the Elbe, where the American army was being slowly driven toward the Rhine. Potsdam was a backwater. The army and the correspondents officially referred to it as the Potsdam perimeter or the Potsdam pocket, but the soldiers referred to it as Goddamn Potsdam. Miller rather liked the latter term.

"Well," Miller said, "at least the Russian planes are tied up as well." Leland nodded. Except for the occasional scout plane, the sky over Potsdam had been empty for the last several days. The only bad part of that was the fact that the supply drops had also ceased. Temporarily, they all hoped.

"Oberst von Schumann, what is the Russian general, this Bazarian, going to do now?" Miller asked.

The news of the outside world was radioed in and the latest stories had been of the cessation of hostilities between Germany and the remaining Allies. This had changed von Schumann's status. He was now an official member of Miller's staff and his presence was accepted at all times. If some resented it, they did not voice their objections in Miller's presence. Even Leland seemed reconciled to it.

"General, I think we can assume that the Russian commander is not a fool. The Russians had a number of incompetents in command at the beginning of our invasion in 1940, but the realities of warfare took care of them. While it is likely that this General Bazarian is not at the head of his class, he has several advantages and will use them effectively."

Von Schumann looked around the headquarters. They were all looking at him as if he were a schoolmaster delivering a lecture. There might not be anything new in what he was going to say, but they wanted to hear it again.

"The Russian," von Schumann continued, "can mass his army and his tanks wherever he wishes and without our knowledge. He will attack in overwhelming strength at a place and time of his choosing, while we have to anticipate his attack occurring anywhere along our perimeter.

"Therefore, I believe he will launch a number of probing attacks before the major attack. He will not be looking for a weak spot—he knows there aren't any—but he will be seeking to confuse us, make us expend ammunition, and, perhaps, make us commit our reserves to a wrong location, which would hinder their redeployment."

Von Schumann looked about for disagreement and saw none. "When he does launch his main attack, it will be with what he hopes will be overwhelming force at that particular spot. His advantage is in numbers, nothing else. He will hope to get his soldiers inside our defenses and commence a battle of mutual slaughter in which his men can inflict enough casualties on us so that we will be unable to continue as an effective force."

Leland blinked in disbelief. "But that means he would be destroying his own army in order to do so."

It was a statement that had been made before, and it was still a difficult concept for an American, bred to conserve life, to accept. The appalling ruthlessness of the Russian army and its almost total disregard for human life when it needed to gain an objective had appalled Germans as well.

"But Bazarian would be saving face, his career, and possibly his life if he were to eliminate what he perceives as a cancer," von Schumann admonished gently. "He will most happily pay that price in the lives of others."

At that moment, yelled messages interrupted them. Tanks were reported approaching the very western flank of the perimeter, where it reached the shallower lake.

"What models?" von Schumann inquired, and he was told they were older-model BT5s and not the dreaded T34s. "Your dug-in Shermans will be able to handle them."

"Are there infantry?" Miller barked, and received an affirmative response. "Then that's it. We get the reserves ready to move out. So much for probing attacks."

Von Schumann was uneasy. The perimeter's reserves consisted of the equivalent of one platoon of Shermans, a handful of M10 tank destroyers, and two battalions of infantry. Other tanks were dug in and hidden around the perimeter. Once ordered, the reserves would move out to preplanned and well-dug-in positions and be difficult to destroy, but awkward to extricate if the attack were not the main one.

"How many tanks?" von Schumann asked.

"Outposts are pulling back so they don't get overrun, but indications are maybe twenty."

"And they are definitely not T34s?" Miller asked.

"They don't absolutely know, sir. They say they aren't all that familiar with Russian tanks, but they're reasonably certain they ain't T34s."

Damn, thought von Schumann. The inability of the Americans to pick out Russian tank types was something they hadn't thought of.

"Tell them this is important," he snapped, and the radio operator jumped. "Ask them if the Russian tanks look like the German Panther." He could only hope the lookout was familiar with German armor.

"No, sir. They don't."

Von Schumann chuckled. "This isn't the main attack, General Miller. They are not using T34s, therefore this is only a face-saving diversion by this Bazarian."

"You're certain?" Miller asked.

"The German Panther tank was a Nazi response to the Russian T34. The silhouettes are very similar. I believe the attacking tanks are indeed the BT5s we know he has. Their primary use nowadays is for scouting, not heavy combat." He thought quickly. "Perhaps Bazarian doesn't have any modern tanks? Perhaps Moscow considers this a backwater?"

"But sir," said Leland, surprising himself by acknowledging the German's higher rank. "The Russians do have heavier tanks than the T34. Could these be their heavies, the JS series?"

Von Schumann pondered. "But we have seen no indication that any of their JS, or Josef Stalin, heavy tanks are in the area. It is highly unlikely that they would be utilized here. I also think your scouts would recognize those monsters."

Miller chewed his pipe. "The reserves sit tight and wait. I think von

Schumann's correct, and we'll let our local defenses handle this. We won't tip our hand unless we absolutely have to."

A FEW HUNDRED yards away, Jack Logan peered through the firing slit of the bunker. Russian artillery was trying to chew up the barbed wire strung about fifty yards in front of him, and where the ditches didn't obstruct the route to the bunker. The cannonade didn't seem to be having much effect on the interlaced strands of wire. In front of that barrier was a series of overlapping antitank ditches. The engineers who had planned Potsdam's defenses said the Russian tanks couldn't cross them or climb them as long as the ground was dry, so their tanks and their supporting infantry would have to maneuver around them. This would place both Russian armor and men in the barbed wire and mines.

Beyond the ditches and wire was a clear field of fire that extended a quarter mile to a road that was obscured by bushes. The Russians, if they came at him, would come from there, which was why Captain Dimitri had put outposts just beyond it.

"The captain reports tanks approaching the road," yelled Crawford. Dennis Bailey, the new platoon sergeant, took the walkie-talkie from him and spoke quickly.

"Captain says the lookouts are coming back and we should watch for them," Bailey added. "But he said they see a lot of Red tanks—not the big ones, thank God—and a whole horde of infantry."

How many in a horde? Jack wondered. He thought that the lookouts could have stayed a little longer and given a more precise count, but quickly realized it really didn't matter. They had not been ordered to commit suicide, which is what would have happened had they stayed. What was important was that a large number of Russians was headed his way. They would know the precise number soon enough.

The rumble of guns firing behind them was followed by explosions beyond the field as American guns hit the advancing Russians, who were still hidden from their view. "About time," someone yelled. The one-sidedness of the artillery fire had been galling. Several Russian tanks were hit and exploded.

The Red artillery fired a few more salvos and slackened, then ceased. Tanks burst through the shrubs and were followed by a mob of Russians.

"Open fire," Logan yelled, and all the machine guns, BARs, and rifles in the bunker commenced to chatter. Other bunkers in the defensive line opened fire along with his. Logan put his rifle to his shoulder and emptied an eight-shot clip, replaced it, emptied and replaced that one. He could see the infantry falling and littering the field with twitching bodies. There was the muffled bang of mines going off, killing more Russians to add to the din, but the remaining tanks kept coming and the infantry was being replaced by a second wave. Logan saw that some of them were carrying ladders just like in the Middle Ages.

The wave of humanity reached ditches and slowed, as did the tanks. Temporarily foiled, the tanks opened fire on the bunkers confronting them with cannon and machine guns while the soldiers with ladders lowered themselves into the ditches as others tried to find their way through the maze of wire. Logan fired again and again, and had the angry satisfaction of seeing more Russians fall.

Another Russian tank burst into flames. It had taken a direct hit on its side from a protected tank destroyer. More American tanks fired and another Russian tank shuddered. Smoke commenced to pour from it. The Russian tanks lifted their fire from the bunkers and sought out the dug-in and well-hidden M10s and the Shermans that were now joining in the battle. The Red Army tanks tried to snake their way between the ditches, which again exposed their more vulnerable flanks to disabling fire from U.S. antitank guns, and a couple more were halted by damaged treads.

Mortars, machine guns, and rifle fire continued to rake and slaughter the Red infantry while the mines killed still more. The Russians, unable to climb through the wire, continued to pour into the ditch, and Logan could see the tips of ladders appearing on the American side.

The Russian soldiers scaled the ladders and, although numbers of them were shot and dropped back into the pit, the survivors ran the few yards toward the bunkers, wildly hip-firing submachine guns as they came. The sheer volume of rifle fire caused bullets to find their way through the slits, and Logan heard the sound of screams beside him. He wanted to look but there wasn't time.

A man's face appeared in front of the slit. The Russian looked puzzled, almost curious. Logan fired and it disappeared in a spray of red and gray. Explosions told him that American artillery was landing directly in front of him. Someone, most likely Dimitri, had called down fire almost on their own position.

The deafening concussions shook and caused him to drop to his knees. There were more screams inside the bunker but they seemed to him to be coming from another world.

Then there was silence. At first they didn't believe it. Jack recovered quickly and ordered the men back to the firing slits. Logan looked out and saw the world outside blanketed with the bodies of Russian soldiers. Some of them were still moving and, as his hearing improved, he could hear their moans. In the distance, he could see the remainder of the Russian infantry running back through the gaps in the shrubs. There were damn few tanks with them. He could see at least a dozen burning hulks from his bunker, and one had its turret ripped off as if it had been a toy.

With the Russians no longer an immediate threat, Logan checked for casualties—he had one dead and one wounded in this bunker. A check of his platoon's other two bunkers showed four wounded. They had won the fight but he had lost six men. One or two of the wounded might return in a couple of weeks, but the platoon had paid a price.

Logan opened the bunker's rear entrance and stepped cautiously outside and into the smoke-filled air. The other bunkers had informed him there were no Russians hiding on his roof, so he felt reasonably safe. He took a couple of men and checked the dead lying around him. He found the man he had shot in the face. The back of his skull had been blown out and his brains were all over the ground.

Cautiously, they walked to the edge of the ditch and pointed their rifles down. Who knew what might be waiting there. The bottom of the ditch was covered with dead and badly wounded Russians.

"Jesus," said First Sergeant Krenski, "how many of them did we get?"

There was the sound of vomiting nearby as one of his men was overcome by the scene. "I dunno," Logan mumbled, stunned by the sight. "It looks like it could be hundreds of them right here alone."

Krenski squatted by the side of the ditch. He was exhausted, and Logan realized he was as well. "Lieutenant, you don't think we'll have to do this again, do you?"

Logan shrugged. "Your guess is as good as mine, top, but I just wonder who has to clean up this mess."

•   •   •

JOSEF STALIN WAS nervous and agitated, a situation that immediately transferred itself to Molotov and Beria. Despite their exalted status in the Soviet hierarchy, they lived their daily lives in terror.

"France," said Stalin. "France is foiling us. They must cease."

Molotov nodded. He was the foreign secretary, so the problem Stalin perceived with France would be his to resolve. He did not glance at Beria, who would be relieved that they had not been summoned on a matter of national security, his area. The situation with the unfaithful Korzov had been bad enough.

Molotov knew that Stalin was frustrated by the slow progress against the Americans and British. It had been almost two weeks since the assault across the Elbe, and there was not much to show for it in the way of territorial gains.

Yet, Molotov thought, why should Stalin be surprised? The Allies were strong and would not fold immediately. They would have to be crushed. Zhukov had protested, although rather tamely it now seemed, that the Red armies needed time to reorganize, rest, and refit after capturing Berlin and destroying the remnants of the German armies facing them. They had not been given time to recover, and now they were paying the price for it.

Worse, Molotov was aware of rumors that the Red Army had paid more heavily in men and material in the destruction of the Germans in Berlin than they had expected. Zhukov was already making plans for troops to be moved from the other, smaller fronts to reinforce his assaults. It was not the best of signs.

Then too, Stalin had been outraged by the armistice between the Allies and Germany. He was not in a mood to distinguish between those Germans who had been Nazis and those who had disavowed them. He saw the agreement as a further betrayal by Truman and Churchill.

Stalin stood and began to pace, an act that Molotov found even more frightening. It meant that his leader was close to losing control.

"France is the weak link in the Allied front," Stalin said. "France is living in the past with delusions of grandeur, and this buffoon de Gaulle is the worst of the lot. Yet France does hold a key that can open up Europe to Zhukov."

Stalin jabbed at the tobacco in his pipe with a dead match and looked at the two men. "Comrade Molotov, you will contact de Gaulle and very bluntly inform him that we require France to leave the war. While the French have only a few divisions available to fight us, American and British supplies are coming through the French ports. Zhukov is correct in that Antwerp must be taken, but we can further damage the Allied effort by driving France into a separate peace with us."

Molotov understood. "We can make contact rather quickly, in a day or two at worst, but, Comrade Stalin, I have a concern."

"And what is that?"

"De Gaulle, comrade, is a most antagonistic and prickly sort of person. A truly obnoxious ultranationalist Frenchman. He is likely to see a slight or an insult in any attempt by us to disengage him from those countries that helped liberate his beloved France from the Nazis. He has already managed to be offended by the actions of the Americans and the British, who are supposed to be his allies."

Stalin lit his pipe and puffed on it. "Then remind him that his enemies, those Nazis who occupied and enslaved his country, are now, thanks to Churchill and Truman, his newest allies. Ask him how he likes that. I do not think he does very much, do you?"

"No," Molotov answered, and Beria nodded.

Stalin chuckled. "And if that does not work, do not for a moment be subtle. Remind him that, with or without his help, the Soviet Union will win this war against the capitalists and the fascists. All he can do is prolong or shorten the inevitable. If he prolongs it, he will make himself and France our sworn enemy. If he closes the ports and shortens the war, he will have proven that he and France can be our friends. The choice will be his. If he does not close the ports, then he will, inevitably, have an angry Russian army crossing his border with what had been Germany. De Gaulle can rest assured that we will exact our revenge, our pound of flesh, for his intransigence. Tell him we will devastate Paris and its people as we did Berlin." He chuckled at the thought.

Molotov did not relish the thought of giving de Gaulle what amounted to an ultimatum. Ambassador Andrey Vyshinsky would be responsible for actually dealing with the tall and absurd-looking Frenchman. Despite his fear of failure, Molotov could almost smile at the thought of Comrade Andrey confronting that arrogant bastard Charles de Gaulle.

Stalin was not finished. "Comrade Beria."

Beria almost jumped. "Yes, Comrade Stalin?"

"For you we have a special assignment. Let us suppose that the French are either so stupid that they reject our offer, or, as is most likely, try to defer making a decision until the last possible moment. Should that occur, we cannot be inactive. We must make life miserable for the Allies as well as the government de Gaulle is trying to form. Don't you agree?"

Molotov noted a bead of sweat forming on Beria's forehead as his head bobbed quick agreement. How, he wondered, could the second most feared man in the Soviet Union be so mortally afraid of the first? Simple, he answered himself: everyone in Russia lived each day in gut-wrenching fear of that one man with his stinking pipe.

"Comrade Beria," Stalin continued. "I want you to make every effort to stir up trouble in France. We have a sizable Communist Party there, and I am certain they would be happy to cause work stoppages, barricade streets, protest the war, and do anything else to show that de Gaulle's hold on the French people is less than solid."

Beria smiled tightly. It would be a fairly easy task. He would call for the French Communist Party to rise in protest against the alliance with Germany and the war with Russia. He was confident they would respond. Perhaps, he thought quickly, he could develop a guerrilla war between the French people and the Allies as they arrogantly rode across France in their long lines of trucks and trains. Perhaps he could carry it over into Italy, where the Italian Communist Party had been fighting the Nazis.

Beria glanced quickly at Molotov, whose face, as usual, showed nothing. Beria envied Molotov's ability to apparently live without fear in a country dominated by Stalin.

"Comrade Stalin," he answered solemnly, "it will be done. The French people will rise in support of the people's revolution."

Suslov checked again to see that his tank was hidden from the prying eyes of the American planes. They were east of the city of Brunswick, and it was nearly dawn and not time to be caught on the road by American fighters and bombers. He did not know which he hated most, the stubby P-47 Thunderbolt or the newer, sharklike P-51

Mustang, or even the B-17 and B-24 bombers, which had been known to dump their lethal and immense loads on the unwary. The tank crews had familiarized themselves with silhouettes of the planes, but it really mattered little. Each plane could be devastating, particularly since the fighters had figured out that tanks were vulnerable to their rockets and ceased wasting machine-gun fire on them.

Most disturbing to Suslov and the others was the fact that there seemed to be so damned many of the American planes in the air lately. They had been used as protection from Nazi planes by the Soviet air arm, and this was no longer the case; thus, the need to hide during the day and to travel only at night. A tank column in the open during the day would surely attract American planes like flowers draw bees.

The political officers had tried to downplay Russian tankers' concerns by saying that the Russian airplanes were pounding the hell out of American staging areas and supply depots, and, when that task was completed, they would return to sweep the skies of the remaining Yanks.

Suslov and his crew had listened solemnly to these comments during the periodic lectures and exhortations, but even Latsis had agreed that they would have much preferred to see more of their planes overhead and fewer lectures when they made their attacks on the stubborn American defenses. No one said any of this to the political officers. Anything other than enthusiastic support for their drivel would result in being sent to a penal battalion, which was the same thing as a death sentence. Those troops led the way during suicide charges or were sent to clear minefields with their feet. Whatever doubts anyone had were kept to themselves.

At least, Suslov thought as he rearranged a tree branch over the turret, they were getting some precious time to rest and refit. As a result of almost continuous combat, the battalion had been bled down to only seven operational tanks. Not all the others had been destroyed by the Americans. Several had been left behind because of mechanical problems. Fuel, while not overly plentiful, was not yet a concern and there was the promise of reinforcements. Word had it that at least a dozen fresh tanks and crews would be arriving within a day or so. In the meantime, it was an opportunity to catch a little rest and do some maintenance on the remaining tanks.

Suslov almost didn't hear Martynov, his gunner, come up behind him. "Pavel, if you were trying to scare me, you almost succeeded. Do you have any cigarettes?"

Martynov handed him a Lucky Strike. They were starting to liberate American cigarettes from prisoners and bodies. Suslov would have preferred a Camel but took the Lucky. Anything was better then the paper-wrapped shit that passed for cigarettes in the Soviet Union.

"Sergei, there is something I want you to see."

Suslov was about to make a witty remark when he saw the look on Martynov's face. He was almost distraught. "What is it, Pavel?" he asked with genuine concern.

Martynov shook his head as if it was difficult to speak. "Just come. Please."

Suslov walked with him across a field toward a farmhouse and barn. Beyond it he could see the tops of a row of trees. As he walked the field, he looked nervously skyward in case an American fighter appeared. He did not think it likely that anyone would waste ammunition on two people walking, but one could never be certain. They were not that far from the front, only a handful of miles, and they could hear the rumble of artillery in the west and the sound of bombings in other directions. It was not the time for a carefree hike.

Martynov directed him to walk around the farm buildings to where he could see the row of trees. Suslov stopped suddenly and gasped. "Sweet Jesus," he whispered.

There were about ten trees, large and lush with fresh spring growth and with strong limbs. Each limb was festooned with the naked bodies of dead women and young girls hanging by their necks. He wanted to puke. Behind him he heard Martynov weeping. There had to be at least fifty bodies swaying in a macabre dance to the tune of the gentle breeze.

He willed himself to walk among them. They were of all ages, from the very young to the withered and shockingly old. Some had been mutilated before being hanged, with their breasts cut off and bellies slashed open so that their entrails hung down toward the ground. A couple had had their eyes gouged out. Except for blackened faces caused by the slow strangulation they'd endured by hanging, they had not yet begun to bloat or discolor. They hadn't been hanging there all that long.

"Who was here before us?"

Ivan Latsis arrived and stood beside him. He was grinning at the sight. "I believe they were Siberians. I've heard about these Hitler Christmas Trees, but I've never seen one before."

Suslov had also heard of this particular atrocity. Some Red Army soldiers, almost always the Asian savages from places such as Siberia, had picked up the habit of murdering their victims after they were through with them and leaving them as macabre decorations on trees. A brigade of Siberians had passed through the day before, as his tank battalion had been taken out of line. This must have been the Siberians' previous encampment.

"God help us," muttered Suslov.

Latsis laughed bitterly and lit his own Lucky. "There is no God, or had you forgotten, Sergei Alexievich. Religion is the opiate of the people and we live to serve the state. You think this is horrible, don't you? Do you want me to tell you again what the Germans did to my family?"

Suslov did not want the story retold. "It doesn't make this right."

Latsis sneered. "I can't wait until the first American women get passed around and used as ornaments like these. The Yanks do have women in their hospitals and with their rear units, don't they? They'll squeal as well as the Germans when we get our hands on them."

"You would do this to Americans?" Martynov was shocked.

"With pleasure," Latsis answered. "They betrayed their true colors by becoming allies with the Germans. It was one thing for us to fight just them. That could have been an honorable war, if there is such a thing, but by making a treaty with the Nazis, they betrayed their true colors. They are as bad as the German scum."

They had been joined by the fourth member of their crew, Popov, the part-Asian loader. "We are wanted back at the tank."

"Why?" asked Suslov.

Popov grimaced slightly. "The political officers want to give us another lecture." At first Suslov had thought Popov was a spy for the NKVD, but he no longer did. He had proven too reliable.

I can hardly wait, Suslov thought. Perhaps we should tell them to hold it in the shade of these trees. "Yes," he said instead, "let us go and hear why we must win this war."

CHAPTER 15

General Marshall accepted the cup of coffee from his subordinate and friend, Dwight Eisenhower. The two men were alone in Ike's tent near Reims while Burke and a number of aides waited outside, chatting, smoking, and wondering what the great men were talking about.

Marshall sipped his coffee. "I had planned to be here sooner, but it was necessary to travel circumspectly to avoid Red planes."

Ike smiled slightly. The danger from Russian planes had become a fact of life to those in the European theater, but was something new for someone coming over from the States. Marshall and his staff had also been delayed by the violent peace riots taking place in war-fatigued Britain. They were a clear message that their main ally, Britain, was no longer as reliable as she had been.

Marshall refused an offer of more coffee. "Ike, what's the latest on the ground war?"

Ike lit another cigarette. "We are fighting them every inch of the way and making them pay. In a couple of days we'll have to quit Brunswick and be back to the Leine River north of the Harz Mountains. The Reds are beginning to flank Montgomery."

"Can you hold them at the Leine?"

"No."

The simple statement silenced both of them. Ike briefly explained that the Leine River was not a major obstacle. Even though there had been time to prepare defenses and fortifications, the river was not particularly wide or deep.

"We can delay them," said Ike, "but that's about all."

Marshall sighed, accepting the fact. "You are still hoping to stop them at the Weser?"

In some places the Weser, a wider and more formidable stretch of water, was only twenty-five or thirty miles west of the Leine. Neither man felt it would be long after the Russians forced the Leine that they would be on the banks of the Weser.

Ike shrugged. "We will make a hell of an effort to stop them there. If that doesn't work, it'll be at the Rhine, which is about a hundred and fifty miles away from the Leine. If they cross the Rhine, well, they won't have much left in the way of natural obstacles to stop them before Antwerp, or much left of Germany for that matter. It'll have to be flesh and blood that stops them, not rivers."

Both men paused and pondered the potential cost.

"Get me more troops," Ike said simply.

"Not likely," said Marshall. "The only available force is Clark's Fifth Army in Italy, and it was stripped and nearly cut in half to support the campaign in France. The Fifth is a mere shell of itself and cannot supply the reinforcements you need, especially since the Italian Commies and the Italian government have decided to start killing each other.

"Do you have any good news?"

"A little," Ike said. "Potsdam is still holding out. They were attacked by a pretty large Russian force, but they managed to defeat it although they took a lot more casualties and the city is pretty well destroyed. There is long-term concern about supplies since we've had to stop air-dropping, but right now they're in pretty good shape."

"Good. Now, what about the Germans?"

Ike paused, then brightened slightly. "Well, with very few exceptions, the German armistice is going well. German units under General Blaskowitz are passing through the British on their way to Holstein and the Kiel Canal defense line without incident, and are joining some other Wehrmacht units under the overall command of Kesselring. Only a couple of fanatics have caused any trouble and just about anyone with an SS background has tried to disappear, probably to South America. Some other German forces are lying low in Austria and likewise behaving themselves."

Ike leaned forward. Marshall stiffened. He knew what his general was going to say. "General Marshall, what do you think about incorporating German military units into our defenses? We have hundreds of thousands of them as prisoners and a large number of units are still fairly intact. The Germans will fight for their country if we let them and all they need are weapons. It's repugnant, but necessary if we are to win this war."

Marshall nodded. He had already come to that unwelcome conclusion. However, there were problems that transcended politics, problems that Eisenhower was overlooking.

"Ike, we can scarcely take care of our own boys. We do not have the resources to organize, equip, and supply any large numbers of Germans, at least not in enough time to influence the fighting now going on."

"I know. But I would still like to use them where and how I can. We could put existing German units into defensive positions and let them fight for their homes. I think they would fight like bandits to get the Soviets out of Germany after all the atrocities the Reds are committing."

"I will talk with Truman. His meeting with Speer may have given us the opening we need. And yes, it is repugnant."

Ike brightened. However small, a weight had been taken off his shoulders. "Did you hear what happened to Goering?" he said, changing the subject with a grin.

Marshall smiled despite his own fatigue. Ike's grin really was infectious. "No."

"Well, a couple of our MPs caught him as he neared the Swiss border. The fool was disguised as a woman. A magnificently fat, ugly woman. What a marvelous ending for the Third Reich."

Marvelous indeed, thought Marshall. Now all he had to do was confront Truman.

ELISABETH SMILED TENTATIVELY. "Jack, which of us smells worse?"

Jack Logan grinned. They were seated outside her shelter on a low cement wall. She was lightly touching him, and he found the gentle intimacy to be intoxicating. The question, however, was not one he had expected.

"Lis," he said. He liked using the diminutive he'd heard Pauli call her, spelled with an *s* and not a *z*. She had smiled when he first started using it, so he had continued. "I think both of us smell, and rather badly, but where I come from we usually wouldn't have brought it up. Discussing body odor isn't some quaint European or Canadian custom, is it?"

She chuckled. "I think you're right about both of us being offensive, and no, it's not something I usually talk about with handsome young men, but it is becoming a problem. Now that it's getting warm, the shelters are almost unbelievably rank."

Water in the civilian part of the perimeter was either carefully rationed or nonexistent. Despite the nearness of the Havel and a number of ponds, there was a real shortage of water for anything other than drinking and cooking, and then only after boiling. Russian snipers had made life too dangerous for those who would have even dreamed of bathing in the polluted river, and the number of wells dug by engineers and others had not yet met the hygiene needs of the population.

"I got a shower last week," he volunteered.

"I got Pauli cleaned up a couple of days ago, but it's been a while for me. An occasional sponge or wet cloth helps but not that much, and I haven't been able to wash out my clothes. I'm not sure how you can stand being near me."

"It's not exactly a problem, Lis. Remember, I'm used to living in a bunker with a dozen of my closest and most aromatic friends." Besides, nothing as trivial as body odor was going to keep him from seeing Elisabeth Wolf.

He looked forward to her company on the brief times they could be together. Finding a young and intelligent woman to talk to and think about was something totally unexpected in a combat area. It was a luxury to be cherished. Besides, she really was pretty and he really was fond of her. The handful of kisses they'd exchanged made him think they were beyond the stage of simply liking each other.

After the Russian attack, Jack had been sick with worry that something might have happened to Lis and Pauli, but could not leave his post to check them out. As a result of the battle, so much of the city of Potsdam not already in ruins was either destroyed or in flames. Thus, he was greatly relieved when she and the boy simply showed up at the bunker, smiled and waved from a short distance, and left. It occurred to him that she might have been relieved as well at finding him safe and unhurt, and he found that thought comforting.

"God, it's got to be rough for you," he said. Pauli was asleep on a mat a few feet in front of them. He was pale; it was obvious that no one was getting enough sunshine.

"Rough? No, Jack, as I said before, this is not rough."

He laughed. Having learned English from a Scottish-Canadian mother, she tended to pronounce his name as "Jock," which she denied and he found amusing.

She squeezed his arm. "Stop it."

"All right, but I am worried about you. Are you getting enough food?"

Now it was her turn to laugh. "Jack, even on the reduced rations your army is providing, we are eating better than we have in a year or more. We endured more hunger and privation in Berlin from the bombings and the Nazis than anything that has occurred here. We have learned to cope."

He had heard some of the stories. He knew that her father, when he was not working as a diplomat, had been a block captain in charge of providing shelters for everyone in the apartment where his family lived. He was also in charge of the surrounding buildings. Elisabeth had told him how they and most people in and around Berlin were so terrified of being trapped and buried alive by falling rubble that they all dug tunnels to the other buildings and locations as possible escape routes. In a way, Berlin became a city of tunnels, and this was beginning to happen in Potsdam.

Jack also knew that her father and Pauli's parents had been killed in the more recent bombings, while Elisabeth's mother had died from a fever the year before. Yes, he realized, the life she had now was not as rough as it had been or as rough as it might be in the future, should the food run out or the Russians attack in real force.

She rested her head on his shoulder. "In its own way, Jack, this is the nicest time I've had in a long while. I just want to enjoy it while I can."

He took her hand in his. It was astonishingly thin, yet she said she was eating better. "Me too." It seemed trite, but he didn't know what else to say.

"Jack, did you have a girl back home?"

"Not really."

He thought briefly of Mary Fran Collins. They had dated a few times before he'd gotten drafted, even went to bed the week before he shipped off to basic training. There had been a couple of letters from her, but they had stopped. Or had he stopped writing her? He couldn't remember. It was another world.

"How about you?" he asked.

She sat up and looked at him, wondering what his reaction would be. "There was a young man. I was very fond of him, but mainly as a very nice and decent friend. He was a good student and naïvely thought the army would never take him because he was short, near-sighted, weak, and had a serious stomach disorder. Ulcers. Well, the Reich was very well organized and they drafted him into a regiment that consisted entirely of people with stomach disorders. Can you believe that? An entire regiment of people with bad tummies? Last year he was on his way to Normandy, where the regiment was stationed, when his train was strafed by your planes and he was killed. Poor little Hans never had a chance."

"I'm sorry." He wondered how many times he would use that phrase.

"Before he left, I let him be my first lover, my only lover. We were so innocent I still don't know if we were doing the right things."

Jack laughed softly. "Lis, there's not too many wrong things two lovers can do."

She flushed and giggled. "He was so terrified that he would never come back. We would make love and later he would sob with fear and I would hold him and comfort him. I was immensely saddened by his death, but I did not love him." She touched his chin with her finger. "Are you shocked?"

"No," he answered, tapping her finger with his.

He had no idea what Mary Fran Collins was doing right now and didn't care. He briefly wondered if the lovemaking between him and Mary Fran had been like what Elisabeth and Hans had done, an act of desperation rather than love. What concerned him now was Elisabeth Wolf.

She reached across his chest and grabbed his arm tightly. "Sometimes I feel so greedy. I don't want my life to end like this. I want to grow up. I want to have a real lover, a husband, someone strong and gentle like you. I want children. Do you know I haven't even had a period in a year because of the lack of food? I don't know if I'm still a woman."

Jack held her to him and felt her shudder. "It's okay, Lis."

She relaxed slightly. "When I was little, I wanted to be a ballerina. I studied dance for years. I was heartbroken when I found that I really didn't have the talent. Then I decided I wanted to be a scientist. A biologist. To everyone's surprise, I found I had a natural talent for it. Now I wonder if I'll ever see the inside of a school again."

"Me too," he said and explained about his years in night school in a dingy junior college in Port Huron. "I was at the point where I had to make a decision. Should I declare my schooling finished and get a job, or should I move away and complete my education at a four-year school?"

"What did you want to be?"

"Either a lawyer or a teacher. Maybe I'd compromise and teach law. At any rate, there's a world for us if we can only get out of here." He sighed. "Lis, you wouldn't mind putting your head back on my shoulder, would you? That is, if you can stand the smell of me?" She smiled and complied and they held on to each other with a quiet desperation.

A LITTLE WAY off and unseen by the young couple, General Miller walked with Major General Rob Wayne, the commanding officer of the badly mauled 54th Infantry Division. They had been inspecting some of the damage caused by the Russian attack.

Miller paused. "Rob, isn't that one of your boys with that German woman?"

"Yep. And if my memory serves me, it's one of the boys you gave a field commission to."

"And Rob, don't we have a nonfraternization rule that forbids Germans and Americans from socializing with each other?"

Wayne snorted. "Yeah, Chris, we sure do. But why not pass a rule outlawing rain on Sundays? Everyone's living with the knowledge they could be dead at any time, and those two aren't the only ones who've found each other. They are young and lusty and lonely and scared to death all at the same time. Just a couple of days ago they endured an afternoon of hell and another couple hundred of our boys became casualties along with a large bunch of civilians. Hell, if those two or any others can make the day a little more pleasant for themselves, well, why not."

Miller laughed. "Rob, are you telling me my rule isn't being followed?"

"Shit, Puff, it's being totally ignored! By the way, nobody's gotten any mail in a helluva long time either. I know your nonfraternization rule is the same as Ike's, but nobody's paid any attention to that one either. Look, I've told my boys to watch out for prostitutes and thieves, but if two kids want to sit in the sun and hold hands and talk nice to each other, well, God bless 'em. Besides, my old friend, just who the hell is our enemy nowadays? It sure as shit isn't Germany anymore, is it?"

Miller thought of his own family back in the States. When would he see them again? Once again, rules were meant to be broken. Seize the day, went some saying, and it was right. Tomorrow you could be dead.

GENERAL MIKHAIL BAZARIAN seethed with inward rage as the pale-skinned young Russian colonel fussed with the papers he'd taken from his briefcase. The man had been poking around his command for a day now, and had become a total nuisance. It was made endurable only by the fact that the little shit was from Zhukov's staff, and was not NKVD or from Stavka, the interservice general headquarters outside Moscow.

Colonel Fyodor Tornov had been sent by Zhukov's people to find out why that tank column had been ambushed and destroyed by the Americans in Potsdam. Apparently the column's late commander had been related to someone important. Bazarian knew that this little cretin of a colonel was also related to someone high up in the party.

Bazarian outranked him, but Tornov treated him with the genteel contempt reserved for inferior beings. After all, Tornov was a Russian and destined for greater things. It was evident to Bazarian that Tornov thought Bazarian and his army would all be growing beets when the war was finally over.

Worse, Tornov had written a report that was going to be highly critical of Bazarian. It might even get him booted from his command.

"In summary," Tornov said, "I can fault the tankers for not heeding your warnings, but you should not have permitted the Americans to be in a position to have caused such damage. They should have been eliminated by that time."

"Those were not my orders," Bazarian reminded him. "I was given a force sufficient to contain the Americans, not destroy them, as was proven by my subsequent attack on them. The Americans have dug themselves into a very strong position in what is virtually a peninsula, thanks to the twists of the Havel and the presence of some lakes on their flanks. And, as I am sure you will note in your report, I did use the forces at my command to attack them very shortly after that unfortunate incident. That my attack failed simply points out that any earlier attempt would have been futile."

Tornov blinked at the convoluted logic. "There is no question that the attack was made and that the attack failed. You lost half your tanks and two thousand men. You are no longer strong enough to attempt anything further against them. Can you even continue to contain them?"

"Certainly," Bazarian said.

They had been over this before. Of course he could contain them. Where could the Yanks go? Even if they did attempt to break out, the American lines were receding into the west and they doubtless didn't have enough gas to push their tanks and other vehicles that far anyway. No, the Americans were still solidly trapped in Potsdam.

Bazarian tried another tack. "Colonel, when will Zhukov send me replacements for the men I've lost?"

Tornov thought for a moment while Bazarian raged behind a placid façade. Did the little shit think he was the one who would make that decision?

"General Bazarian, replacements of good quality are in short supply. Headquarters might be able to get you another division or two of Romanians."

"Romanians! Those human dung!" Bazarian was outraged. How dare they even think of sending him people with such minimal military value. Worse, the Romanians had once been allied with the Nazis, but had turned coat and now fought with the Soviet Union. Would they turn again? Once the Romanians had been fairly decent soldiers, but these were the leftovers.

Tornov smiled, and Bazarian realized just how little his force was thought of if they would only send him help from that source. Calmly, he said he would take the Romanians.

"Good," said Tornov, putting his papers into a briefcase. "I'm sure you will put them to good use." Tornov checked his watch. "It is almost noon. I should be off shortly to return to headquarters."

Bazarian smiled. *And there to deliver your report, which will ask for my head.* "Must you leave so soon? Have you had a chance to actually watch the Americans?"

Tornov was intrigued. He had never even seen an American "No, I haven't."

After careful inquiries, mainly through Tornov's driver, a Ukrainian who thought the colonel was an incompetent asshole, Bazarian had earlier found that Tornov had never seen any action of any kind. He had only recently been assigned to Zhukov's headquarters, and was tolerated only because of his highly placed uncle. The driver felt that he had been sent on this fool's errand to get him out of truly important people's way.

Thus, while it was possible his report would be ignored, it was not a chance that Bazarian was willing to take.

"Colonel," he said soothingly, "you must see them. I will take you. It's safe and it will be something you can tell your friends. After all, how many of them have actually seen Americans?"

Bazarian could see Tornov calculating the options. He had said it was safe and, yes, it would certainly impress his peers.

Tornov beamed. "Yes, I would like that very much."

They took Bazarian's vehicle, an American jeep that had been sent to Russia as part of an aid package. He was very proud of it and his driver, another Armenian, kept it spotless. His previous staff vehicle had been a captured German Volkswagen, which had not impressed him in the slightest.

It was only a few minutes' drive to the spot Bazarian had chosen. "We will watch them from Outpost 7."

They were met by a couple of men and an officer, who came over and started to speak. A glare from Bazarian changed his mind and made him back off, a confused and sullen expression on his face.

They walked down a well-trodden path in a deep trench until they came to a sandbagged platform. Bazarian climbed to the top and Tornov followed. "There," he said, "use my binoculars and you will see them quite clearly."

Tornov didn't comment that the binoculars were German and not Russian. He took them and placed his elbows on the top of the platform. "I can't see anything."

"Then step up a little higher. Don't worry, they're well out of range."

Tornov did as he was told. "I still can't see."

The sounds of the rifle firing and the bullet impacting on Tornov's head occurred almost simultaneously. Tornov jerked backward, dropped the binoculars, and slithered to the ground. Bazarian turned him over with his foot. The American bullet had penetrated just below Tornov's right eye, creating an absurd three-eyed effect, and exited the back of his skull, leaving a gaping hole. Thank God the binoculars were undamaged, Bazarian thought as he picked them up.

Bazarian shook his head sadly as his driver and the others came running up.

"The poor man. I told him this was a dangerous place but he was brave and insisted on seeing for himself. He also told me he thought a periscope was a coward's tool."

The last comment was aimed at the officer whose comment Bazarian had shushed. It was common knowledge that the Americans had a sharpshooter with uncanny skills in the area. As a result, most observers had devised and used crude periscopes.

The soldiers nodded solemnly while Bazarian's driver stifled a grin. He'd known Bazarian for a very long time.

Bazarian turned to his driver. "Anatol, bring me the colonel's papers. I must see if there is anything important in them that should be passed on." Or burned, he thought. "We will notify headquarters, of course, and bury the poor man here." And I will get those divisions of Romanians, he added silently, and perhaps some others. Then we will settle with the fucking Americans.

CHAPTER 16

Steve Burke was delighted at the turn his great European adventure had taken, all the while admitting that he was perplexed by what he was discovering. The camp for Russian POWs had been established just outside the German city of Bitburg, which itself was just inside the border with Luxembourg. He was actually in Germany, and the thought made him exultant. He had convinced others at SHAEF that he would serve a good purpose if he went and interviewed Russian captives.

But, after interviewing a number of Soviet prisoners and reviewing the scanty records of others, what he was finding disturbed him. He was trying to sort it out as he walked near the stockade in the fading light of the mid-May evening.

"Colonel Burke?"

He turned and gasped. The thing before him was an apparition from hell.

"Oh dear," it said. "I've done it again. I've gone and startled you, haven't I?"

The accent was decidedly British and so was the uniform, Royal Air Force to be specific. The creature's apology seemed totally without remorse.

"Only slightly," Burke said, gathering his composure. "I was thinking and didn't hear you come up behind me." It was partially the truth. He had been deep in thought.

"Are you certain it isn't the fact that I have no face?"

Burke wondered, was he being teased? The RAF officer before him lacked a nose and eyebrows, and his skin had the appearance of stretched and shiny rubber. There was little hair on his head and only lumps that might have once been ears. Burke glanced down and saw that the man's hands were claws. Each hand had thumbs, but only one or two other fingers on each hand to oppose them. Despite himself, he shuddered.

"Yes," he answered truthfully. "I was shocked."

The man laughed. "Well, finally someone who admits the sight of me scares the shit right out of them. So many are so terribly polite and assure me they see abominations like me all the time and aren't affected at all, which is patently a fucking lie. I am Major Charles Godwin and I would shake hands with you but I really don't have any hands left to shake with. I know you're a colonel, but don't expect me to salute. I stopped that a long time ago as well." He shrugged. "Just what the hell can anyone threaten me with, eh?"

Burke managed a grin. "Sounds fair. By the way, how did you know who I was?"

"Easy. You are the visiting Russian expert from the states. I looked you up because I wanted to ask you some questions and share some thoughts. Perhaps a drink might help things along."

Burke thought that both were wonderful ideas. Godwin had parked his jeep just a short distance away and had a bottle of brandy and a couple of glasses in it.

"Cheers," he said after pouring. "Now, before you ask or start wondering, I lost my face and some other very important body parts in 1940 when the Hurricane I was piloting was shot down by a Messerschmitt over Plymouth. Unfortunately for me, the Hurricane turned into a flamer before I could get out, and I had to actually land the bugger since there was serious doubt whether my parachute would open under the circumstances." He bowed. "Thus, the medical marvel you see before you."

Burke sipped his brandy. Martell, he thought, and Godwin confirmed it.

"Since I cannot fly, the military lords often send me on errands like this one, and I hope I have been valuable to them. I am currently serving as air liaison with General Montgomery. I do not speak Russian but you do. I would like to learn what you have found out about our imprisoned ex-allies. But first, I would like to know about the London you passed through. In particular, the riots. London is my home."

Burke recalled the incidents all too well. For a while he had been in real fear for his life. The worst incident had occurred while they had been driving along the Thames Embankment in a caravan of vehicles that included Marshall. It had begun when they had turned right onto Birdcage Walk and headed toward Buckingham Palace.

"We weren't actually going to the palace, just by it on the way to our living quarters after a day of meetings."

At that point he said they had been blocked by an unexpected sea of angry humanity. They were confronted by thousands of men and women of all ages who bore signs critical of Churchill and the government, but, most particularly, they were against the war with the Soviet Union. They had been protesting in front of Buckingham Palace and were, he found out later, slowly but firmly being pushed away from the palace by the London police and right into the path of the American convoy.

For a moment, the crowd just stared at the short line of slow-moving cars, but then the vehicles stopped and started to back up. At that point someone in the crowd started yelling that the fucking Yanks were here and that the Yanks were the cause of it all.

Burke shuddered and took some more brandy. "Major, it then got horrible. They started pounding on the cars and rocking them. Rocks were thrown and some of our men got dragged out of their cars and beaten. I found out later that a couple of Americans were killed by the mob, beaten or trampled. The MPs protecting General Marshall opened fire and some of the rioters were killed as well. Then the rocks and bottles started really coming down. We got Marshall's vehicle turned around and we tried to keep the other cars between his and the mob while he got away. It didn't work all that well. They just flowed around us like water around boulders. Somebody punched in the car window right by me and I was showered with glass and some blood where the bastard had hurt himself."

"Where were the police?" Godwin asked. "On the other side of the crowd, right?"

"Of course. They finally came and started fighting the crowd, which was now trapped between two lines of cops. Then someone in the mob started setting fires and they spread fairly quickly to a number of buildings nearby. I saw people—police and at least one American—get thrown into the fires by the rioters. It was unbelievable. After that, we finally got away."

"Who was doing the rioting?"

"Everyone says it was socialists and left-wing radicals. I don't think that's entirely correct. Some of those people looked too middle class to be typical radicals. I saw a lot of older people, grandparent types. You know what I think? I think it's true that a large number of Britishers are totally sick of the war and scared it won't ever end. You know what else?" The Martell was starting to warm him. "I'm not sure I blame them. The thought of this going on forever scares the shit out of me too."

"Nor do I entirely blame them," Godwin said softly. "Thank you for the telling. I lost a young cousin in those riots and I wanted to know how, if not why. I'm not sure anybody knows why. A number of them have broken out in Manchester, Liverpool, and other British cities. God only knows where it will end."

Burke sighed. "Now, you said you wanted to know about the prisoners. Well, I've noted something peculiar."

Before he could elaborate, the sound of sirens filled the air and searchlights quickly pointed brilliant fingers upward.

"Goddamn air raid," snarled Godwin. "Find a shelter. The bloody Russians are going to bomb us."

The nearest shelter was a slit trench about fifty yards away, and they piled into it. They could hear planes coming closer and there wasn't time to be choosy and search for something more substantial. Antiaircraft guns opened fire, and they could see the Russian bombers outlined in the sky by searchlights while the tracers sought them out.

"Ilyushin 4s," Godwin said. "They don't have much of a bomb load, only about two tons, but they have pretty decent range, which is why they are currently overhead."

"Marvelous," said Burke, trying not to let the gut-tightening fear he was feeling control his voice. Two tons of bombs might not be much to Godwin, but it was an enormous amount to him.

Godwin continued. It was as if he was delivering a lecture. "No, not marvelous at all. Frankly a rather shitty plane flown by inexperienced or unskilled pilots. Do you see they are in following groups of three? Well, that's so they can follow the leader. Otherwise they'd get lost because they are so bloody stupid."

As they watched, one of the bombers exploded in midair. The others began dropping their bomb loads, which Burke realized were going to impact primarily on the prison camp.

Godwin thought this amusing. "What wonderful intelligence they must have. They are killing their fellow Russians."

"Do they know this is a prisoner camp?" Burke asked.

"I would hope so. We have notified the Red Cross and the Swiss, who are supposed to inform everyone, and there are signs on the roofs of the buildings, but that presumes the Russians can read. Poor bloody bastards."

Burke ducked as the sound of the bombings washed over them. Good God, people were dying and he was actually seeing combat. Again, he tried to keep his voice steady. "That's what I was going to tell you. Many of them aren't Russians."

"What?"

"Well, a lot of them are from other, non-Russian parts of the USSR, and many of them can't even speak Russian. I don't understand it."

He explained about trying to communicate with them in Russian and receiving blank stares in return. At first he'd thought it was his American accent and maybe he was talking in an elitist way to some peasant, but he was wrong. The few Russians who were there had understood him fairly easily. The non-Russians, he finally managed to ascertain, understood only a handful of Russian words, and these basically represented commands or obscenities.

A bomb went off nearby, and they ceased talking and hugged the ground at the bottom of the trench.

They waited as the sound of the planes receded and the explosions ceased. Godwin stuck his head out of the trench. "Bloody hell! My jeep's gone. Blown off the road, I would think. Thank God I had the foresight to bring the brandy with me."

Yes, Burke thought. Thank God that we are alive and able to have a drink. It was occurring to him that he had been in no particular great danger, but that many others in the camp had been killed or wounded. The irony that Soviets had killed their own did not mitigate the horror of the deaths.

Godwin couldn't find any glasses so he politely passed the bottle before taking his own liberal swallow. "So," he said, "you don't understand the prisoner situation."

Burke took another swallow. "Yes. First, there is the sad fact that there are so few prisoners. Only a few thousand, as far as I can tell. I guess it's logical since they are the ones who are attacking and would have less of an opportunity to lose manpower as captives."

"True," said Godwin.

"And most of them are not Russians."

"True again."

"Charles," Burke said, "what, in your opinion, does that mean, if anything?"

They thought on it for a while. Then it came to them.

SOME DAYS NATALIE Holt was sick with worry over thoughts of what could be happening to Steve Burke. The very idea of him going into a war zone was almost ludicrous. He didn't belong there. He belonged in a classroom. Actually, she thought with a satisfied inner smirk, he belonged in her bed, where she could take damned good care of him.

Her concern for him sometimes did affect her work at the State Department. On a couple of occasions her bosses had gently chided her about her lack of attention to affairs of state, and she had apologized sincerely. After all, it wasn't as if she was the only staffer with a loved one in harm's way.

Fortunately, most of her work was interesting enough to keep her distracted. There was an incredible amount of information surfacing from Russian émigrés in various countries, and it needed to be reviewed. It also seemed like everyone with Russian relatives wanted to be assured that they were all right, which was impossible to determine.

Like Gromyko and the rest of the Russian diplomatic corps in the United States, Ambassador Averell Harriman and his staff were confined to the embassy grounds in Moscow and dependent upon local government to provide them with food and other necessities. Consulates had been closed in both countries and a number of Soviet citizens had been detained, as had Americans in Russia.

Detained, she knew, was a euphemism for being imprisoned. Russians were being held at American military posts and were being treated well. She wondered just how Americans who weren't ranking diplomats were faring in Russian hands. Not all American prisoners of the Russians were military or diplomatic personnel. A number of civilian American merchant marines had been either in the port of Murmansk or so close to it that they could not turn back when the war started. They too had been interned, and she did not think they were being treated gently.

Despite the constraints, both embassies were still functioning. Ever so correctly, the respective host governments did not cut off telephone or cable links and both embassies communicated with their home countries by diplomatic pouches which were carried by neutral Finnish, Swiss, or Swedish couriers. She also knew that the U.S. embassy in Moscow communicated with its counterpart in London via shortwave radio, an advantage the Soviets in North America did not have.

Of course, everything was listened to and phones were tapped, but life still went on. She understood it was because it was hoped that the presence of diplomats on one another's soil might someday facilitate an end to the war.

Natalie prayed that it would end before something happened to poor, dear Steve.

"Miss Holt?"

Natalie looked up to see the unwelcome presence of Special Agent Tom Haven, a stocky man in his late thirties with bad breath. He also seemed to dislike everyone in the State Department and made little secret of it. He'd been heard saying everyone in State was a queer or a Commie. Haven and others from the FBI had been reviewing everyone in her group, and it was getting on their nerves. Natalie was thankful that the problem with her mother had finally been satisfactorily resolved and she no longer had to undergo interrogations by people like Haven.

"Where's Barnes?" he asked. Walter Barnes was her immediate supervisor.

"I haven't the foggiest idea, Agent Haven. I don't spend my time watching him," she snapped.

"I mean, is he on vacation today?"

Natalie checked her watch. It was already nine o'clock and Barnes, an early starter, was very late. "No, he's not. Have you called his apartment?"

Haven nodded. "No answer. His boyfriend doesn't know where he is either."

This last was said with a sneer. Barnes was a frail and middle-aged homosexual. He had gone to great lengths to try to hide that fact, but everyone knew. Nobody said a word, but he always took lunch and breaks with a young man ten years his junior from Personnel. He had been a special target of ridicule and scorn by Haven ever since the agent found out. Natalie looked away so Haven would not see the look of contempt in her eyes. Why couldn't they let the poor man live his own life and pretend that his precious secret was intact?

"We had an appointment with him this morning, Miss Holt. We were going to go over some of his conversations with a few of his friends. There are those in the FBI who think he might have discussed some very sensitive matters with people who shouldn't have been told about them."

Natalie folded her hands on her lap and made sure Haven didn't see too much of her legs. "And what would you like me to do, Agent Haven?"

"Do you know anywhere else he might be?"

"No."

"Are you certain, Miss Holt?"

Natalie stood. She was almost as tall as Haven, and he backed up a step. "Are you accusing me of lying?"

"No, ma'am. But he is your boss and your friend. You might have been tempted to do something to protect him."

"From what?"

Haven recovered and managed a tight smile. "Maybe from being arrested, Miss Holt, if he did tell some of his queer friends about his work. Do you know where he lives?"

"Yes."

"Good. I'm new here and not familiar with all of Washington and I'd like you to come with me."

"No, Agent Haven, I will not. You're a rude and bullying man and I will not take you to see where Mr. Barnes lives. You know how much you terrify and upset Barnes, and I think you take great pleasure in it."

She was also reasonably certain Haven would make a pass at her if he got her alone in a car.

To her surprise, Haven actually laughed. Maybe he thought being disliked was a compliment. "Okay, have it your way. Will you take Forbes?"

The other agent was across the room and grinned affably upon hearing his name. Forbes was easygoing and friendly. The father of three kids, he was not always trying to mentally undress her. She quickly agreed.

Half an hour later, they pulled up in front of the undistinguished apartment building where Walter Barnes lived. Forbes used his FBI identification on the manager to gain access to the building and quickly found Barnes's apartment. After a number of futile knocks on the door, they got the manager to give them a key.

"Should we be doing this alone?" Natalie asked.

"Probably not," he said. The door opened to a darkened room and he flipped on a light. "But I'm not going to phone for help for what is most likely an empty set of rooms. My money says he's run off. The Bureau's having a field day picking on fags in State and he probably panicked. Stay here."

After a moment he told her to come in. The apartment had a living room, a small kitchen, and a bedroom. All three rooms were fastidiously clean. The bed was made and everything on the dresser was standing as if on display. There were no socks on the floor or anything out of place. Instinctively, she knew that Steve Burke would not be so neat. Even the closets were open and the clothes hung with care, as if their owner knew someone else was going to see them. A photo of the young man from Personnel was proudly displayed on the dresser. Forbes picked it up, looked at it for a moment, and put it down.

"Have you checked the bathroom?" she asked.

"I didn't see one. Isn't it a shared one down the hall?" Forbes said.

"No," she answered, "you don't know Barnes. He was an extremely private person, especially so about any personal ablutions. It was almost a joke. He wouldn't clip a fingernail if he thought someone might see him doing it."

"Aw shit," said Forbes as he looked about the room. Something was wrong and he'd missed it. He walked to a drape on the wall and jerked it aside. A door was behind it.

"So fastidious that he even hid the entrance to his damned john? Good grief," Forbes said with nervous laughter. He had almost made a big mistake by missing the room.

He tried the door. Both he and Natalie looked at each other in growing horror. The door was locked from the inside. Forbes was a big man and he put a shoulder to it, and the cheap wood shattered immediately. He reached in and turned the knob and opened the door.

Forbes groaned and Natalie strained to see inside the bathroom. When she realized what was lying pale and naked in the brown-red water of the bathtub, she vomited on the floor and ran into the hallway outside the apartment, where she began to cry. Behind her, she heard Forbes talking on the telephone. After a moment he came out in the hallway and stood beside her.

"I'm sorry you saw that, Miss Holt."

"So am I."

"Are you going to be okay?"

She lit a cigarette and drew heavily. Belatedly, she offered one to Forbes, who accepted. After all, it wasn't his fault.

"I'll make it. How did he do it?" she finally managed to ask.

"Very creatively," Forbes said wryly. "I would say he ran the bathwater nice and warm, got in, made it as hot as he could stand it and then, as the hot water numbed his nerves, used an extremely sharp knife to slice open his wrists and then bled to death. There's something that looks very much like a scalpel on the floor by the tub. The ancient Romans used to do something similar to commit honorable suicide."

"Leave it to Walter to think of something like that," she half sobbed. "He always did have a flare for the dramatic."

"There was a suicide note," Forbes added. "In it he said he'd been blackmailed by the Russians and he couldn't stand the thought of being without his lover or going to prison."

The FBI had found what they wanted, proof that there was a leak in the State Department. Now they would dig harder. She wanted to curse her poor dead boss, but couldn't. His life must have been so tormented with the Russians coming at him from one direction and the FBI from another.

With a start, she realized that this was how Gromyko knew so much about her. Damn Barnes.

A car had pulled up outside the apartment, and she saw Agent Haven and another man come running up the stairs. Neither looked at her as they entered the apartment, and she realized she was no longer needed. She told Forbes she would take a cab and left. She would go home and not to work. Today had been long enough and she wasn't ready for the stares and talk of the people in the office. The war had claimed another casualty and she had yet another friend to mourn.

It was time to write another letter to Steve. Of course she wouldn't tell him about this. It might upset him and worry him, and she would never do that. Letters overseas should contain only happy news, comforting words. She could do it. She started crying again.

"Come back to me, Steve" she whispered.

CHAPTER 17

*T*he supply trains began in the port of Cherbourg each day and originally consisted of twenty freight cars each. They ran to Paris, where they picked up more cars with more supplies and headed east. The trains were considered priority traffic and rolled along at a fairly high rate of speed. As they went, they used their whistles frequently to warn of their coming. As a result, someone with a sophomoric sense of humor had labeled the whole thing the "Toot Sweet Express."

This time, the Toot Sweet train that swept toward Verdun and the French border with Germany also contained two squads of American soldiers under a young second lieutenant, John Travis. What used to be a milk run had turned potentially deadly, and Travis's job was to protect the valuable train from attack by Soviet airplanes. For this purpose he had two flatcars with raised platforms carrying a pair of 20 mm antiaircraft guns each. He did not think it much of a deterrent. Darkness, he felt sincerely, was the best protection from the Reds.

Nor was Travis thrilled about the men he was commanding. Most of the ones in the security detachment had been culled from the stockades, where they had been serving time for various minor offenses, or from labor battalions where there was not a high premium paid for intelligence. Only his gunners seemed above average. He felt that all of them looked down on him.

Travis had doubts about himself. Only recently commissioned as a ninety-day wonder straight out of Officer Candidate School, he had never seen combat. Instead, he had been working in a personnel office in England when the call came for more officers to help free the truly qualified soldiers to fight the Russians.

Even though he had taken the express only a couple of times, the route was beginning to become familiar. He looked about through the grimy windows of the caboose and, even in the night, knew roughly where they were. He figured they were about twenty miles from the border and that the closer they came to Germany, the more danger there was from the air.

Travis put on his helmet, left the relative comfort of the caboose, and stepped over to the rearmost gun platform on the adjacent flatcar. It was also the only gun he could safely reach. He was not going to clamber over more than fifty freight cars to get to the first one just to be told that everything was fine. Instead, he depended on a walkie-talkie to communicate with both the sergeant in charge of the front gun and the train's engineer.

Travis was about to call them when he both heard and felt the train slowing. Then the squeal of brakes became an insistent howl and he had to hang on while the train came to a complete and sudden halt. He looked around. They were out in the country.

"What the hell?" he asked. The gunners, also surprised, only shrugged. Then one pointed. The train had stopped on a curve and they could see a barricade about a hundred yards in front of the engine.

Travis picked up the walkie-talkie and called the French-speaking soldier in the old steam engine with the engineer and fireman.

"Lewis, what's going on?"

"Sir, we got a pile of stuff on the tracks and it looks like people around it."

Travis began to get nervous. "Well, tell them to get the hell out of our way. And tell them to move that shit off the tracks." He wondered if the train could push its way through the barricade if it had to. If the people who manned the barricade were looters, this could get dangerous. He drew his .45 automatic.

There was silence as Lewis tried to communicate with the leaders of the crowd, who were now alongside the engine. Travis saw women as well as men. The men on the front gun platform called in and said they were being surrounded by Frenchmen, some of whom were armed.

What the hell is going on? Travis thought. Aren't the French our friends?

Lewis's voice, tinny and distant, came over the walkie-talkie. "Sir, they say they're taking the train from us because we're fighting their Communist brothers. Sir, they're coming on board!"

"Stop them," he yelled.

Immediately there was the sound and flash of small arms as the French and the Americans fired on each other. Then the front antiaircraft guns, depressed as low as they could be, opened up on the crowd. Because of the curve in the tracks, the rear guns could see the barricade and they began to chop it up with their weapons.

A fire quickly started, lighting up the night sky with a fierce glare. French civilians, men and women, tumbled about in death. Travis saw well-armed Frenchmen firing on the exposed American soldiers on the train. He heard screams and knew that his men were dying as well.

Thousands of feet overhead, two Yak-9 fighters saw the sudden conflagration. From the Soviet 16th Air Army, they had been part of the large fighter escort for a hundred Ilyushin bombers that had been formed to attack the railroad yards at Cologne. It was a long attack run for fighters whose range was far less than that of the bombers, and they had been worried about having enough fuel to return to their base.

Their concerns were justified. Well before Cologne, they had been jumped by a horde of American and British fighters who had pushed the fighter-bomber swarm south while they cut the bomber force to pieces. If any bombs had fallen anywhere near Cologne, it would have surprised the two pilots immensely. Their respect for the Allies' air power increased with each day and each bloody incident.

As a result of the air battle, the two Yak fighters had been separated from the remains of their force and pushed both south and east. Petr Dankov, the senior of the two, flew close to the other plane, turned on his flashlight, and gestured with his hands. He did not want to use the radio lest it give away the fact of their existence. Dankov had flown combat against the Nazis and had shot down fourteen of them. He had a great respect for the Luftwaffe, and the actions of the Americans over Cologne and other places had shown them to be formidable enemies as well. Two American fighters had fallen to his guns.

Dankov signaled that he wanted to take a look at the fire. They dropped to a thousand feet and flew parallel to the train, which he quickly recognized as an American supply train and not one loaded with passengers. He signaled that he would lead the attack. It was strange, he thought, that the American train would be stopped by some kind of fiery accident in front of it. And why were all those people swarming over it?

No matter, he chuckled. If the Yanks wanted to make a gift of the train before he was forced to bail out from lack of fuel, then he would thank them. There was no way he could now make it safely back to base, so he decided to end his last flight as a free man by doing something useful.

They came on a front-to-rear pass. They had no bombs, but their 37 mm cannon chattered and the shells walked the length of the train. First the engine exploded in a billowing cloud of steam, then one of the boxcars flamed. He saw the men on the rear gun platform look for him, and he was over them before they could react.

On the train, Travis watched in horror as the first Soviet plane streaked overhead. He had seen them seconds earlier as they flew alongside. His fervent wish was that they were Americans. The dimly seen red star on the wings disposed of that wish.

As the shells ripped through the boxcars, he tried to remember the train's manifest. There was ammo in three of the cars!

"Run for it," he shrieked. He jumped off the train and ran across the field. He saw a couple of his men do the same thing as the second plane flew overhead. The men on the front car were ready for it and the Yak flew into a wall of shells and commenced to fall apart. Travis watched as it fell into the ground about a half mile away and explode.

Explode! He remembered the ammo. Getting to his feet, he began to ran as fast as he could. His urgency communicated itself to a couple of Frenchmen who dropped their weapons and ran with him.

The first ammunition car blew up while they were running. The force of the blast flung Travis to the ground while the shrapnel from the exploding shells ripped his body to lifeless shreds as he tried to get to his feet.

Petr Dankov, now alone in the dark sky, watched the conflagration below. He was now truly alone in a strange land, and with about half an hour's worth of fuel and very little ammunition left. Another explosion from the ground distracted him so that he never saw the first of four RAF Spitfires, also attracted by the flames, take up position on his tail and open fire at a range of a hundred feet. He felt the bullets impact the plane and then, for a brief, final instant, his body.

•   •   •

THE CORPSE LAY where it had been found that morning. By this time the number of curious had diminished to only a couple of people and only one bored American guard was still on duty. He straightened to something resembling attention as Logan approached with Elisabeth Wolf beside him.

"How much longer is he going to stay there, Private?"

The soldier glanced nervously at the bloody corpse. "I've been told about another hour, sir. I guess somebody might want to take a picture or do some kind of an investigation. Not that it'll do much good."

Elisabeth leaned over the restraining rope, stared at the dead man, and grimaced. "I remember him only slightly. Of course, back then his head wasn't bashed in. I'm glad Pauli isn't here to see it, although I'm afraid he's seen much worse."

They had walked the short distance upon first hearing of the violent death. This was the first time that a refugee had been killed by another refugee since the siege of Potsdam had begun.

"Lis, I've already heard a number of rumors. Was he a thief or something else? I heard that he was a Nazi murderer."

Elisabeth looked at the blood-matted blond hair of the dead man. "No. Not a thief, although there are those who say he stole people's lives. He was identified by one of the Jews here in Potsdam as having been a concentration camp guard she'd seen about a year ago. The person who identified him recalled him as being particularly cruel and despicable, even for an SS man."

"And he was certain it was the same person?"

"The woman told the others you always remember the man who kills your child."

Given so calmly, the comment chilled him. "Jesus."

"In order to be certain, I understand they sprung a trap. They waited until last night, when he went out in the dark to relieve himself, and then they called his name, the one they knew him by at the camp. Like a fool, the man responded. The Jews here in Potsdam are still weak and sick compared to others, but there were a dozen of them and they dragged him down and beat him to a bloody pulp. It didn't take long. If anyone heard the fight or the man's screams, they did nothing. I don't think anybody will remember anything either."

Logan looked again at the body. The man's skull was distorted, like a melon that had been dropped. There were only about a hundred Jewish refugees in the Potsdam perimeter and, understandably, they stayed together as a group and did little mingling with the others. Mostly male, with only a handful of women and no children, the Jews were thin and appeared tormented. Logan again wondered if the terrible rumors he'd been hearing about how the Nazis treated the Jews were true. They were almost too awful to believe.

Elisabeth took his arm and pulled him away from the scene. "What happens now?" she asked.

"Probably not much. If the man was as much of a pig as they say, the killers probably did the world a favor. Our generals might think it's smart to separate the Jews from the others so it can't happen again, or worse, someone might try to take revenge on them. God, what a crazy world we're in."

He stopped and pulled her around so that she faced him. "Lis, did you know what was happening to the Jews? Is it true? They're saying millions died."

"Last question first." She took his hand and they seated themselves on the ground, where they could look at a couple of trees and not at the devastation around them. "Jack, what happened to the Jews defies belief. It was so awful as to be almost incomprehensible. The Nazis wanted to exterminate them and did so with such calculated cruelty that the world may never forgive Germany."

"Incredible, almost impossible to believe. Now, what about the first question?"

"We knew from the beginning that something awful was happening to the Jews. Or, in the case of German Jews, had already happened to most of them by the time my family returned to Germany from Canada. Everyone knew the Jews were disappearing, and most said good riddance because they were different. Remember," she said sarcastically, "they killed Christ and they talk funny and they have big hooked noses.

"The official word was they were going to resettlement areas or work camps for the duration of the war. After the war they would be expelled and sent to some other country. Somewhere I heard that Madagascar would be their new home, but the war interfered, and it never happened."

She leaned against him and he put his arm around her. "But did I know they were being systematically murdered? No. Most Germans didn't know that. I know my father didn't. At least not in the beginning. He may have suspected that things weren't as they should be, but you didn't voice your suspicions too loudly in the Third Reich. Besides, what could he have done? My father was a good man and, like just about everyone, he originally thought Hitler was going to do good things for Germany. It wasn't until we returned, and Hitler took over Czechoslovakia, that he began to have doubts. Many Germans knew the Jews were being mistreated, and thought that it was good. But I truly think that the emerging awfulness and extent of the exterminations is a shock to the majority of Germans. The ones who perpetrated the crimes must pay."

"Like the dead guy did?"

"It's rough justice, but effective."

"Lis, is there any chance the Jews were wrong last night? What if the guy had been forced to do some of the things he did?"

She smiled up at him. "You Americans are so trusting, aren't you?" She reached up and touched his cheek. "That's why I like you so much. Even for a soldier, you are still so innocent. Jack, there was no doubt that he was the brute from the concentration camp. Before they killed him they stripped him and found the SS tattoo on his arm. As to his being forced to do what he did, no. All the SS men were volunteers, and only the cruelest and most malevolent were sent to the camps as guards. We know this now."

"And he killed that woman's son."

"That and more, Jack. Did you know it was against the laws of the Reich for a German to have sexual intercourse with a Jew?"

"No."

She laughed bitterly. "Do you think such rules would stop a prison guard? He and several others violated her after they killed her child. The Nazi sex laws worked the other way as well. Did you know that it was customary, almost a law, for a German woman to have sex with an SS man if he asked?"

"Are you joking?"

"Hitler wanted to breed more Aryans as quickly as possible, so he let his golden-haired Teutonic knights have any woman they wished."

A sickening thought overtook him. "Did they come after you?"

Surprisingly, she laughed. "No, all those goats wanted was some blond Brunhilde, and I am too small and dark-haired for their tastes. I was definitely not what they had in mind to perpetuate the master race. For once, not being a buxom blonde worked in my favor. Besides, the law was not that widely observed."

Jack squeezed her arm slightly and tried to joke. "Well, I like you anyhow even if you're not a blond Brunhilde."

She didn't smile. "Pauli and I will leave Germany as quickly as we can when this is over. Somehow, we will make our way back to Canada. I still have dual citizenship, but Pauli is only German. It doesn't matter," she said determinedly. "We will get there. And"—she kissed him on the cheek—"I will use that address you gave me and find you."

ASSISTANT SECRETARY OF State Dean Acheson was shown into the elaborate Paris office used by the acting president of France, Charles de Gaulle. De Gaulle rose and, at almost six and a half feet tall, towered over the smaller Acheson. De Gaulle also had a huge nose, and the effect was to make him look more like a horse than a great general and a brilliant intellect. Acheson recalled that de Gaulle's family traced itself back to before the battle of Agincourt and that his love of France went beyond the extreme. He also recalled that, as a student, de Gaulle had been nicknamed "The Big Asparagus" or Cyrano by his unloving peers.

Acheson spoke passable French, but de Gaulle either did not speak English or chose not to; thus the presence of translators.

"I knew you would come," de Gaulle said. "As soon as you heard the Russians were here, I knew you would follow them."

"Indeed," said Acheson. The presence of Vice Premier Andrei Vyshinsky in Paris had come as a shock to the U.S. government. Acheson, who had been in London, had been quickly dispatched to Paris. One question involved the manner in which Vyshinsky had arrived in Paris. After all, weren't the Allies at war with Russia? But the Russian had traveled to neutral Finland and taken a plane to equally neutral Sweden and then to France. Acheson had to remind himself that there had yet been no formal declaration of war, and that the various embassies were still functioning in the various capitals, no matter how incongruous that might be.

De Gaulle gestured for Acheson to be seated. "Do you know what that man did?" he asked through the translator. "He reminded me of all of the many slights I had suffered at the hands of the Americans and the British. As if I would ever forget them!"

Acheson winced. Along with being a brilliant man and a devoted patriot, de Gaulle's ego was as huge and as sensitive as any man's could be. Worse, in the beginning the Allies had done almost everything wrong in their dealings with the pompous Frenchman. First, Roosevelt had not taken him seriously as a leader of the Free French, although Churchill had given him his early support. Why should they have concerned themselves with his apparent delusions of grandeur? He had been a fairly low-ranking and unknown general at the beginning of the war. Then, when the Americans began to realize his importance, they chose instead to deal with the traitorous Darlan and others. It hadn't helped that Roosevelt thought de Gaulle was an insufferable boor and had disliked him intensely.

What made de Gaulle even more difficult to deal with was his insistence that France was still a world power when just the opposite was true. In Acheson's and most others' opinion, France had slipped to being a second- or even a third-rate power. Thus, de Gaulle's pronouncements about France's right to a sector of Germany and her right to be at this or that bargaining table, or the right of the Free French Army to cross the Rhine when it had no longer been necessary, were particularly frustrating. Acheson thought him galling and smiled to himself at the pun.

On the other hand, Acheson did feel he understood what Charles de Gaulle was actually up to. He was a patriot and wanted France to lift herself from the ashes of disgrace and defeat. The morale and self-esteem of France were so low as to be virtually nonexistent. If de Gaulle must make an obstreperous fool of himself in order to help the land after which he and his ancestors had been named, then so be it. Somehow, he would breathe life into France.

"Mr. President," Acheson said, "I had hoped that all those mistakes were in the past and that we could get on to the future."

De Gaulle grunted. "The past is our history and we must be reminded of it. The Russian made me an offer. Do you wish to hear it?"

"Of course." The very thought of a Russian proposal to France was frightening. The Soviets wanted France out of the war. What would they offer?

"Not surprisingly, Vyshinsky said that the Soviet forces would win this war and that the Allies would be forced out of Germany. He then said what happened to France after this was up to me. If I wanted France to live as a free and independent country, then I would have to sever relations with Britain and the United States. In particular, Russia would require me to forbid your armies to supply themselves through French ports and via French rail. Air bases would also have to be closed. In effect, France would become a neutral nation, just like Switzerland."

Acheson was aghast. Such actions would cripple the Allied effort. "Mr. President, I cannot see how France could exist alongside a Germany dominated by Russia. It would be a nightmare of contradictions."

De Gaulle leaned back, an effect that gave Acheson an uncomfortable view of the inside of the taller man's nostrils. "Vyshinsky said I had no choice. He said that my country was in a state of revolution as a result of his Communist brothers wanting peace with Russia, and that the French people were sick and tired of war. If I did not acquiesce to his demands, then the Russians would not stop at the French border when they finally defeated the Allies in Germany with their Red Inferno. Instead, they would invade a helpless France and turn her into a satellite of the Soviet Union." De Gaulle glared at Acheson. "What would you have done had you been confronted with such a proposal?"

Acheson wondered if he was being tested. He dared not scold or patronize the man. Or worse, misjudge him as so many others had. "I presume you told him you understood that France could not be a free country with Russian armies on her border, and that a Soviet victory would result in a de facto occupation of France in any case."

De Gaulle smiled slightly. "That is what I thought, but it is not what I said to the foolish Russian. I told him he had given France much to think about and that I would respond presently. You are, however, quite right. In either event, a Soviet victory would represent the death of a France that is already very ill. It cannot be permitted to happen. If pressed for an answer, I will tell him to tell Stalin that we will not betray our alliance with Great Britain and America, even if it results in our being invaded and occupied again. I already fought one war from exile, and I will do it forever if I have to."

Acheson let out his breath. The heavy-handed Russians had insulted de Gaulle and not intimidated him. "We are honored, sir, by your loyalty."

"Which is to France," de Gaulle snapped, "not to England or the United States. Vyshinsky was correct when he said I was confronting a revolution. The Communists have risen in France and are trying to take control. Many of them fought the Germans as members of the underground, and they are now fighting the Americans and trying to interrupt the supply efforts that are so essential to the war. Worse, they appear to be coordinating with the Russian air force. Did you not hear of the train that was stopped by Communists near Namur, and then assaulted from the air?"

Acheson had been briefed by military experts who had quizzed both French and American survivors, and it was their belief that the apparent coordination had been an act of fate and not a planned occurrence. De Gaulle, however, obviously thought otherwise.

De Gaulle continued. "I know some do not believe it occurred that way, but I cannot take a chance on that being the truth. If you want your supplies to get through, then they must be guarded by French troops. While Frenchmen might fight Americans, I am reasonably certain they will not fire on their own countrymen. Therefore, I will be taking my divisions from Italy as soon as possible and, if necessary, de Tassigny's First Free French Army away from your General Devers. They will be retained in France for as long as necessary to quell the Communist revolution."

Acheson nodded. He understood full well what de Gaulle had just done. First, he would protect the supply lines. Second, he would do it with French troops, which meant they could not be involved in the bloody meat-grinder battles that were commencing and from which the French had largely been spared. It was a trade: French lives for American supplies. The net effect of the trade was to weaken the overall war effort against the Russians. Damn de Gaulle.

On the other hand, blunt Russian diplomacy had failed to make de Gaulle their ally. They had offended the prickly Frenchman. Speaking of pricks, Acheson thought more happily, de Gaulle may be a prick, but he's still our prick.

• • •

DAYS BEFORE, THE near-dawn explosions had awakened Tony from a fitful sleep. For an instant, he thought he was back in his tank and under attack by the Russians. Then he recalled where he was—Ketzin, Germany, and in a Russian work gang. As the explosions drew nearer, he and the others tried to take shelter in a ditch. Not much use, he thought, if something came down close to them, but it was better than nothing.

The drone of airplane engines backgrounded the blasts, and they realized that something nearby was under attack from bombers. Jubilantly, he realized the bombers had to be either American or British. As dim shapes flew overhead, he strained to identify them as they flew on, seemingly impervious to the antiaircraft tracers reaching up for them.

"Wellingtons," Vaslov whispered. "British."

Tony didn't care if they were Mexican. His side was striking back. It was a wonderful feeling and he could see by the looks on the others' faces that it was shared.

It was not until later in the day that he learned that he would have a price to pay for the bombers' success.

It was now the third day of their ordeal in the work gang, and Tony's arms and back ached from the strain of constantly lifting and carrying the dirt and rubble to fill in the road craters created by the Allied bombers. He thought he would collapse, but he would be shot if he did so. He'd seen it happen. His only consolation was that everyone else in the work gang seemed to be in as bad a shape as he. Perhaps, he felt with a twinge of guilt, even in worse shape. After all, he had not spent the last few years on a starvation or minimal diet. On the plus side, it seemed that, with the task nearing completion, the Russians were nowhere near as demanding or as security conscious as they had been.

While filling in the roadway, he was shocked and mildly depressed at how many craters there were in nearby fields and just how many bombs had fallen nowhere near their targets. Bombing, he concluded, was a very inexact art.

Tony stumbled and swore. "Quiet," Vaslov hissed. They looked to where the fat little Russian guard stood. He was not looking at them and had heard nothing. Both men thought of him as Ivan the Hog.

Tony tried to recall just what he had said when he almost fell. Probably nothing more than a grunt instead of something in English that might have given him away. He had spoken no English out loud since the Russians had swept them up.

It was only good fortune that Tony had been wearing German civilian clothes while they foraged, and that they had earlier hidden their weapons and the uniform they'd taken from the NKVD officer. In a fit of brilliance, Vaslov had told a Russian that Tony was an Italian worker the Germans had drafted and transported to Berlin for use as slave labor. Since Tony could speak passable Italian, and the Russians none at all, the ruse had worked so far, as Tony obligingly jabbered away incomprehensibly. Vaslov had told Ivan the Hog that he would look out for the imbecile Tony, and the Russian had shrugged his shoulders in disinterested agreement.

Tony looked up. The guard had walked away. "We gotta get out of here. I can't take this too much longer."

"Who can?" Vaslov whispered bitterly. "I think we are almost done with this section of road. If that is the case, security might be a little lax. Perhaps we can slip away tonight."

"Where do you think the others are?" Of the band of ten, only he and Vaslov were in this particular work group. Tony was less concerned about their personal safety than he was about the others getting captured and talking about the American who was their nominal leader.

Once again Tony glanced about to see if anyone had heard him speak English. He knew that any number in the crew of dozens of Germans and other nationalities would gladly sell him to the Russians if they found out, and the strain was beginning to tell on him. He was particularly concerned about a dark-haired man in his late twenties who, while thin, looked healthy and appeared to have been doing all right by himself until recently. This man would periodically stop and glare at Tony.

A whistle blew and they all froze. What now? It was far too early to quit. Nothing good was going to come of this. With abrupt gestures, the Russians urged them to form up in a semicircle. When they were gathered, a line of nine men and three women were led in front of them and forced to their knees. Their hands had been tied behind their backs and they were all linked like human sausages by a long rope.

Tony gasped as he recognized three of them as his people, two of the Jews and one Pole. Even worse, a Russian officer with the now-familiar NKVD insignia stood off to the side with a swarthy-looking man who was obviously a high-ranking officer, maybe even a general.

The NKVD man began to speak. His voice was a flat, ominous growl that needed no translation to communicate its threat. He identified himself and introduced the general, someone named Bazarian, who was in charge of the area. These people, he said as Vaslov whispered a translation, had been caught either stealing or sabotaging Russian equipment. The NKVD man also said that they had admitted to signaling the location of Russian targets to the American bombers.

Tony looked at their bruised and swollen faces. They had been tortured and doubtless some would have agreed to anything to stop the beatings. But what about the two Jews who had been with them? Had they told the Russians anything about the group? One of them looked up and appeared to make contact with Tony through blackened and swollen eyes. The man's mouth distorted slightly in what might have been a smile and he lowered his head.

The NKVD man finished speaking. He drew a pistol and began walking down the line. At each prisoner, he paused for a ghoulish second before he fired once into the back of each person's head. He paused only to reload. When he was done, the workers were ordered back to their tasks. No effort was made to pick up the bodies. They lay there swelling and stiffening in the summer heat.

As he passed the rest of the afternoon working, Tony's eyes would unexpectedly begin to water. The two Jews had not said a word. They had not told on him, not even to save their lives or end their suffering. What had he done to deserve that loyalty?

At night, they were given bread and thin soup. After everyone was asleep, Vaslov turned to him and nodded. It was time. They stood and walked to where the stinking latrine trenches were. They looked about and saw no Russians, although they could hear them carousing nearby, hopefully drinking themselves into a stupor, and continued walking. Their escape was absurdly easy. They just walked away.

Very soon, they found themselves in the middle of a small Russian motor pool. Tony paused and began unscrewing gas caps.

"What are you doing?" Vaslov hissed. "We've got to get going."

"I'm fucking up their cars. This is for the two Jew boys."

Vaslov looked aghast, then chuckled and began to help pour dirt into the gas tanks. With only the smallest amount of luck they would ruin about a dozen Russian jeeps and trucks.

Vaslov left the motor pool and dashed across an open field first while Tony watched. Just as Tony was about to rise and sprint away, he felt a hand on his mouth and the blade of a knife on his neck.

"Don't move," he was told. "Make a single sound and I'll slice your throat. If you understand me, nod."

Tony nodded. It was only then he realized that his captor had spoken in clear English.

CHAPTER 18

Sirens went off just as the sound of machine guns shattered the night. Logan jumped off his cot and tried to orient himself. Yeah, he was in the bunker and it was the middle of the night.

More gunfire, and it was coming from the lakefront. It was in their rear. Dear God. Had the Russians gotten behind them?

Dimitri burst in. "Logan, I'll take over here. You find out what's happening. The radios are in chaos with everybody yakking away."

Logan dashed out of the bunker and grabbed a bicycle. With gas and vehicles at a premium, many civilian bikes had been confiscated. He pedaled as quickly as he dared. The roads were cratered and the only light came from the sky, although explosions improved visibility as he got closer to the waterfront.

Searchlights from both sides of the Havel swept the area and illuminated scores of small boats heading toward him and coming from the Russian side. The Reds were attacking what they hoped was the vulnerable American rear. A lot of people had said the Commies wouldn't attack across the water, and they were very wrong.

Logan spotted a very anxious General Miller giving orders. Several of the Russian craft had been hit and were either sinking or burning, but the remainder were pressing on. In the inconsistent light, it was impossible to figure out how large an attack it was. A Sherman tank rumbled beside him and stopped. The main gun fired and the shell landed between two boats filled with Russian soldiers, spilling them into the water. The tank's machine guns raked several other boats. Logan gulped, recalling his crossing of the Elbe. That could have been them when they'd crossed that river an eternity ago if the Germans had tried to contest the crossing.

More American tanks arrived and joined in, while additional infantry with machine guns and BARs began to rake the Russian boats. There weren't as many as before and the survivors were turning back. It was over.

Jack pedaled back to the bunker and his captain. After hearing the brief report, Dimitri nodded. "We were lucky. We were able to send our reserves to the water rather quickly. What do you think might have happened if the Reds had been smart enough to coordinate that attack with a land one?"

Logan told the captain that he really didn't want to contemplate that. Instead, he again went looking for Lis and told her what had gone on.

She started to shake. "One of these days they will succeed."

Jack held her tightly until she calmed down. He told her everything would be all right, but he knew that was a lie. Food was becoming short and so was ammunition. A few more attacks and they'd be defending Potsdam with rifle butts.

And when was the last time they'd seen an American plane? As the Soviets moved westward, they made the flight from the American lines ever longer and more treacherous. Hell, it'd been a long flight for American fighters when they'd crossed the Elbe, and that river had been crossed by the Reds a long time ago.

"We'll make it, Lis, I promise."

"How can you say anything like that?" she asked with a tentative smile. She wanted to believe his brave words but knew better. "Are you telling me you have a plan?"

"Sure. Actually, I have several plans."

This was a true statement. He spent much of his free time devising plans. The only problem was, none of them appeared workable. He kissed her quickly and headed back to his platoon.

He had the sinking feeling that Goddamn Potsdam had been forgotten by the rest of the world.

GENERAL MARSHALL SHIFTED in his chair and looked at Steven Burke. They were surrounded by boxes and other evidence that, once again, SHAEF headquarters was going to be moved in deference to the Soviet air force, whose planes were constantly searching for it.

"You requested five minutes of my time, Colonel; well, you're in luck. I can give you fifteen."

"Yes, sir."

"Now sit down and tell me what went on at Bitburg."

Burke was just a little surprised that the chief of staff would have known of his trip to the Russian POW camp. But only a little. Marshall had a reputation for knowing exactly what was going on, particularly regarding members of his staff.

"Sir, one of the reasons I went there was to talk with the so-called average Russian POW and find out how he felt. A second reason was to try to confirm or refute a rumor that a great number of recent prisoners were not Russians; that, instead, they were Asians from places like Uzbekistan or Kazakhstan, or even Siberia."

"Yes," said Marshall, "we had picked up on those rumors as well."

That statement somewhat deflated Steve, who had hoped he had stumbled onto something new. "Well, sir, I can confirm the presence of the non-Russians in large numbers. I can also say that those Russians we have in custody are very confused and not particularly enthused about the war against the United States."

"Few prisoners would be," Marshall said drily.

"General, based on my own interrogations and, after reading the reports of others, I believe the Russians may have suffered far greater losses in the last offensive against Germany than we first believed. I heard too many stories of depleted units, massive casualties, fuel and ammunition shortages, and lack of food for all these rumors to be lies. They all fit too well together. Simply put, they are running out of good manpower as well as supplies."

"So are we," Marshall said, "which is why we are drafting eighteen-year-olds. And I suppose it explains the use of Asians by the Reds. They'll make good cannon fodder until the Russians reconstitute their army."

"Yes, sir. Or at least that's part of it. I believe that the Soviets are letting their second-echelon troops both inflict and take heavy casualties in an effort to wear us down. When the time comes, I believe the Reds will use their remaining elite Guards to great effect, but not until the second- and third-rate soldiers, the Asian rifle divisions or penal units, have bloodied us very badly, even though they would have destroyed themselves in the process."

Marshall nodded. "That pretty much confirms what the others have been saying. Now, tell me what's going on in Stalin's mind as a result of all this."

"Sir, it is totally unlike him to do anything impulsive or irrational, so I think he's thought this out very clearly. He has a dread of being surrounded and attacked simultaneously by non-Communist, or capitalist, countries. This would include a resurgent Germany and an American presence in Europe. By taking all of Germany, he can eliminate at least one of his major problems. If he forces us out of Europe, he will have eliminated the second. The other countries of Europe will fall to him like dominoes."

"A charming picture."

"He would then be free to incorporate the resources of a Communist Germany as a military ally."

Marshall arched his eyebrows. "What makes you think Germany would become Communist? Would the people do that after experiencing fascism?"

"Sir, they would have no choice. In one of his speeches he said something to the effect that an occupying or conquering power will always impose its own economic or social system on the occupied. This would be consistent with his stated aims of exporting the Communist revolution to all corners of the globe. Sir, give him a decade and every good little German will be a good little Communist, instead of a Nazi."

Marshall stood and leaned over the desk. "But what if we stop him, Colonel? What if our defenses hold, as I believe they ultimately will?"

"Sir, this is where his ruthlessness and his ideology meet. Let's say we stop him before Antwerp, which is his obvious goal, and he is also unable to cross the Rhine. Well, we then have a stalemate and he is the winner because he will still have conquered the lion's share of Germany."

Marshall's eyes were hard. "But Burke, what if we attack and drive him back to Russia?"

Burke managed a small smile. "General, despite what I've heard about General Patton's recent quotes about burning the Kremlin with Stalin inside, I don't think that's going to happen and neither does Stalin, and I don't think you do either. It's all rhetoric."

This time Marshall's voice had an edge to it. "Go on."

"Sir, we still have Japan to finish off. In the event of a stalemate, we would be on the horns of a dilemma. Either we negotiate an armistice with the Reds and then invade Japan, or we sit here with our army and ignore the Japs. Sorry, sir, but I don't see the American public standing for a long-term stare-down between the two armies while the Japs go scot-free. I also don't see the American public permitting its armies to suffer hundreds of thousands of casualties so we can liberate a bunch of ex-Nazis from the clutches of a man we just recently called 'Uncle Joe.' I don't know the figures, but I would guess we have suffered a lot of dead and wounded in the last few weeks. Rumor has it at a hundred thousand. I hope to God it's not true."

Marshall sat down. A look of sadness crossed his face. "Burke, it's more like a hundred and fifty thousand. About forty thousand more are missing and most likely prisoners of the Reds and will be pawns in any peace negotiations. And that doesn't count those surrounded in Potsdam."

Burke was shocked. "I didn't know it was that bad."

"If it's any consolation, the Russians are suffering far worse, but then, that was their plan, wasn't it? They have the numbers and the will to absorb all we can give them and keep on coming, don't they?"

"Yes, sir."

"Stalin's a cunning and ruthless bastard, isn't he?"

"Yes, sir. I should also add that he probably thought of the previous war between the Allies and Germany as little more than a civil war among capitalist nations. The fact that he had been dragged into it was fairly irrelevant, although very inconvenient. Again, sir, he is willing to throw away lives in the taking of an objective now because he feels it might not be achievable in the future. Why he feels that way right now, I do not know."

There, thought Steve, once again there was that almost imperceptible flicker across Marshall's face. He decided to try something. "Sir, it would almost seem that he fears we have some sort of secret weapon, just like the Nazis were always bragging about."

Marshall's mouth twitched and the façade of stoniness quickly returned. "Thank you, Colonel, that was well presented and has given me much food for thought. I will be returning to Washington in a day or so. I think you would be a valuable addition to Eisenhower's staff, so you will remain here. Contact Beetle Smith regarding your duties."

Burke saluted and left. He had done his best. He had hoped to return to the States and Natalie, but that would have to be put off for a while. He would write her and, without giving away too much detail, let her know that he had just delivered another lecture to the chief of staff.

But he did still think there was something funny about Marshall's reaction to his comments about secret weapons. Could there actually be one?

STALIN WAS OUTRAGED, but this time Molotov and Beria knew where the anger was directed. This served to calm them, but they knew that the direction of Stalin's fury could change at any moment.

"De Gaulle," said Stalin, "is a fool. A big, oafish lump. It has been almost a week since Vyshinsky's meeting with him and there has been no response to our demands."

Molotov took the tirade in stride. Stalin and de Gaulle had met briefly a couple of years earlier and had formed an instant dislike for each other. Stalin thought de Gaulle was an arrogant snob and Molotov concurred with that opinion. What de Gaulle thought of Stalin was of no concern to Stalin.

Stalin puffed on his pipe, sending yet another blue-black cloud toward the high ceiling. "When we have finished with the Americans and the British we will take care of France. I will have de Gaulle shot, or, better yet, spend the rest of his life freezing his nuts off in a Siberian camp. Comrade Beria, when will your revolution of French Communists topple him?"

Beria looked furtively about the room before he spoke. Stalin did not like to hear of failure, and he knew that was what he had to report. There was no second French Revolution. "Comrade Stalin, I must report that the enthusiasm of our French brothers for supporting us is nowhere near as high as I had been informed it would be."

"Why?"

Molotov thought he could smell the odor of Beria's perspiration and tried not to look at the man. "Comrade Stalin," Beria said, "while there were some initial attempts to interrupt the French transport system, these were very few and far between; therefore, the French police and army were quickly able to put them down. Further, we have now confirmed that French troops are beginning to ride the trains and protect the highways, as well as the oil pipelines that the Americans have laid across France. While our brothers in France might have been willing to assault the Americans or the British, there is a very real reluctance on their part to attack their brother Frenchmen."

Stalin nodded. "But that means our intelligence reports are correct; the French armies are being pulled out of Italy and Austria."

Beria's head bobbed. "Yes, comrade, it does. Although it does not appear to be occurring in any great numbers yet, the withdrawal of the French has begun."

"Comrade Stalin," said Molotov, "it would appear that the time for any diplomatic initiatives is not yet at hand. The military aspect of this war must play itself out a little longer before anyone will be willing to negotiate. We have been deeply involved in the French question and have been out of touch with the military. How does Zhukov progress?"

Stalin placed his pipe in an ashtray with a sound that made a distinct crack. "Slowly, far too slowly. The Allies are putting up too good a fight, particularly in the air. However, we are bleeding them and we will prevail."

The admission concerned Molotov. He had often heard Stalin say that the democracies were weak and would not fight either hard or long. Now he was granting them a grudging level of respect. In that regard, there was no other choice. The Russian armies had not yet broken through the Americans.

"Zhukov," Stalin said, "predicted a war of three to six months. He is confident that the Allied lines will crack under our pressure and this current war of small gains will soon become one of movement and great leaps." Stalin chuckled. "Zhukov also reminded me that the Red Army is now without its greatest general, Adolf Hitler."

Molotov and Beria laughed along with Stalin. It was common knowledge that, but for the incredible military blunders ordered by Hitler, the battle against the Germans might have had a different ending.

"The Americans and British fight, give ground, and fight again," Stalin said. "Sometimes they throw us off balance with counterattacks and bombing raids. I have to give them their due; they are much better and more determined than I thought they would be. We will, however, still win."

With that, Stalin dismissed them. Alone, he pondered the information he'd received through his intelligence services. For almost a year, the German-born scientist Klaus Fuchs had been working at Los Alamos, New Mexico, and had been passing American nuclear secrets to Russia. Prior to that, Fuchs had been living in England and passing British secrets to the Soviet embassy. It was amazing, Stalin thought, just how much damage one man could do if he really tried. Incredibly, it seemed to be a matter of ideology for Fuchs, as he had refused all offers of money.

Normally never one to look back on past decisions with regret, Stalin wished that he had ordered the development of an atomic energy program such as the Americans had. From all of Fuchs's accounts, the project was titanic. Worse, if Fuchs was correct, it would soon be successful. He wondered if Soviet physicists and other scientists would have been able to develop an atomic weapon as rapidly as the Americans had. At least they now knew that the bomb was feasible. That would save them from making so many wrong turns into scientific dead ends as the Germans had done with their nuclear program under Werner Heisenberg. When the time came, Russia would develop an atomic bomb much faster than the Americans were now doing.

Before that, Stalin knew he needed two things. First, he needed to establish hegemony in Europe to protect the Soviet Union and enable him to project the revolution. Second, he needed time to develop his bomb. The information Fuchs had provided would shave years off the task.

ALTHOUGH EVERYONE IN the Soviet Union knew that their nation was at war with the United States and Great Britain, the implications of that fact did not affect everyone's thinking in precisely the same way. Baku, a city south of the Caucasus mountain range and on the edge of the Caspian Sea, was literally on the border between Europe and Asia as defined by geographers who felt that such a distinction was necessary. Baku itself was only about a hundred miles from the border with Iran, which was now under British control after having flirted with the Nazis. Somewhat as a result, portions of Iran's oil-rich northwest had been occupied by the Soviets at the start of the war. Despite the drama of the Barents Sea convoys, Iran had long been the main entry point for Allied Lend-Lease supplies to the Soviet Union. Supplies entered at the Persian Gulf port of Abadan and were shipped overland from there.

Baku and the surrounding oil fields had been the target of Germany's 1942 offensive. The German goal was to either take the area or seal it off from the rest of Russia. Either way, they wanted to deprive the Soviets of a major and critical source of petroleum.

The Germans had failed, although they had come very close. They had directly threatened the oil fields around Grozny before being pushed back. The defenses of both Baku and Grozny logically faced northward to where the German menace been launched. As the war had drawn away from the Caucasus, so too had a large number of the implements of war. Many of the antiaircraft batteries had been removed, as had most of the defending aircraft. The war was far away. The oil fields were safe.

If the fact that a new war was raging over the horizon was any concern of Major General Vassily Guchkov, he did not show it. If he wondered why he had been left behind with a rump section of the Fourth Air Army, consisting of five hundred obsolescent fighter planes, it was no concern of his. What did concern him was that he hated Baku. It was full of black-ass Muslims whose faith was the Koran and not Lenin, who spoke a hideous Turkic type of language, and who hated Russians with an unspeakable passion.

It was not yet midmorning and he was already thinking of the private session he would have with the big-breasted blond typist from Kiev who functioned as his daytime mistress. As usual, she would serve him a light lunch in his office and then perform oral sex upon him. He felt it refreshed him for the rigors of the rest of the afternoon, which invariably concluded with bouts of heavy drinking. His adjutant would then drive him to his palatial quarters and turn him over to his night mistress, a plump local woman with very basic tastes who hated oral sex. She was also afraid she'd have her throat cut by her fellow Muslims if she ever left Guchkov's employ, and she was right. Left alone on the streets she wouldn't last thirty seconds.

All in all, he thought, it wasn't a bad life. Let the others get shot at by the Yanks. He, Vassily Guchkov, would enjoy life despite the vulgarities of Baku and its people. The weather was nice, the women pliant, and he had several thousand men who saluted him.

His reverie was jolted by the distant sounds of low-flying aircraft and attendant explosions. Belatedly, the air raid sirens started to howl, sending civilians and noncombatants running frantically to the shelters.

What the hell is going on? Guchkov thought. He ran the few dozen yards to his combat command center, huffing badly, and received word that strange planes were overhead and dropping bombs. He looked out the window just as one of the planes flew past and was horrified to see the insignia of the United States Air Force on a P-51 only a few hundred feet above him. The fighters were bombing and strafing his airfields and the antiaircraft defenses.

"Scramble the planes," he yelled, and he was informed that it was already happening, but too late. Most of the planes he commanded were being destroyed on the ground, as were the antiaircraft guns.

The fighter attack lasted only a few minutes, then there was blessed silence and the sound of the all-clear. He wondered who had decided it was safe, but his thoughts were again interrupted when the sirens shifted to the danger sound, sending the civilians screaming and running back to the shelters. The planes were returning.

"Where are my fighters?"

His adjutant, a slim young major named Brovkin, shrugged and looked at him with something bordering on contempt. "Either destroyed on the ground or unable to fly because of craters in the runways. Those few who did make it up appear to have been shot down. Oh yes, General, they've been strafing and bombing our antiaircraft positions."

Guchkov sat down hard in a chair. He was fifty years old and had been in the Soviet military for more than thirty of those years, and never had anything like this occurred to him before. Even when the Luftwaffe was slaughtering the Red air force in the early days of the Great Patriotic War with Germany, he had been safe in a training command near the Urals.

"This time it's their bombers and we can't stop them," Brovkin practically sneered.

The sky was clear, and overhead they could see the sunlight reflecting on the American planes. The effect was a silver twinkling of what looked like scores of tiny flying fish. He fervently wished they had been fish. Guchkov knew he was safe where he was because he now understood what was happening. The Allies had built up an air army of their own near Tehran and were going to use it to do what Hitler and his Panzers could not—destroy the oil fields!

All day long, the bombers came in waves, and he could see, hear, and smell the effects of the bombing. He could also see the fires where the wells and storage tanks had been set aflame. Dozens of dark, greasy fingers of smoke searched for the sky and many more fires must have been unseen in the distance.

At night the fighters returned, vectored in by the flames. They crippled attempts to repair the runways and hit anything they could see. They also denied sleep to the exhausted Russians and the terrified people of Baku. In the morning the bombers returned. Communication lines were damaged so Guchkov had no detailed information, but he did manage to find out that the bombs were falling all over the Caucasus region.

In his frustration, Guchkov got roaring drunk and beat up his night mistress, while the blonde stayed prudently out of his way. As the communications situation improved a little, he managed to find out that virtually the same thing was happening to the refining center at Ploesti and the oil fields in Romania. Although the battles for those areas were not as one-sided as the devastation around Baku, the reports of destruction mirrored his.

It didn't matter. His command and his career had been destroyed. If his planes and guns had inflicted any real damage on the American tormentors and their airplanes he was not aware of it.

When, after a couple of days, there was a real lull in the attacks, he took a quick tour of the area. Most of the wellheads had been destroyed and were burning furiously, as were the refining and storage areas. The main rail lines from Baku to Rostov had been severed in a score of places and would require major reconstruction before any oil could be shipped. That is, if oil could ever again be brought from the ground in the first place. The totality of the disaster appalled him.

There were very few reports of bombers being shot down, and when he did find one crashed on the ground, he went to it and stared at the scattered rubble of the giant plane. It was a B-29. Soviet intelligence had said they were in the Pacific. This meant they were coming to Europe to join in the war. He calculated the range. Based in Iran, they could hit most of southern Russia. The cities of Odessa, Sevastopol, Kiev, Kharkov, and Stalingrad could be bombed, perhaps even Moscow.

"Did we get any prisoners?" Guchkov asked.

"Half a dozen," Brovkin replied.

"Kill them."

Brovkin disagreed. "I would like to interrogate them first, comrade General."

"Of course," Guchkov said. He didn't see the look of relief on Brovkin's face. No prisoners would be murdered if he could help it.

Stunned, and in a drunken near-stupor, Guchkov allowed himself to be driven back to his office. There were radio messages from Stavka on his desk asking for information about the disaster. How badly were the fields hit? they asked. Would the flow of oil be interrupted? If so, for how long? When will oil be shipped again?

What they didn't directly ask was who was to blame. Everyone knew who was to blame. Major General Vassily Guchkov, that's who. Guchkov sobbed. He sent a coded message that the fields had been destroyed, as had all the supporting facilities and the transportation lines. Yes, he said, the fields could produce oil again, but not in this year of 1945. Maybe in 1946, but he doubted that.

Guchkov knew he was to blame and would be punished brutally. They had left him five hundred planes and he had failed. That the planes were shit, the pilots were poorly trained, and that the best mechanics had left as well, so that at least a third of the planes had been grounded for mechanical problems at the time of the assault, was no excuse. That he had no radar and his inherited antiaircraft guns faced north and not south was his fault as well. He was doomed.

Guchkov told his staff he did not want to be disturbed. He went into his office and closed the door. He took a seat behind his desk and pulled the Tokarev automatic pistol from its holster, stuck it in his mouth, and pulled the trigger.

Outside Guchkov's office, his staff jumped at the sound of the shot. A couple of them rushed for the office but were stopped by Brovkin. "Why bother hurrying?" he said. "Just another of his messes we'll have to clean up."

Later that night, his nighttime mistress tried to make a run for it. She got about a hundred yards before she was caught and had her throat slit.

TONY SIPPED HIS thin potato broth and looked across the small fire they'd lit to warm their food. If he lived to be a hundred, he would never forget the feel of that knife alongside his throat. The man on the other side of the fire had said his name was Joe Baker and would give neither his rank nor his branch of service. But he did say he was with the Office of Strategic Services, the OSS. To Tony, the OSS was the stuff of legend. Cloak-and-dagger boys trained to kill and destroy. They made movies about the OSS, and here he was with one of those people. It was even more comforting than the bombing attack during his captivity at the work camp that had gotten him into so much trouble in the first place.

Baker was the man who had been watching him in the Russian camp, and now looked innocuous enough. Like Tony and the others, he was a little on the small side and thin, although unlike the two Poles who were now Tony's only other companions, Baker looked like he was in fine shape, like an Olympic distance runner.

After Baker had been convinced that Tony would not betray him, they had located Vaslov, who then found the other Pole. The remaining refugees had already scattered.

Baker, it turned out, had also been rounded up by the Russians and forced to work and had chosen that same evening to make his break. He had suspected Tony was an American by the fact that he looked fairly healthy, and then had confirmed it by reading Tony's lips when he was trying to communicate with Vaslov.

Baker had assumed leadership of the little group. No one had argued. Baker could be lethal when he wanted, as the incident with the knife had proven. He had told them that it was better they remain few in number so as to not attract either attention or people who might talk under torture. When Tony had told him about the two Jews, Baker had been deeply touched. Tony, who didn't think Baker was his real name, now thought that the OSS man might be Jewish.

Baker said he had a job to do and he could do it either alone or with the help of a handful of others. Too many would get in the way. His assignment was to cause as much harm as possible to the Russian transportation system. Specifically, he was to find their local oil stores and call in air strikes on the small shortwave radio he'd parachuted in with and hidden. As a last resort, he would try to destroy the targets himself.

To Tony, it seemed like a wonderful idea. He was now firmly convinced, if there ever had been a doubt, that he would never see home and family again if the Russians weren't defeated. Oh, they had talked about trying to gain the relative safety of the Potsdam perimeter, but that had been decided against for some very good reasons. First was the fact that they would have had a helluva time getting through the Russian and American lines without being shot. Second, what would they have gained? Baker had said it best: "All you would be doing is changing one prison camp for another."

Baker was right, of course. While they would not have been alone in Potsdam and the sound of more American voices would have been nice and comforting, Potsdam was surrounded and there was little he could do in there to help the war. Potsdam was also possibly doomed. Out here he was free. Sort of. Tony kind of liked that better than being sort of not free.

Baker had earlier been out scouting and had reported the location of a couple of tanker trucks hidden nearby. Hardly enough to call in a flight of bombers, but something that should be taken care of.

"Hey, Joe, what are you gonna do about them trucks?" Tony asked. "Can't leave 'em there, can you?"

Baker smiled slightly. "Haven't decided."

"You speak Russian?"

"Maybe."

"Bullshit," Tony laughed. "I'll bet you speak it real good."

Baker took out his knife and began to sharpen it. "I'll bet you're right, Tony. I'll bet I speak German too, and maybe a little French. Why? You got an idea?"

Now it was Tony's turn to smile. He knew Joe didn't think much of Tony's brainpower although he did respect him as a survivor. "I was thinking, Joe, why don't you just walk up to them trucks and blow them up."

Joe shook his head and grinned tolerantly. "And what would you

put on my tombstone? That the dumb shit thought he could get away
with it?"

"Joe, what if you were wearing a Russian uniform? One of their
NKVD things that seems to scare the shit out of the regular Russians."

"Tony, if I had one of those I could cause so much damage it would
make your head spin."

Tony laughed and told him about the uniform they'd taken and
hidden, along with the weapons. Joe's jaw dropped. Then he too
started laughing.

CHAPTER 19

*E*lisabeth Wolf was entranced. It had been years since she had seen a baseball game and she had forgotten how much she liked the sport. It was like a touch of an earlier home, of Canada, a time and a land that belonged to another her. Pauli, however, was simply confused by all the running and yelling. He would much rather have had a ball that could be kicked.

Jack Logan had explained to her that the baseball tournament had been a source of controversy for some time. There was the real fear that the Reds would either bombard or attack during a game and cause needless casualties, while others had feared that the exertion of playing might unnecessarily weaken young men who were already on short rations.

General Miller had asked a number of the men what they had thought. They had frankly and tersely responded to both fears. "Fuck it, General," one soldier had summed it up, "we all gotta die sometime. If it's gonna be here, I'd just as soon be playin' ball as hiding in some goddamn trench waiting to starve to death or get hit on the head by a Russian shell."

Thus inspired, the engineers had used lathes to fashion a kind of bat and made baseballs out of discarded tires. Gloves and catcher's masks were in short supply, so the rules of the tournament were adjusted to fit the fact. Even so, the games were a huge success and a boost for morale, and now football games were being planned.

Ball hit bat with a solid thwack and there were cheers. Pauli looked up and tried to figure out what was happening as a runner slid gracelessly into third base. Elisabeth looked up from where she was sitting on the ground and noticed a number of German women cheering on their particular soldiers. It would appear that she was not alone in having an American friend.

Logan trotted over from the field and plunked himself down beside her. "You look great," he said.

"Thank you." For the first time since he'd met her, she was wearing a skirt. She had made it from some blue drapes she'd found in a house. It was a little long, but it did make her feel a little more feminine than the men's clothing she had been wearing. She knew she had nice legs and knew that the reduction in food hadn't created any problem for her in that area.

"How come you stopped playing?" she asked.

"I took myself out. I wasn't playing all that well and I really should let the enlisted men have their fun. Besides, I'd rather sit here with you."

Elisabeth smiled. Jack had made two errors in the field and struck out once. Captain Dimitri had yanked him and sent him off with a swat on the rear while his team hooted in good-natured derision. He hadn't pulled himself out; he'd been booted.

Elisabeth shifted, and Jack caught a quick glimpse of knee and thigh that widened his eyes despite the fact that women wore far shorter skirts in the States. God, he thought, am I that horny? Yes, he answered. I am.

A familiar shape darkened their horizon. "Am I intruding?" It was Lieutenant David Singer. His one hand rested on a cane.

"Hardly," Elisabeth answered as she gestured for him to take a seat with them. "How are you feeling?"

Singer, still wan and thin, looked far better each day. "Almost ready to go out there and play. Don't laugh—don't the St. Louis Browns have a one-armed outfielder?"

"If anyone would, it would be the Brownies," Logan said.

Singer beamed. "I got a letter from Marsha." Two nights before, they had been overflown by a bomber flight that had dropped some essential supplies and, surprise of surprises, a number of sacks of mail. Once again, morale had soared. "It was written before I got hurt and we got stuck here, but it was really good to hear from her. She's working in Boston as a waitress and she's gone back to college. When this is over, she'll get a job and support me while I go back to school and finish my education."

"Good idea," said Jack, thinking of his own interrupted studies. But that had been in another world, hadn't it? "How are you doing at the hospital?"

"Well, they're still letting me work with the more badly wounded. I either read to them or help them to try and realize they still have a life to live."

"That's great, Dave," Jack said. Elisabeth had slipped her hand into his. It was a wonderfully comforting feeling.

"Jack, you have no idea how good it feels to be useful. After all, I still have two of the three arms I was given—right arm and short arm." Logan grinned and Elisabeth smiled tolerantly. She got the joke. "Seriously, I do have a life to live and a career to build when I get home and, no, I was not going to be a surgeon or a paperhanger."

Elisabeth laughed. "Then what?"

"An accountant. And like I once told Jack, I can juggle figures just as well with one arm." Singer looked around and saw some friends, said he'd talk to Jack and Lis later, and went over to visit.

Elisabeth squeezed Jack's hand again. "Did you get any mail?"

"Nope. A lot of people didn't. I was hoping, but what the heck, I'll live."

"Does that upset you?"

"I'll live. Really, I'm used to it."

Despite his denial, there was a hint of sadness in his voice. There was a moment's silence while Elisabeth reached into the pocket of her skirt and pulled out a plain envelope.

"Here," she said.

"What's this?"

"A letter. It's from me. See, you do have someone who cares for you and writes to you."

Elisabeth turned her head so that she could not see the stunned expression on Jack's face and so that he could not see the look on hers. He pulled her closer and said how much he appreciated it and yes, he really did want letters from home, but this was even better. He said he would read it later, which was what Lis wanted. Despite being a soldier, Lis thought he was such a good and gentle man. Perhaps this was one way of letting him know that she felt that way about him.

On the other side of the playing field, Wolfgang von Schumann confronted General Miller. "Well, General, have you made up your mind?"

"Ike would crap."

"But wouldn't he also crap if he found out that you looked a gift horse in the mouth?"

"True enough, Herr Oberst." Miller looked longingly at the ball game and thought of gentler times gone by. He knew he now had a decision to make.

A belated survey of the Potsdam area had revealed the existence of a large number of German antiaircraft guns and a quantity of ammunition. They had been Potsdam's defense against bombers. Von Schumann had also located a warehouse that contained, among other things, a quantity of *panzerfausts,* the shoulder-carried antitank rockets that could be useful at close range.

Almost simultaneously, a census of the remaining German population of Potsdam had revealed several hundred veterans or soldiers in hiding, along with the crews of most of the antiaircraft guns, which included a number of the splendid 88 mm guns that could stop most tanks as well as shoot down planes. The German soldiers had stayed to defend their city and been swept up by the advances of the Russians and the Americans.

Von Schumann had reviewed the situation and made a modest proposal that they all be put to use in the defense of Potsdam. The Germans were willing, and the American soldiers had no apparent qualms, so what was the problem? Miller asked himself. Certainly, no one was concerned about using the other side's weapons. That had been done many times in the war.

Von Schumann had argued that it really didn't matter that use of German personnel wasn't yet authorized by SHAEF or Truman or anyone else, although there were rumors that it soon would be. What did matter was that they use every means possible to defend themselves. War is hell, he reminded Miller, and it contains no rules except to destroy one's enemy. He was reminded that the Germans in Potsdam would be slaughtered by the Russians if they broke through and would, therefore, fight like tigers. He added that they had a right to have weapons to defend themselves, and Miller couldn't rebut him.

Miller smiled and patted his pocket for some tobacco. Once again there wasn't any. "Advisers," he said smiling.

Von Schumann blinked. "What?"

"They cannot be allies and they cannot be part of the American army. At least not officially and not yet. However, they can be advisers. Someone must teach my soldiers how to use those nice antiaircraft guns of yours and how not to shoot themselves in the foot with the *panzerfausts*. Therefore, they will advise our soldiers."

Von Schumann thought it over. "Should it become necessary, or even helpful, can these advisers man guns and shoot them?"

"Of course, Herr Oberst," Miller said sweetly. "How better to advise?"

THE PLANES THAT had ravaged the oil fields and other vital areas of the Caucasus had come from airstrips in Iran and Iraq. There had been as many as a thousand fighters—P-51s and P-47s—and they had simply overwhelmed the inadequate defenses of the area and destroyed virtually all the planes left to defend the precious oil-producing area. These had been followed by the bombers, hundreds of B-17s and B-24s along with a few score of newly arrived B-29s.

For the Russians, the final tally was 139 of their planes shot down, and nearly 350 destroyed on the ground. Even allowing for the wildly inflated claims of the surviving aircrews and those gunners on the ground who had found targets worth shooting at, the Americans had lost only about fifty planes of all types. To make matters worse, it appeared that the Americans had overflown Turkey and then entered Russian airspace from the Black Sea. They had been wolves among the Russian sheep before there was any reaction from the Russian defenders, even the handful who had been looking westward.

The simultaneous raid on Ploesti had been staged from bases in Italy and North Africa, and the planes, again more than a thousand, had crossed the Adriatic, and then Yugoslavia, and been above Ploesti only seconds after the alarm had been sounded. It was noted by the Soviet leadership that the Yugoslav Communists under Marshal Tito had not been terribly efficient or prompt in communicating the presence of Allied aircraft to Stavka. It was a lapse of fraternal socialist brotherhood among ostensible Communist allies that Stalin swore he would remember. It seemed to some observers that Tito did not look with total favor upon the thought of Russian hegemony in Europe.

Stalin, Beria, and Molotov had traveled from Moscow to this dismal German city of Kustrin on the Oder to acquaint Marshal Zhukov with the new realities confronting him. At least the place for the meeting was better repaired than the last time. Now the windows were glassed over and there was electricity. Otherwise, Kustrin was still a city in ruins.

But first there were matters that had to be settled in the traditional Soviet matter.

"This motherfucking Guchkov," Stalin asked, "it is confirmed that he is dead?"

Zhukov saw the dread look in Stalin's eyes and was glad he was not Guchkov. It was the look of a snake stalking its prey. Stalin was openly expressionless but his eyes gave him away. He looked to be mad for revenge. Zhukov replied. "Yes, Comrade Stalin. He is dead, a suicide."

Stalin turned to Beria. "Then he has cheated justice. Have his family picked up as well. They must be considered equally guilty for his actions." Beria nodded. He guessed there would be a score of people, women and children included. They were as good as dead. A few years in the gulag and they would be dead in fact as well as theory.

"And who," Stalin continued, "commands the Fourth Air Army? Who is the fool that left the idiot Guchkov in charge of such a sensitive and important area as the Caucasus with such limited resources?" Stalin knew the answer. He just wanted someone else to say the name.

"Vershinin," said Zhukov. Stalin gestured to Beria, who nodded. Another casualty of the raid.

"And Ploesti?"

Zhukov wondered where it would stop. "The Fifth Air Army is under Goryunov." Again the gesture to Beria. Both generals would be arrested by the NKVD within two hours and be shot within three. The price for failure—or stupidity—was high in the Soviet Union.

The feral look left Stalin's eyes. The beast had been sated, tamed at least for a while. "Now, Marshal Zhukov, do you understand the situation with oil?"

"What I understand is that there will be very little more oil for the foreseeable future. How long are we talking about? Weeks? Months?"

Molotov spoke. "Perhaps much longer. I spoke with the minister of the interior, and it is his early estimate that there will be little more than a trickle for about three to six months."

Zhukov nodded. With his intimate knowledge of Soviet efficiency, he knew that the actual length of time would probably be at least a year before any new oil appeared. He also knew that the Germans had been fairly successful in the expensive task of transforming coal into oil. Sadly, these facilities had been destroyed a long time ago and were doubtless in worse shape than those in the Caucasus. Another source, Lend-Lease from America, was obviously severed. The Allies had provided the Soviet Union with more than three million tons of oil, primarily by truck and pipeline, from the Middle East. Worse, the Americans had been a primary source of gasoline and aviation fuel, which the Soviets made poorly even when they had the resources.

When the war started, the USSR produced 10 percent of the world's oil, virtually all of it from the now ruined Caucasus fields. The United States, on the other hand, produced more than two thirds of the world's oil. The Soviet Union would run dry in a very short while and the United States would continue to be flush in petroleum.

Zhukov remained impassive. "It will make sustained operations very difficult, perhaps impossible. We must begin hoarding and rationing immediately and at all levels."

"It is being done," said Beria. Further reductions in oil for the civilian population meant a reduction of what was already almost nothing. "We are somewhat fortunate that our trains run on coal, and we have plenty of that. Most of our factories are also coal-heated, as are our homes, so there will be little reduction in production or transportation as a result of this disaster."

Beria knew the need for warmth in homes was considered incidental by Stalin, but the Soviet Union did need fairly healthy workers to man the factories.

Stalin blinked slightly at the use of the word *disaster*, and Beria continued. "There will be no impact on food production. The troops will not go hungry."

That presumes, Zhukov thought, that the food not currently in hand can be shipped safely under the increasing pressure of Allied air attacks. Without fuel, how could the air force defend the army from American planes?

Instead, he said, "We have already taken steps. As you know, the Russian soldier is very resourceful. We have appropriated food and livestock along the way and are in no danger of going hungry for quite some time." He smiled. "Chuikov said we appear like a Mongol horde."

Stalin nodded his approval. He had seen the effects of such appropriations of German food. Russian armies were almost literally eating their way across Germany, but not like Mongols who butchered cattle and people indiscriminately. A plague of omnivorous locusts would be more like it. Millions of Germans would starve this winter, but that did not matter to Stalin at all. What did matter was that, for the first time in years, food was being grown in the Ukraine and elsewhere to keep the workers fed and working; thus, his soldiers would eat while they destroyed the capitalists. Let the Germans die, all of them. If only they could solve the oil problem.

"Zhukov," he said. "What will you now do?"

"Comrade Stalin, I will continue as planned. We have little choice. We are approaching the Leine River and will continue across while Koniev continues as a blocking force in the south and Rokossovsky to the north. The Leine is not a great obstacle, and the Americans will not hold it for long or in force. As before, we will continue a measured advance against what will doubtless be strengthening American defenses until we reach the Weser. At that point it will be necessary for us to pause and regroup."

"For how long?" Stalin asked, suddenly tense. He did not want his armies stopping and giving the Americans their own chance to recover.

Zhukov's face was impassive. "A couple of weeks. Perhaps more. The situation with the oil will complicate matters."

"So long a pause?" asked Beria.

Zhukov answered. He disliked Beria and was scarcely civil. "Even despite the oil problem, our armies are in desperate straits. They have been fighting continuously since crossing the Oder, first against the Nazis and now against the Americans and British. I must admit that our losses in men and equipment in taking Berlin were much greater than we first thought."

He turned to Stalin. "What we thought were missing units and personnel caused by the confusion of battle have, in too many instances, turned out to be actual dead and wounded. Many of our divisions are almost out of ammunition and are physically exhausted as well as greatly reduced by casualties. We have whole brigades that have become separated from their major units and haven't received orders in weeks. They continue west because that was the last order they received. As a result, many of our attacks against the Allies were piecemeal and poorly coordinated. If we try to force the Weser under those circumstances, we will not be successful."

Molotov looked grim. "But the Americans are retreating. I thought we had defeated them."

"No, comrade, we have not. Eisenhower is no fool. He anticipated our actions and pulled many of his units away from the Elbe and our initial attacks. It wasn't all that difficult for him to do as, in many cases, all he really had on the Elbe was advance units. Since then, we have been moving forward a few miles at a time against their flexible defenses. All the while, they have been preparing for a strong stand on the Weser."

"What else will you do with that time?" Stalin asked, the displeasure evident on his face.

"As I said, our armies are worn out. We must replace some units. I have given orders that the 7th Guards, as well as the 27th and 53rd Rifles, be sent from the Second Ukrainian Front. From Yeremenko's forces, I have ordered the 1st Guards along with the 18th and 40th Rifles. Fortunately, manpower is not an issue in the Red Army, even though it means we will be further stripping Koniev's and Rokossovsky's armies."

Stalin saw the logic and gave his grudging approval. Zhukov sensed his opportunity. "Comrade Stalin, I will require more."

Stalin was surprised. "More? You have stripped every front under your command to support your attacks. Where will you find more?"

Zhukov permitted himself a small smile. "In the Far East, comrade Stalin, where we have an army preparing to attack the Japanese. It is essential that the Japanese assault be deferred and those resources, including two air armies, shipped to me."

"They are second- and third-rate troops, but they are yours," Stalin said. "But there are some things you cannot have. I will be rebuilding the facilities in the Caucasus and we will start immediately. We cannot wait for the end of this war to commence reconstruction of our oil fields. Therefore, I will be protecting them, and Ploesti, with sufficient air and antiaircraft strength to ensure the success of our rebuilding efforts, and that includes the two air armies you wished."

Zhukov was not pleased. He would need everything possible to defeat the Allies. The armies from Siberia would take a long time to arrive, while the movement of the air armies and the antiaircraft batteries to the Caucasus would weaken his air support. Worse, the two air armies would use up precious fuel, both when traveling to their new stations and when flying patrols over the Caucasus. When he started to protest, Stalin silenced him with a glare. He had gotten more than enough, the look told him. He would win with the resources available or not at all.

"One last comment," said Stalin. "I would hope that your armies will not be totally inactive during this wait along the Weser."

Zhukov was glad to change the subject. "Hardly, comrade. Marshal Rokossovsky has been moving his forces so they now directly confront the British."

The move of those armies had also been at great cost in fuel, Zhukov now thought grimly. He could only hope that Rokossovsky could crush the British fairly quickly and, hopefully, push them out of the war. The British had been retreating slowly under limited pressure from Rokossovsky for some time. Now let's see what happens when the full fury of the Red Army hits them.

With the meeting concluded, Stalin sat alone in the little room. He was satisfied. As usual, he had contrived a situation in which he could do nothing but win. If Zhukov overcame the problems with American tenacity and his own lack of fuel, then the Allies would be defeated and he and the revolution would be the masters of most of Europe. The rest of the continent would fall shortly after.

If Zhukov failed, a potential rival would have been disgraced. If Zhukov wins, Stalin thought, it will be necessary to eliminate him anyhow. But even if he failed, the cost to the Allies would still be huge and the Soviet Union would remain in control of almost all of Germany west of the Oder to at least the Weser. Probably all the way to the Rhine, he thought. He was confident that, whatever transpired, the Allies would be too weak to attempt a reconquest of Germany, and Zhukov would not be a potential rival.

Stalin smiled. Outside the open door, Molotov saw the expression on his leader's face and wondered what terrible thing would now occur.

CHAPTER 20

Brigadier General Leslie R. Groves was ushered into the Oval Office. He saluted briskly and Harry Truman returned it. Groves was powerfully built, stern-faced, and had a well-trimmed mustache that was becoming his trademark. More important than his appearance, Groves was a brusk and no-nonsense administrator who spearheaded the Manhattan Project—the building of the atomic bomb. Along the way, he had offended a number of very sensitive academics and scientists. At one point, Groves had gotten so frustrated that he had proposed drafting all the physicists into the military and prohibiting them from speaking with one another in order to protect the project's security. His lead physicist, J. Robert Oppenheimer, had sat him down and told him just how scientists worked and how they needed the free flow of information to turn ideas into realities. Groves had grudgingly relented. He knew there was a war on and the first priority was to win it. Then he would kill the damned scientists.

Prior to taking on the Manhattan Project, Groves had been in charge of the construction of the Pentagon.

Truman had decided to speak with Groves and not one of the scientists, such as Oppenheimer or Fermi. Although very well read and self-educated—he read the classics in Latin and even spoke the dead tongue—Truman's formal education was that of a high school graduate, and he knew next to nothing about nuclear physics. He was concerned that the scientists would either condescend to him or talk in terms he would not understand. The pragmatic and honest Groves was an obvious choice to function as an intermediary, a task he had ably fulfilled since the inception of the Manhattan Project.

"General, be seated." Groves did as he was told but still managed to remain at attention.

"The bomb, General. Where do we stand?"

"Specifically, sir, we have three bombs. One is scheduled to be tested next month at Alamogordo in New Mexico. As you are aware, the test is called Trinity."

"Three bombs?"

"Yes, sir."

"And when will we have the fourth, fifth, and so on?"

"Sir, what we have now are prototype weapons. Each is unique, and we have no idea which will work best. Nor," he admitted reluctantly, "are we totally confident either will work at all. This is all unexplored territory. Someday we may be able to wheel atomic bombs off an assembly line like Ford does cars or tanks, but not now. I doubt that we could have any more bombs for another several months."

Truman thought that over. "Then we cannot afford to run leisurely scientific tests, can we?"

"Sir?"

"General, I do not think we can afford to waste one third of our atomic resources on a field test. The scientists may think it desirable, and, under other circumstances, I would also. But we do not now have that luxury. How long would it take to crate the things up and ship them off to Europe?"

If Groves was surprised by the idea of them going across the Atlantic he didn't show it. While the whole atomic bomb project had been started to counter the possibility of the Nazis having an atomic bomb ahead of America, the apparent collapse of the Third Reich had changed everyone's focus from Germany to the Pacific. Now the president wanted them shipped to Europe, with the Soviets as the new target. God help the Russians. Did they have any idea what they were getting into? For that matter, did the United States?

Groves explained that the scientists were in wide disagreement over what might happen when an atomic bomb was detonated. Some felt it would simply be a large bomb, a big bang that left a large hole in the ground, while others forecast the end of the world. As a practical man, Groves leaned toward the former opinion. A lot of the scientists were concerned about radiation, something he barely understood, but many leading scientists said it would dissipate quickly and be of little or no consequence. The simple truth was that no one really knew what would happen when an atomic bomb detonated. Theories were wonderful things, but the truth would come out when the first bomb went off. If it went off.

Groves took out a notepad and scribbled. "I'll have to check. If we shipped them by boat, perhaps the scientists could work on them en route."

"Good." Truman decided he liked the testy but aggressive Groves.

"We will have to get the B-29s off Tinian." Groves referred to the squadron that had been rehearsing carrying and dropping very large bombs and was now in the Pacific. Only their commander, Colonel Paul Tibbetts, knew what type of bomb was contemplated. "If you're not aware, Mr. President, we planned to use the B-29s because of the bulk of the bombs, as well as the range of the planes."

"I had wondered, and assumed something like that."

"The B-29s also require much longer runways. I spoke with General Marshall, and he assures me that runways in England are being lengthened as we speak. Some Eighth Air Force staffer actually used his brain and anticipated the arrival of B-29s."

"Excellent. Now, General, in your opinion, do the Russians know what we are doing?"

Groves paused. The scientists were all security nightmares. They had little understanding or concern regarding the political world. Many were so downright utopian regarding the universality of science, they'd be on the phone blabbing everything they knew in a minute if they hadn't been sealed off in New Mexico.

"Sir," he said solemnly, "if I were a betting man, I would say it's almost a sure thing that the Commies know what we're doing. When we cleared these people to work here, their early socialist leanings weren't important because Russia was our ally and we were fighting the Nazis. We desperately needed their brains and didn't much care about their politics. Now that the Reds are our enemies, the FBI is scrambling all over the records of some of our people and having a field day trying to trace their personal contacts. I can only say that I would be very surprised if Russia doesn't know what we are up to and that we are extremely close to success."

Truman nodded thoughtfully. "Thank you, General."

The meeting was over. He stood and saluted again. Truman rose and shook his hand. "General, we may have it in our power to end this war and change the world for a very long time. I sincerely hope your bombs work and that you can get them into use before it is too late."

Seconds after General Groves left the Oval Office, Secretary of State Ed Stettinius and Secretary of War Henry Stimson entered.

"You heard?" Truman asked, and the two men nodded. He had decided not to have the other men present for his meeting with Groves. He had thought it might intimidate Groves into being less than candid. Now he thought that Groves might be intimidated by a grizzly bear with hemorrhoids and not much else. God help the errant scientists who got in his path.

Stettinius took a seat. "At least we now have a clearer understanding of Stalin's motives in attacking now. He wants victory before we get the bomb." Stimson nodded agreement and reached for coffee.

"Yes," said Truman. "In a little while we will have the greatest weapon man has ever known." If the damned infernal thing works, he thought. "With that in mind, that son of a bitch Stalin has struck now while we don't have that weapon deployed. He is trusting that this war will leave him with most of Europe as a fait accompli, and that we won't use the bomb to help retake what he has stolen. What a calculating bastard!"

Stimson shrugged. "It is pretty much as we suspected."

"Damn."

"Mr. President," Stimson continued, "we are now trying to figure out who has been passing on information regarding our atomic project. When we are successful, we can assess the amount and quality of the data we have lost and then forecast just when the Soviets might have an atomic bomb of their own. My own guess, however, would be within three to five years."

"At which point," said Truman, "we would be equals as nuclear powers. If Stalin has control of Europe when that occurs, we will have no opportunity of defeating him militarily."

"That's right," Stimson agreed.

"Then," Truman said thoughtfully, "it's now or never for us, just as it is for him."

"One other thought," said Stimson. "What will Churchill say when he finds out that these atomic bombs are going to be in England?"

Truman grinned. "I have no intention of telling him."

• • •

GENERAL MIKHAIL BAZARIAN looked at the gutted vehicle a few feet in front of him on the road to Potsdam and tried to stifle his rage. The tanker truck was totally destroyed. Even the tires had melted, leaving the truck's axles on the ground. The blackened and grinning skeleton behind the steering wheel mocked Bazarian's growing impotence. This was the third oil or gas tanker truck he'd lost this week and he would not be getting any more vehicles or fuel to replace them. If this kept up, the situation for his army could quickly go from annoying to critical.

Just a few days ago, he had gotten the word from Zhukov's headquarters—no more oil or gas. For the foreseeable future, he would live with what he had. Bazarian had heard rumors of a massive attack on Soviet petroleum sources but had discounted them as enemy propaganda. Now he wondered. He always understood that a great deal of oil had come through Lend-Lease, although that had been officially discounted by political officers who denied the Soviet Union's reliance on outside sources as being contrary to the spirit of the revolution. Bazarian sniffed. Some people still thought the world was flat.

But what he had not counted on was the destruction of his precious reserves by saboteurs. The corpse in the truck cab would give him no answers. The dead Russian soldier could not even tell him how he had died. Had he been stabbed or shot? Poisoned or strangled? Bazarian's money was on him having been stabbed. It had happened before.

At least, Bazarian thought, the situation was not totally dire. He had received and kept two divisions of Romanians. They were shit soldiers whose country had surrendered and changed sides. They were poorly trained and equipped, but there were nearly 25,000 of them and they would make marvelous cannon fodder when the time came to storm Potsdam. They would go first, and his own men, still numbering more than 20,000 themselves, would follow into whatever breach the Romanians managed to make.

His artillery was still intact and their ammunition stores were adequate to support the attack. His tank strength, however, had not been fully restored. While he had managed to pick up a half-dozen precious T34s and their crews as replacements for the older tanks he'd lost, the same fuel restraints had denied him the opportunity to work with the new troops and increase their effectiveness. The only reason he'd gotten the T34s was because they were in bad mechanical shape.

Again on the positive side, the powers that be seemed to have totally forgotten about the foolish Russian colonel they had sent to report on him and whose sudden death had been so shocking. Obviously, the powers had better things to do.

So that left him with the matter of the saboteurs. He suspected that they were infiltrating his lines from Potsdam and causing the havoc in front of him. Bazarian briefly considered an artillery barrage to remind the Americans that he was still their master and they were effectively his prisoners, but decided not to. The directive to hoard resources was too specific for him to take a chance on disobedience. For the time being, at least, the people in the perimeter were snug and secure and would remain so. He would not attack or bombard, and was unable to do much about the now almost daily flights that had recommenced dropping supplies to the Americans. The flights infuriated him. How could the Americans get supplies and he could not?

So what to do about the saboteurs? First, he had to catch them. Then he would skin them alive and have one of his few scout planes drop the corpses into the perimeter. The thought made him smile. That would get their attention. He recalled that it was how his ancestors dealt with enemies and unwelcome visitors during sieges of castles.

Bazarian's adjutant approached him and snapped to attention. "So?" Bazarian asked.

The adjutant, a young captain, was glum and nervous. Bazarian's rages were becoming more and more violent as his frustrations increased. It would not be unusual for Bazarian to lash out and punch or kick someone who gave him news he did not want to hear.

"I'm sorry, sir, but the second guard died of his wounds."

There had been two guards protecting the tanker. One was the corpse in the vehicle while the second, stabbed in the chest and throat, had been left for dead. While the saboteurs had been preparing to blow up the truck, the remaining guard had regained a level of consciousness and, through superhuman effort, managed to crawl away before passing out again. The saboteurs had probably looked for him to put in the cab with his comrade and given up quickly rather than take time searching and risk discovery.

It had been Bazarian's fervent hope that the man would shed some light on who his adversaries were and just how they operated. For instance, just how did they manage to overcome two alert and well-armed guards? This was the third time this had happened, and the guards were all on their toes. After all, didn't their lives depend on it?

"Did he say anything before he died?"

"Yes, General, he did."

There was an uncomfortable pause. Bazarian stared at the young captain. "Do you intend to tell me?"

Bazarian saw that his adjutant was almost trembling. Good God, he thought, what on earth did the now dead guard manage to say, and why does this dolt think I will be angry upon hearing it? Doesn't the idiot realize that I will be angrier if he persists in this nonsensical silence? Finally, the captain gathered his nerves.

"General, the guard said that the man who attacked him was an NKVD officer."

Bazarian staggered as if struck by a blow. "Impossible."

The captain was insistent. "Sir, that's what he said, and then he died."

"Are you certain?" Bazarian asked. After all, the creature had his throat sliced pretty badly. Perhaps he had been misunderstood.

The captain shook his head. "Sir, he was pretty hard to understand, but I repeated it and kept asking if that was what he was trying to tell me. He kept nodding yes."

Bazarian was as superstitious as the next man, and he regarded a person's deathbed confession or statement as being sacred holy writ. Therefore, the statement stunned him. An NKVD officer? Why?

He dismissed his adjutant, who almost ran in his haste to get away from his temperamental leader.

Why?

He tried to think. First, the guard was doubtless sincere in what he saw, or at least thought he saw. He had to think it really was the NKVD, and that would explain just how the terrorists had managed to get so close to the guards. The NKVD were gods in the army and could do what they wished and go wherever they desired.

That led to the second question: Was it really an NKVD officer? Again, he had to presume yes. Their uniforms were distinctive, and everyone who valued his life knew them. No one would make the mistake. Once they saw the crimson piping on the collar patches and the shield with the vertical sword in a blue oval, they knew that even the most trivial act of perceived disobedience could result in instant death through summary execution, or a frozen eternity spent in Siberia.

Therefore, why was the NKVD doing this to him? Was it revenge for the fool colonel whose name he could no longer even remember, or was it revenge for the failure to take Potsdam in the earlier assault? While attractive as motives, neither seemed credible. It had to be something deeper.

Of course. The explanation was clear and simple.

The Russian command wanted him to fail. He was one of the few non-Russians in a position of authority and he had been entrusted with the ultimate conquest of Potsdam. He knew that the siege was being given a high degree of publicity in the capitalist press and even in Moscow, and was a key part of Operation Red Inferno. If he succeeded, he would be a hero and probably even be promoted to lieutenant general, a rank he felt he richly deserved. If he succeeded, Stavka would be practically forced to recognize his efforts, and all Armenia would bathe in his glory.

But what if he failed?

Well, people would simply shrug and say, "What did you expect from some black-ass from the south, an Armenian, no less?" His disgrace would result in his loss of command and banishment to protecting some obscure border with a nation more despicable than Romania. If he failed, he would be replaced and his army removed so the Russians, the golden boys, could take the city and reap the renown.

It was so obvious. But what could he do? First, he would have to prove it was the NKVD. He would have to catch their man and then he would decide how to handle it. But what to use as bait?

PLATOON SERGEANT BAILEY lowered his binoculars and wiped his sweaty brow with a dirty cloth. He, Logan, and a handful of others were in a small fortified observation post dug into the ground just past the road from which the Russians had launched their earlier assault. General Miller had decided to extend the perimeter to provide earlier warning of the next Russian attack. Even though the Reds had been quiet for some time, everyone considered the resumption of the battle as inevitable. Thus, they had spent much of their time improving their already formidable defenses.

"Lieutenant, are sieges always this boring?"

Logan laughed and shifted the still unfamiliar weight of his Luger, which was holstered on his waist. Like many Americans, he had taken to carrying extra weapons from the liberated German stores. "Now just what makes you think I would know? And what makes you think this is boring? Why not consider it a vacation from reality?"

Bailey grinned. They had been friends before Logan's promotion. "Because now you're an officer and supposed to know all these things. Besides, I thought the army was a vacation from reality in the first place." Logan genially punched him on the arm and returned to watching the inactive and invisible Russians.

They had been on the outpost line for two days and were just about ready to rotate back to the main defense lines through the myriad of tunnels and deep trenches that made movement along the defensive lines fairly safe.

As he shifted, Logan felt the rustle of paper in his pocket. It was the letter from Elisabeth. He had read it a score of times and would read it again tonight. It was a very sensitive and eloquent statement of just how fond she was of him. At no time, he noted, had it mentioned the word *love*. They were both aware that their situation was both too sudden and too precarious for two very logical people to let their emotions run rampant. It wasn't easy, however.

On a number of occasions, Logan had tried to sort out his feelings for her. His first thought was that she wasn't what he'd always thought of as his type of woman. Mary Fran Collins had filled that bill. Larger-bosomed and taller, the naked Mary Fran was a lusty delight and they had reveled in each other's bodies in those frantic days before he shipped out. Lis, on the other hand, was petite.

Mary Fran had not been the first girl he'd had sex with; she was the second. That distinction went to a girl in high school—her name was Florence Something-or-other—and getting her in the sack was no great trick. Instead, it was more of a rite of passage. Short and plump, she had screwed just about half the boys in his senior class. "Just tell her you love her," one of his friends had instructed him, "and she'll hurt herself trying to get out of her dress." As it turned out, even that wasn't necessary. Florence What's-her-name, Jack recalled, just plain liked to screw.

That brought him back to Lis and what attracted him to her. She was short and he preferred tall. He liked blondes, and her hair was almost jet black. He also liked a woman's hair long and hers was, of necessity, chopped short. She was small-breasted, and he preferred them bosomy. She was thin, almost skinny, and he liked a little meat with his potatoes, as the saying went. The diet deprivations had blotched her complexion so that pimples were an almost constant problem for her. Well, they were for him too, so what the hell.

Even more surprising, since he had never been around little kids, Jack found that he actually liked Pauli, who seemed to like him too.

Given all that, why did he care for her so much? Sometimes he suspected the obvious, that they were lost souls who had been thrown together by nearly tragic circumstances. But he knew better. The relationship had expanded beyond that. She was, in her own way, very attractive and, by anyone's definition, intelligent, cultured, and mature. When he thought of that, he wondered just what she saw in him. Then he recalled the letter. Not too many people had ever called him good. Or honorable.

As to sex, he knew that she'd had one lover. He wasn't jealous, which surprised him, but he was envious and that did surprise him. He definitely did find Lis sexually desirable. So much for Mary Fran Collins and her great breasts.

They had talked about some of the others with them in Potsdam and their open sexual activity, and she had firmly stated that she would not have sex during the siege. "I will not copulate in a sewer or in a ruined house like so many of the German women are doing."

So were the American men, Jack thought, but declined to add. "When it happens," Lis continued, "it will be in a lovely room with a real bed and with a man I love very deeply."

"Anyone I know?" Jack had asked with mock innocence.

"Quite possibly," she had answered impishly. "I just adore Captain Dimitri. He's so manly; don't you think?"

Before he could reply, she had kissed him, fully and deeply.

Then, miracle of miracles, the next mail drop had brought Jack letters from his parents and his brother. All was well on the home front although everyone was shocked by the sudden and tragic turn the fighting had taken. They loved him, they were concerned for him, and they were all praying for him and wanted him to come home. The world knew that, along with the fighting now raging up and down Germany, there was a bunch of lonely GIs in Potsdam and all of America was concerned for them. Potsdam had become a symbol of American pride and resistance. He had sat there and wished there was some way he could tell his family that he loved them as well, but while mail could come in, it could not go out. He had missed so many opportunities in the past. Sometimes he had been such a stupid kid.

Unbidden tears had welled up and he had commenced to cry in a way he hadn't since he had been a small child. Elisabeth had started crying as well, and they had held each other tightly for comfort and protection from the rest of the world. When they stopped crying, they still held on to each other. Jack had never felt as close to anyone in his life as he had to her in those moments. He knew he would remember them forever. However long that was.

"Lieutenant?" It was Bailey again, snapping him out of his reverie. The binoculars were at his eyes but he wasn't seeing a thing. Hell, he had been so deep in thought the whole Russian army could have sneaked up on him. At least Bailey had been alert.

"Yeah, Sarge."

"While you were watching the Russians so intently, we got a message from the captain. We're being relieved in a couple of minutes."

Logan wondered if Bailey was being sarcastic about his being intent, and the twinkle in Bailey's eyes confirmed it. "Sergeant, there are a lot of Russians out there and I didn't want to miss any."

"Sure. But we are pulling out."

Logan scratched his beard. Not shaving was another result of being cut off from the rest of the army. They were out of razor blades and just about everyone was growing a beard. Elisabeth thought he looked like a Viking. She called him Jack the Red. "I don't think I'll miss this place."

"Me either," Bailey said. "You think Elisabeth will be waiting for us?"

Logan rattled around, gathering his equipment. "I hope so." He understood what the sergeant meant. Elisabeth and Pauli had started to hang around the platoon, and the boy had been adopted by the soldiers while they all tried to talk with the skinny, dark-haired waif with the bad complexion who always responded graciously. The platoon had adopted her as well, although Logan thought their collective feelings weren't quite as paternal as they were for Pauli. At any rate, they seemed to like her and weren't jealous of his much closer relationship with her. Bailey said it was just so nice to be able to talk to a woman who spoke English, even though it was with a screwy Canadian accent.

Relieved, the platoon snaked their way back to the main defensive line and the bunker they had built more than a month ago. At first it had been a chore; now it was their home. He settled his gear in the bunker and exited through the rear door. As Jack had both hoped and expected, Pauli and Elisabeth were waiting, and she had a big smile for him.

TRUE TO SOVIET military tradition, the headquarters of the Russian field armies was closer to the front lines than its allied counterparts would normally be. Soviet generals felt they had to smell gunpowder to show bravery to their soldiers. This often led to higher than ordinary casualty rates among Russian generals.

The city of Brunswick, only thirty miles from the Elbe River, had fallen two weeks earlier to the Red Army and was still a smoking ruin. It was less than fifty miles from Brunswick to the Leine River, the next natural obstacle the Russians would have to cross on their way to the Weser, the Rhine, and Antwerp. In the distance, the sound of artillery could be heard.

Marshal Zhukov looked at the numbers the report indicated and was appalled. The fight for Brunswick had cost nearly fifty thousand casualties. It was small comfort that they had badly mauled the American 19th Corps. The Soviets had been suckered into a street fight for a city the Yanks had never intended to hold for long. It was the result of his second in command, Vassily Chuikov's relative inexperience in handling large forces. The city should have been surrounded and left to rot like Potsdam. Chuikov was a good general and he would learn. He would have to. Zhukov was learning as well. The Americans were nasty fighters.

"This cannot happen again," Zhukov said firmly.

The smaller, darker-haired Chuikov nodded glumly. "I thought we could trap them. I was wrong. But"— he sighed—"wouldn't it have been wonderful to have bagged four American divisions, one of them airborne?"

Grudgingly, Zhukov had to agree. It was probably something he might have attempted had he been put in Chuikov's position. The victory that didn't happen would have punched a great hole in the American lines and bloodied them terribly, perhaps badly enough to make them pull out of the war. However, it hadn't worked out that way. The American general had sniffed out the trap and led Chuikov by the nose through the streets of Brunswick while he and his corps escaped largely intact. Even the lightly armed American 17th Airborne Division that Chuikov had so badly wanted to capture had only been wounded, not mortally damaged. It had been a mistake, but Chuikov was an aggressive bulldog who would fight again.

"No more," Zhukov said. "We cannot afford victories at such cost. A few more of these and we will have no army."

Chuikov accepted the rebuke in silence.

"Now," Zhukov said, "we must continue to plan for the future as Stalin and Stavka have defined it. The Americans have found our Achilles' heel and attacked it with great success. As you are aware, the oil situation has gone from merely bad to critical."

"Marshal Zhukov, I have already instituted a program of hoarding and rationing. I am confident that we will have enough for this campaign."

"As am I, but only if dire steps are taken. I have ordered all available fuel reserves shipped to you. Other armies will be allocated enough for defensive actions, but not enough to go on the offensive."

"Koniev and Rokossovsky will not be happy."

Zhukov flared. "I do not give a fuck if they are happy or sad! I only care that Operation Red Inferno is a success. I do not care if their soldiers starve or have to walk into battle carrying spears. I only want to drive the Americans out of Germany and take Antwerp!"

Zhukov brought his anger under control. "I am fairly certain that the Americans will withdraw quickly to the Weser when the Leine is crossed. The battles from the Elbe to here have given them ample time to prepare their defenses along the west bank of the Weser. I think you will advance rather quickly for the next few days after crossing the Leine. No, that is not my main concern."

"Then what is, comrade?"

"The war in the air, Vassily. I am afraid we are losing it. I had feared that would happen. We have been losing planes and men at a faster rate than I thought would occur. Stavka thought, and I agreed, that it would take the Americans far longer to move additional planes from the Pacific than it has. Worse, the fuel situation will be more critical for the air force than it will be for us."

Chuikov found neither statement hard to dispute. Since realizing that fuel depots were high-priority targets for the Allied planes, he had introduced a system of fuel distribution within his armies, which, although less efficient than depot storage, did have the benefit of disbursing the precious commodity. Some of his commanders had carried it to an extreme. They were reintroducing the expedient used in the early days of the war of strapping fifty-five-gallon drums of fuel to the outside of the tanks as a ready reserve. Many tanks carried more than one drum since no one was really certain when the next shipment would arrive from the scattered division or corps reserves.

Even though the T34s ran on diesel, which was less combustible than gasoline, storing it on the outside was still a dangerous practice. A rocket or a .50 caliber tracer could easily ignite the diesel and turn the tank into a very large iron torch. Even the American bazookas, ordinarily ineffective against a T34's armor, could prove lethal if they found the fuel.

Yet what had Zhukov meant when he said it would be even worse for the air force? "Comrade, how can it be harder for the air armies? After all, they do not have to drag their reserves around under the noses of the enemy like we do."

Zhukov chuckled. He was fond of Chuikov, who had fought and won at Stalingrad and then led the storming of central Berlin. "Correct, Vassily, but the difference is more subtle. We can manufacture large numbers of planes as replacements, but what about the replacement pilots? If they are to be effective, pilots must be trained in all aspects of flying.

"Vassily, we still have the vast spaces where they can be trained, and thousands of young men eager to die for Mother Russia, but we no longer have the fuel needed to train them properly. We have just given directives that the pilot training flights will immediately be cut by two thirds. Therefore, when replacements arrive at the front, they will be scarcely know how to take off and land. They will be easy prey for the

Allies. The same restrictions will be true for tank drivers, but it will not be as serious a problem to overcome."

Chuikov was dismayed. If that occurred, the aerial cover he counted on to support his massed armor and infantry attacks would be shredded and the enemy planes could rain hell upon his formations.

Chuikov was aghast. "Comrade, I need air support. If the air force continues to deteriorate, the Allies will do even more to savage my transportation system. If they are successful at that, it will not matter how many tanks and guns they produce in the Ural Mountain factories; they won't get here! It makes no sense to protect properties in Romania and the Caucasus that have already been destroyed and cannot be fixed in time to be of any help to us! Did you not explain this to Stalin?"

Zhukov was not put out by the younger man's vehemence. It was something he felt himself. "Stalin was adamant."

Chuikov rubbed his forehead in frustration. "Does this have anything to do with the rumored American superweapon?"

Zhukov blinked. How the devil did Chuikov know about that? "I don't know. Perhaps."

Chuikov laughed derisively. "Well, comrade, let me tell you something. I do not believe in superweapons any more than I believe in goblins and ghosts."

"I hope you are right," Zhukov said.

Zhukov was not certain what the Americans were up to. He knew only that it was supposed to be a giant bomb. But what sort of giant bomb? He had seen the effects of giant bombs, blockbusters, but the size of the bomb was limited by the weight and bulk that a plane could carry. The blockbusters were impressive, but not that devastating and surely limited by aircraft technology.

Zhukov was puzzled. Just how much larger could the American monster bomb be? If it was larger than the mammoth blockbusters, just what would they use to carry the monster? he wondered. Perhaps Chuikov was right. Perhaps it was all a deception on the part of the Americans to scare first the Germans and now Russia. How could there be such a thing as he had heard rumored? And how could it be that Stalin had fallen for the deception?

CHAPTER 21

*T*here were two sets of hospitals in besieged Potsdam: military and civilian. Most of the medical personnel were military but still found time to help out at the main civilian hospital, located in a ruined hotel. Work had been done to seal windows and roofs, but the building was still stark, drab, and poorly ventilated.

With the need for her services as a translator diminishing, Lis found herself with time on her hands and a need to do something useful. Working at the hospital was an easy choice.

"Look at them," she said to Logan. "This shouldn't be happening in the twentieth century."

Lis was wearing a dirty smock and her short hair was a mess. She was tired, but appeared satisfied. She admitted that the work took her mind off the terrible things she'd seen and it permitted her to help others.

Jack couldn't argue. Rows of beds were filled with people whose conditions wouldn't normally exist in the type of civilized society he was used to. Starvation, malnutrition from bad food, dysentery from contaminated water, and even a few cases of scurvy were present. In addition there were numerous cases of wounds from the intermittent shelling and from gunfire. Civilians were always getting killed or wounded, but, other than the occasional callously ignored body by the roadside, this was the first time he'd seen real evidence of it.

Thanks to the renewed airdrops, there was minimally sufficient food and the military was providing bandages and medicine. One colonel had complained about scarce resources going to their former enemy, but the doctors had basically told him to shove his complaints up his ass. They reminded the colonel that they had taken an oath to help, regardless.

In a separate room she would not let him enter were a group of women. They had been gang-raped, beaten, and sometimes mutilated by the Soviets as they took revenge for similar atrocities committed by the Germans during their advance in Russia. Unspoken was the fact that such would have been her fate if the Reds had taken her and would still be if Potsdam fell.

"Most of them are not ready to come out into the world, and certainly not to be stared at by a strange man. Some will never be ready. They will be put in asylums once this is over." She smiled wanly. "I hope."

She showed him the children. There were only a dozen of them. "The children and the old people are the weakest and most have simply died. These are the lucky ones."

"As was Pauli?"

"Yes."

Several children stared at him, shyly and hesitantly. He was an American, and they were now taught that the Americans were the good guys. Some had casts and bandages and all looked reasonably well fed.

A couple, however, stared blankly into the distance. "They've walled themselves off, haven't they?" he asked, and she nodded.

Finally, they passed a family of five, two adults in their thirties and three small children. They were gaunt and filthy, although otherwise they appeared unhurt.

"Every now and then a miracle occurs," Lis said. "These people arrived yesterday. Somehow they managed to make it through the Red Army lines and up to your defenses without being hurt. They said their guardian angel was watching over them, and I believe it."

Jack could understand getting through the Soviets. They were overconfident and sloppy and ripe for a counterattack if only the Potsdam defenders had the resources. The real luck came in not getting shot by nervous GIs. He didn't ask if the woman had been assaulted. It was far too common an occurrence to even think of asking.

"These refugees said that the Russians are stripping the land bare of food and leaving the Germans to starve. You Americans are so unlike them. You wouldn't do anything like that, would you?"

"That might depend on how hungry I was," he said grimly. "So don't canonize us just yet."

But he would relay the offhand comment to General Miller's headquarters. Were they aware that the Reds were out of food as well? Scrounging and stealing from locals could feed the Red Army only for so long. At some time, they would run out of food and get very, very hungry. And what would they do then? Of course, by that time everyone in Potsdam could be starving as well if the food drops were cut off.

Or would the presence of any food at all in Potsdam make it a more desirable target by this Bazarian person?

Lis squeezed his arm, and they stepped outside and breathed in the fresh air. "I wanted you to see the hospital. If the Russians make it in, they will all be brutally murdered. I've heard what happens when they storm a hospital. It will be an orgy of horrors."

Jack shook his head. That could not be permitted to happen.

COLONEL PAUL TIBBETTS sucked in the mild, cool air of Iceland. After the stifling heat of Tinian in the South Pacific, he found it refreshing. He did wonder just how cold it would get in winter if this was what they called summer.

Considered one of the best pilots in the air force, Tibbetts had flown as personal pilot for Generals Mark Clark and Dwight Eisenhower, and was now the commanding officer of the 509th Composite Group. A demanding and superbly organized taskmaster, Tibbetts had received his orders to pack up and right away move halfway around the world. He had loaded the massive B-29 Super Fortresses with essential supplies and a number of ground personnel and, after several refueling stops, had landed on the cold ground of Iceland. None of his men were surprised at the suddenness of their change of orders and direction. They all knew what was happening in Europe.

The rest of the 509th's people and equipment would come over on slower C-47s. The 509th consisted of 15 aircrews of 9 men each and an enormous ground crew of 1,700 men, all experts in maintaining and servicing the B-29s.

One thing about Iceland did please him. There were few other air force personnel about to give him and his men a hard time. On Tinian, they had been the butt of jokes and teasing from other bomber crews since all the 509th seemed to do was train or go on reconnaissance runs over Japan. They never went on real bombing runs and they never appeared to go in harm's way. While just about everyone assumed they were training for something special, the fact that they never shared in the danger of bombing Japan frankly pissed off a lot of other aircrews.

Tibbetts's men did know they were training for something special, only they didn't know exactly what either.

Training had begun in Wendover, Utah, and then moved to Tinian, and now, with the Russian menace on the horizon, to Iceland. Technically, Iceland was part of Europe. The part that shits, one of his sergeants had said upon seeing the place, and to a certain extent Tibbetts had to agree.

Training for the 509th generally consisted of taking off, maneuvering, and landing with enormous weights in the bomb bay. The pilots also had to contend with extra quantities of reserve fuel which made the Super Fortress a difficult plane to handle. They had also made practice runs with a strange-looking bomb that was filled with ordinary explosives. Without anything being said, the pilots clearly understood that they were training to drop some other, new kind of bomb.

Tibbetts had proven scathingly demanding of his pilots with regard to accuracy and timing. Only he knew that the decision had been made to use pilots to guide the bomb and not drop by radio control, since no one knew just how the atomic bomb would behave.

All in all and despite the confusion resulting from the sudden move from Tinian, he was satisfied. His men were responding magnificently, as he'd known they would. That left only the question of a target, and his men were speculating openly on the obvious—that the new bomb would be dropped on a Russian target. Only he in the 509th knew that they would shift to England before their attack and that it would not be on Moscow or any other major Russian city.

Use of the bomb, therefore, would be tactical and not strategic. It also meant revising and rethinking the tactic that had the pilots of the 509th flying in isolated groups of three over the Japanese islands. The purpose was to get the Japanese used to the sight of the small groups of bombers and their relative harmlessness. He would have to reinstate it over Europe, where Russian airpower was much stronger than that of the depleted Japs. It saddened him to think that some of his planes might be lost in such training, but it was a price they would have to pay. The B-29's maximum ceiling was 36,000 feet, which put it at the same maximum as some of the Red fighters.

One of his pilots, a very young major, walked up to him, grinning. "Hey, Colonel, we're getting up a group that's gonna find a sauna in town. Are you interested?"

"Not now, thanks," Tibbetts responded politely. Sweating in a sauna didn't appeal to him. He'd sweated enough on Tinian.

"By the way, sir, I drew Berlin in the target pool. I think I got screwed out of five dollars. There's nothing left in Berlin to bomb, is there?"

Tibbetts smiled slightly. "Nothing that I know of. Consider yourself thoroughly and royally screwed."

The major walked away. They both had known that Tibbetts wouldn't be interested in finding a sauna, and he hadn't given out any information regarding a target. What the major hadn't known was that Tibbetts didn't know the target either. It didn't matter. Someone would tell him when the time came. He had too many other things on his mind to worry about that.

WHEN THE SOVIET infantry reached the Leine River, they did not stop. Instead, the shock troops swarmed across in an assault that was effective because it was so unexpected and illogical. Logical thinking dictated at least waiting until the launches and small boats were ready, or until the soldiers could be covered by artillery and air, or if their armor could cross with them. In this case, General Chuikov had told his men to grab anything that would float, and swim, wade, or paddle their way across.

It helped that the Leine was not a major obstacle. In some places, a man could have stood on one bank and thrown a rock to the other. Thus, the Americans had been shocked and confused by the sight of hundreds of Russian soldiers running into the water and emerging wet and bedraggled on the other side. It simply wasn't the way Americans fought, and many a local commander was caught off guard.

American retaliation came quickly, and the Soviet infantry on the western bank quickly found themselves scourged by American artillery and mortars. Attempts to reinforce the tenuous foothold on the western bank were mauled and few reinforcements reached the other side. Those that did dug in and waited for help. It was the armor's turn.

Suslov looked through the hatch as the column's lead tank gingerly approached the water. The battalion's colonel thought the river could be forded, and there was only one way to be certain. If that was the case, they could save hours that would otherwise be spent waiting for engineers to build a bridge, hours in which the American planes and guns would continue to pound the bridgehead, shelling and bombing the other vehicles that were lining up to cross.

Suslov opened the hatch a little higher so he could see just a bit better. He was not going to poke his head all the way out. There was too much danger from snipers and from all the shrapnel and lethal debris that was flying around

The tank selected to test the river eased itself into the water like some giant jungle beast. Maybe a hippo, Suslov thought. It paused as the water deepened and its treads churned brown mud and froth. The tank got about halfway across when it lurched, settled deeper into the water, and stalled.

"I think it hit a mud pocket," Suslov commented.

"Fairly logical," said Latsis drily. "After all, it is a river."

"Aw, shit," snapped Suslov. "Look at those damned fools."

The tank in the middle of the river had quickly attracted the attention of machine gunners on the American side, and the water around it was splashed by bullets. While in potential danger from American artillery or an airplane, the crew of the stuck tank had nothing to fear from machine guns. Even if bullets should hit the fuel drum strapped behind the turret, the possibility of explosion was not all that great. As Suslov and the others knew, those drums were now fairly empty and they were awaiting replenishment. The tanks would have to go forward on what they had in their internal tanks.

The driver's hatch on the grounded tank opened and a man climbed out. He was quickly followed by a second while the turret hatch opened and the other two crew members joined them. They paused for a moment on the tank as if they were afraid to jump into the water.

"Hurry," Suslov hollered even though they were too far away to hear.

Almost immediately, one of them went limp and fell into the river. Suslov could hear the sound of bullets hitting metal as the machine guns rained shells on the tank.

"Help them," he yelled, and the machine gun by the driver began to chatter as it searched for the source of the American fire. He presumed it was Latsis doing the shooting. It was too late. As if swept by a wind, the remaining crewmen fell into the water and slowly floated away.

"Damn it." Suslov pounded his knee. "What a waste."

Latsis ceased firing. There had never been a real target. He had been trying to provide indirect cover for the now dead tankers. The Americans were too well hidden. "At least the comrade colonel used his head. That was one of the replacement tanks and crew, inexperienced chicklings."

"What do you mean?" Suslov had a feeling he was not going to like the answer. Latsis had been acting even more strangely lately. Just the other day Suslov had caught him slashing an American corpse.

Latsis chuckled. "Haven't you noticed? Whenever something like this comes up, the colonel sends out one of the new chicklings. If we lose one of them, who cares? They had no experience anyhow, and another new tank with four or five warm bodies will show up sooner or later. But if he loses one of us, his elite, then his loss is irreplaceable."

Suslov thought of telling Latsis he was full of crap, but the man was probably right and Suslov wasn't particularly upset about not having to take on the muddy little river. He scarcely knew the new tankers. They had arrived a couple of days ago, all fresh-faced and eager, and now they were dead.

Latsis was right on one count. The new crew had been almost ludicrously inept. They knew little more about their T34 than how to drive it. Even that skill had failed them when they had attempted to cross the river. Suslov had the nagging feeling that he and Latsis could have navigated the Leine with little problem. Now they would have to wait for a bridge to be built. Perhaps it was better. Maybe the colonel was making the right decision by husbanding his dwindling supply of skilled human resources.

A little while later, the engineers made an appearance and a bridge started to take shape. As this occurred, the fire on the Soviet soldiers who had crossed earlier slackened as the bridge became the primary target. More infantry crossed, again using small boats. Several of them were hit and more bodies floated gently on the Leine. Overhead, there was a second battle as Stormoviks, protected by Yaks, tried to take out the American positions. The Americans called on their fighters, and P-47s dived among the Yaks. The American planes were better but the Yaks more numerous, and this permitted the armored Stormoviks to do their bloody work.

Even so, Suslov kept his hatches closed and his tank buttoned up. Whenever his men complained about the stifling heat, he told them to be quiet and listen to the sound of rain on the hull. Only it wasn't rain. It was the clatter of small pieces of metal impacting on the armor. Inside they were safe. Outside, the poor, bloody infantry and engineers were having their flesh penetrated.

After what seemed an eternity, the bridge was completed. First across was another swarm of infantry to finally reinforce the earlier river crossers—if, that is, any were still alive.

Suslov's tank was the fourth one across. He noticed that the lead tank in this effort also belonged to a replacement crew. Latsis was right. The colonel was very consistent. Reinforcements had brought the battalion up to twenty tanks, and many of their crews were very inexperienced indeed.

There was no real embankment on the other side of the Leine. The river had been channelized by the industrious Germans. Suslov's tank was soon on the flat plain and he was watching a line of buildings a quarter mile away. It looked like another of the damned little villages that speckled the landscape in Germany. If defended, it would be hell to take.

"What do you think?" Suslov asked Latsis. The man was probably crazy but he did know his tactics.

"They have an observation post in the church and they're dug in along the ground levels of the houses. It's just like every other time we see a setup like this. Hell, there's only so much they can do."

Someone must have agreed with them. The church erupted as shells hit it, tumbling the steeple. Latsis laughed. The entire armored battalion was now across. The tanks began to fan out and move forward, accompanied by trotting infantry who tried to hide behind them. They had to move quickly. To sit still was to die. They had no idea how long the Yank planes would stay preoccupied with the Stormoviks or what evil was hidden in the village.

The answer came quickly. Suslov saw the flashes of antitank guns coming from the buildings. There was an explosion nearby as a T34 took a hit. "Faster," Suslov urged. His tank surged ahead and the infantry were running to keep up.

There was another blast and then the feeling of heat. "What the hell was that?" Martynov, the young gunner, asked.

Suslov turned the turret and squinted through his view port. A great cloud of smoke and flame was enveloping two of the battalion's tanks. Smoking bodies lay on the ground and he saw a couple of men tumbling and burning, trying to put out the fires. It had to have been either a mine or some goddamn thing dropped by a plane. Intuitively, he decided it was some kind of incendiary bomb. There was a banging, clattering sound as bullets struck the turret and hull from close range. Aside from the noise and the terror they inflicted, they did no harm.

Martynov fired the cannon at a building that was coming up quickly. The front wall disappeared, but there was nothing to indicate any damage to an American fortification. The Soviet infantry moved into the village. They crouched over, cowering as if they expected to be shot at any moment. He watched as a couple of them had those expectations fulfilled and fell to the ground. The Red Army had crossed the Leine but was paying a terrible price.

Finally, they were through the line of buildings and the firing from the ground slackened off, although American planes still whirled through the sky. They had defeated the Stormoviks and Yaks, and were now after prey on the ground. After a short while, even they pulled away, their bombs dropped and their bullets fired.

The exhausted tank crews found places to pretend they were hiding their iron steeds. Hell, the Yanks knew where they were and could come back at any time. Suslov checked the number of remaining vehicles in the battalion. There were fifteen. In one skirmish they had suffered 25 percent casualties. Worse, not all of them were Latsis's inexperienced "chicklings"; a couple were fairly experienced crews. Fire from the sky, Suslov concluded, could not differentiate the elite from the chicklings.

Suslov opened the hatch and climbed out. It was a profound relief to be outside. He checked the tank for damage and found nothing serious. The extra fuel drum, however, had been shredded. Even though it had been 80 percent empty, it was a small miracle that there hadn't been some sort of fire.

Latsis yelled down to him that the colonel wanted to see him immediately. Suslov trotted over to the command tank and presented himself. He knew he looked like hell and didn't care. He noted that the colonel looked like he had been wallowing in dirt as well.

The colonel, an older man of almost thirty, nodded to him. "Good to see you made it."

"Thank you, comrade Colonel. It's good to see you as well." He meant the comment. The colonel was a good man who tried to care for his troops, even the new ones when he could. Suslov was shocked at the lines of fatigue on the other man's face. He wondered if that was how he looked to Latsis and the rest of his crew.

"Your captain's dead. You will take over for him. And by the way, we have a new political officer. He likes to be called Comrade Boris." The colonel rolled his eyes. That communicated enough. Comrade Boris was an asshole.

"Yes, sir. Thank you." Suslov wheeled and returned to his vehicle. Shit, he thought, ten minutes ago all I had to worry about was one tank. Now I have five tanks to watch out for and we don't have any reserve fuel. Worse, two of the crews are raw trainees. Latsis had laughed at them yesterday and said they didn't even know how to wipe their asses without hurting themselves or getting shit on their feet. He had to admit that Latsis, crazy or not, was again correct and had a way with words.

Perhaps he would let Latsis help out with the training of the new crews. Maybe they would even get some more replacements, although he would rather have some fuel. A T34 had a supposed range of 250 miles, but reality pushed that down considerably. Every second with the engine idling, or every time a tank had to backtrack or maneuver, ate into the distances they could cover. He also wondered when they would start to get some of the improved T34s or the Josef Stalin monsters. He would settle for a new T34, the improved version of which had an 85 mm gun instead of a 76. It also had an additional crewman, and he was curious as to how another human being would fit into the already cramped, hot, and stinking quarters. Maybe he would get Comrade Boris and find out?

Well, rumor had it that the Yanks would now pull back to the Weser and concede this last move to the defensive line they'd been working on for two months. If true, that would give him some time to whip his litter of young pups into shape. When the time came to cross the Weser, only the fit and cruel would survive.

Is this what I've become? he suddenly thought. Cruel? Well, he had survived, hadn't he? All the way from Stalingrad to this dirty little river in the middle of Germany. If it was necessary to be cruel to survive, then he could live with that. Perhaps he could someday change into the human being he had been so many years ago. At least his cruelty was not the same insane variety as Latsis's was. Suslov recalled that Latsis had not always been that way.

"The war has made us all monsters," he said.

Latsis stuck his head out of the tank and grinned cheekily. "All hail comrade tank commander, captain and leader."

Suslov shook his head. He would gather his chicklings and get to work. Lives were at stake, and one of them was his own.

CHAPTER 22

Wolfgang von Schumann eyed the scruffy-looking group of American GIs carrying supplies from the depot up to their units. More and more, he thought, the Yanks were beginning to look like nothing more than a bunch of pirates. Perhaps it was the beards, which were totally out of character. Americans were supposed to be clean-shaven and boyish. These men looked like genial thugs. Then there was the question of their uniforms. Despite the fact that resupply efforts had picked up, many were in rags and tatters, and sometimes wore a miscellany of civilian clothing and liberated German uniforms when necessary or simply convenient. Uniforms in June had a lower shipping priority than food, medicine, and weapons.

Even when there was a choice, the young Americans had shown a marked preference for German equipment to replace theirs that had worn out or to enhance what they already had. While they had not started wearing German helmets, they had no qualms about using German submachine guns, machine guns, pistols, and antitank weapons. The discovery of the Nazi weapons cache in Potsdam had given the American warriors a chance to shop and they had taken advantage of it. Antitank *panzerfausts* were now a part of every unit's arsenal, and the enlisted American infantry had started carrying sidearms along with the officers. Von Schumann had never been able to see the reason behind the rule that prohibited enlisted men from carrying pistols. Give them every advantage they could, he thought, even if it was only psychological, as he thought pistols were relatively useless in modern warfare.

The advantages of the German antitank weapons were far more than psychological. The American tank-killer weapons were deplorable. Neither the bazookas nor the towed antitank guns could penetrate the armor of a T34. Thank God he had convinced General Miller to use the Nazi 88 mm antiaircraft guns, which could double as extremely effective antitank weapons. Rommel had figured that out in North Africa and nearly destroyed the British armor in the process.

Having come late to the ground war, the Yanks had not had to face the wrath of either the German Panthers or the Luftwaffe when they were at full strength. Now they had to deal with the Russians, who had largely destroyed both the Panzers and the Luftwaffe. It was not a healthy situation, and the Americans were paying for it with the blood of their young men.

Von Schumann snapped to attention as General Miller emerged from his command bunker with Captain Leland. The look in Leland's eyes told von Schumann that he was still having a hard time getting used to Germans being on his side. Did he think von Schumann felt all that comfortable saluting an American?

"Herr General, good morning," he said to Miller, and he nodded to Leland, who nodded back. "May I talk to you about supplies for a moment?"

"Let me guess," said Miller, "you'd like some more for your people."

"If it is possible, yes. Even though most of the population of Potsdam fled before your arrival, there are still several thousand civilians in the perimeter and, while we are grateful for your generosity, many are still hungry."

Leland responded. "Thanks to the brave men of the Eighth Air Force, Oberst, we are only now beginning to reach what we consider minimum food standards. I think it is premature to increase rations, particularly for civilians, until we have a reserve to fall back on in case the Russians sever that lifeline again."

Von Schumann agreed with Leland and took Miller's silence to indicate that he agreed as well. It was what he had expected, but he felt he had to ask. As yet there was no real hunger problem among the civilians, but they were very definitely on the edge of it. The two Americans started to walk away and von Schumann fell in step with them.

The reintroduction of the airlift had come as a surprise to the men, although Miller had been informed that something of the sort would be attempted. Someone at Bradley's HQ had brilliantly decided that a

B-17 could carry several tons of supplies instead of bombs and had reconfigured a number of them for that purpose. For a couple of weeks now, thirty or forty of the Flying Fortresses would fly overhead and hundreds of packages of supplies would be parachuted down. The bombers were protected by hordes of fighters as well as their own guns, and the Red air forces nearby had apparently decided they had better things to do than attack bombers that weren't bombing anything. The flights were also erratically timed to keep the Reds from setting up an ambush.

Along with rations, medical equipment, ammunition, and replacement weapons, they had also dropped mail and other items of a personal nature to the besieged army. The result had been a surge in morale as the soldiers realized that they were not forgotten and alone. Everyone knew that any major Russian effort could stop the supplies, or the American armies could be pushed too far west for the effort to take place, but for now they were a godsend.

Miller paused and turned. "By the way, I caught hell when Simpson and Bradley told Ike I was using your men."

"Does this mean we must cease?" Von Schumann sincerely hoped not. The Germans fully understood the weapons while the Yanks, willing learners, did not have the experience. Besides, using his soldiers would free Americans for other tasks.

"Naw. I was told that it was my responsibility, a command decision on my part, although I would have to answer for it at another time. I told them I sincerely hoped they would get my ass out of here so I could be called on the carpet for it, and that sort of shut them up. Just their way of admitting there's nothing they can do to stop me. I think they agreed with me, and I wouldn't be surprised to see Ike do something like it with the rest of the army."

"Good." Von Schumann meant it sincerely. Anything to defeat the Russians.

"But more food, Oberst? That, I'm afraid, will have to wait like Leland says. We have to build up a stockpile and hide it from possible harm."

Again, von Schumann had to agree with the assessment. In the two months since they'd been trapped in Potsdam, he had been awed by the manner in which the Americans had dug and tunneled their way throughout the perimeter until it was a veritable honeycomb of underground passages. Other than the psychological need for sunshine, there was no need for them to be standing around outside right now.

There were now three lines of interconnected defenses, all supported by antitank guns, dug-in tanks, and tank destroyers, and protected artillery. Every possible target outside the perimeter had been calculated and mathematically zeroed in on. Sometimes the zeroing had been done with live ammo when the Reds gave them something to shoot at. Potsdam had truly become a citadel.

The American engineers had excavated large underground rooms for storage and for living. Although they were heavily reinforced, von Schumann had doubts whether some of them could stand up to repeated hits by Russian big guns.

All they could do was hold on and hope the Americans won the war. It was so frustrating knowing that events were so totally out of one's control. Whether they were ultimately liberated, killed, or became prisoners depended on events taking place far to their west.

"General, one other thing. That correspondent wants to do a story on me. Do you think that is wise?"

Miller chuckled. "No, Oberst. Not at this time. Tell him to leave you alone. But I will have to give the little bastard credit for thinking about it. I may just solve the problem by having him shot and dropped into the Havel like I thought about doing when we caught the guy who was printing up the Commie literature."

Even the dour Leland smiled at that. The Communist sympathizer with the mimeograph machine they'd caught had turned out to be a boy of fourteen. He'd been turned over to von Schumann, who had slapped him around until he cried and then convinced him he was lucky not to be shot. He was now working in the hospital dealing with people who'd been brutalized by the Red Army, and perhaps gaining a new perspective on life.

The correspondent, Walter Ames from Los Angeles, had successfully flown a two-seat Piper Cub all the way in from Hanover. He had stayed at treetop height to make himself invisible to the Russian planes as well as to fly over any trigger-happy infantry before they could aim and fire. With incredible panache, he'd had to land in Russian-occupied territory to refuel from five-gallon cans he'd carried on board his tiny craft. He'd also saved enough fuel to fly himself back. Or so he hoped. Much depended on where the American armies might be when he decided to leave.

Ames had also brought his own shortwave radio and generator, which he used to file his stories. This had necessitated the use of an American officer to function as his censor to ensure that he didn't divulge anything important. As befitted the risks he had taken to get to Potsdam, Ames was pushy and aggressive.

Miller, however, could not argue with yet another leap in morale brought on by the presence of the reporter. He'd gone from unit to unit and taken down names and relayed information by radio about the soldiers to their loved ones. He was particularly insistent that the wounded be the first to send messages back home that they were okay, and Miller had quickly concurred. When the fighting first started, the wounded's next of kin had received only a telegram stating that their loved one was wounded in action. Normally, this would have been followed up by further information, or even a letter or phone call from the soldier as he was evacuated to the rear. Because they were cut off this hadn't happened, and Miller totally sympathized with the frustrations that the families must be feeling.

But now was not the time to let Ames tell the world that an ex-Nazi held a position of authority and influence in Potsdam.

"Leland," Miller said, "I've changed my mind. Let Ames live for a few more days. Just keep him out of my hair."

THE MOVE OF SHAEF's field headquarters from Reims to nearby Compiègne had been necessitated by the fact that the Russians had located the first site and launched several very strong bombing attacks against it. When these had been beaten off, the Reds then tried sending in single planes, hoping they could sneak through and kill some Allied leaders. When one lone plane succeeded and a bomb fell on a mess hall and killed more than fifty men, wounding many others, including several generals, it was decided to move to a safer location.

Burke parked his jeep and immediately noticed the tension and bustle. There had always been a sense of urgency in the headquarters but this was different. Something had happened, and the tone of voices and the sense of grim urgency said it wasn't good. He knew better than to approach Beetle Smith in a time of crisis, but he did want information as to what was happening.

Luck was with him as he recognized the disfigured British officer, Major Charles Godwin. He walked up to the man and grabbed his arm.

"Charles, what on earth's going on? Everyone seems in such a panic."

Godwin's scarlike mouth opened in a smile. "Nothing so important as to make one do away with politeness. Now, how have you been? Met any interesting Russians lately?"

Burke shook his head in disbelief. "As a matter of fact I've been away for several days checking prisoners, and returned to find SHAEF moved and the new place in an uproar. The Russian POWs had nothing new to add."

"Nothing?"

"Well, they did complain about supply shortages and they definitely feel the Russian air force has let them down, but nothing new of a political nature. The Reds still seem to be hoarding most of their elite soldiers for future battles."

"Ah," said Godwin, "not so much anymore."

Burke felt a twinge of dread. "What do you mean?"

"What I mean and why I am here is because the Russians have gone and right royally buggered Montgomery. Were you familiar with the tactical situation regarding the British Army?"

"A little," Burke admitted. "I know they are to the north of us."

"Well, they still are, only not quite as many of us as before. As we were still holding on to Hamburg, British lines were rather extended and there were some calls from Ike to Monty that he should give up Hamburg before he got outflanked. At any rate, Monty declined and the Russians hit the point where your army connected with ours and rammed its way in between. It was a typical Russian attack. They swarmed and probed until they found a weak point, and then they blasted their way through. The Reds are now racing toward Bremen, and eight British divisions have been cut off and are retreating into German-held Holstein while your army pulls back to the south. Hamburg, of course, is belatedly being abandoned and Montgomery is having a snit, complaining about being abandoned by Ike."

"Is it as bad as it sounds?"

"Perhaps worse. There are almost a hundred thousand British soldiers in jeopardy. We estimate that Rokossovsky, the Russian commander, has at least half a million against us. Thus, there is no chance that we will be able to go on the offensive and rescue them. Our soldiers will have to continue to retreat north through Doenitz's rump republic of Germany."

"Good."

"Ah, Steven, but it will remind everyone of the possibility of another Dunkirk. As you are well aware, there is a large antiwar movement in Britain, and this will fuel their fire. It may even cost Churchill his job."

"Unbelievable how much trouble you've gotten into while I was gone."

"Ike, however, is pushing for a second alternative. He wants the British to link up with the Germans and fight alongside each other instead of contemplating a humiliating withdrawal while our ex-enemies cover our backsides. It is causing an absolute uproar in London."

Godwin smiled wickedly. "On the other hand, perhaps we'll get lucky and Montgomery will be relieved of his command."

Burke was shocked. He had known that Montgomery was not held in high esteem by the American command, but was Godwin speaking heresy about the hero of El Alamein?

"Charles, I thought he was your best general?"

"Then God save Britain. No, Monty is an adequate general who can perform well when he is given time to plan an act accordingly. When he has to create, he fails. He won at El Alamein because he had two months to plan the battle and he outnumbered and outgunned Rommel. He failed at Arnhem because it was too ambitious and novel, and he made it work too slowly. Personally, I thought it ludicrous that he wanted to be the overall ground commander and lead a narrow-front drive to Berlin. It would have been disastrous." He smiled his ghastly smile. "I will never admit such heresy in public, of course.

"And when I said Monty was in a bit of a snit, I said so with typical and elegant British understatement. The shock of the Russian attack has brought him to a state of near hysteria and collapse. He is scarcely able to function, and General Crerar, another second-rate intellect who doesn't get along with Monty, is in effective control of Monty's

21st Army Group, which now includes the First Canadian Army and what's left of the British Second Army. If he doesn't get control of himself, Monty may be evacuated to England."

Burke was stunned. Yet another reversal for the Allies, who had been in almost continuous retreat since the first week of May. It was now the end of June and it looked like the Allied defensive lines were beginning to crumble. He knew few Englishmen, but if the typical soldier was anything like Charles Godwin, he must be a truly formidable fighting man, and the British, too, were giving ground.

"What happened to the idea that the Reds were too low on fuel for an attack against Montgomery?" Burke asked.

Godwin laughed. "It appears there was sufficient for Rokossovsky to knock my beloved England out of the war with his sudden and unexpected attack."

"What shall we do?" Burke asked.

"Well, since both of us are too unimportant to be involved in anything significant at this point, let us go and renew our acquaintance. I believe it is your turn to provide refreshments."

Burke chuckled. Perhaps it wasn't the end of the world after all. "I managed to salvage some cognac on my travels. Had I not taken it, it might have fallen into evil and irresponsible hands. Will it be adequate?"

"Beggars can't be choosers, Steven, although I will beg if I have to. Cognac sounds marvelous. Lead on, Colonel Burke, and I do hope it is a large bottle."

TONY LAY ON his belly in the tall grass and peered through his binoculars at their intended target. Joe Baker, the OSS man, was beside him with Vaslov and Anton waiting farther away at their camp.

"What do you think?" Baker asked.

Any sort of request for an opinion from Baker pleased Tony. The man obviously knew a lot about how to wage war on a small scale, and usually the shoe was on the other foot with Tony asking the questions. He also thought Joe was testing him. Tony refocused the binoculars. It was only one tanker truck, but it wasn't very well guarded. One sentry outside and one in the cab who looked asleep. The outside sentry didn't appear to be paying much attention to the world and stopped every now and then to take an unsteady sip from his canteen. Tony chuckled. It sure as hell wasn't water.

Tony looked around at the deepening shadows. It was getting darker with every moment. "Let's go get it," he said.

"Look again, Tony."

"At what?" Tony was chagrined. He had missed something important and Joe was now going to tell him exactly what it was. He hated this part of their relationship, but it was making him a better soldier.

"Look at the tires on the truck. What kind of shape are they in?"

"They look fine to me, nice and round."

"That's right, nice and round and full of air. If that tanker was full of fuel, don't you think it would flatten out the tires just a little bit?"

"Shit, Joe, that fucker's empty."

"That's right, and this place is a trap."

Tony swore silently. It had been his fault that the sentry had gotten away the other night. He could have sworn the man was dead. After all, his throat had been cut and he was bleeding like a pig the last time Tony saw him. Joe had sliced him, but it was Tony's job to make sure that the man was dead and he had failed. There should have been two corpses in the burning cab that night, not just one. Now it looked like the Russians were on to them.

"Sorry, Joe."

"Don't worry. It was only a matter of time before they did something like this. Look, we still don't know if the guy died and told them about the uniform. All that's certain is that the Russians are getting tired of us blowing up their tanker trucks. That was bound to happen."

The comment made Tony feel a little better. "So what do we do now?"

"Follow me."

Tony did as directed and the two men circled around the truck, always maintaining their distance from it. They quickly found three places where a full squad of Russians soldiers lay in wait. "Too dangerous," Baker said in understatement, and Tony heartily concurred.

It was now very dark and they had no difficulty exiting the area without being seen. "Well, what the hell do we do now?" Tony asked.

"Are you up for some adventure?"

What the hell have we been doing? he wanted to ask. "Sure."

It turned out that Joe Baker's idea of adventure consisted of prowling through the Russian encampments and looking for targets of opportunity. With a dozen men waiting to ambush them at the truck, he concluded that the security might be lax elsewhere. He was right.

As on the first night they had met, they located several small motor pools and truck parks and this night they entered them stealthily. Unwilling to risk an explosion, they satisfied themselves by pouring dirt in the gas tanks. Tony killed a Russian who, apparently drunk, had wandered into a grove of trees, while Joe sliced the throats of two men who had fallen asleep too far from their comrades.

As Tony wiped the blood from his knife, it occurred to him that he was a far different animal than had lived in New Jersey. At first, he found that taking a life was awful. Now it was awful because it was so damned easy. He wanted to talk to someone, a priest, for instance. His big brother Sal was a priest. When he got back home he would have to talk to him and find out whether he was committing some sort of sin. In the meantime, killing Reds helped provide a slim chance that he would get home to go to Confession.

If he didn't stop thinking about home and stuff and stay alert, he reminded himself, he might not make it away from these Russians, much less home. Neither man had any doubt regarding their fate if the Russians should capture them. A quick death would be fortunate.

It was the middle of the night before they called a halt and returned to where Vaslov and Anton waited. They quickly packed their gear, buried the uniform, and commenced to move. It was also time to get a long way from the Russians. Whoever had set the ambush at the truck would be very angry and just likely to start a manhunting sweep that would uncover them. Vaslov and Anton had told them just how ruthless the Russians could be when dealing with partisans or irregulars. Anyone they caught who might be a suspect, they would simply execute and hope they got the right person in the crowd of deaths. He realized their actions might cause innocent men to suffer if the Russians did start sweeping up people, but he couldn't help that. He had a war to fight and war was hell.

They would lie low and rest for a couple of days and start the process all over again.

"Hey, Joe. Fourth of July's comin' up soon, ain't it?"

"Yeah?"

"What'ya say we set up for some special fireworks."

Joe laughed. "That, my friend, sounds like a marvelous idea."

Tony could have purred. Joe Baker had just called him his friend.

CHAPTER 23

Harry Truman glared at the two men sitting with him. He was still reeling in disbelief at the proposal put forward by Stimson and Marshall, both of whom he trusted, and concurred with by a man he trusted not at all, Winston Churchill.

Churchill had telephoned his opinion earlier. He was back in England and trying desperately to hold on to his position as prime minister, which was in jeopardy following the debacle along the North Sea.

Truman shook his head. "I cannot believe we are ready to countenance the use of Germans in our armies, however limited your proposal is. Yet we know that Churchill agrees with it and that this Miller fellow in Potsdam is already doing it. I can't blame him there. He has a unique situation. But you're telling me that the Russians are too?"

Stimson answered. "Everything is true, sir. Miller began to use Germans to crew German antiaircraft weapons properly, and Ike would like to extend the practice to the rest of the army."

Truman turned to Marshall. "And you condoned this? Is there no way you could have stopped Miller?"

"Sir," Marshall responded, "Miller is the commander in the field and, as such, is given considerable latitude regarding decisions. The fact that he is surrounded and outnumbered by his enemies, and hundreds of miles from contact with the American armies, makes the situation both more complicated and more desperate. Besides"—he smiled slightly at the memory—"Miller as much as told me we would have to come and get him if we wanted to court-martial him for disobeying orders."

Truman grunted. Sight unseen, he had to admire this General Miller. He must have a fine set of really brass balls. Not too many military men would have had the temerity to tell the army's chief of staff where to get off. Truman had also been appalled to find that the Reds had drafted Germans to man the antiaircraft guns around Ploesti and other places. Worse, there appeared to be an effort to create a German Communist army out of the multitudes of prisoners of war the Russians held. Just how successful this would be remained to be seen. However, it was thought that many German prisoners would likely choose the opportunity to live as a soldier instead of starving in a POW camp or being worked to death in the gulag.

"And now, gentlemen, you're telling me that Ike wants to do the same thing?"

Stimson sighed. They had already been over this. "That's correct. Ike feels we are winning the air war, but that the Red air force is still a formidable adversary. Despite the fact that we are producing almost three times as many airplanes as the Reds, they still have a mighty host. We made a big mistake last year. Ike ordered the disbanding of a hundred battalions of antiaircraft guns because the Luftwaffe was such a weakened threat, and everyone concurred. Now these battalions have been reconstituted in light of the still dangerous strength of the Reds, and we need much more to protect our boys. Thus, Ike is proposing that we utilize German soldiers to man the antiaircraft guns and other weapons that we have captured in great abundance."

Truman did not respond. His expression was stern. Marshall took over from Stimson. "Sir, if you are concerned about our boys serving with any war criminals, I do not consider that likely. The antiaircraft guns and gunners were part of the Luftwaffe, their air force, and not the SS or even their regular army. Even if they were so inclined, I doubt that the gunners and others in the Luftwaffe would have had the opportunity to commit many war crimes."

Truman stood and looked out the window behind his desk. "And Churchill concurs after all the Germans did to England? Well, I suppose he would, considering the mess his army is in. Has it been confirmed that Montgomery has been replaced?"

"Yes, sir," Marshall answered. "By Alexander."

Field Marshal Sir Harold Alexander had served with distinction in North Africa and Italy. Marshall had just received confirmation from the British chief of staff, Sir Alan Brooke. The choice did not displease the American high command. After first being almost insultingly critical of the American military, Alexander had proven quite easy to work with and had strengthened the alliance between Britain and the United States.

The public had been told that Montgomery had been a casualty of the battle and had been evacuated to a hospital near York. Only a handful knew that he had suffered a nervous breakdown.

Churchill had made the decision that the mauled remnants of the British Army would continue to remain in German-occupied lands and fight alongside their former enemies. Wounded were being picked up by the Royal Navy from a multitude of beaches and small fishing villages along the west coast of Denmark. The British had lost most of their armor and artillery and practically all of their supplies, which meant they would be relatively helpless for the foreseeable future.

Marshall continued. "In a small way, using Germans in any capacity will help resolve the problem of numbers. We are still badly outnumbered at the point of battle."

"I know," said Truman.

In the nearly two months since the start of the war, the United States had managed to scrape together only a few new army divisions to throw at the Reds. Two each from Okinawa and the Philippines were en route to Europe. This did not mean that the four American divisions from the Pacific were in any shape to fight the Soviets. They'd been worn down by battle and disease. Physically, the soldiers were suffering from a score of ailments, and their equipment was shot and needed replacing.

Then there was the problem of getting any of Clark's already reduced Fifth Army across the Alps. The Swiss and their neutrality were a large roadblock. A trickle of Clark's army had made it across from Italy into Austria, but the price had been high, too high. Others were wending their way around Switzerland by way of France, while a lucky few got to take ships from Italian ports and thence around Europe to Antwerp. Either way there was a dreadful delay and moving any of Clark's troops meant ignoring the fact that they were in Italy to prevent a Communist-inspired civil war from breaking out there.

"And what are the Russians doing?" Truman asked.

Marshall stole a look at his notes. "Sir, our intelligence sources say that the Reds are stripping their other armies in Europe for the coming battles, which we all assume will be decisive. We have also confirmed that they are using Romanians and Bulgarians in some locations, although these cannot be the best soldiers in the world. We further believe they will be using those so-called German volunteers wherever they can as shock troops. That's been their tradition. They've always utilized penal battalions and released prisoners for suicide attacks. The men actually do volunteer because they know they will definitely die as prisoners, while there is the small chance they will survive as soldiers."

Truman looked puzzled. "Under those circumstances, I would think a great number of them would desert. God only knows, I would."

It further boggled his mind that Stalin would take the Russian men released from German POW camps, hand them guns, and send them straight back to battle as poorly led, untrained, and half-starved mobs. He had to remind himself that Stalin, early in the war, had said that surrender was punishable by death. He was just enforcing his decree.

"They might desert," said Marshall, "we just don't know how they would manage it. They would be closely watched and not have very many chances under any circumstances. We aren't certain the German volunteers will be used against us. I consider it more likely they will be used as a police force to maintain order in Poland, Czechoslovakia, and Hungary. All of those countries are now in rebellion against the Russians. Thus, more armies can be taken from the forces occupying those countries and sent to the front. Further, the OSS reports that their operatives have sighted trainloads of soldiers coming back from the Far East."

"Makes sense," Truman said. "How many men are we talking about?"

Marshall again referred to his notes. "These are estimates, but at least half a million from Siberia and maybe another half million from other sources."

Truman groaned. Counting both the reinforcements from the Pacific and Clark's army, if either got there in time to help in the next battle, they would total less than a fraction of what the Russians were bringing up. There had been some talk about lowering the draft age to seventeen and raising the upper end from its current high of thirty-five years of age to forty. The potential for the greatest numbers would come from the lower end, but, like Roosevelt before him, he was already catching hell because eighteen-year-olds were in combat. If seventeen-year-olds went to war, the political effects might destroy the entire war effort.

At any rate, it wouldn't work. First, as they had discussed before, there wasn't enough time to draft and train large numbers of men. Second, the decision had been made to hold the size of the American military at a certain level in order to keep the economy going, and that made sense. What good did it do to put all these men in uniform if there were no weapons being produced for them to use? There were very real limits to what the Arsenal of Democracy could do.

"Damn," Truman muttered. "We can shoot down their planes and make more aircraft than they do, and we can make more tanks than they, but their tanks are much better. That pretty well evens out, doesn't it?" Stimson and Marshall nodded. "Therefore, until and if we can get that bomb of Groves's working, the difference in this war is numbers, isn't it?"

"That and supplies," Marshall corrected. "If they take Antwerp, our resupply effort will be crippled."

"Well," said Truman, "we cannot speed up the ships bringing in the Pacific reinforcements and we cannot enlarge the army by changing the draft. If we could get at least some of the Fifth Army across the Alps, it might help take pressure off, wouldn't it?"

"A little," Marshall admitted.

There was a pause as a courier knocked and entered with a note from the secretary of state. Truman opened the envelope and read the one-page document quickly.

"Well," he said with a wide grin, "it would appear the British defeat has served one purpose, other than to get rid of Monty, that is."

"And what is that, sir?" Marshall asked. He declined to remind the president that the Fifth Army had been stripped to support the invasion into southern France.

Truman handed him the note. "It seems to have scared the bejesus out of the Swiss. The idea of a possible Russian victory seems to have made them change their neutral little minds. They are going to let Clark's boys transit through Switzerland in order to preserve their financial system. All right"—he chuckled—"if the British can decide to fight alongside the Germans, and the Swiss can give up their neutrality, you can use your Germans as antiaircraft gunners."

• • •

TIBBETTS WATCHED AS the flight of three B-29s circled for a landing on the isolated air base outside Reykjavik. Once again, another flight had returned unharmed from the long sortie over Germany. After a couple of false starts, he had devised the tactic whereby each trio of bombers would fly over selected areas of Europe just after a major bombing raid had taken place, either there or nearby. Thus, they would usually catch the Reds on the ground refueling and rearming as the American bombers disappeared to safety. In the first few days of this effort, there had been some attempt by the Russians to attack the bombers. This had cost him two planes, but the attacks had ceased as the Reds realized the bombers weren't bombing. He presumed the Russians thought they were out for photoreconnaissance purposes. It was as if they didn't want to waste precious fuel on them. Well, he decided, who cared what they thought? It worked, didn't it? Now they were over Europe each day. It was as if the planes of the 509th had been given safe-conduct passes.

Tibbetts was pleased that the temporary base was pretty well complete. Men and supplies were housed in a host of Quonset huts. His ground crews had all been shuttled in and he had a full complement of supplies. Even better, the scientists had arrived, and that meant the nuclear material would soon arrive and then be flown to England. He understood that it was coming by warship, the heavy cruiser *Indianapolis*. Since the Germans had surrendered all their U-boats, the Atlantic was as safe as a pond. Arrival of the nuclear material would end his crews' period of training and put them into the cauldron. Perhaps, if this bomb worked as the scientists expected, they would be the cauldron itself.

Everyone who knew about the atomic bomb, including Tibbetts, wondered what their target would be. He didn't think it would be a German city, as they were already pretty well destroyed. He had seen the figures and they staggered him. Bremerhaven was 79 percent destroyed, and Bonn 83 percent, and Hamburg 75 percent. Ironically, Berlin was listed at only 33 percent destroyed by bombing, which was a testimony to the futility of trying to wipe out truly large cities from the air. While he sometimes wondered who went around and counted ruins, he had no reason to doubt the results. The major German cities no longer existed as viable targets. Besides, he reminded himself, we are now at war with Russia, not Germany.

Most of his people had put their money on targets inside Russia, and he had to admit some fondness for that idea. Moscow and Leningrad were everybody's favorites and there had been some conventional bombing attacks on them. Leningrad was closest and much easier to hit, but there really weren't many military targets around there, except some navy bases, and the Russian navy, such as it was, had stayed home for this war. Moscow was the capital and contained the military headquarters, and would normally be a juicy target. Unfortunately, it was so far inland and, therefore, so well protected by guns and planes, that the few attempts to bomb it had suffered badly.

There had been three attacks on Moscow totaling 500 bombers that had lost a total of 135 planes. Unacceptable, Tibbetts thought, totally unacceptable. If he were to launch a nuclear assault against Moscow those numbers meant there was the high probability that he would lose a bomber that carried a nuclear bomb, whether it was disguised as a photo plane or not. With so few bombs available, not to forget the highly trained crews, he could not risk the huge cost of failure.

Logically then, that left tactical targets, and they were in a constant state of flux. Tactical targets had the annoying habit of moving.

Tibbetts would have to give considerable thought to what he might suggest as a target. That is, he thought wryly, if anyone would accept targeting input from a mere colonel, even if he was supposed to fly the plane and head the mission. Well, he knew he had access to Ike and he had information about how the bombs might cause damage when they detonated. Perhaps it was time to call in some favors.

ELISABETH WOLF TWIRLED in her skirt and laughed as Logan stared at her white thighs. "Thank you for the razor, Jack. That's the first time in months that I've been able to shave my legs."

Logan flushed. "You're welcome." He still wasn't comfortable talking strictly feminine topics. First body odor and showering, and now leg shaving. What was his world coming to? Apparently such discussions came more easily to Europeans than they did to comparatively puritanical Americans. The last time Lis had worn the skirt, he had noticed the obvious fact that she hadn't shaved her legs in a long time. While some of the blond German women could get away with it, a dark-haired girl like Lis could not. He'd been told that many European women didn't shave as a matter of course.

An airdrop had brought them an abundance of safety razors and blades. More than enough to share, especially since General Miller had not revoked his permission to grow beards. Many of the soldiers, Logan included, had gotten fond of their furry growth, and Miller was keenly attuned to what he could do for his men to make them happy in what was now openly referred to as Goddamn Potsdam.

Once again, they were outside in the warm sun. Elisabeth stopped her impromptu dance routine and sat down beside him on the rickety bench. Technically, he was still on duty but the bunker was only a short distance away and in plain sight. Bailey would call if anything came up. Casual arrangements like this were common up and down the perimeter, and Jack wasn't the only one in the company doing it.

"You know, Jack, it wasn't always like this. Once upon a time, my family and I were really quite comfortable. Regardless of where we were and even in the depths of the Depression, we always had enough money to buy both necessities and a few luxuries. Father was high enough in the diplomatic hierarchy to command a decent income, and we had rental properties that provided other money. I never had to do without pretty dresses, nice shoes, cosmetics, books, anything." She lifted her foot, again showing a little bit of leg. "I was even able to shave my legs whenever I wanted to." She laughed wryly. "Of course, as a young girl I never wanted to because it burned my skin. I tried to convince my mother that only evil women shaved."

"Did it work?"

"Of course not. She said if I didn't I would look like a bear. Did I look like a bear?"

Jack put his arm around her waist and pulled her more tightly to him. "Yeah, and the type of bear I wanted to hibernate with."

She jabbed him in the stomach. "Be nice. Besides, it isn't even winter."

"I just hope we're not here in the winter," he said sincerely. Like most of the men in the garrison, he was astonished at the length of time they had been in Potsdam and the fact that no end was in sight to their precarious existence. As he had thought and said so many times before, these days in the sun were a blessing to be enjoyed while they could, since they surely could not last.

"Me neither," she said. "I want to get back to someplace that's real. Not just for me, but for Pauli. He deserves a better life than this. He needs a home, playmates, and a school. I may have been spoiled with what we had amid the privations of the Depression, but it wasn't an evil spoiling. Surely there can't be anything wrong with having loving parents.

"We weren't plutocrats," she added, "just normal people trying to live their lives. Now look at us. We've been reduced to little more than beggars living in caves and wearing rags."

She rested her head on his shoulder. Sometimes she was overwhelmed by the enormity of the disasters that had befallen her, and who could blame her. She was still only twenty, an age when many young women of her social and economic class were still single and in school. Instead she found herself in a refugee camp in a besieged city, wearing cast-off clothing made from curtains, eating a foreign army's rations, washing infrequently, and being unabashedly grateful when a friend gave her something so she could perform an act of personal hygiene.

Worse was the feeling of helplessness. What would the future bring? For her and the others with her, was there a future at all? At any time a Russian shell could crash down and end any discussions of the future. It was something they had to live with and deal with. Thus, they were relatively unconcerned about sitting outside. If death came, so be it. Otherwise, there was still a semblance of life that had to be lived.

"Jack? Tell me about your home again."

"America? It's not like Canada. America's a magical land that's full of good things to eat and the streets are all paved with gold."

"Jack. Please?"

He hugged her and nuzzled her cheek. "Okay." Softly, gently, he again told her of his life. It had been rough but not desperate. His father had worked for the railroad and spent a couple of years riding the freight trains as a railroad cop chasing off the bums and tramps. He did not tell her what his father had told him of the starving young teenage boys and girls he came across and what they did to survive. That didn't sound like America. He also didn't tell her of the times his father had to club a vagrant senseless because he wouldn't leave, or because the bum wanted to throw his father off the moving train. That wasn't America, either.

He told her how his family had persevered, how they had grown some of their own food, sewn worn clothing, and lived as frugally and as moneyless as they could during the dark years of the early and mid-thirties. Jack's father had never really lost his job; however, there had been long stretches of time when the railroad "didn't need him" and he waited at home for circumstances to change. There really wasn't much use looking for another job; there weren't any.

Finally, in 1940, things got better. His father got a job in the administration end of the railroad and they moved to a small house in Port Huron, not far from the tracks. They could see Sarnia, Ontario, across the St. Clair River, which formed the boundary between the United States and Canada. It was easy to watch the cars and people on the other side and wonder where they were going and what they were doing. It was also easy to take a small boat across or take the Bluewater Bridge, which had connected the two countries since 1938. Until the war came, crossing to Canada, either officially or unofficially, was quite easy.

"Did you ever go there, to Sarnia?" he asked.

She shook her head. "Montreal and Quebec, yes, but not Sarnia. And the only time I got to the States was a visit to Niagara Falls when we went across to the American side for a couple of hours. We were disappointed. The best view is from the Canadian side."

Jack agreed. He had been there too. Idly, he wondered if he might have seen her. They compared dates and found they were years apart on their visits.

"I'll take you back there," he said.

"I'd like that." Her voice was soft and he realized she was falling asleep. He guessed there wasn't much rest for her some nights in what amounted to a crowded barracks. Sometimes it wasn't so pleasant sleeping in that bunker with his men when one of them had a bad night or got hold of some liquor. Not all the gardens being grown were for food crops. Some enterprising souls had started making a near-lethal variety of moonshine.

That he could handle. Drunks were easy. But it was difficult to deal with a man his age who had suddenly given in to despair at the thought of ever leaving Potsdam. It was fairly easy to maintain a degree of bravado during the day, but ugly truths and nightmares came out during the dark hours. When that occurred, even the strongest of men was known to cry. No one mentioned it in the morning—their turn might be next.

Jack knew that he had to get Lis and the boy out of Potsdam. He had no illusions. The American army had been defeated and was retreating away from them. Sure, they might come back at some time in the future, but, based on what had happened in the Pacific, that could be years. The Russians would not grant them years of safety and the airdrops could not last forever. Sooner or later the Russians would attack again. Maybe the next one could be beaten off as well, but what about the following one, or the one after that?

As a soldier, he could hold out some hope that he wouldn't be killed, that, instead, he would be taken prisoner and someday returned to America. He might live, and where there is the possibility of life there is hope.

But what about Lis and the boy? Pauli would probably be lucky. He would likely be killed outright. But Lis? He had heard the stories. Most of the German women in Potsdam had been raped by Russians and had made plans to kill themselves before that happened again.

Lis hadn't mentioned anything—some topics were still taboo—but he knew she must have considered it. He could not bear the thought of her spread-eagled on the ground while a line of grinning Russians waited their turn.

He had to get her out of Potsdam. How? he bitterly asked himself. They were surrounded by a river and tens of thousands of Russians. If she could sprout wings she might have a chance.

"Did you say anything?" she asked groggily, and he realized he must have said something out loud.

He kissed her on the forehead. "Nah. Must've been mumbling to myself."

Elisabeth shook her head and roused herself. "I have to get up and see your dear Sergeant Krenski."

Logan chuckled. He saw nothing dear at all about First Sergeant Krenski, who seemed to worship Lis. "Why?"

She stood and stretched like cat. "Because I am teaching the nice man how to read. He isn't dumb, you know. He just was too embarrassed to do anything after he succeeded in leaving school without learning a thing. Really, you ought to do something about your schools."

Jack swatted her on the rear and she stuck out her tongue. Lucky Krenski, he thought, and what the hell is he doing with my girl?

BURKE AND GODWIN waited in the chill dawn alongside the hastily built airstrip. It was long, very long, and Burke wondered just what the hell needed so much real estate for takeoff and landing.

Godwin was there as a representative of the RAF, and Burke was there because it was presumed he was an emissary from Marshall. Basically, this was an American Eighth Air Force show, and scores of air force personnel ranged the area. Antiaircraft guns pointed skyward, although their crews stood several feet away from their weapons lest there be some tragic mistake.

"I still can't believe this is happening," Godwin said.

Burke chuckled. "Hasn't happened yet, now has it?"

"If this is a trap," Godwin said. "We are dead."

It wasn't a trap, Burke reassured himself. There weren't that many important people present to make it worth a trap or a betrayal. At least that's what he hoped.

A large flight of P-51s flew overhead with a roar. They were the van of the escort. Even though unseen, a multitude of other American fighters provided flank and rear support.

Godwin jabbed Burke's arm. "There."

A dark shape had descended from the clouds and was approaching the landing strip. Instead of the roar of a propeller plane, this had more of a singing sound. "Oh my God," muttered Burke.

The strange plane touched down gently, showing the pilot's obvious skill. "I can't even get into bed that softly," Burke said.

They openly gaped at the plane. It more resembled a shark than anything else. And there were no propellers. The plane was a jet, the dreaded ME-262.

Behind the first plane came a second and a third, and others queued up for their turn to land. The hatch of the lead jet opened and a man in his thirties wearing the rank of Luftwaffe general climbed out and jumped down. He looked around and spotted Burke. Godwin stepped behind. The turnover was to be from the Germans to the Americans.

Burke was a little befuddled. He knew what was supposed to happen, but there was an air corps general a mile away who was in the wrong spot and wondering how the hell to get to the right one without losing his dignity. Additional German jets were landing and lining up alongside the first one.

The German held out his hand, and without thinking, Burke took it. He'd never shaken hands with a Nazi before. But then, this general was supposed to be one of the good guys. That is, if there really were any good Germans.

"Colonel, I am Lieutenant General Adolf Galland, and you Americans will soon have all the German jets I commanded. At least those that survived," he said sadly. "I trust you will use them wisely. I also trust you have fuel for them."

Godwin responded. He noted that Galland was not shocked by his face. Obviously, the Luftwaffe had its own share of burned wretches.

"General, we have fuel for our own jet program and our scientists are confident it can be modified for your jets."

Development of the British Meteor jet lagged well behind the ME-262. "I hope so," said Galland. "If not, we might as well have blown them up on the runway."

CHAPTER 24

Natalie Holt responded impatiently to the sound of the doorbell. It was ten o'clock in the morning, and she was up and about cleaning the large apartment. Ordinarily on a holiday like the Fourth of July she would be preparing to visit friends, and she still intended to see her mother later in the day, but so much of the time this morning was being spent in busywork to keep her mind off of how much she missed Steve Burke.

"I'm coming," she hollered, and she heard a muffled masculine response. She opened the door a crack and saw the grinning face of Special Agent Paul Forbes.

"Can I come in?"

Natalie opened the door. Forbes had been with her when they had discovered Walter Barnes's suicide, and the shared experience had helped an easy bond to form. The fact that neither was too fond of his boss, Tom Haven, was another plus. She noted he was wearing a dark business suit on Independence Day, so the visit was not social.

"Paul, unless I miss my bet, today is Wednesday, the Fourth of July. I know there's a war on, but don't you people get any time off at all?"

"Rest is only for the wicked. Not good guys like me."

Natalie offered coffee, which he accepted, and she slightly regretted that she was dressed so casually in old white tennis shorts and a T-shirt that said U.S. Navy. She had been mopping the floor, not preparing to be a hostess.

"I'm assuming the obvious, Paul, that your visit is official and rather in a rush."

"Very true on both counts. I got a call at home about an hour ago from your favorite lecher, Agent Tom Haven, who informed me that I had to leave my wife and children and see you immediately, Fourth of July or no Fourth of July."

"How charming. About what? Have you discovered another closet homosexual or unrepentant socialist in the State Department?"

"I hope not. I want to talk about Steven Burke."

Natalie was shocked. "Good lord, why? He hasn't gotten into any trouble, has he?"

The only thing she could think of was that he might have blabbed something. It seemed unlikely. Steve understood the need for secrecy as much as she did. The only reason they talked about their mutual interest in the Soviet Union was that both had equal security clearances. Even his letters, which implied that he was doing something important for Eisenhower since he hadn't returned with Marshal, had been appropriately circumspect.

Forbes shrugged. "I admit it's a possibility, but not a very good one. If he was in trouble, he would be under guard, if not arrested, and we wouldn't be having this conversation on a holiday. Frankly, Natalie, I really don't know the reason for either the questions or the haste. I was just told to do a quick review and do it now. I think there is the possibility that he might be being considered for higher clearances than he now has."

"I thought he was as high as he could be."

"Nope, within security clearances, there are degrees within degrees. Now, let's get this done so I can go home and burn hamburgers. How long have you known him and so forth?"

Natalie quickly answered all the statistical questions, and Forbes wrote her responses on a small pad. She stumbled at only one point. "Paul, I just realized I don't know his birthday."

Forbes laughed. "September twelfth. He'll be forty-one. Some girlfriend you are." He put down the pencil. "I'm sorry, but I have to ask this next question. Have you slept with him?"

"Paul, he's in his forties and I'm in my thirties. Neither of us is a virgin." Although, she thought, he might have been. "The answer is yes. Now, does that make him an immoral and degenerate reprobate?"

"I'd say it makes him damned lucky."

Natalie laughed. Thank God even that pig Haven had enough sense to send the easygoing Forbes to ask questions like that.

"Natalie, this next line of questioning is a little more serious. In your opinion, why was he so interested in the Soviet Union in the first place? After all, not very many middle-class, Midwestern academics find the subject interesting. With your Russian ancestry, your interest is obvious, but the reason for his is somewhat more vague, and we'd like to know more about it."

"Are you concerned that he might be a spy for Stalin? I can assure you he finds both the man and his regime to be highly repugnant. As to why he studied it, he told me he found the Russian Revolution to be one of the most dramatic events of this century, perhaps in several centuries. In his opinion, it ranks up there with the French Revolution of 1789 for its potential impact on the world; and, by the way, there are a lot of people still studying that ancient phenomenon, the French Revolution. It intrigued him and the more he studied, the more intrigued he became."

Barnes put away his notes. "Sounds like what I expected. A harmless academic nut with the most beautiful woman in town as a girlfriend."

Natalie laughed, then turned serious. "I cannot believe how paranoid the FBI is about people who are different. What they did at work to some very good people was awful."

"I can't argue that too much, and I sure as heck can't say anything publicly, but I largely agree with you. By the way, I'm sorry you didn't get the position vacated by your boss Barnes's death. I guess the State Department isn't ready for a woman in management."

"Thanks, but I'll live. It was what I expected. There are a lot of people unready for women in power. But I'm still angry at the way your FBI hounded that poor man who was already being beaten up psychologically by the Russians. Why is Hoover so afraid of homosexuals? From the rumors I've heard, he's not always walked the straight and narrow in that regard himself."

Barnes flushed and looked over his shoulder as if someone might be eavesdropping on them in her living room. "Natalie, there are some things in this world that we just don't talk about."

"Okay, I get the message. But I still don't understand all the attacks on people who experimented with communism back in the twenties and thirties, and even later when the Russians were our Allies."

Barnes helped himself to more coffee. "Natalie, I know a little about the Russian Revolution too. I know the cruelty of the old regime made revolution as inevitable as rain on a cloudy day, and that the Bolsheviks stole it from the majority, who wanted a less radical form of government. I also understand how people in the depths of despair caused by our Depression could be seduced by a theology that seemed to promise food, shelter, and dignity to people who had none. While a lot of my colleagues disagree, I can see that those people's motives were caused by frustration and hunger."

He shook his head. "They are the ones who couldn't or wouldn't see the evil that Stalin had become, and the ruthless manner in which the revolution was enforced. Hell, you know as well as I do that many of those American workers who joined the Communist Party could barely read. All they saw was the glitter of hope and not the substance. You know that some of them even went over to Russia to work in their factories and most of them have returned? Well, a few of them are still there, either because they still believe, or because a couple of wars have trapped them in a strange land.

"But it's the other type, the academics and the scientists who were highly educated, intelligent, and, therefore, should have known better. They read the theories of Marx and Lenin, but they closed their eyes when they heard about the massacres committed by Lenin and then Stalin. When hundreds of prominent people disappeared, they should have wondered, and even a dunce could have seen that the trials of so many were charades leading to death. But while many of them left the Communist movement disillusioned and really are of only minor concern to us, a number of others didn't quit. They are totally unrepentant and rationalize their beliefs by saying that the excesses are either lies or just growing pains, like the Terror in the French Revolution. They feel that communism will, in the end, prevail and create a classless paradise in which people will be free to learn and teach to their heart's content. The fact that Stalin is a dictator is a mere inconvenience. These are the people who are dangerous because many of them are in positions of leadership and can influence Allied policy. Worse, some of them might be able to give secret information to the Reds. They would be traitors to us, but a true believer in communism wouldn't be worried about that label."

"And you thought my Steven fell into that category?"

"Someone thought it was possible. I read his record and thought it very unlikely. Now, if you'll excuse me, I have to give this report verbally to Haven at his house and have it typed up first thing in the morning. Maybe I'll still have some time to play with my kids or their mother. Have a nice holiday, Natalie."

Forbes showed himself out, leaving Natalie seated on the couch. Oh, Steve, she thought, what have you gotten yourself into now?

LIS GIGGLED AS Jack pulled her along in the night. She had a change of clothing in a pillowcase and she felt foolish with it. "Jack, you're going to get in trouble."

"I don't think so. Besides, what can they do? Fire me? Don't I wish."

It was after midnight and the evening was warm. They found the building clearly marked "Officers' Showers" and slipped inside. "You want to clean up or don't you?" he asked, laughing.

Water tanks lined the ceiling and the wall and showerheads emerged below. Lis looked around. "There's not much privacy."

"In the army, there's no privacy whatsoever, which is why we're doing this in the middle of the night. Hey, if you want to go back, we'll go."

Jack's taking her to the officers' showers was a follow-up to her earlier lament about cleanliness. The engineers had finally repaired the damaged plumbing and set up a flow of clean well water, which had been put to use for cooking, laundry, and bathing. The showers closed down at night to give the water tanks a chance to refill.

"How much is this costing you?" she asked.

"Nothing, actually. The sergeant in charge is an old friend of mine. Now, here are the rules. You hang up your clothes on the hooks over there, and you stand under the shower. You pull the rope and you will get thoroughly soaked by very cold water in a very short time, so be prepared and, for God's sake, don't scream."

She laughed. "I'm too old for cold showers."

"I thought I was too, but then I met you," he teased. "Now, when you're wet, you take the soap and lather up real quickly, which I'm sure you'll do because you'll be freezing. When you're done, you pull the rope again and another torrent of cold water will rinse you off. It's crude and fast, but it works."

"All right," she said, looking at all the plumbing in the room.

"I'll be out front making sure nobody stumbles in."

As soon as Jack was gone, Lis stripped and hung up her clothes. The evening breeze felt refreshing. It occurred to her that not only had she not bathed in a long time, she'd also not had any opportunity to be naked, and it felt good. She wondered what Jack was thinking, just the other side of the wall. She hoped it was about her.

She stood under the shower, took a deep breath, and pulled. Gallons of icy-cold water drenched her. She gasped and grabbed the soap. This was not going to be a long, leisurely shower. She lathered quickly and thoroughly, took another deep breath, and pulled the rope. This time the water flowed more slowly, but equally cold. Shivering, she grabbed the towel that someone in Jack's platoon had liberated from the ruins and dried herself off. She dressed as quickly as she could and ran to Jack.

"I'm freezing. Warm me up," she ordered, and he wrapped his arms around her and felt her shivering against him.

"Was it worth it?"

Lis squeezed closer. "You tell me, kind soldier. You were the one who said I stank."

Jack burrowed his nose in her still-damp hair. "I don't recall saying any such thing. But I will say you do smell bloody marvelous." He looked around and grabbed her hand. "Now, let's go."

As Jack walked her back to her quarters, Lis smiled. He hadn't insisted on watching her or even sneaked a peek. Maybe sometime in the future she would let him watch. She stifled a giggle. Maybe she would let him help.

But next time the damn water would have to be warm.

THE SUMMONS TO meet Eisenhower had been totally unexpected. Burke had only a couple of moments to straighten himself up before he reported to Beetle Smith at SHAEF headquarters near Compiègne. At least he was fairly presentable and had shaved that morning. He hoped the irritable general would take into account the fact that they were in a war zone.

Steve snapped to attention and reported to Smith, who looked at him curiously. "Relax, Colonel, no one's going to bite your head off. Now, have you ever met Eisenhower before?"

"No, sir." Burke had seen him, of course, and been an attendee at meetings, but he had never met Ike or spoken to him.

General Smith continued. "So I suppose you wonder just why you were ordered here to meet with him."

Burke forced himself to relax. "It had crossed my mind."

"Well, normally I would brief you on what Ike is going to say so you don't make a complete fool out of yourself, but this time the general hasn't asked my opinion or given me any clue about what he has to say to you. In other words, I have no idea why you're here. Does that make sense to you?"

"No, General, it doesn't." But it did sound like the army, he thought.

"In fact, Ike didn't even know your name. He just asked me if the skinny professor who specialized in Stalin was still around, and I assured him you were. I told you that so you won't get a big head just because Ike wants to talk to you. It may be important for national security, or he may have a bet with Patton about what Stalin eats for breakfast. Anyway, that was a couple of days ago, and then he had me review your security credentials. You passed, by the way."

"General, I promise you I won't get a big head over this."

Smith forced a small smile. "I didn't think you would. For an intellectual, Burke, you're not half bad." He gestured to Ike's office. "He's expecting you."

Steve knocked and entered. He snapped to attention, saluted, and reported. Ike was seated behind his desk. He returned the salute and told Burke to stand at ease but did not offer him a seat. This, Burke decided, was going to be a very short meeting with the great man and he was probably going to get his ass chewed. But why the security review if that was the case?

The look on Ike's face was grim. This was not the happy, smiling face in the newspapers and magazines; this was the hard-driving war leader, the man who could send thousands of men out to be killed. Ike's eyes were cold and his voice flat when he spoke.

"Colonel, I am giving you a special assignment of utmost importance and secrecy. You will note the obvious, that we are alone and not even General Smith is with us. This task, Colonel, is indeed that secret. Upon leaving here, you will be flown immediately to Iceland to see a Colonel Paul Tibbetts. He will provide you with information that you will share with no one, absolutely no one, without my permission. Is that clear?"

Burke assured him it was. Ike continued. "While in Iceland, you will take directions from Tibbetts and speak only to those he directs you to, and only about what they tell you. Within reason, you may ask questions if Tibbetts permits it, but you may not have to as Tibbetts is putting together a presentation for my benefit with you acting as my surrogate."

Burke could only stammer, "Yes, sir."

"When you return, you will be asked to give that information to me at a time and place of my choosing. There may be others present at that time or there may not. I haven't yet decided. Again, I must repeat that you are forbidden to talk about what you learn or even take notes. If you disobey, or even inadvertently fail to maintain security, I will have you court-martialed for treason. Is that clear?"

"Yes, sir." Burke felt himself sweating. What the hell was going on?

"Colonel, you are doubtless wondering why you were chosen for what appears to be a particularly thankless task. Well, General Marshall left you here thinking that your particular knowledge of Stalin and the Russian mind might prove useful. I agreed, although I had no specific need at that time. Now I have a use for that knowledge and it might help me make some very important decisions."

Ike's expression softened. "Notice, I said I will make the decision. You will provide information that may help me."

"I understand, sir."

"Burke, Tibbetts is an old friend of mine who is part of an incredibly secret project involving a weapon whose potential is so devastating that it could affect the war, perhaps all mankind. Not even I know the details, and your task is to learn what you can readily assimilate about that weapon's capabilities and limitations, and then advise me as to how it might best be used against Stalin and the Russians."

So that's it, Burke thought. There is a secret weapon. Burke's expression must have given him away. Ike stood and glared at him from across the desk. "You didn't look surprised. Did you know about it, and, if so, who the hell told you?"

"Sir, I didn't know anything specific, only a hunch." He quickly recounted his two conversations with Marshall, and Marshall's reactions when he speculated there was more to Stalin's motives than pure greed. He told Ike that he felt Stalin knew there was a limited window of opportunity and for reasons that were not readily apparent.

Ike nodded, his anger dissipated. "Good guess. I can see why Marshall recommended you." He checked his watch. "I laid on a plane for you, and it should be fueled and ready about now. You probably won't have to stay more than a day to learn all you need to know about this weapon. When you get back, keep yourself available at all times. I'll tell Smith not to send you on any errands. Now get going."

Burke saluted and started to turn. Then he saw Ike's hand was out and he grasped it. "Do a good job, Colonel." This time Ike was grinning slightly.

CHAPTER 25

"**H**ere they come again," Holmes yelled. It was all that an exhausted, hungry, and filthy Lieutenant Billy Tolliver could think of as he looked through his binoculars. How many times had he thought that phrase during the last couple of months? A dozen? A hundred? Only this time, it was a mob scene with people close-packed and making easy targets. What the hell kind of commanders did the Russkies have?

Tolliver's platoon was dug in as a rear guard with the Weser River to their backs. Behind them, a steady column of American trucks and tanks crossed the temporary bridge that had been constructed only a couple of months prior in happier times, when the army was whipping the Nazis. Now it was used so Americans could retreat. When the last vehicle was safe, Tolliver and the rest of the rear guard would cross to the west bank and the bridge would be blown up.

Holmes grabbed his sleeve. "Lieutenant, take a closer gander. Those look like civilians, not Russians."

Tolliver shook the fatigue from his brain and looked again. As usual, Holmes was right. It was a mob of civilians heading toward their position. That would complicate things a bit. They would have to frisk them and let as many of them as possible cross before making their own escape and destroying the bridge. What the hell was the matter with those people, didn't they realize the field they were crossing might have been mined? It would have been had there been more time. Then he realized the awful truth, the reason for the advancing wave of civilians.

"Holmes, are those soldiers behind them?"

Holmes moaned. "Aw Jesus, the Reds are pushing them in front."

Tolliver looked at the approaching horde of panic-stricken people. The closer they got, the better he could see the Russians pushing them, prodding them forward with gun butts and bayonets. Worse, there were women and children among them. I'm going to be sick, he thought. But what choice did he have?

"Tell everyone to open fire," he ordered, then turned to Holmes, who, as usual, had the radio. "Then get mortars on them, fast. Come on. If you don't we'll be overrun!" Holmes paled but complied, quickly relaying the message to the weapons platoon.

For a moment, there was no rifle or machine-gun fire from his platoon. No one wanted to kill women and little kids. At least, no one wanted to be first. The wave of people was only a couple of hundred yards away and Tolliver could see faces. Their mouths seemed to be open in frightened Os. He also thought he could hear a kind of collective singing moan coming from them.

Tolliver jumped out of his foxhole and stood upright. "See," he screamed, "this is how you do it!" He fired his carbine at the advancing host, emptying the clip. Even though it was a long shot for a carbine, the mob was difficult to miss and he saw several people fall over, and the moaning turned to screams. It was enough. The rest of the platoon opened up and bullets cut the advancing people down in rows, not discriminating between soldier and civilian, adult or child. Within seconds, the mortars arrived and bodies and parts of bodies were hurled into the air as the shells exploded.

Holmes paled and sobbed, but he too kept on firing. With macabre satisfaction they saw that Russian soldiers were lying dead among the fallen civilians. Holmes wondered if he could ever have been the first to kill those people, like Tolliver had. Then he saw that Tolliver too was crying.

The Russians stopped advancing and began to withdraw, leaving the dead and dying civilians. Tolliver lifted fire and directed the mortars to follow the retreating enemy infantry. Along with the civilian casualties there was a number who were unhurt. These milled about in confusion until a couple of them realized that the Russians had abandoned them. Then some of them started to walk slowly toward the American positions while a few of the other survivors searched among the bodies for loved ones.

A runner appeared beside Tolliver. "Captain says the last truck is about to cross and we should get ready to leave."

"Did he say anything about this mess?" Tolliver asked.

The runner gulped at the sight of the slaughter. "He said he understands, and that you should still get out right now. He said battalion thinks there's Russian armor coming up real fast."

Which means, Tolliver thought as he gave the order to withdraw, there will be no aid for those poor wounded civilians lying there. It was funny. Just a few weeks ago, he would have thought of them as Nazis, the enemy, people to be punished. Now he thought of them as flesh-and-blood human beings, just like himself.

It took only a few minutes to reach the bridge and sprint across. Tolliver found his captain and asked for orders. The captain said nothing, only pointing. A line of civilians was crossing the bridge. They could see safety in their grasp and some began running. Then he saw the first Russian tank starting to cross the field a couple of hundred yards from the bridge. Oh no, he thought.

Suddenly, the lead tank exploded, its turret flying off. Seconds later, Tolliver saw the blur of a barrel-chested P-47 Thunderbolt pulling out of its dive. The air force had arrived.

"Hey, Captain. Now we can delay blowing the bridge, can't we?"

The captain started to say something, but it was too late. Both ends of the bridge disappeared in a cloud of smoke and flame. The civilians were thrown off by the explosion and soon disappeared in the water. Tolliver shook his head in mute anger and sorrow. He already knew why some of the old guys back home who had fought in France in 1918 wouldn't talk about their experiences in that war. If he ever made it back to Alabama, there was no way he could speak and let mere words try to describe what he had seen and what he had done.

SUSLOV WAS CAREFUL not to get too close to the Weser, staying instead in a line of trees a half mile away. There wasn't much cover for the tank column from air attack, and he had heard what had happened to a couple of tankers who had strayed too close. The Yank army had retreated across the Weser and taken all their bridges with them. The Americans had escaped.

As if there was a doubt, he thought. After crossing the Leine, it seemed that the American resistance had suddenly collapsed. Gains that had been measured in yards suddenly became miles. While it had taken two months to go from the Elbe to the Leine, it had taken only a little more than a week to go from the Leine to the Weser.

Had the Americans broken and collapsed? Suslov didn't think so. The withdrawal across the river had been done without any panic that he could see. They had left neither their equipment nor their wounded. No, it was obvious to him that the slow fight to the Leine had permitted them time to build up defenses along the Weser.

Ivan Latsis opened his hatch. "Well, Sergei, that is a real river, not one of those piss trickles we've been crossing all this time."

Suslov could not recall any piss trickles. The Oder had been real, as had the Elbe and even the smaller Leine. He estimated this one at somewhere between two and three hundred feet across, deep, and flowing fairly quickly. While there were no truly steep embankments on either side, there would be no testing of the depths to see if a tank could cross. Instead, they would have to do it the hard way. Again.

"What's our fuel status?" Suslov asked.

"Less than half and nothing in the drums," Latsis replied.

Popov reported they had only a dozen shells for the 76 mm gun and a hundred rounds total for the two machine guns.

Latsis shrugged and smiled. "I don't think we'll be leading the attack this time. Not unless they want us to run dry right away. This time I think the rumor is true."

Suslov agreed. The scuttlebutt was that the brigade would again be pulled out of line, reinforced, and refitted for a while before attempting to force a crossing. It only made sense. They had been fighting constantly since the assault on Berlin in April, and the wear and tear on men and equipment had been horrific. Once again, their numbers were down. The entire battalion numbered only eight functioning tanks. Two had been lost to aircraft the day before, while the rest all needed major overhauls. Suslov wondered if he could get a replacement engine for his tank. The existing one was running hot and making strange noises.

They needed ammunition and fuel. They needed food. God, Suslov thought, when did they last have a good, hot meal? Their uniforms were smelly rags that sometimes barely covered their private parts. There was no way his brigade was going to help force a crossing of that river in their current condition. Even though the infantry would likely lead any assault, as it had in the past, it was imperative that the armor rest and refit in order to support them.

Suslov knew his geography. The Weser ran north-south well into the mountainous regions below them. Behind the Weser was the mighty Rhine. It seemed dumbly improbable that they would be able to force the Rhine. He had heard it was wide and deep, and protected by steep cliffs. Logically, he thought that the plan would be to force the defeat and the destruction of the Americans on the relatively flat terrain he'd been told lay between the Weser and the Rhine, and then drive on to the ocean. Amsterdam or Antwerp seemed the most probable ultimate targets. Maybe then they could stop fighting.

Suslov climbed out of his tank and landed awkwardly on the ground. His whole body ached. He stretched and tried to loosen up. It scarcely worked.

"We need some food," Suslov said.

"I'd like a cigarette and something to drink," said Latsis. "Some schnapps if we can't find some decent vodka. After that I'd like a piece of ass and a bath."

Suslov shook his head. At least Latsis hadn't begun his tirade about killing Germans. Perhaps he was getting over his hate. "Ivan, something tells me if you bathe first you might be more likely to get the piece of ass than if you bathed after."

Latsis actually laughed. "Fuck you, comrade Commander."

Comrade Boris, the political officer, heard that and scowled disapprovingly at Latsis. "You should be thinking more of destroying our enemies than your own comforts."

Suslov could almost feel Latsis's contempt for their new commissar. Some of the political officers shared the privations of the men they were there to inspire, but not so Comrade Boris. His uniform was clean and his belly looked full.

"We will be resting and refitting here for a few days," Boris said, "and then we will lead the final assault that will destroy the capitalist allies of the Nazis."

Latsis smiled. He had picked up on the word *we.* "Ah, Comrade Boris, does this mean that you will be with us when we cross this fucking river? If you'd like, we'll be happy to make room for you in our tank so you can inspire us properly."

Boris flushed. "I will be with you, although not likely in your tank." Then it was Boris's turn to smile. "I don't think you need me to lead you. All you have to do is think of the Americans' treachery." With that, he turned and left.

Latsis shook his head. "Suslov, were you impressed?" he whispered.

"I was more impressed that you didn't tell him to go fuck himself like you do me all the time."

GENERAL GEORGE PATTON raised a glass of red wine to his guest, Dwight Eisenhower. "Here's to victory," he said, "and to hell with the Russians." They were at Patton's headquarters near Bamburg, Germany.

Ike smiled. "Simple and elegant, George. Just like yourself."

"Just my way of saying I'm ready now. Why don't you turn me loose?"

Ike shook his head. As usual, Patton was being overoptimistic regarding the capabilities of his reinforced Third Army.

"George," he said tolerantly, "you know why I can't let you attack just yet. We don't have the strength. Hell, I don't know when we'll ever be strong enough to attack the Russians."

"Even a small attack would delay an attack on Antwerp," Patton insisted stubbornly. "It'd make them use their oil, and maybe some reinforcements would arrive for us."

Ike had known Patton for decades and they had been the closest of friends, even to the extent of sharing wild and improbable peacetime adventures when they were both in their twenties.

But sometimes Patton was exasperating. That, of course, was part of Ike's reason for being present at Patton's HQ—to make sure Patton understood exactly what was expected of them.

"But that's what we want them to do," Ike insisted. "The last thing we want is for them to dig in along their bank of the Weser and proclaim the end of the war. Do you think anyone relishes the thought of attacking the Russians while they are still so strong? They have to attack and we have to wear them down. They stop attacking and we have lost."

Prior to the Soviet assault, Patton had received heavy infusions of men and equipment that made his Third Army almost the same size as an army group. The Soviet attack had pushed Patton slightly to the south while Simpson was bearing the brunt of Zhukov's attack. Both armies were heavily outnumbered by the Soviets.

"George, we are starting to kill the Reds in the air, and that's where you're going to win the tank war. For some reason, probably lack of fuel, the Russians aren't as aggressive anymore in providing cover for their tanks, and that's when you are going to start chewing them up. We estimate our tank losses to date have been roughly equivalent to theirs, but about eighty percent of our kills on their armor have been from air strikes. That's where they are vulnerable and that's where you are going to kill them."

"Ike, don't you think they're saving their planes for their big push? I would."

"I don't know. I would save them, sure, but not at the price they're paying in armor and men. No, I've got a feeling we are really winning the air war. I'm getting reports that their pilots, when they do go up, aren't as good as they used to be either. When you attack, your planes will make the difference, not your tanks."

"I know," Patton said grudgingly. He was a cavalry man and wanted his outgunned Sherman tanks to run wild against the Soviets. He knew it wasn't going to happen that way as things currently stood.

"One other thing, George. I'm sending you several hundred more fighter planes that had been on jeep and escort carriers for you to use as tactical support. With the U-boats gone, we have total command of the seas. We no longer have to worry about convoy escorts in the Atlantic."

Patton nodded. "Excellent. And I can use German antiaircraft weapons and crews as well?"

Ike smiled. He would give Patton an inch and knew he would take a mile. "Yes, George."

Truman's rules of conduct regarding the usage of German personnel were being stretched beyond the breaking point.

Eisenhower tried to hold off the worries that consumed him. He had done everything in his power to try to stop the aptly named Red Inferno. Was it enough? He doubted it. Despite growing advantages and Patton's exuberance, the American armies still weren't strong enough to defeat the Soviet juggernaut.

"I SWEAR IT, Lis," Jack said fervently. "I will get you and Pauli out of here. I don't know how, but I will do it!"

Elisabeth smiled tolerantly at him and moved a little farther into the doorway to stay out of the rain. It had been a depressingly gray and gloomy mid-July day, she thought, and this must have helped to bring on the sudden declaration of concern from Jack. Normally, he was cheerful and upbeat, making her laugh and keeping her from becoming despondent.

"Jack, if any of us could leave, we would. But we can't fly, can we?" she said soothingly. Elisabeth stood on her toes and kissed him gently on the lips. He pulled her closer to him and she felt his lean body against hers through the thin clothing that was all she owned. He hardened and she pulled back just a little. She didn't want to tease him, although she was not displeased that, skinny though she was, she could still arouse him.

"Maybe I'll steal that reporter's little plane," Logan said. He realized the incongruity of the statement and forced a smile and pulled her to him again. This time she didn't pull away. "Of course, I don't know how to fly it."

Elisabeth shifted and tucked in beside him. The wind had suddenly shifted and they were getting a little wet. "I don't either, and I don't think Ames will teach us. If we asked, it might make him a little suspicious as to our intentions."

"It's just that this can't go on forever, Lis. Something has to give, and I don't think it'll be for our good."

Deep down, Elisabeth agreed. It was fine to be optimistic, but word of the battles in the west and the continuing American retreat had not been held back from the people in Potsdam. General Miller felt that everyone had a right to know exactly what was happening. Again, and despite the continuing bad news, morale stayed high.

"The Russians will attack again," Jack said.

"Perhaps not."

"No. They have to. If they win the big battle that's coming up they will turn and finish us off. Even if they lose that battle, they're likely to take out their anger on us. We'd be such a convenient target. Lis, I am just so afraid for you. I can't stand the thought of anything happening to you. God, I just found you."

"Well, I'm worried about you too."

"Yeah, but I've thought about it and there's an ugly irony in all this. I'm a soldier. If the U.S. is defeated in the west, Miller may just think this whole thing is hopeless and surrender. In a way, it would be the only honorable thing to do, If that happens, I'll be a prisoner of war. Maybe I'll be in Siberia, but at least I'll be alive."

Although maybe only for a while, he thought. "As a civilian, God only knows what might happen to you. There's no way the Russians would protect what they see as German civilians."

Again Elisabeth could not argue. She had talked to too many of the women about their experiences at the hands of the Reds. While the better frontline Russian soldiers were likely to treat civilians with a degree of respect, the ones that followed—the Asians, penal battalions, and others—were the ones who raped and murdered, and these were the ones surrounding Potsdam.

"Jack, I should tell you something. Don't worry about me being taken by the Russians. It won't happen."

"Why?" he asked, dreading the answer.

She turned her head and looked at the rain. It was too difficult to face him directly. "Dear Jack, in the shelter we have formed a number of small groups. When the time comes, one of the group will help the others to commit suicide. We have accumulated a small supply of poisons and some very sharp scalpels and knives. The leaders will kill anyone who wishes it, quickly and in the most painless manner possible, and then commit suicide themselves. I've arranged for that to happen to both Pauli and me, and no, I'm not one of the leaders. I don't think I could go that far."

Logan sagged from the pain the thought gave him. It was just all too awful. Elisabeth Wolf was the most wonderful person he had ever met. She was not just a desirable woman; he thought of her as a beautiful, warm, and intelligent human being. It was just too horrible to think she might die in this ruinous place without ever having lived a full life, which, greedily, he wanted to live with her.

A part of him said she was right. Was she obligated to permit herself and Pauli to be violated and then murdered, which they both knew would be their fates if Potsdam was either surrendered or conquered? When he considered the alternatives, he saw there were none. He knew he too would consider suicide in battle as an alternative to a lingering and horrible death if he had to. At least in battle he could go down killing some of the enemy. Perhaps that would be an acceptable alternative to life in a Siberian camp? Everyone had heard rumors that the labor camps were almost as awful as the Nazi death camps. How could he even think of living as a prisoner if Elisabeth was dead?

Jack wondered what a priest or minister would say to her and the others in these circumstances. What other alternatives would a man of God give her, since just about every faith condemned suicide? He had no doubt that a merciful God would understand; that is, if any God that permitted all this to happen could be considered merciful.

Elisabeth separated from him and shook his arm. "No more talk of death. I can't handle it any more than you can." She reached behind her neck and pulled out a flat package she kept on a string around her neck. He had noticed the string before, and she had commented only that it was a special necklace. "Take a look at this."

The package contained a small number of documents. He recognized her and Pauli's birth certificates. Hers confirmed that she had been born in a small hospital in Toronto. There were two other items: her Canadian and German passports.

"There," she said, handing him one. "Have you ever seen anything quite so silly?"

Elisabeth was younger in the Canadian passport. He checked the dates. She had been twelve years old. A dark-haired and bright-eyed child stared out at him. Despite attempts by the photographer to dehumanize her, he could see the sparkle of humor in her expression.

The German passport was three years newer, when she was fifteen. This time it was a girl on the verge of womanhood. Once again, the photographer had failed to imprison her.

"You're beautiful," he said.

"I was skinny and flat-chested." She thought for a second. "Just like now." She took the documents from him and put them away. "I always carry them, along with a couple of photographs of my parents and Pauli's. If we should get out of here, those documents are my proof that I can go to Canada. The photographs will always remind me of the family I've lost. Even if I never leave, they are talismans that tell me there is another world, and it's just my bad fortune to have to live in this one at this time. At least I'm not alone, Jack. I have you. I don't think I could face anything without you."

With that she moved into his arms and they held each other. They said nothing. There was nothing more they could say.

CHAPTER 26

"**H**ey, buddy. I'm Chuck Ames and I'm with Reuters News Service. Mind if we talk?"

Logan shrugged. The reporter was staring at him as if daring him to say no. "Sure, but you might not find anything interesting. I don't know too many military secrets. Even my family thinks I'm dull."

"You'd be surprised how interesting you might be, Lieutenant. Along with the big-picture news, I'm filing a bunch of stories about ordinary soldiers. Kind of like what Ernie Pyle was doing, only he was a lot better."

At least Ames hadn't said he was better than Ernie Pyle, the legendary correspondent who'd been killed a short while back in the Pacific after spending most of his time writing about the war in Europe.

"I met Pyle a couple of times," Ames went on. "Helluva loss. Regardless, I want to do a little of what he did and talk to regular Joes. If my editors like what I write, it'll be published and your folks at home will get to read about you."

Jack nodded. "That, I'd like."

General Miller had given Ames permission to use the army's radios along with his own during downtime and subject to censorship. He was writing copious notes and planned to turn this adventure into a book when he got home. He was almost forty and thought it was about time he did something to get really noticed. Sneaking into Potsdam in a "borrowed" plane might just have been his last chance before the war ended and he went back to being a small-time reporter.

Ames asked routine questions, and Jack responded about his home, family, schooling, ambitions, and a ton of personal stuff he hadn't thought about in a while, and he started to get emotional about it. Ames turned away and gave Jack a moment. He'd seen that reaction all too often. Home was another world, and many GIs had walled themselves away from it.

"And maybe finally," Ames said, "what about a girlfriend? Got one?"

Jack smiled. "I hope so."

Ames continued to scribble in his notepad. "She back home in Michigan?"

"Nope. She's here."

Ames blinked. "What? Oh, Christ, now I know who you are. I've seen you with that young German girl."

"Are we that obvious?"

Ames laughed. "Damned straight, you are. You're either the luckiest man in the world or the smartest. How the hell did you find a young woman like her in a hell hole like this?"

Jack gave him a summary of how they'd met and a little of her background. "If you want some more personal stuff from her, I think it'd be better if she told you and not me."

"Nasty?"

"Some of it. Even so, she was luckier than most."

Ames understood. The girl hadn't been raped. They shook hands. Ames checked his notes. Ordinarily it would be just another human-interest story, but Logan's finding a girl in Potsdam was a good one. He would look up the girl and interview her as well. Maybe something about love and romance in the middle of war and the squalor of Potsdam would play well back home.

He hummed happily. If he played this right and he actually got out of Potsdam before the shit hit the fan, he might just win himself a Pulitzer. First, however, he had to figure out when was the time to leave and how. Miller had already made noises about taking his plane for reconnaissance purposes. No sir, that couldn't be permitted to happen. That was his ticket out and a chance to win Mr. Pulitzer's little prize.

"I AM ANGRY," declared Chuikov. His jaw was set and his eyes burning with rage. "No, I am furious. Comrade Zhukov, we need men and we need fuel. Someone is failing us."

Zhukov looked about him in the small room he'd commandeered in Hanover. He looked grim. "Be careful. You run the risk of being accused of criticizing comrade Stalin." Unspoken was the fact that anyone could be listening and could turn on them. No one was safe in Stalin's Russia.

Chuikov started to say something more, then smiled sweetly. "Of course I would never criticize our beloved Josef Stalin, comrade Marshal. How could you even infer such a thing?"

"Good. Now let us understand that we will deal with the Allies using the tools at hand, not the tools we wish we had. The high command believes that these tools will be more than enough to ensure victory. Do you not agree?"

"Comrade Zhukov, Stavka and comrade Stalin are far, far away. At risk of again being accused of criticisms, I am afraid they do not understand the full complexities of the task before us. We have been resting our men and hoarding supplies for two weeks now and are ready to begin the assault on the Americans on the other side of the Weser. Have no doubt, we will cross that damned river. When we accomplish that task, next we will be up against the Rhine and the Maas before we reach Antwerp. I am afraid that we will again be forced to pause before we even think of eliminating the Rhine barrier. I shudder at the thought of sending our armies against American-occupied heights along the west bank of the Rhine."

Zhukov agreed. He'd reminded Stavka of the hard-fought and costly battles against the Germans on the Oder when the Nazis fought hard for Berlin. He assured them it would not get easier. The Rhine could prove to be a mighty barrier. All the more reason to destroy the Americans this side of it.

Unlike the Germans they'd fought on the Oder, the Americans were neither disorganized nor demoralized as they continued their withdrawal. They had fought tenaciously and well for every inch of ground since the Red Army crossed the Elbe, retreating only when it was militarily expedient. Whoever said the capitalists wouldn't fight was wrong.

The Americans still had the cream of their youth in their lines and they were pouring weapons into Europe. Weapons, not men. Spies had told Stavka that the Allied numbers had been only slightly augmented by new arrivals. Zhukov smiled. Perhaps there was a limit to the American horn of plenty, after all.

There was, however, a very real limit to what the Red Army could accomplish and that concerned him greatly.

Zhukov put his hands behind him and began to pace. "I have stripped both Koniev and Rokossovsky of much of their armor and air cover in order to make this final push successful."

"I know, and I am grateful. But all of these tanks and planes need fuel, and we are not getting it. What little we have in reserve is not enough, and what is in the rear areas is just not getting through. The same is true of heavy weapons. We both know there are literally hundreds, perhaps thousands, of tanks, T34s and Stalins, in hiding in eastern Germany and Poland because we cannot transport them safely to the front. The damned Yank bombers have disrupted road and rail traffic for hundreds of miles. We can repair most damage within a day or two, but the bombing occurs continuously and, worse, they keep destroying the bridges. Those, we cannot rebuild quickly. Nor can we simply drive them, because we lack the fuel."

Chuikov took a deep breath. "Comrade Zhukov, with your permission, I am changing the immediate goal of the army."

Zhukov was surprised. "You are what?"

"We will not be driving straight for the Rhine. Instead, we will be aiming toward Dortmund."

"But why? That would have your armies veering north toward Amsterdam, not Antwerp. Why on earth are you interested in a detour toward Dortmund?"

Chuikov's craggy face lit up with a smile. "Because the Americans have recently turned the area around Dortmund into a massive supply and fuel depot. Our planes have confirmed the existence of resources beyond our dreams. If we can take Dortmund, we will have all the American fuel we would ever need to complete our offensive, not to mention food and vehicles."

Zhukov shook his head. "I do not recall that area being serviced by enough roads and rail lines to make the existence of such an immense depot likely."

Chuikov smiled and passed over some eight-by-ten photographs. "Look at these. They have built major arteries to the depots and have done so just recently. These are the supplies the Americans will need to stop us. If we take them, the Americans will either be forced to retreat precipitously or will have to die protecting them."

Zhukov studied the photos. What they showed was an extraordinary and sudden buildup. "Chuikov, I've seen your supply figures. If you make that detour and fail, you run the risk of running on empty fuel tanks."

"That will also happen if we do nothing, comrade," Chuikov said grimly. "The supply figures you've been provided from Moscow are, shall we say, optimistic? We've calculated everything more realistically, and there is no way we can force the Weser and reach the Rhine without the supplies the Americans have at Dortmund."

Zhukov continued his pacing. Did they have a choice? He had nearly two and a half million men ready to attack the Americans. Despite losses, there were still thousands of tanks and thousands more pieces of artillery as well as additional thousands of planes to hurl at them. The Americans had hurt the Russian advance, but not stopped it. Only the threatened lack of fuel could stop the Red Army.

Perhaps also, Zhukov thought, the Americans would finally be put in a position where they could not refuse a battle of attrition, which the Red Army would certainly win. He and Chuikov had tried hard to make the Americans stand and fight to the death, but the Yanks would have none of it. No one in their right mind would want to fight the Russian bear at close quarters.

But sooner or later they would have to. Would it be at Dortmund? If so, perhaps Russia could win and end the war. This could occur if they could kill enough Americans on the east side of the Rhine so that the rest would lack the will to fight. American soldiers might be brave, but their political leaders were not, and they must be cringing at the thought of the losses they were incurring.

After all, it wasn't as if the Americans were fighting for their homes. For that matter, he realized grudgingly, neither were his own troops. He had begun to notice a distinct lack of enthusiasm on the part of his soldiers and even some of his generals. He would have to deal with that, and very ruthlessly.

"The Americans must bleed," Zhukov said.

"They will. The preparatory bombing will begin shortly, although with great care not to hit the Dortmund area. We will pretend we don't know it exists. We will use every plane in our possession and hammer them along the Weser. This will be followed by an intense and prolonged artillery barrage, something the Americans have never endured. The Americans may crumble under the weight of the metal thrown at them."

Zhukov concurred with Chuikov's revisions to the original plan. He had to bow to the tyranny of logistics. They simply could not push on to the Rhine without the supplies Chuikov insisted were at Dortmund. As to the Americans crumbling, let Chuikov think that would occur if he so desired. Instead, he would have to prepare for the longer battle.

In the next few weeks, it was imperative that certain things occur: first, Chuikov would have to have some measure of success driving toward the Rhine while, second, Koniev would have to halt the inevitable counterattack that would come from the south. With many of his tanks stripped from him to support Chuikov, this would be a difficult challenge for Koniev.

Zhukov smiled inwardly. At least, he thought, if Chuikov's armies were stopped in the north, Koniev was likely to get a bloody nose in the south. If that were to occur, his despised rival could not claim the upper hand in jockeying for the position of most favored general with Stalin.

TONY TOTELLI SHRIEKED in horror as the Russian emerged from behind the tree and, equally astonished, confronted Joe Baker. It was their worst fear come true. It couldn't be happening. Tony had checked the area and there had been no Russians around. Where the hell had this one come from?

Tony was more than a hundred yards away and he could only watch as Joe's knife suddenly emerged in his hand and was driven into the chest of the Russian.

The Russian fell forward onto Joe and there was a sudden flash and the sharp crack of an explosion as the stick of dynamite Joe had been carrying detonated.

"No!" Tony screamed and stood up. It couldn't be. Joe Baker was immortal. He couldn't die.

Anton ran up to him, gasping. "I saw the Russian at the last moment. He had been taking a nap and must have just awakened. At least he was not part of an ambush."

"We gotta help Joe," Tony moaned. In the last few weeks, Joe Baker had been more than a leader to Tony. He had become a big brother to him, and Tony began to sob with the sense of loss.

Anton grabbed his arm. "Tony, we must leave. There's nothing we can do for him and the explosion will surely bring more Russians."

Reluctantly, Tony agreed. All they had been going to do was blow up a lousy telephone line using dynamite they'd stolen from the Russians. They had done it many times before and it was no great deal. Yet, this time, something had gone wrong. Joe had killed the Russian, but somehow the charge had detonated.

The smoke was clearing and Tony and Anton could see the misshapen and fragmented lumps that had once been Joe and the Russian strewn about on the ground. Neither man looked like anything human.

"Tony," Anton insisted, "we must leave."

"Yeah." Tony shook the anger and sadness from him. What a fucking horrible break for Joe. "Let's go."

As they made their way from the danger area, they hid behind trees and were passed by a couple of trucks loaded with Russians who were heading quickly for the area of the explosion. The sight of them infuriated Tony and he wished he was carrying a weapon that he could use to avenge Joe. But he was unarmed. That was another of Joe's thoughts. If you're not carrying a gun or knife, you won't be tempted to do something stupid with it. Even in his saddened state, Tony knew that attacking truckloads of Russians would certainly qualify as stupid.

After long detours, they made it away from the area of immediate danger to where Vaslov had stayed back at their last encampment. Their activities were somewhat protected by the fact that refugees of all types, ages, and nationalities were wandering Europe; thus, there was safety in the sheer numbers of people uprooted by the wars.

"What now?" Vaslov asked on hearing the sad details.

Tony had to think. For the longest time, other people had been doing most of his thinking for him. First it was his parents, then his teachers, and then his sergeants and officers. Joe Baker had taken over from them, as Tony really had made no long-term plans for staying alive in enemy-held territory.

Now it was time to do something on his own behalf. Sure, he had made it after his tank had been destroyed, but that was mere survival. Now he wanted to fight.

So what were their strengths? First, they had a couple of weapons and that NKVD uniform buried not far away. Second, they had the radio Joe had brought and they knew how to use it to contact his OSS superiors. All they had to do was decide how to use these resources in the best manner.

Oh yes, Tony thought, we are alive and free. They had survived the months since that fateful day of the ambush. That ought to count for something.

LIEUTENANT GENERAL ADOLF Galland of the Luftwaffe felt the incredible surge of power beneath him. It was invigorating to be in a plane again and going to battle against the enemies of Germany even though he didn't quite understand his status. Was he still a Luftwaffe general or, he laughed to himself, a prisoner of war out on parole? What the hell, he thought, he was flying the best plane ever made and the Americans were going to let him kill Russians while using British jet fuel. What was happening to his world?

Galland was forty thousand feet above the Weser River and stalking prey, this time Russian instead of American or British. It struck him as incredible that he and the other pilots had resumed working at their craft. He had fully expected to have been executed by Hitler either for insubordination or for having failed to stop the Allies, or, later, imprisoned for many years by those same Allies.

Instead, the war between America and Russia had brought him and his fellow pilots a reprieve. It had also brought the world's first operational jet, the ME-262, back into the war, this time with American markings. It had only made sense to use the Germans who had piloted them, although there were a handful of Americans in the formation. Thank God he and some of his comrades spoke fairly good English and had been able to give the Yanks some solid but quick training.

The ME-262 was a weapon incredibly superior to any fighting aircraft other nations had. Unlike most of Hitler's other attempts at a superweapon, the ME-262 actually worked. Heavily gunned, with four 30 mm cannon and twenty-four rockets, it could fly at 560 miles per hour, almost twice the speed of some of the Russian planes and still much faster than anything the Americans or British possessed. If only Hitler had permitted quantities of them to be built instead of the thirteen hundred or so that had finally been completed. It hurt Galland to realize that the majority of them had been either destroyed on the ground or captured in hangars because there was no fuel to fly them and no safe place for them to land. He was not aware of more than a few that had actually been shot down in battle.

The tactics were simple. The jets would be the first to attack the enormous Russian bomber stream that radar said was approaching the American defenses along the Weser. The jets would dive from on high and rip through the Russian air fleet at blurring speed, killing as many as possible and throwing the meticulous Russian formations into confusion. When they were finished, the other Allied fighters would take over and continue the battle. With luck, he and the others would be able to refuel and attack again and again. Jet fuel had been in short supply in Hitler's Germany, but the Americans, even without any operational jets of their own, had devised a way to adapt British fuel and were well on their way to making their own.

There. He saw them. A long, ugly smudge of what looked like locusts coming in below him from the east. The hundreds of Russian bombers, quickly identified as Ilyushin IL-4s, were, as usual, flying in tight formation, close up and three abreast in a serpentine line that stretched for miles. Russian fighter pilots could be quite good, but their bomber crews generally were not.

He hand-signaled to his wingman, another German, a man who'd shot down more than two hundred Soviet planes, and received acknowledgment. They had kept radio silence and it was unlikely that the advancing Russians suspected their presence. They would logically expect American propeller-driven fighters, not jets.

Quicker than he dared think possible, they were over the Russians. Galland made another signal and the scores of sleek-winged jets began their attack, like wolves ripping into the herd of sheep below.

Tolliver winced and closed his eyes as the earth shook again. It was impossible to think clearly, much less hear. He glanced at Holmes and the couple of others in his trench on the west bank of the Weser and saw the pale terror on their faces. Did he look like that? God help us.

After a few drinks, some of the older men in the bars of Opelika had told of the incredible artillery barrages of World War I and how men went mad under the incessant thunder, knowing they could be blown to pieces, or turned to jelly by a near miss, or buried alive at any time. How long before that happened to his men? Or to himself? Buried alive was the worst of the three terrible choices. It was the stuff of nightmares.

The Russian barrage had commenced only an hour earlier, and that hour now seemed like forever. They had been fired on before by German artillery, but it had been nothing like this Russian effort. There must be hundreds of Russian guns zeroed in on his position, churning up the earth and lifting clouds of dust and smoke that made it nearly impossible to breathe. As any fool knew, it was part of the softening-up process that would precede the Russian assault.

Incredibly though, he didn't think anyone had been seriously hurt. When they had retreated across the Weser, they had been directed to preplanned and preconstructed defenses that had been well sited and built to withstand Russian artillery. His respect for the army's engineers had always been high. Now it was astronomical. Despite the noise and thunder, he was fairly safe from anything but a direct hit by a very-large-caliber shell, or a lucky piece of metal coming through a gun port. Neither seemed all that likely. All they had to do was stay sane.

Earlier in the day, the Russians had tried their luck at bombing the dug-in Americans. It had been a curiously ineffective attempt. While a lot of Russian planes had appeared overhead, their attacks had been disorganized, and it seemed to him that a lot of bombers had been content with dropping their load in the general direction of the ground and getting the hell out of there. Of course, the presence of large numbers of American fighters certainly had something to do with it.

Despite warnings not to, many soldiers, he and Holmes included, had stuck their heads out to watch the battle in the skies above. The sight of hundreds of planes circling like angry bees in the blue sky above had stunned them. So too had the numbers of smoking aircraft streaming earthward like smudgy banners in a macabre dance of death.

Holmes had tried to put it in perspective. "At least foxholes don't fall down and crash." Tolliver knew it was a play on a recent Willy and Joe cartoon that had appeared in the soldiers' newspaper, *Stars and Stripes*. In it, Willy and Joe assured a sailor that they preferred the army because foxholes don't sink. Tolliver thought Holmes had a very good point for a damn Yankee.

"On the other hand," Holmes had continued in his aggravating nasal manner, "foxholes can get crashed into."

At that point, their observations had been interrupted by the sight of a small black object streaking across the sky at an incredible rate of speed. It made the other planes appear like they were standing still. "What the hell is that?" Tolliver had asked.

"A plane, sir," Holmes had said cautiously. "Only, I don't know what kind of plane could move that fast."

Mesmerized, they watched the dark bug dash in and out of the fray. They thought they saw its guns fire, and they saw planes disintegrate and plunge from the sky as the deadly bug whipped through the battle storm.

Holmes grabbed Tolliver's shoulder. "Lieutenant, there's a couple more!" This time the strange planes came out of their dives and flew close enough to the ground to give them a fair look. "Jesus, sir, those are jets."

Tolliver laughed aloud. "And they have American markings."

Tolliver had heard rumors of the German jet, but had thought it was a flight of Hitler's fancy. Now they had emerged on the American side of the war. As he tried to think out the implications of that, a couple more Russian planes began their death spiral to the ground, courtesy of the American jets. Sometimes, when a plane was destroyed, there was a parachute with a pilot dangling forlorn and vulnerable beneath it, and these floated to the ground like pods or seeds from some strange tree.

Sometimes, though, the parachute didn't quite open and the pilot was sent on his own death spiral, screwing himself into the ground at high speed. Tolliver could only wonder what last thoughts went through a man's mind as the ground rushed up to squash him like a bug on a windshield. He shuddered. Foxholes don't crash, he continued to tell himself.

Another Russian shell landed close, bringing him back to the present. Once again they were covered with dirt that had blown in, but had escaped unscathed.

"Lieutenant," said Holmes, "I am getting fucking sick and tired of this."

Tolliver thought it was a dumb comment to make, but let it go without a sarcastic rebuttal. Maybe Holmes just needed to get it off his chest. "So am I, Holmes."

"No, I mean it, sir," Holmes insisted. "Do you realize we've been fighting for more than two months straight? We haven't been pulled for any rest or refit, we haven't gotten reinforcements, nothing. It's like we've been sent out to fight until there's nobody left."

"Holmes, I don't think that's quite what's happening."

"Yeah, sir? Well, how many's left in the platoon? I'll tell you: fifteen! And I checked, and there's only sixty-two in the company. After all this, who the hell knows how many'll be left."

Tolliver hadn't thought of it in quite that way, but Holmes's numbers were correct. They had gotten their share of supplies and ammunition, but there hadn't been any fresh, warm bodies to fill in the gaps made by fallen comrades. Was the rest of the division in as bad a shape? What about corps? Or Bradley's whole army group? Two thirds of his men were down. If that figure carried over to the rest of the army, just what the hell would they do to stop the Russians when they crossed the river only a couple of hundred yards to their front?

Another barrage of shells shook them and showered them with fresh debris. At least, he concluded, they were knocking the Russian planes out of the air faster than they could come at them. But he wondered about artillery duels. If the American big guns were returning fire, he was unaware of it. He was totally focused on the thundering Russian efforts to snuff out his young life.

"Y'know, sir," Holmes continued when there was a breathing spell and they could better hear each other, "I almost wish the Reds would actually attack."

Tolliver rubbed the dust out his eyes with a damp cloth. "Why?"

"Then at least this bombardment shit would let up."

Billy Tolliver of Opelika, Alabama, thought for a minute and concluded that he agreed with the annoying little Yankee. Let's end this shit. Let's get it over with one way or the other.

CHAPTER 27

After a solid day of intense, ground-shaking artillery bombardment, the first Russians had come by night as paratroops descended behind American lines along the Weser. Thus, instead of being able to concentrate totally on the advancing hordes to his front, Tolliver had to detail a couple of his few remaining men to watch the rear of their defenses as word of the enemy airborne force reached them. Tolliver swore. He didn't have enough men to fight on two fronts. The paratroops to his rear kept some of his men occupied while darkness and man-made smoke hid the enemy to his front.

With the arrival of dawn, he was able to see what the Russians had accomplished throughout the night's fighting. Almost oblivious to American shells raining down on them, Russian infantry massed on the other side had pushed a horde of small boats into the water and paddled across. Some of the boats held only two or three men and had apparently been taken from local fishermen, while others held a dozen or more. He was further surprised to see Russians pushing horses into the water and urging them to swim across while other soldiers hung on to their manes and saddles for dear life. There was no apparent organization to their efforts. Wherever they reached the other side was their objective. The effort was crude and insane, but effective.

Many of the Russians died in the attempt, and the Weser, not quite a hundred yards wide where Tolliver's unit had dug in, was stained red and littered with human and animal debris that slowly drifted away. Tolliver was close enough to the water's edge that he could hear the screams of wounded horses and men. Despite the carnage, the Russian numbers prevailed and some small beachheads were established.

When this occurred, the Russians manhandled barges into the water. When a barge was safely floating, ramps were connected and a tank loaded onto it. While the barges crossed, other Red Army tanks on the east bank laid down covering fire. Since this was direct fire, it was disconcertingly accurate, and Tolliver and his men had to keep their heads down. Again, the Russians suffered heavily, and Tolliver saw a couple of tanks disappear into the river and sink like stones as the barges were hit. No crewmen emerged alive when this happened.

Tolliver yelled at Holmes to report the situation up the line. Holmes shook his head. "Phones are down, sir. I guess their paratroops cut the line."

Yeah, Tolliver thought. They probably did, although the phone lines could have been severed by Red artillery as well. They couldn't go around suspecting there were Russians behind every tree. Hell, he thought bitterly, there weren't many trees left standing. Holmes used the walkie-talkie and got through to the next platoon, which had already sent the information to the company commander.

In front of them, a Russian tank struck a mine. The explosion lifted the vehicle and sent pieces of tread flying into the air. In a perverse way, Tolliver felt sorry for the men in the tank. They would have to stay where they were until the battle passed them by before they could attempt repairs. All the while they would be vulnerable to American fire. The disabled tank's main gun barked and the shell hit a few dozen yards to his left. So much for sympathy, he thought bitterly. That tank could still kill.

Tolliver's men opened fire on the advancing Russians, cutting down about a dozen before the others dropped and hugged the ground.

"Keep it up," he yelled. "We got 'em stopped."

Holmes put down the walkie-talkie. "Second platoon is pulling out, sir. Word from the CO is the Reds punched a hole down a ways in G Company and we're being flanked."

Tolliver was shocked. They had stopped the Russian advance. An enemy tank was dead and so were a bunch of Reds. "They want us to retreat? You're bullshitting me, aren't you, you damned Yankee?"

"No sir, no bullshit. The word is retreat. Now."

Tolliver swore. A fat lot of good all the defenses the engineers had built had done them. They'd withstood the bombs and the artillery, but after only a couple of minutes against the exposed Red infantry, they were going to have to pull back. At least there were more defenses built and prepared behind them.

"Let's go," he ordered, and the handful of men he commanded emerged from their trenches and burrows into the smoke-filled sky. They hunched their shoulders as they trotted back, as if that would protect them from shells or bullets.

There was a short, angry stutter of automatic weapons fire, and Tolliver saw a man in a baggy uniform standing directly in front of them. A Russian, his mind screamed. It was one of the paratroops, and he was fumbling with reloading a deadly looking submachine gun, a look of panic on his face. Tolliver fired his carbine from the hip and a number of his men did the same thing at the apparition, who lurched backward from the sudden storm of bullets and lay still.

"Shit!" Tolliver said. He had never been that close to an enemy soldier before. The Russian had been only a few feet away. "Anybody hit?"

There was a few seconds' silence while his shocked platoon checked themselves. "One," said a voice. "Holmes."

Tolliver whirled and looked at his fallen radio man. The bullets from the Russian's submachine gun had stitched a hideous pattern across his chest, exposing bone and organs. Holmes's eyes were open but blank.

"Should we take him with us, sir?" It was Barrie, his senior surviving NCO.

Tolliver thought for only an instant. They were still out in the open with a long way to go. "No," he said sadly. "We leave him here."

Tolliver reached down and pulled off one of Holmes's dog tags. Then he looked down at the Russian. Angrily, he fired several shots into the dead man's chest. "That's for Holmes, you motherfucker."

As they turned to continue their withdrawal, Tolliver noticed some activity around the damaged Russian tank. Were they trying to fix it?

"C'mon, Lieutenant. Let's get the hell out of here."

"Barrie, what are the Russians doing to that goddamn tank?"

Barrie looked for a moment, spat on the ground, and grinned. "Yeah, Lieutenant, I see what you mean. They're siphoning gas or whatever the fuckers run on."

Tolliver laughed. The Russians were so short of fuel they were cannibalizing their own disabled vehicles on a red-hot battlefield. Not only that, they were ignoring the fuel drums strapped to the back of the tank, behind the turret. Why? Because they were empty, that's why.

"Who's got the walkie-talkie?" One of his men waved a hand as they commenced trotting away. "See who you can raise, and tell them to report back what we just saw. Tell them the Russians are running out of fuel."

Poor Holmes, he thought, glancing back at the limp body on the ground. You bugged the shit out of me sometimes, but I will miss you. God damn the Russians.

GENERAL ADOLF GALLAND searched the empty skies for a target and found nothing. He was not surprised. The Russian planes had paid a terrible price since the assault on the Weser had begun. It had been only three days since the first bomber wave had fallen prey to his jets, and now the Allied fighters almost totally ruled supreme. He alone had accounted for fifteen Russian planes confirmed killed, and several others damaged, and his was not the best total. Some of his younger pilots had double his amount.

The former German jet fighters had more than decimated the ranks of Ilyushin bombers along with Yak and MiG fighters who'd tried to escort them, and even killed a few armored Stormovik tank destroyers. After the first day, the slow, blundering bombers had not been seen again. He was not aware of any ME-262 having been shot down by a Russian. A few had been lost, but he thought that might have been due to equipment failure, and there was one report of a jet colliding with a Yak that was too slow to get out of the jet's way. If true, that was a shame, but it was also war.

On the dark side, about a third of his planes were grounded because of mechanical problems. The jet was a fairly fragile kind of weapon that needed to be maintained much more carefully than the ground crews were used to. The American P-47s and P-51s, on the other hand, were unfeeling brutes by comparison, needing comparatively little maintenance and repair. The jet, he concluded, was the rapier, while the P-47s, P-51s, and others were the broadswords and battle-axes.

Galland understood that the victory in the skies had not been his alone, and that the Americans would have won it sooner or later. But he did know that the Luftwaffe's jets had made it possible for that victory to occur with astonishing swiftness. Statistically, the relatively small number of jets had killed an average of twenty Soviet planes each, while the Americans had a four-to-one kill ratio.

The Russians, however, were not totally done. Galland thought they would lick their wounds and hoard their remaining planes and save them for the proper time and place—like last night, he thought wryly. Who would have suspected a Russian attack at night? All their other attacks had come during the day. Thus, the order to scramble from their supposedly secret American-run base had been a surprise, and many of his men had taken far too long to get their planes in the air.

Vectored into the Russian airplane stream by radar, they had chewed on the formations and then watched incredulously as transport planes disgorged hundreds, perhaps thousands of paratroopers onto the American defenses.

Galland had reviewed German airborne operations, such as the disaster on Crete, where an entire German paratroop division had virtually been destroyed, and knew that the attacks by his and American planes, however belated, meant that Russian paratroops would be landing nowhere near their intended drop zone. But was that important to them? Wherever they landed they could spread chaos. Had they misjudged the Russians once more?

Others in his squadron continued to report a lack of targets. In a little while, they would have to return to base. Despite its superiority as a weapon, the ME-262 did have one major drawback. Its maximum range was only 650 miles, and that didn't leave much time to search for an enemy.

Galland looked at the ground below. They were almost directly above the river and he could see small, dirty clouds where explosions had already taken place as well as the flashes of new ones. Poor bastards, he thought. Who the hell would ever want to fight down there? Give me a plane and the blue sky anytime. If I have to die, let it be as a bird in flight, not a rodent in a burrow.

BAZARIAN SMILED AT his guest and offered the disgusting creature another drink of liberated schnapps. It was readily accepted. The Russian was well on his way to getting totally stinking drunk.

"This is piss" was General Vladmir Rudnev's response. He had been making the same comment for each of the six very large drinks he had consumed. Rudnev might not particularly care for the German liquor, but he accepted it as an adequate substitute for his normal quart of vodka per day. Either that or, Bazarian thought, the pig actually liked to drink piss.

"Of course it is, dear comrade General." Bazarian oozed warmth. Even though he slightly outranked Rudnev, he needed him, or at least what Rudnev could bring with him in the coming battle for Potsdam.

Rudnev belched and Bazarian recoiled from the stench of the man's breath. Rudnev was a short, stocky man in his early forties. He had piggy little eyes and a small, tight mouth. His peasant background was evident in everything he did. His hands were large and coarse and he smelled of unwashed skin and old underclothing. For Bazarian, who considered himself somewhat of an aristocrat, it disgusted him that such a creature could have risen to a position of authority within the Soviet Union. Under normal circumstances, he would not have acknowledged Rudnev's existence.

But these were not normal circumstances. Rudnev commanded a brigade of armor that was hidden and stalled on railroad tracks a few miles away. Bazarian had told him that the rail lines to the west had been destroyed in a hundred spots, and Rudnev had accepted that as fact and promptly commenced drinking.

Bazarian had not quite told the truth. In fact, it was possible for Rudnev to proceed a good deal farther west toward the climactic battle being fought on the Weser. In all probability, however, many, if not all, of Rudnev's tanks would have been destroyed by American planes before they arrived, and that would have been a terrible waste. They were fresh, new, fully crewed, and, most important, full of diesel and ammo, although with nothing additional in reserve. Rudnev agreed that he would need more fuel when he left the trains and proceeded overland. Both men understood it was unlikely that he would find any; thus, sooner or later and well before the Weser, Rudnev's tanks would run dry.

Bazarian smiled. "It is a stinking shame that you are being deprived of the glory that would surely be yours if you were able to reach the war."

"It is." Rudnev reached for the bottle and poured some more. Bazarian considered the possibility that the man had an iron stomach. "I long for the right to kill the enemies of the state," Rudnev stated piously and belched again.

"I know. And, even when the tracks are finally repaired, the battle will doubtless be over before you arrive, if indeed you arrive at all. And, should you decide to go by road, you will not have enough fuel to make it anywhere near the Weser, and there are no reserves to draw from. I have heard that we have crossed the river and are driving on the Rhine. We shall quickly cross over that barrier as well and storm into Antwerp. With that, the Allied coalition will collapse and the war will end. A shame"—Bazarian sighed—"and you will still be here."

Rudnev slammed down his glass, splashing both men. "I want to fight. I want to kill the fucking Germans—I mean Americans."

When he glowered, as he was doing now, Rudnev reminded Bazarian of a picture he had once seen of an angry chimpanzee. "Comrade General, let me offer you the opportunity to fight and destroy the enemies of the state."

Rudnev blinked. He was having difficulty thinking. "How?"

"My orders have always been to first contain and then destroy the American forces in Potsdam. Because of the needs of the other fronts, I have not been given adequate forces to fulfill the second part of my orders. Now, it is almost fate that you are here with your tanks and no means to get them to the main battle. I invite you to join me in the glory of taking the city that has been a boil or a cancer in our side."

Incredibly, Rudnev took yet another drink. "You make a good point. Everyone is aware of the situation here and your failure to kill the Americans. Frankly, General Bazarian, there are those who laugh at you."

Bazarian's temper flared, but he held it in check. It was still another act of Russian arrogance in dealing with non-Russians. Rudnev might be an animal, but he was a Russian animal and, thus, part of the elite. With the greatest of efforts he controlled himself and did not draw his pistol to kill this little shit of an ape.

Rudnev continued, completely unaware of the effect his comment had had on Bazarian. "I was not aware that your failure was due to the fact that you had been deprived of weapons. Considering the circumstances we both are in, I would gladly use my forces to assist you in reducing Potsdam, but I am concerned about American planes."

"Do not worry, comrade General. I have planned the attack for night, and I have it on good authority that the weather to the west is worsening. There will be overcast skies when we attack." Bazarian was lying. Although he would try to attack at night, he knew absolutely nothing about the weather to the west.

"Then I am your man, comrade General Bazarian."

"I am delighted, comrade General Rudnev." Bazarian smiled like a salesman, and the two men shook hands. He was also aware that the little ape had said he would assist, not place himself under the command of Bazarian. It was half a loaf at best, but he would take it.

Rudnev stood to leave. He was a little unsteady but otherwise able to navigate his way out of the cottage Bazarian was using as his personal quarters.

Rudnev stopped and turned. "I want a woman."

"I'll send a couple over for you to choose from." Bazarian amused himself by pretending to be surprised. He thought fucking a horse or cow might be more up Rudnev's alley. The thought of one of his women rutting with the little ape upset him a little. It had taken him several weeks to round up enough young and attractive German women to make life interesting. It hadn't taken much effort to get them to agree to giving him sex. All he had to do was offer the carrot of food and shelter, and the stick of being turned over to his troops to be gang-raped if they said no.

Well, he thought, let Rudnev screw his little brains out. Bazarian had seen Rudnev's brigade. Eighty tanks, in all, and sixty of them the giant new JS model. There was nothing in Potsdam to stop Stalin tanks if they were used properly. Finally, he would take that city and still the laughter coming from the arrogant shits in Moscow.

"DORTMUND," GENERAL BRADLEY said. "There's no doubt about it; not that there ever was. They've been driving straight toward the depots at Dortmund and they are not even attempting a pincers movement to reach the Rhine. They've given up all attempts at trapping us on this side of the Rhine."

Ike had earlier come to that conclusion. The lack of an enveloping maneuver had confirmed it. The Russians had used a pincers strategy whenever practicable. They'd done it at Stalingrad and, later, at Berlin. Their change of strategy in the north had come as a slight surprise, although not totally unexpected considering the prize the Russians saw awaiting them at Dortmund.

Bradley frowned. "And they're moving in great strength. We've identified two rifle armies, as well as two tank armies. It also looks like another tank army, the Third, has been moved up in reserve and will be crossing the Weser at any time."

The 3rd Guards Tank Army had previously been identified as belonging to Koniev. That meant, in the week and a half since the initial assault on the Weser, the Russians had successfully put five armies on the American side, with a sixth about to cross over. It was only seventy-five miles from the Weser to Dortmund; Russians had already taken Paderborn and were more than halfway there. According to intelligence, the Russians, despite the enormous casualties they'd sustained, still had more than a million men thrusting toward that city like some giant convulsive animal.

Yet the attack was on a relatively narrow front with Simpson's First Army as it's focus, which left it potentially vulnerable to attacks on its flanks. Inside the Russian attacking front was an immense compression of men and equipment. So far, the U.S. Army had been unable to contain its advance.

Ike puffed on one of the cigarettes he chain-smoked. "It certainly proves that our attacks on their supplies and transportation network have paid off. It looks to me like a move based on sheer desperation. They must be in even worse shape than we dreamed of for them to distort their offensive objectives like they have. I'd say they've totally forgotten about Antwerp as their primary objective. At least for the time being."

Ike's thoughts were interrupted by a clerk informing him that they had Patton on the line. Ike took the telephone handed to him. "George, how's it going?"

"Ike, we kicked off just before dawn and are making some gains against damn stiff resistance."

Patton's limited counterattack had been reluctantly approved and was planned merely to disrupt the Russian offensive, which was proving far stronger than expected. It was hoped that the Russians would have to shift some troops to defend themselves from being cut off, or that Patton would be allowed to run wild in their rear. All of this supposed that Patton would be able to punch through them. Patton was saying the going was slow, which meant that he was failing.

Bradley slipped Ike a note. He read it and his face turned crimson.

He looked at Bradley, who turned away. "George," he said grimly, "are you using German tanks in your attacks?"

"Hell, yes. Got me a couple hundred Panthers and about fifty Tigers heading up my Shermans. They're a helluva lot better than anything we have. The kraut tanks were scattered all over southern Germany, and it took us a while to assemble and repair them, and put U.S. designations on them just like the air force did with the jets, but they're working just fine. Why, is that a problem?"

"I don't know," said Ike. "That might just depend on who's driving them."

There was a pause. "Aw, hell, Ike, do you really want to know?"

Eisenhower thought that one over. Did he really want to know what the devil his most irrepressible and irresponsible subordinate was up to?

"George, are you using Germans to crew those tanks?"

There was another pause. Finally, "Yes."

"George, you know we can't do that."

"Yeah," Patton interrupted, "and it makes no sense. We get to use the krauts as pilots for their jets, and as antiaircraft gunners, but not as tank drivers to fight the Russians. And don't tell me Brad's not using those German-crewed antiaircraft guns as antitank weapons, either. Hell, I know I am."

Ike shook his head. Patton had a point. The policy regarding Germans was inconsistent and flawed. And, yes, Bradley was indeed using German-crewed antiaircraft guns to kill tanks. But a promise had been made, both by Ike to Marshall and by Patton to Ike. The Luftwaffe was considered probably clean of war crimes, while the ground troops were the ones more likely to have committed atrocities. Although he realized that most of them probably had not, some doubtless had. The thought of GIs serving alongside some of the people who had butchered Jews and other innocent people was as repugnant to him as it would be to the American people.

Patton continued. "Ike, I won't bullshit you. I always had every intention of using every weapon I could possibly get my hands on to defeat the Russians. But I'm only using regular German soldiers and not the SS. This isn't tiddleywinks or football, Ike, this is war, and I don't give a damn what or how I have to do to win. I will do it."

Patton actually laughed. His normally high-pitched voice sounded tinny over the phone. "Y'know, I kinda think Marshall suspects what we're doing. After all, isn't he the one who conned Truman into letting us use the antiaircraft guns and crews in the first place? Don't tell me he didn't know they could be used to kill tanks as well.

"As to Truman? Hell, let him fire me. Ten dollars says he won't do anything until the war's over and then he's going to try to hush it all up. Not even Truman would fire a general whose only crime is cheating to win a war."

Ike quietly admitted that Patton had a point.

"Hell, Ike, you can never have enough weapons. Besides, if I want to make a real mark on history, this is my only time around."

Eisenhower hung up. He would deal with Patton later. After all, there was the possibility that Patton would be proven right. Winners are honored and losers face humiliation. It was entirely likely that Patton would get a medal for his act of disobedience. It wouldn't be the first time. But now he would work with Bradley as he dealt with the main thrust of the Russian armies nearing Dortmund. At the rate they were going, the Russian armored columns would be there in a couple of days.

What would the Russians do when they reached that town? What would their reaction be?

THE LONG BARREL of the 88 mm gun was twisted back as if it were a toy destroyed by a large and malevolent child. Beside it were the blackened and torn bodies of its crew. Germans, Suslov thought. God-damn Germans. They wore American uniforms, but their ID said they were German. They were not the first dead Germans in American uniforms he had seen in the last few days, nor, he surmised, would they be the last.

German ground participation on the American side had come as a bitter surprise to them all. So too had the manner in which the Germans had fought them. The 88 mm guns that had proven so effective against Russian armor in the past had been arrayed against the onrushing Soviet tanks. Flashes of light from their dug-in positions and the crash of hot metal against Soviet tanks brought back terrible memories. He could still hear the screams of crews from those tanks with radios as they cried out for help from the flaming hell their tanks had become.

Yet the Red Army had persevered and punched through still another defensive line. In a little while they would reach the Dortmund area, where they had been told all manner of supplies waited for them to feast on, supplies that they desperately required. Suslov thought it would be heavenly, except there was no heaven in Stalin's Russia.

First and foremost the tanks needed diesel and the other vehicles needed gasoline. Next, they needed weapons and ammunition. Many of the Russian guns had been destroyed. Some didn't particularly like the idea of using American weapons, but there was no other alternative.

Food was also in short supply. Much of their supplies were brought up to the front on horseback and, therefore, not a prime target for the menacing planes, but even that flow had slowed down lately as there was little food to bring. A good number of the horses had already been eaten and many men were becoming weak from hunger.

The Yanks had proven to be no fools. While not exactly incorporating a scorched-earth policy, they had made certain that there was little to sustain an advancing army. It was August, and there was no sign that any crops had been planted in the fields they passed, which also meant there would be mass starvation if the war continued much longer.

They drove forward. There was only sporadic resistance. They concluded that the last line of guns they'd confronted and destroyed must have been the final Yank defenses before Dortmund. After a few more miles, they saw evidence of a major military presence in the form of heavily traveled roads and military signs they couldn't read. They followed one road and soon came to a sight that took their breath away. Thousands of fuel drums and thousands more large wooden crates were stacked in an open area that covered hundreds of acres. For Suslov and the others, it was a vision of paradise.

Almost shyly, Suslov and the other tankers drove toward their salvation. Grinning like children, they stopped, hopped down, and ran to a fuel drum. It was heavy and the contents sloshed.

"Open it and see if it's diesel," Suslov ordered. "I can't read this shit the Americans call writing."

Latsis and Popov pried open the small lid where the spout would go. Latsis almost stuck his nose inside. He looked up, puzzled.

"What is it?" Suslov said, walking over and looking in.

"I don't know." Latsis tilted the barrel so that some of the clear liquid ran out. "Shit, it's water."

Quickly, they checked some of the other barrels. They all contained either water or sand. They pried open a number of crates and found them filled with earth or rocks or junk. They heard cries of dismay as other tank crews made the same discovery.

Suslov felt dread. "They fucked us. The Americans totally fucked us. There's nothing here but shit. We fought all this way to get here and there's nothing."

Suslov and the others sat on the ground by their tank. Despair hung over them. There was no food and no fuel. They could not go forward and they wondered if they could go back. Back to what? Suslov wondered aloud, and the others agreed. They looked at the sky.

For the time being at least, they were free of Yank planes. Even the Americans got tired once in a while and had to stop. But the planes would be back. And so too would the American armies that had been retreating all this time. The dummy supply depot meant that the Americans knew how critical the Russian supply situation was.

"Latsis, how much fuel do we have?"

Latsis used a twig as a dipstick to check the tank. The scowl on his face was half the answer. "If we're real careful, don't have to detour, and don't have to ride fast, we might make it back to the Weser."

"What about the Rhine? We're actually closer to it than we are to the Weser, aren't we?"

"Yes, comrade Commander, we are. But the Yanks will probably resist us, which will prevent us from driving in a straight line. Therefore, we will likely have to get out and push before we reach it."

Disheartened and hungry, they waited through the night. Their only orders told them to capture the supplies that were supposed to be outside Dortmund. They could only guess that higher-ups were trying to figure out their next move.

At dawn, Boris the commissar arrived from brigade HQ. He was riding a mangy-looking horse, and not driving a jeep or staff car. He was also drunk and nearly fell down while dismounting.

"Comrade," Boris told Suslov in a slurred voice, "because of treachery, we have to stop our attack on the capitalist pigs for the time being. You are to pull back to defensive positions as soon as possible. You will receive more details later. On the way you will double-check every vehicle you find for fuel and ammunition and take whatever you can. Please convey that to the rest of your battalion."

Suslov was astonished. "My battalion? What happened to the colonel?"

"Oh, you didn't know? He's dead. He killed himself this morning. You're next in line. Congratulations. Of course," Boris said with a tinge of bitterness, "your entire battalion consists of six tanks." He checked his watch and blinked. He was too drunk to see the time. "You'd better get started. This retreat has got to be orderly or it could be a disaster."

Suslov wanted to scream that it already was a disaster. "What else do you know?"

Comrade Boris scoffed. "Do I look like Zhukov?" He gestured and Suslov followed. He put a beefy hand on Suslov's shoulder. "Seriously, comrade, Chuikov met with our general and others. He said we would hold bridgeheads on the Weser. The fuel shortage is worse than awful, but there is hope that it will be rectified. The people of Russia will not let us down."

It was Suslov's turn to scoff. "Really?"

Boris looked around. "Careful." It was a clear warning that what he said might be held against him once the fighting ended. "Chuikov said the Amis are attacking from the south but that we are holding them off. According to Chuikov, the Amis must attack us because they cannot leave us holding most of Germany. When that time comes, we will crush them."

"Do you believe that, comrade Boris?"

Boris tried to mount his horse, slipped, and fell into the mud. He wiped the filth from his face and grimaced. "Truthfully, comrade Suslov, I now believe that as much as I believe you have a battalion to command."

CHAPTER 28

Logan crawled on his belly behind Crawford. "Lieutenant, why the hell are we doing this? Didn't anybody believe me?"

"If nobody believed you, we wouldn't be out here crawling on our bellies like snakes. Your info was passed up all the way to General Miller himself and all he wants is confirmation."

"So why do I have to go?" Crawford asked as he slithered forward under the barbed wire.

"Because, Corporal Dummkopf, you're the one who found it and you're the only one who knows where it is."

They moved forward in the shallow ditch Crawford and others had dug weeks before. It enabled them to slide under their own wire and snoop around Russian areas. Their faces were darkened with mud and dirt, and dark cloth bands secured their clothing and kept their equipment from rattling. Logan thought they moved like ghosts but Crawford told him to stop making so much noise.

Finally, they were through the wire. They crouched low and moved slowly. Sudden motion in the night attracted attention. They reached a dirt road and Crawford signaled a halt.

"Now we crawl across?" Logan asked.

"Hell no, Lieutenant. Right now there are people awake and looking around but not for us. You try to sneak and you'll stick out like a big red pimple on a fat girl's ass. No, you and me we stand up and walk across like we lived here and had a right to."

Logan swallowed and did as directed. His estimate of Crawford was rising. The little man from the piney woods knew exactly what he was doing. It was also a reason why von Schumann's spies were ineffective in this case. German civilians in a built-up military area would be easily spotted and summarily executed.

"If we see anybody, we just walk casually in the other direction."

Logan thought that was fair enough and started walking. "How much farther?"

"Little bit."

Half an hour later, Crawford halted in a wooded area. "It begins here. They're kind of spread out and there are men either in tents or sleeping on the ground, so we're gonna go around the area and not through."

Logan tried to make out the shapes in the night. Crawford was right. He'd found Russian tanks, lots of tanks. They moved around the tank park's perimeter and made a rough estimate of close to a hundred tanks, many of them behemoths that could only be of the Stalin variety. The remainder were T34s. To date, they had confronted neither kind, only the older, smaller, and less-well-armored models. The Stalins and T34s spelled major-league trouble.

Crawford grabbed Logan's shoulder and pointed. "See the roads, Lieutenant? They have to use the roads to get to us because the ground is so boggy. Big-ass tanks like those will get stuck otherwise. There's lots of wooded areas down here, and I'll bet if we chopped down a big bunch of trees near Potsdam we could slow them down a lot, maybe even get them to go where we want them to."

Logan's estimate of Crawford went up yet another notch. If the bombers couldn't take out the tanks before they moved up, then artillery from Potsdam could straddle the roads as they got close. Regardless, it was imperative that General Miller get confirmation of Crawford's discovery. They could notify the air force and begin zeroing in on the roads that led to Potsdam.

"Maybe we could mine the roads," Logan said, and Crawford chuckled.

A woman's scream pierced the night. She screamed again, groaned in agony, and whimpered. The raucous sound of men laughing followed.

"What the hell is that?" Logan asked.

"Some fucking Russian general. I think his name is Rednuts. He gets German women and that's what happens. Heard it before. Kind of wonder what's going on, but maybe I really don't want to know."

Jack agreed. It was time to get back inside the wire and report.

• • •

HARRY TRUMAN STARED at the microphone on his desk and took a deep breath. He envied the late FDR's calming voice and mellow tones. He knew he sounded tinny and had a tendency to speak too quickly and clip his words. Comedians and mimics were already having a field day with him. So be it. Sometimes their efforts were actually funny, although on some occasions it was merely spiteful. He thought it would be nice to punch one of the sons of bitches in the snoot.

The hell with them. He was president and they weren't. The sound engineer signaled. He was on.

"Fellow Americans. I am taking these few moments to speak to you about the way the war with the Soviet Union is progressing. As you are aware, our boys are fighting bravely and well as they withdraw to more defensible positions. Despite the fact that we continue to withdraw, we are gradually winning this conflict and will continue fighting until final victory is ours.

"However, that is not the purpose of this address. Some of America's enemies are planting the lie that we have signed a separate peace with Nazi Germany. This is absolutely false. There has been no treaty or understanding with the Nazis.

"Let me tell you what has actually happened. Before the savage and unprovoked attack on our boys by the Soviet Union, Germany was already fighting Russia and that has not changed. Germany continues to fight Russia, so, to that extent, she is on our side. Please recall the old saying that the enemy of my enemy is my friend. Well, Germany's enemy is now our enemy as well.

"During the past couple of months, we have taken possession of many excellent pieces of German equipment, including planes, tanks, and antitank weapons. We are using and will continue to use those captured weapons against the Russians. It just makes good sense and will save American lives. It also makes good sense to use captured German personnel to train American soldiers in their use. And, if that means German military personnel sometimes wind up fighting alongside Americans in a highly fluid military environment, then so be it. Our job and my duty is to end this war quickly and decisively. It would be sheer lunacy to be choosy when American lives are at stake.

"Please be assured that no SS, Gestapo, or suspected war criminals will be allowed to work with American soldiers and airmen.

"Does this mean that our policy of unconditional surrender regarding Germany is being reevaluated? Yes, it does. Following Russia's brutal attack on us, any agreements previously made went down the drain. When the war is over, we will base treaties with Germany and other countries on current realities rather than the Soviet Union's lies.

"Let everyone be assured that this does not mean that war criminals will go unpunished. They will be tried by an international court and the guilty will receive justice, which is not what is being meted out to the German people by the Soviets. The Russian armies are committing unspeakable acts of barbarity on the German civilians. They say that they are doing so because this is the way the SS acted in Russia. Yes, the German SS did behave brutally, raping and murdering innocent people, but what the Russians are doing is revenge, not justice. By torturing and killing innocent civilians, they are behaving like Mongol hordes, not a twentieth-century civilization. Justice will be meted out after a fair trial and not indiscriminately against innocent civilians.

"Finally, we will use every weapon at our disposal to bring this war to a successful conclusion, and I do mean every weapon."

Truman took a sip of water as the radio people disconnected him. "Well," he said to General Marshall, "do you think Uncle Joe understood me?"

Marshall smiled tightly. "We'll find out, won't we?"

CHAPTER 29

Immediately upon his return from Iceland following his daylong conference with Colonel Tibbetts, Burke found himself held incommunicado at SHAEF headquarters. He was given no tasks and told not to talk to anyone or leave the compound. Meals were brought to him by an unsmiling cook and he had his own bathroom facilities. He had been ordered by Beetle Smith, who still did not know anything but the roughest outline about his assignment, to prepare notes and thoughts. Very soon after, he'd had a one-hour meeting with Eisenhower, who listened thoughtfully, then took Burke's notes to read at his leisure.

Burke wasn't surprised that the high command wanted him out of circulation so that he would not even inadvertently tell about his trip. The secret he had been told in Iceland had been so vast and significant that the knowledge of it had almost rendered him speechless. Thus, Burke felt a degree of anticipation when Beetle Smith entered his tent and returned the stack of papers Eisenhower had taken from him.

Smith was subdued. He had read them and understood their significance. "Burke, there will be a meeting in half an hour at Ike's conference bunker. You are to be there and you will bring these papers. Eisenhower has made a lot of his own notes, but he feels he may have to call on you for something specific. Now, there will be a lot of very senior officers there, so you know exactly how you are to behave, don't you?"

"Absolutely, General. I am to sit with my hands folded in my lap and I will not speak unless called upon by my betters."

Smith grinned. "I knew I could trust you."

The meeting was held in a sandbagged and heavily reinforced underground bunker that was as bombproof as such a place could be. Even though the Red air force had crumbled, there were still enough scares to make such security efforts a good idea, and there was always the fear that a suicide bomber might try to plunge through.

Of the other men in the room, only the scarred Godwin was even remotely of Burke's own relatively low rank. Godwin winked, an incongruous act considering his lack of eyelids, but said nothing. Like Burke, he took a seat in the rear. The furnishings ranged from folding chairs to overstuffed couches.

Eisenhower, Bradley, and Field Marshal Alexander were the most senior officers present. Simpson, Patton, and Smith were the only other men who weren't either a field marshal or a full general. It was a fairly exclusive meeting of the Allied high command, and one the Russians would have loved to have bombed. After only a few moments, the room was thick with cigarette and pipe smoke. The ventilation system was totally inadequate and the air turned stale very quickly.

Eisenhower began the conference by giving them a ten-minute summary of the atomic bomb and its estimated capabilities. The others were stunned and there were exclamations of shock. While there had been suspicions regarding the possible existence of a super-weapon, the extent of its potential destructive power left them incredulous. Even though Burke would have bet good money that Bradley had already been informed, he apparently hadn't, as he too looked surprised and even dismayed. Burke was also flattered by the fact that Ike's information was almost word for word from what Burke's notes had said.

"Gentlemen," Ike went on, "we believe that we have, in this bomb, a weapon that can shorten, if not end this war. We have been ordered by the president to use it at our discretion. All we have to do is decide when and where."

Ike looked to where Burke was seated. "A few days ago, I sent Colonel Burke to meet with Colonel Tibbetts, who will fly the plane that carries the bomb. The information I received from Colonel Burke is the basis for this discussion and he is here if he is needed to amplify anything. While I will welcome all comments, the final targeting decision is mine."

Patton spoke. "I guess we can assume that this atomic bomb will be used in Brad's area since that's the main thrust of the Commie attacks."

"Correct," said Ike. "Further, we have only three bombs, so it is imperative that we use them wisely. By the way, the physical size of the bomb is so great that it can be carried only in a B-29. The bombs will be loaded at one of our bases in England."

Bradley still looked concerned. "Logically, that leaves the Russian perimeter to the west of the Weser. Since their high-water mark at Dortmund, they have pulled back about a third of the way to the river and there are several areas where there are very large concentrations of men and tanks."

Everyone glanced at the map. It showed a Russian perimeter that was still seventy-five miles wide at its thickest point near the Weser, and between sixty and seventy-five miles deep, depending on the curvature of the river. The American forces shown were not in direct contact with the Russians. It had been Ike's choice to not engage in force until the bomb was used.

The map also showed that Patton, to the south of the perimeter, had reached but not crossed the Weser. Farther to the east, one lonely marker indicated the besieged garrison at Potsdam. Burke thought it interesting that the map showed no attempts at advances from the British and Germans who had crossed the Kiel Canal north of Lubeck and Hamburg and were probing the Soviet armies.

"Ike," asked Bradley, "just how on earth does Tibbetts plan on delivering one of these things safely? If that B-29 should crash with the bomb on board, there could be a catastrophe."

"Brad, there's always some risk, but the scientists and Tibbetts have gone out of their way to minimize it. The bomb will not be fully armed and ready for detonation until just before they approach Russian-held territory. Some very brave or foolish man in Tibbetts's crew has volunteered to do the final assembly while the plane is actually airborne."

Patton chuckled. "How about both brave *and* foolish."

Ike continued. "For some time now, Tibbetts has been misleading the Russians into thinking his planes were for harmless photoreconnaissance purposes. He has been flying them at high altitude and in groups of three, and the Reds have been ignoring them for the past couple of weeks. In one way, they have been lulled to sleep, but it also reflects on their lack of fuel and planes. They probably consider attacking Tibbetts's few B-29s a waste of their limited resources. There will be a high probability of success that he will deliver the bomb safely and accurately."

"But will it go off?" Field Marshal Alexander asked. "And will we not be giving away all our secrets if it does not?"

"There is an altimeter in the nose of the bomb," Ike said. "When it registers that it is just under two thousand feet from the ground, it is supposed to detonate. If that fails, or if the bomb just doesn't work, it is our fond hope that it will be destroyed when it impacts the earth. We are, however, very confident that it will detonate. We just don't know exactly what the results will be. Tibbetts will be dropping the bomb from an extremely high altitude to protect himself and his planes. Since pinpoint accuracy is not essential, this is an acceptable tactic. It's hoped that the distance he can gain by banking and diving while flying away before the bomb goes off will save him and his crew from destruction. For safety reasons, I will be grounding all of our planes that day and I will be ordering all our men to stay heads down at a certain time of that day to protect themselves from burns and blindness."

"You won't possibly reach all of them," Bradley said sadly.

"I know," responded Ike. "I know."

Alexander seemed nonplussed. "Gentlemen, I find it difficult to comprehend that a plane flying at nearly 32,000 feet and at a speed of 320 miles an hour might be in danger of damage from a bomb it drops nearly a minute earlier." He looked at Eisenhower for a correction to his statement. There was none. "Great God," he murmured.

Patton looked distressed. "Explosions, burns, even blindness from the glare are things I can understand, but what the hell is this radiation thing you mentioned? It sounds like some goddamn death ray."

Ike checked his notes and decided to defer. "Burke?"

Steve stood up. His knees were shaking. Even though it was intoxicating, he still wasn't used to this kind of audience.

He focused on Patton. "Sir, as you doubtless know, atomic material in the bomb, uranium, gives off invisible rays called radiation. In years past, people died from what they thought was harmless radiation, such as those workers who applied radium to watch faces to make them glow in the dark. I was told by Colonel Tibbetts that a couple of scientists developing the bomb in New Mexico got exposed to radioactive material and died after becoming quite sick. He said the effect is very much like some kinds of cancer. What the scientists don't really know is exactly what the effects will be when an explosion takes place and the radioactive material within the bomb is disseminated over a wide area, making anyone and anything in that area radioactive to the degree that they are exposed. Tibbetts said that some of the scientists believe that the effect will diminish to nothing within a couple of days, while others feel that the effects could linger on for years, even decades. Perhaps," he said, suddenly aware of the utter silence in the room, "for centuries."

"Jesus Christ," said Patton. "That's not war. That's fucking slaughter. Burke, are you implying that the ground that the bomb radiates might not be livable for years, even longer?"

"Yes, sir. At least, that's what some scientists feel."

"And what about the people affected by this radiation?" Bradley asked, his face pale. "Will all of them die?"

"General, there is the strong possibility that many apparently unhurt people will sicken and die within a couple of months, while others might not show the effects for years."

Bradley was stunned. "And we're going to use this thing, this death ray?"

Eisenhower responded and was firm. "Yes, Brad, we are. Truman has ordered it and I concur. We all believe that the current pause is just so the Reds can resupply and that they'll commence their attacks as soon as possible. Using the bomb will save American lives, and that's all there is."

"What do the Germans know about this?" Alexander asked.

"Very little," Eisenhower admitted. "We told them we were going to intensify the bombing in the area and that there would necessarily be many civilian casualties. They accepted that."

Patton chuckled. "Gawd, are the Russians going to be surprised. I just hope we can someday drop one right down Stalin's throat." Burke noted to himself that Patton had quickly gotten over any reservations regarding the use of the bomb.

The discussion then focused on the matter of selecting a specific target. Alexander wondered whether conventional carpet bombing of an area wouldn't be as effective and less sinister than an atomic bomb. Ike agreed to a point but insisted that the shock value of a single atomic bomb would be so much more effective.

Within the Russian perimeter west of the Weser, there were three major areas of concentration. Ike reviewed the virtues of each and decided on the northernmost area and that the bombing would occur as soon as possible. The next morning if it could be done. All were in agreement that the sooner the terrible bomb was used, the more devastating the effect would be, as the current massive troop concentrations could easily disperse.

With that, the meeting began to break up. Burke was concerned. The generals had missed a point.

"General Eisenhower," he said, "may I speak?"

This earned him a deadly glare from Beetle Smith that told him whatever he was doing had better be worth it.

"About what?" asked Ike.

"Sir, it's about the Russian command psychology and how using the bomb might affect that."

Eisenhower, who had risen, sat back down and smiled slightly. "All right," he said and turned to the others, who had paused. "Gentlemen, before joining us Burke was General Marshall's resident expert on the Soviet Union and, most particularly, an expert on our antagonist, Josef Stalin. He is also the man who brought Marshall the warning that the Reds were going to attack the Potsdam column what seems an eternity ago."

Burke saw many eyes staring at him with surprise. Even Patton seemed respectful. "General," he began after taking a deep breath, "the Russian command structure is very tightly controlled. The Russians are taught to obey their orders and not to deviate from them. In the past, anyone who deviated in the slightest from Stalin's orders was dismissed, even executed."

Patton whistled. "What a nasty bastard. And he was our ally?"

Burke continued. "When their war with Germany started, most of the Russian generals were sycophants who had survived on their loyalty to Stalin, not because of their military abilities. Stalin is a pragmatist, so, when the defeats began to pile up, he replaced those toadies with real generals like Zhukov, but the psychology of the structure remains the same. You obey your orders, no matter what they are. Disobedience can be fatal, even if that disobedience results in victory. Stalin cannot stand the thought of a rival."

Ike leaned forward. "What will happen after the war to men like Zhukov?"

"Sir, Zhukov and others have been given considerable latitude in order to win the war against Hitler, and now against us. As a result, they have become personalities and heroes. In my opinion, they will either be banished or executed when their usefulness is over."

Patton laughed. "Shit, I think I prefer our method of retirement, even with the lousy pay."

After the chuckles stopped, Ike asked Burke just how that would affect their target selection.

"Sir, if you can take out their commanders as well as cause casualties, the survivors will be a leaderless mob until such time as Stalin is able to correct things. If the bomb is as good as it is supposed to be, that might be never."

"Burke," said Bradley, "are you suggesting we murder Zhukov and other leaders?"

"Yes, sir," he responded without hesitation.

"Why not?" chided Patton. "They're all soldiers, aren't they? Didn't we go after and kill Yamamoto in the Pacific? And didn't we spend some tense moments last December when it appeared that the Nazis were going to try and kill Eisenhower?"

Ike tapped the table with his pencil. "Brad, do we have a good idea where Zhukov is?"

Bradley nodded. "Yes. The OSS people we left behind have reported that he is with Chuikov and they are just east of Paderborn. We can't pin it down to a precise place, but we are pretty sure they are in the center cluster, not the northern one. It makes sense when you figure that the center is where Zhukov's old command is."

"Then," Ike said grimly, "it's decided. We hit the center group. Brad, see if you can get more specifics on Zhukov's possible location and convey them to Tibbetts. I still want them hit tomorrow, if possible. The sooner we kill Russians, the more Americans are saved."

The generals left the bunker, and Burke found he was almost alone. "Now you've gone and done it," said Godwin. "You've given yourself a place in the history books, at least the larger ones. Not bad for a clerk or scribe," he teased, "but do you really understand what you've caused?"

"I'm not certain," said Burke.

"To begin with, you've just been instrumental in determining the place where the weapon that will change war and history will be used."

"That I understood."

"But, by helping to change the target from the northern group to the middle one, you also just condemned men who were scheduled to live to instead die a horrible death, while others, whom Ike had previously determined would die, get to extend their lives. In short, you've played God, just like a real war leader. Rather much for a university professor, wouldn't you say?"

Burke walked up the stairs and into the night. It had gotten dark since the meeting started. He walked briskly to his tent. He would have to write down everything that had transpired at this meeting before his memory dimmed. Somewhat against regulations, he had been keeping a journal since that fateful night in Washington when the Russian colonel slipped him the message.

If the atomic bomb did work and wiped out the Russian command, his comments could have indeed affected history. What would Natalie think of what he had done? And, he thought, what about his future students? They would be told as well. What would their reaction be? Would they consider him a hero or a murderer? Suddenly, he had doubts.

He could hide behind the fact that the ultimate decision was Ike's, but his comments had affected the choice of where the most horrifying weapon in mankind's history would be used. He had the feeling that the date of August 6, 1945, was going to go down in history.

A MACABRE PREDICTABILITY developed regarding the Russian artillery barrages at Potsdam. Although infrequent, the bombardments always began during the night and shook Logan and his men out of their sleep, so that they spent the rest of the night either cringing from the shells or awaiting the infantry attack that they all knew would someday follow. With the fighting on the Weser coming to a head, it seemed logical that the Russians would soon decide to end the siege of Potsdam once and for all.

But the bombardments, although heavy, came at intervals. The shells would land all along the defenses and then the Russian artillerymen would walk their following rounds through the perimeter and in the general direction of the river. It was as if, lacking solid knowledge of specific targets, they were going to try to destroy everything. As before, American counterfire was limited to specific targets to conserve ammo and not give away the guns' locations. The American command wondered if the Russians had gotten more ammo or they were using up all they had.

By midafternoon it seemed apparent that this day's softening-up process would continue for a while, although the outposts had noted no signs of any major Russian troop movements in the direction of the American positions.

"We got us another lull," said Bailey. He was covered with dirt from earthshaking near misses, as were Logan and the others. "You gonna check?"

Logan was in agony. Were they safe? But could he leave his men?

"Lieutenant," snapped Bailey in a low voice the others couldn't hear, "get the fuck out there and find out. All of us want to know. You're not the only one who likes her."

Logan darted from the bunker and found one of his men's bicycles undamaged on the ground. He mounted and pedaled furiously to where Elisabeth and Pauli had been sheltered in the basement of a church. When he arrived, there was a crowd around the entrance and there were bloodied bodies on the ground.

"No," he said, and then he saw Lis and Pauli, bedraggled but unharmed, standing a short distance away. He dropped the bike and ran up to them, and they hugged.

"What happened?" he asked, although the answer was fairly obvious.

"Part of the roof collapsed under the shelling. It was terrible. The screams of the injured were awful and the blinding dust made helping them almost impossible. So many are dead. It was just like Berlin." She started to shake, and he held her again to calm her.

After a moment, Logan grabbed her arm and she pulled Pauli along. "Let's go."

"Where?" she sobbed.

"If I can't find anyplace else, I'll take you back to my bunker." At least, he thought wryly, the roof had held up so far. The sight of the ruined shelter confirmed his worst nightmare. The military bunkers were far better constructed than those for the civilians, and the carnage among nonmilitary personnel was bound to be awful.

The three of them ran, painfully aware that the Russians could begin shelling at any time. They were in the misleadingly calm eye of a military hurricane. Suddenly, Logan stopped and stood in amazement. An airplane was coming straight down the street at him. It was Ames the reporter in his Piper Cub. He had found a stretch of level ground and was planning to take off.

"He's leaving," yelled Logan. He ran directly in front of the slowly moving plane and waved. Ames, looking pale and confused by the interruption, stopped, but did not cut the engine.

"Get out of my way, soldier."

Logan opened the passenger door and grabbed Ames by the arm. "You're taking two people out of here."

"Bullshit, this plane is full."

Logan pulled his pistol, cocked it, and placed it next to Ames's skull. Ames paled and tried to pull back. With his free hand, Logan yanked on Ames's duffel bag and threw it on the ground. "I say this plane has room." Logan grabbed another sack and flung it to the ground.

"Hey," screamed Ames, "some of that stuff doesn't even belong to me."

"Tough shit. And don't move this plane when I take this gun off your head. If you even try, I'll put a bullet through you or that gas you got stored in the back. If it goes up, you'll be just another large grease fire."

Ames glanced back at the stack of five-gallon cans loaded for extra fuel, gulped, and nodded reluctant agreement. Logan picked up an unprotesting Elisabeth and pushed her into the plane. Then he handed her Pauli, and the boy settled in on Elisabeth's lap on the seat behind Ames.

"Now," Logan snarled at Ames, "get the fuck out of here."

A relieved Ames needed no further encouragement. Logan stepped away as Ames turned the little craft in the direction of the clear ground. Logan stared as Elisabeth looked at him through the small window. Neither attempted to say anything. He tried to memorize her pale and frightened face. It had all been so sudden, and one way or another, she and Pauli were actually leaving Potsdam.

The Piper Cub picked up speed and quickly lifted off until it was about fifty feet off the ground, then it began to settle back down. Logan screamed in horror, thinking it was going to crash, until it steadied at the ridiculously low altitude of only about twenty feet and headed toward the river. It was barely visible when he saw it turn left toward Berlin. He understood Ames's plan. The reporter was going to try to fly northwest toward the Danish border. That way he might stand a chance of staying out of the great battles to the west. As to the low altitude, it would help him stay invisible and avoid any conflicts he couldn't possibly win. Logan could only pray that Ames's skills as a pilot were up to the demands of flying at what was less than treetop height. He also prayed that he had done the right thing for Elisabeth and Pauli.

He heard footsteps pounding up to him. "I ought to court-martial your ass!" snarled an infuriated and livid Captain Dimitri. "That was a dumb fucking trick to pull."

Logan stood up. "Guess what, Captain, I don't really give a shit! I just hope I did the right thing for them and that maybe they'll have a chance to live. You saw what happened at the church. The civilians are going to die. Maybe we'll get lucky and become prisoners, but not them. Even if they survive the artillery, they're going to get butchered if we lose. If I saved them from that fate, then anything you have in mind for me is okay."

Dimitri stared at him, his anger quickly ebbing. "Go back to your bunker, Lieutenant," he managed to say. "We stay out here any longer and the Russians are going to start shelling again. We'll talk about it later. If there is a later, that is."

FIELD MARSHAL GEORGI Zhukov growled as the air-raid sirens went off again and then suddenly cut short, as if someone had pulled the plug. "What now?"

Chuikov put down a field phone and shrugged. "More American planes, comrade. Perhaps it's our turn to be bombed. Shall we go to a shelter?" They were in the basement of a ruined farmhouse.

"How many planes?" asked Zhukov. He waited a moment while Chuikov asked for and got the needed information. Great waves of American bombers had been attacking to the north. These were fairly ineffective attacks, as his tanks were hidden and not parked in tight rows. Even so, they did cause damage. He needed at least one more day to complete the allocation of scarce fuel among the vehicles to ensure a continuation of their attacks on the American positions.

"Just three," said Chuikov. "Probably those damned photo planes they send over every now and then. That is why the sirens cut out so quickly."

Zhukov accepted the comment and dismissed the planes as relatively unimportant. Once again he pored over the maps of the area and how they tied in with the complex plan for the next series of assaults. He would not let the Americans rest and recover, even though his own resources were severely limited.

"Look," someone yelled. "You can see them."

Curious, Zhukov stepped outside and stared upward. He could just barely make out the reflection on the distant belly of the plane. "What kind of pictures can they possibly take from that altitude?"

Chuikov laughed. "I have no idea, comrade Marshal, but should we not smile and wave? Or better, I shall have our soldiers expose themselves."

Zhukov smiled tolerantly at his protégé. "Not now. And didn't you say there were three planes? Where are the other two?"

A staff major was watching the sky with binoculars. "Two others peeled off a moment ago, sir. Oh, look, the bomber has dropped something."

Chuikov was puzzled. It couldn't be just one bomb, now could it? That made no sense at all.

Zhukov snatched the binoculars from the unprotesting major. He found the falling object fairly easily as it reflected light quite brightly. The plane was in a steep banking turn. Whatever the plane had dropped did look like it could be a bomb. But one bomb?

A feeling of sick dread seized him. What had he heard about the Americans and a secret weapon? A superbomb? The object seemed to grow as he watched it draw closer. He knew it was too late to flee.

At under two thousand feet in the sky, a second sun dawned with unprecedented fury. For many who saw it, whether they survived or not, it was the last thing their scorched eyes took in. Those farther away described it as a pink-white incandescent flare and an incredibly glowing orb. Almost immediately, there was a tremendous and deafening clap of thunder. It was followed by a howling, shrieking wind and a suffocating blast of heat.

Within a three-quarter-mile circle from the center of the explosion, everything died.

Outside the circle, the shock and heat destroyed structures and vehicles, started fires, and caused secondary explosions. The force took the debris it made and turned the most innocent of objects into lethal projectiles that seemed to seek out and penetrate screaming and terrified flesh. Above, the fireball turned into a churning black cloud that raised itself into the sky like a horrific, monstrous, living thing.

Almost two miles away, Suslov had been inside his tank, shifting supplies and ammunition. He shrieked when the light brilliantly illuminated him through the open hatches. Seconds later, he felt the tank lift up on its side as the shock wave slammed into it and flung him about helplessly inside. He felt something snap in his arm. With a crash, the tank righted itself and landed back down. Suslov screamed again as his shoulder smashed against the inside of the hull.

He waited a moment for the chaos to subside and for his breathing to become regular. What had happened? The most logical conclusion was that a bomb had landed nearby. Damn the spotters for letting a plane sneak in. And where the hell were Latsis and the others? And what on earth could be burning?

Cautiously nursing his broken arm, Suslov took several minutes to ease himself out the hatch and down onto the ground. The sights surrounding him were appalling. Bodies were everywhere, although some were twitching and trying to move or crawl. Despite the lack of fuel, many vehicles were on fire. A number of tanks were billowing black, greasy smoke, and ammunition was exploding everywhere. Worse and most frightening, he was in the shadow of a tower of flame and smoke that seemed to have engulfed everything in that direction. He froze where he stood, afraid to move.

"Latsis," he finally managed to call. "Popov, Martynov, where are you?" They had been outside when the explosion occurred. He called again, finally getting a whimper of a reply. He moved as quickly as he could without jarring his arm. He found his crew just behind the tank, where what looked like Latsis was squatting on the ground, bent over two other figures.

Latsis looked up and gestured him over. There was a great brown-and-black burn on his face, and his shirt had been torn off showing other burns as well. "We are here, comrade. Come and look at us."

Popov was clearly dead. A piece of wood had been driven through his skull. Young Martynov, if that was indeed him, was a horror. The skin had been burned entirely off his face and his teeth gleamed at them like a smiling horse. There were holes where his eyes should have been. Martynov kept trying to open and close his mouth as if he was trying to say something.

"Let me have your pistol," Latsis said, and Suslov handed it over. He placed it against Martynov's temple and pulled the trigger. "Good-bye, my friend," Latsis muttered. The explosion was puny in comparison with what had caused the devastation about them and no one noticed, even though there were others walking about, most of them in an apparent daze.

"At least we don't have to worry about Commissar Boris reporting us as malcontents," Latsis said, waving feebly to his left. "He's that smoking lump over there."

Latsis helped put Suslov's arm in a sling, but Suslov had nothing to help care for the other man's terrible burns. The pain must have been agonizing. Even so, Latsis made it back into the tank and tried to start it. If they could, they might be able to drive it a few miles away from this awful field of death before they ran out of fuel. They were not in luck. It would not start. The shock wave had caused too much damage. For the first time, Suslov noticed that some of the tank's paint had bubbled from the heat.

Latsis climbed out and shrugged. "I guess we walk."

Suslov looked about him. "Can we make it back to Russia?"

They looked at the sky, which had darkened even more as what looked like rain clouds moved in. "No," Latsis said. "And don't even think about walking. We are much too weak. I guess we stay here and wait for our future, comrade."

It began to rain. The drops were dirty, filled with specks of dark matter. Latsis said he felt dizzy and vomited.

Twenty miles to the west, Tolliver's men had grumbled when they received the order to stay in their holes and keep their heads down for a period of almost an hour. Since the order was not accompanied by any explanation, rumors ran wild, as did a litany of complaints. The most logical rumor was that a Commie ammo dump was going to be blown and the soldiers might get hit by flying shells. The craziest was that Jesus was going to come down from heaven on a shaft of light while riding a white horse. Tolliver put his money on the ammo dump. He had long since decided that Jesus was nowhere near the front lines.

Tolliver was in his foxhole, squatting on his haunches and facing the rear as ordered when the area was bathed with an unholy brilliance. His first thought was that the rumor about Jesus had come true. Then he realized that there had been an enormous explosion somewhere in the Russian area. He waited a few seconds and stood.

"Unbelievable," Tolliver muttered, and the soldiers nearby echoed him. The mushroom cloud was clearly visible as it formed and billowed on its way to the sky. Some of them actually saw the shock wave as it raced across the ground. Fortunately, by the time it hit them, it was a gust of air and virtually devoid of any power to injure. Even so, Tolliver called for a nose count to see if everyone was all right.

One GI was injured. The young PFC had caught a blast of light from a reflection off a mirror he'd had out to help him shave.

"I can't see, Lieutenant."

Tolliver and a medic checked the man over. "Can you see anything at all?" Tolliver asked as he looked in the boy's eyes. There was no apparent damage, but his skin did look a little pink and flushed.

The boy blinked. "A little, sir, around the edges. But there's a dark spot in the middle of my eye and I can't see through it."

The medic bandaged the boy's eyes and guided him back to the rear. Tolliver looked into the distance at the cloud and wondered just what kinds of hell the Russians were enduring. He had no idea what had actually caused the explosion, but he was certain that it had been a bomb and not some kind of accident or natural event like a volcano. After all, wasn't a bomb the best reason for the order to stay heads down?

Tolliver saw a vehicle about a mile away, in the Russian area. It looked like some kind of truck. From a distance, it seemed to move with exquisite slowness, but he realized it was going very quickly and was running all over the road as if the driver was in a panic. Or blind. Who the hell could blame him? Tolliver thought. The truck hit a rock and turned over.

For the first time, he felt a kind of sympathy for the Russians. What the hell was going on?

CHAPTER 30

Lieutenant David Singer simply showed up that evening at Logan's bunker. He looked a little pale, but had regained some lost weight and seemed otherwise healthy. He leaned his cane against the wall and grinned infectiously, like a kid who had just put something over on a teacher.

"David," said Logan as the others looked on, "aren't you supposed to be in the hospital?"

"Hospitals are for sick people. Tell me, do I look sick?"

"Let me rephrase the question. Did the hospital release you, or did you just take off?"

"What does it matter? I'm here, aren't I?"

Sergeant Bailey offered Singer a cup of coffee. "I think Lieutenant Logan is concerned because he is in so much deep shit with the captain for breaking rules that he doesn't want to get in any deeper."

Singer took a swallow and made a face. "This really tastes like hell. All right, I took off and Dimitri doesn't know I'm here. So what?"

Logan took a deep breath. "Why, David?"

"Guys, I wasn't joking when I said that hospitals are for sick people. There's a battle coming, and they don't need me moping around and getting in the way just because I lost twenty pounds the hard way. Besides, unless I've missed something, I'm still an officer in this man's army and I am reporting for duty. And I'm not going to tell the captain. I should also be honest and tell you I've been thinking it may be safer right here with you guys. The hospitals are marked with red crosses, but that hasn't stopped the Reds from shelling them."

"Why not tell Dimitri you're here, sir?" asked Bailey. "You afraid he'll send you back?"

"Because rumor has it he's so pissed at young Lieutenant Logan that he'd replace him with me, one arm or not. After all, I am senior to him in date of rank. Worse, there's the possibility that Dimitri would make me stay with him so as to keep me out of trouble, and that's not why I'm here."

"Okay," said Logan resignedly, "you're our little secret and just one more reason for Dimitri to crucify me. Now, what use can you be to us?"

At that moment, the thundering Russian barrage began again. For a second, Singer looked like he wanted to change his mind and return to the hospital, but he quickly settled down. "Maybe I can help with the radio. If nothing else, I can praise the Lord and pass the ammunition," he answered, mimicking the song that had been popular after Pearl Harbor.

"Hallelujah," said Logan, and he winced as a shell landed near. "Then get on the radio and find out what the hell is happening at the outposts. And David"—he grinned evilly—"don't drop it."

As darkness fell, they got word that the Russians were advancing and that there was a lot of armor headed in their direction. Shortly after, the men from the outposts snaked their way back through the trenches and tunnels, passing through on their way to the rear.

An engineer captain was the last to appear. He was stringing wire and had a detonator, and explained that an earlier line had been cut by the Russian artillery.

"Are all the men out, Captain?" Logan asked. He knew a lot of those people in the outposts.

"All that's coming out, buddy." With that, he twisted the detonator. A second later, the earth a half mile out in front of them lifted in a shower of dirt, destroying the now abandoned outposts. "Well, that's that. I can only hope there were some Commies in there when we blew it."

Logan agreed, but he also hoped there weren't any Americans alive in that hell.

He quickly stopped worrying about others and focused on himself and the bunker. The Russians were indeed coming. American artillery began firing back with everything they had, aiming for the roads the enemy armor had to use. There was no reason for either side to save anything for a tomorrow that might never come. American mortars soon began landing on presighted targets where the Russians had been observed. Soviet artillery picked up the pace and the explosions became deafening, with the vibrations shaking the ground and sucking the air out of the bunker. Worst were the rockets, the Katyushas, the Stalin Organs, which the Russians had not used on them in a while. Shrieking like banshees, the shells came down in hosts, having been launched dozens at a time. Wildly inaccurate, they were, however, devastating psychologically and saturated the area on which they impacted. Worse, they lit up the sky and announced that the main attack was coming.

Logan's bunker was one of a number that were placed at angles to provide enfilading and overlapping fire on an attacking force. As before, there was a pattern of tank traps in front of them and a number of lines of barbed wire; however, there wasn't enough wire. Getting quantities of it into Potsdam had proven a major problem. The area in front was mined as well, but, again, not enough mines had been flown in to really saturate the area and many of those had been destroyed by the artillery. The idea of dynamite had been General Miller's, and it did appear to have slowed the Russians down a little.

By now, the smoke and dust blown into the air obscured their night vision and limited their line of sight to an indistinct couple of hundred yards. American antitank guns and dug-in Shermans had opened fire, but on what? The air outside was filled with flying metal and other objects, and it was inevitable that some would find their way in through the bunker's firing slits, causing cuts and bruises.

"Aw, crap," muttered Bailey, "look what's happening to the tank traps."

Blood was trickling down Logan's face, and he plucked a small piece of metal out of his cheek. He tucked it into a pocket, insanely thinking it would be a nice souvenir. Trying to keep as small as possible, he looked out and quickly understood his sergeant's dismay. The dirt walls of the tank traps were collapsing. They had all been afraid of that possibility. Almost surrounded as they were by the river and the lakes, the water table was very close to the surface; thus, when the earth was damp and muddy, it became very unstable. The shelling had loosened the walls of the traps, and now they were falling in and filling the ditches. Could a tank get through? They would soon find out.

"Tank," yelled Crawford. "Jesus Christ, what the fuck is that?"

An iron monster emerged from the smoke and darkness. It seemed twice the size of any tank they had ever seen before. Logan watched in shock as it moved slowly forward. Infantry huddled around it, but they were quickly swept away by the storm of metal. The tank crept closer. The main gun looked larger than anything Logan had ever seen in his life. A Stalin tank, he thought. It had to be a Josef Stalin model, as if that was important. An antitank shell hit the tank's turret and bounced off. The Stalin was impervious to them.

Like an animal, the tank was testing the ground. The collapsing trap had it confused. The turret turned and seemed to see the bunker only fifty yards away. It fired and the bunker shook from the impact. Someone screamed. Logan picked himself up and took another look at the tank. It fired again. This time, the shell hit the edge of a firing slit and blew it apart, sending debris flying around inside. Now the slit was an open window and there was screaming from inside the bunker.

The tank moved forward. It felt for the slope of the collapsed trap. Slowly, it lowered its bulk into the hole and almost disappeared.

"Get me a bazooka," Logan screamed. The tank would be on them in a minute if it was able to climb out of the hole.

Bailey handed him a *panzerfaust,* the single-shot German antitank rocket weapon. It wasn't a bazooka, but he had heard it was better, and there were a number of them in the bunker. The tank's turret was now plainly visible as it slowly emerged. Logan laid the tube on his shoulder, aimed, fired, and watched as the rocket's shell hit the front armor of the tank and bounced off. He yelled and asked for another, but Bailey was down. The side of his head was open and he could see the sergeant's brains. Logan wanted to gag, but there wasn't time. The tank was out of the hole and beginning to climb over the bunker. They were going to be squashed like bugs and buried alive.

"Here," said Singer with surprising calmness as he handed Logan another *panzerfaust.* "Try for a belly shot."

The ruined firing slit was almost all blocked by the bulk of the Russian tank as it began to churn its way onto the top of the bunker. Did its crew think everyone inside the bunker was dead? Perhaps they hadn't even felt the first rocket when it glanced off.

Logan backed away from the slit. The tank was actually too close for him to fire safely. Tough shit. He closed his eyes and squeezed the trigger. The rocket roared forward and pierced the less heavily armored belly of the Stalin and exploded inside it. The ammunition inside the tank began to detonate and hot metal shrieked into the bunker while the force of the explosions threw men about.

The tank still had enough impetus, or perhaps the driver was yet alive, so that it actually made it to the roof of the bunker, which began to settle under its immense weight.

Logan was on the floor. His arm hurt like it was on fire and his leg was bent at an impossible angle with bone sticking out from his thigh. There was a sticky wetness on his face and he knew it was his own blood. There was little pain from his leg and he realized he was going into shock.

As consciousness faded, he was dimly aware of a couple of things. First, that the explosions outside had reached a new crescendo, as if that were even possible, and second, that the earthen roof above him was collapsing and would soon crush him.

Last, as he felt someone pulling on him, he heard the sound of someone else screaming in terror for his mother. As darkness overcame him, he recognized the voice as his.

BAZARIAN TOOK THE reports of the assault on Potsdam in stride. He had expected heavy casualties and he was not disappointed. While he had hoped that the Stalin tanks would penetrate the defenses of Potsdam, the fact that they had failed did not deter him. The sudden appearance of the American bombers had stopped the assault as the B-25s, flying at nearly treetop level, dropped their loads on the battle below. In some cases, they went so far as to bomb their own lines in order to stop the Red armor. It had worked. Almost all the Russian tanks had been destroyed, along with that obnoxious pig of a Russian who led them. Then, bombs gone, the bombers returned to strafe the Russian positions with their machine guns, again from absurdly low altitude.

However, it was the napalm that had really halted the attack. When the bombers departed, the fighters arrived in swarms and dropped scores of liquid-fire bombs that burned the Russian infantry and incinerated the crews of the remaining tanks. He had heard of the existence of the weapon, but had never expected to see it.

Even so, he was confident that the next attack would succeed. The Americans had nothing left with regard to physical defenses. They had all been blown to pieces by the combination of artillery, Russian tanks, and American bombs. He would use his infantry in waves to overwhelm what was left. By assiduously collecting stray units as he had done with the armor, he still had a force of nearly fifty thousand men. While many were inferior soldiers and virtually all were reluctant warriors, they would still go forward on his orders, which he had told their officers came directly from Moscow. Stalin wanted Potsdam eliminated. Would you deny that to Stalin? None would. Potsdam would fall.

Of more concern to him were the confused stories he was hearing about the battles to the west. While it was common knowledge that Zhukov had been stalled in his campaign to take Antwerp, some catastrophe had apparently befallen his armies. Some idiotic rumors even said that entire Soviet armies had been destroyed, wiped out, and that both Zhukov and Chuikov were missing. Impossible.

Yet something had definitely gone horribly, terribly wrong in that area by the Weser. Thus, it would be best if he eliminated the problem of Potsdam and prepared his army to assist in what was rapidly becoming a general retreat.

There was a knock on the door to the room he was using as an office. "Yes."

A nervous orderly told him he had a visitor. A visitor? Bazarian paled when he saw that it was a captain from the NKVD, a short, stocky, swarthy man with an angry expression and a briefcase. Despite the difference in their ranks, Bazarian knew real fear. What did the NKVD want of him? He stood to greet his "visitor" while the orderly closed the door to give them privacy.

"Bazarian?" the man said. He had a strange accent and pronounced the name with difficulty.

"*Da,*" Bazarian responded. Yes.

The officer smiled and reached into the briefcase. When his hand emerged, there was a pistol in it and he fired twice at point-blank range. The bullets struck Bazarian in the chest, lifted him up and back over his chair. He crumpled on the floor and lay still.

The NKVD officer replaced his pistol and calmly walked out of the room. Outside, he ignored the looks of shock and dismay on the faces of Bazarian's staff. What, they wondered, had their general done? Why had he been executed? Would they be next? As soon as he passed, they all bolted and ran away. Nobody checked on the general.

The stolen jeep with the Russian unit markings painted over with crude NKVD insignia waited a few yards away. Two uniformed Russian soldiers sat in the front. Tony the Toad climbed into the backseat and sat straight, looking forward. The driver started up and they drove down the road.

When they were out of sight, Tony began to shake. "Jesus Christ, Jesus, Jesus."

"Quit praying," said Vaslov. "Did you get him?"

"Twice in the chest. Jesus, I didn't think I could do it. I don't speak any fucking Russian. All I did was act like that shit who killed the Jew boys, and ask for Bazarian. I snapped my fingers, and they almost shit themselves showing me where he was. It was like I had the plague and they wanted to get rid of me."

The late Joe Baker would have been proud. They had no idea what impact the shooting of Bazarian would have on the battle for Potsdam, but he had the feeling they had accomplished something really good.

"Enough," said Anton. "Now let's find a place to hide these uniforms."

TOLLIVER'S FIRST IMPRESSION of the nightmare land was that it was some kind of hideous modern landscape painting by some psychotic artist in which everything was done in black. The trees were black, the grass was black, the vehicles were black, and worse, the bodies were all blackened and shriveled. Maybe it was more like some medieval painting of hell he'd seen in a college art class.

His jeep was the third in the column that drove slowly toward where the atomic bomb—they now knew its name—had been detonated. The first jeep contained a couple of scientists with a machine called a Geiger counter that supposedly told them it was safe to go on. Safe from what? Radiation, whatever the hell that was. The second jeep carried some mid-level brass from Ike's headquarters, and Tolliver and his men in the following jeeps were along to provide security. He had been told that a number of other columns were going to try to penetrate the area and might need protection.

They didn't. The only Russians remaining were vast numbers of the dead and the dying. Those who could still move and who hadn't already surrendered had fled to the east, leaving behind a scene of catastrophe unparalleled in scope. Tolliver had never seen so many dead bodies and so many ruined vehicles in one area before. He now realized that it was true—an entire Russian army had indeed been destroyed by this atomic bomb. Someday, he might feel truly sorry for them, but not now. He thought of dead Holmes and so many others whose lives were wasted by a war that, in his opinion, hadn't had to happen.

A scientist in the lead jeep signaled a right turn, and the column obediently followed. Tolliver saw that they were skirting the actual center of the blast, now referred to as "ground zero." If the bodies strewn about were any measure of the danger they were avoiding by detouring around ground zero, it was okay by him. This was yet another sight he would never forget and never be able to describe. Black death, black fire, black earth, and now the black stench of ruined bodies rotting in the summer sun. He noticed that birds were eating the dead. What effect would radiation have on them?

Someone in the second jeep yelled out that Zhukov was probably in there, in the center of this mess. If he was, thought Tolliver, he wasn't going to be found and he sure as hell wasn't coming out.

As they slowly circled ground zero they began to encounter survivors. Many of those trapped between ground zero and the American lines had already surrendered, while these pitiful remnants had been trying to make it east to supposed safety. The only thing was, they weren't going to make it. Their wounds and burns were ghastly. The flesh had been destroyed, and some of the things crawling on the ground could scarcely be recognized as human.

The column did find signs of attempted mercy. Some few Russian doctors had set up hospitals, which had been overrun by the numbers of wounded.

Tolliver saw a light colonel named Burke leave his jeep and talk to a Russian doctor. The colonel then got on the radio and delivered an emphatic message. Tolliver caught only a few words but he got the gist of it: send help fast. Tolliver also noted that this Burke looked quite shaken.

They drove on a little farther. They stopped when they saw a handful of men who appeared to be relatively unharmed. A scientist got out and waved his magic wand over them and said they were safe to approach but not to touch. The brass got out and Tolliver tagged along.

The Russians were pale and covered with sores. Their eyes looked at the Americans with utter helplessness. The Americans might have been the enemy, but the Russians were in no shape to fight—or to surrender. They just sat or lay there. Tolliver leaned down to see if one of them was alive or dead. His face was all burned up and the skin had peeled off in gobs.

"Don't touch," said the scientist, and Tolliver withdrew his hand like a shot. "Radiation sickness. Don't take a chance."

A few feet away, Burke leaned over and said something in Russian to a soldier who tried to focus on them. The soldier managed to mutter a response, and then began coughing.

"What'd he say, sir?" Tolliver asked.

"He said his friend died an hour ago and he will die soon as well. He said his name is Suslov and we should pray for him."

With that, Burke began to shake and tears ran down his face. It was just too awful to even begin to comprehend.

Tolliver tried to be helpful. He walked over and, instinctively and in total disregard of the difference in their ranks, put his hand on the other man's shoulder. "Hey, Colonel, don't take it so hard. It's not as if this was your fault or something."

FIVE DAYS AFTER the massive assault on Potsdam, two battalions of the 82nd Airborne Division parachuted onto the runways of Berlin's Gatow Airport and secured it. There was little resistance, only scattered sniper fire, which the airborne soldiers quickly eliminated. Additional drops were made and work began immediately on filling in the craters so that at least one runway would be ready for planes to take off and land. All this occurred while additional paratroops continued to descend from the sky. By nightfall, the entire division was on the ground and had linked up with the defenders of Potsdam, who had sent a strong patrol to Gatow.

Early the next morning, C-47 transports began to arrive with supplies, medical personnel, and additional soldiers to protect the expanding perimeter. One of the first planes carried General Omar Bradley and a handful of his staff.

Bradley had not announced that he was coming, so no one was waiting for him at Gatow. That neither surprised nor disturbed him. He was certain his men at Potsdam had more important things to do than arrange a ceremony for him. He and two of his staff hitched rides to Potsdam from an astonished young private.

"Shit," said General Miller as he ran out to greet Bradley. "You could have warned me you were coming." He snapped to attention and saluted. Bradley returned the salute. The two men then shook hands and, spontaneously, embraced warmly. "Good to see you anyhow, Brad," Miller said.

"Good to see you too, Puff. What on earth have you done with this lovely little town?" he said half jokingly. "And what have you done to your head?" he added, commenting on the bandage on Miller's scalp.

Inwardly, Bradley was appalled by the devastation. Few buildings still stood, and the ground was pocked with so many craters that it looked like a moonscape. Broken vehicles were everywhere, as were signs that showed where graves had been dug. Soldiers' graves were marked by crude crosses with dog tags nailed to them, while civilians had been buried in mass graves that were now large mounds on the ground. Worse, almost everyone seemed to be at least slightly wounded.

"It was a helluva fight, Brad. I got off easy."

Bradley took Miller by the elbow. "Let's go take a look around and talk about it."

Typically, the first thing Bradley wanted to see was the wounded. He toured the hospitals and talked to the men for several hours. He was gratified to see the fresh medical personnel moving in to take over from others who looked like they were dead on their feet. As always, he was sincerely moved, and they responded to him. He noticed German and American wounded were together while the Russians were separate. After all, they were still at war and they were still prisoners even though they didn't look like they had any fight left in them. The Russians smiled and nodded at everyone who passed by.

It was much later before he had a chance to sit down with Miller and talk over the situation.

"I lost a third of my men dead and wounded in that last attack, Brad. I really thought they were going to smash their way in. They had those damned big tanks and there wasn't anything we could do to stop them. Behind those tanks they had numbers equivalent to almost a whole field army. We would have killed a lot of them, but they might have killed all of us. When the air force came and started bombing from such low height, I knew the Reds were in for it."

Bradley chuckled. "Some of the higher brass wanted to bomb from greater altitude for safety's sake. The pilots and crews wouldn't hear of it. Many of those boys who bombed the Reds were the same ones who dropped supplies to you during the siege. I think they kind of adopted you people and were angry at the thought of losing you."

Miller nodded appreciatively. "Well, whatever the reason, it worked, even though they had to drop their bomb loads on our own lines and caused some casualties among our troops. It was war and it had to be done. And I have never seen anything as terrible as napalm."

"Then," said Bradley sadly, "you haven't seen what the atomic bomb did."

"I guess not."

"Puff, it was as bad as anything I've ever dreamed. We will never know the total butcher's bill for that first bomb, but it looks like about thirty thousand Russian dead and another eighty thousand wounded. Worse, there are at least a hundred thousand more suffering from various levels of radiation sickness. Many of them will die within the next few weeks and months and there's nothing we can do to treat it. The second bomb, dropped on Koniev's troops, was just about as bad.

"Even with precautions, we still had a couple of hundred of our boys killed or wounded by the bomb. Some were blinded by the flash, while others suffered broken bones from falls and crashes. Saddest were the handful of our soldiers who got too close afterward and got radiation poisoning. We also lost three brave OSS men who pinpointed Zhukov and died for their efforts."

"What about Zhukov and Chuikov?"

"Not found and presumed dead, and Koniev is reported to be badly wounded. There are areas near the center of the explosion that we won't be able to enter for a long time, and only then with protective clothing on. The net result is that the First Belorussian Army Front no longer exists, and Koniev's First Ukrainian Front has been decimated. It's as if my entire Twelfth Army Group had been destroyed."

Miller shuddered. "It's awful. But it's ending the war, isn't it?"

"It appears that way. Let me give you a rundown. The Germans and

British in the Netherlands are now south of Hamburg and have linked up with the British airborne who retook Bremen. Alexander has Dempsey's British troops moving south to meet Patton, who has crossed the Weser and is running free in the Russians' rear. He's approaching Brunswick if he hasn't taken it already. There's very little resistance. When our two armies do meet up, there will likely be a very empty bag, as so many of the Russians were either killed or wounded by the blasts or have already surrendered. The experts were right. Without their senior commanders, the Russians don't know what to do.

"Rokossovsky is pulling his Second Belorussian Front back as quickly as he can."

"Will we stop?"

Bradley grinned. "Did the Russians? No, we will continue on. There have been some political changes. Truman managed to inform the Soviets that we have other bombs and told them we wouldn't hesitate to use them on any target we wanted, and that included Leningrad and Moscow. The air force thinks they are both out of reach and too dangerous, but the Russians don't know that. According to overtures from Molotov, the Russians are willing to return to their prewar boundaries east of Poland if we'll leave them to withdraw in peace. I think those terms will be accepted."

"I think I may have fought my last campaign," Miller said.

"I understand, Chris. Maybe I have too. I mentioned we've been talking with Molotov. Well, no one's heard from Stalin for the last few days. There's a rumor that there's been a coup and he's been toppled. He may even be dead."

Miller chuckled. "That'd be nice."

"You won't get an argument from me, Chris. It also seems that the Japs may have gotten the message. They understand how much we hate them and have figured that if we'd use the bomb on white Europeans, we'd have no qualms about bombing their cities and their culture into ashes along with their yellow skins. They may be as racially bigoted as we are, but they're not stupid. It may be too early, but we'll see."

Miller had mixed emotions about the Japanese. While he wanted no more war, he wondered if they, like the Germans, might get off too lightly considering the atrocities both nations had committed.

Bradley continued. "Where's your German tank commander? I'd like to meet him."

"Von Schumann left yesterday for Hamburg. Too many of the civilians he had been protecting were killed in the battle, and he was having a hard time dealing with it. That and the fact that the man is desperate to find his family."

The thought saddened Bradley. He could barely imagine the torment of someone who had to search a ravaged continent for loved ones who might be dead. Silently, he wished von Schumann well.

"One more thing," Bradley asked. "Are those three boys still under wraps?"

"The soldier and the two refugees who shot Bazarian? Sure, but why?"

Bradley shook his head. "For some reason, the higher-ups want it still believed that a Russian NKVD officer tried to kill an Armenian general. The OSS says that Bazarian will survive his wounds and has linked up with several thousand Armenian soldiers who are going crazy with anger at the Russians. The OSS likes that and thinks it might contribute to the further instability of the Soviet Union. Ours not to judge. Give our boy a medal and a promotion and order him not to talk. As to the two Poles, they can immigrate to the United States if they swear to keep what they did a secret."

They turned as a couple of young men approached them and saluted. They wore the insignia of war correspondents.

"How're you doing, boys?" asked Miller.

"We're doing fine, General," said the older of the two. "We're gonna give this place and these boys the story they deserve."

"That's great."

"But, sir. We're puzzled. What happened to the guy who was here?"

"Oh," said Miller, "you mean Ames. I understand he flew out about a week ago. You mean nobody's heard from him?"

"Not a peep, sir. Damn, that's a shame."

CHAPTER 31

The calendar on Harry Truman's desk told him it was January 7, 1946. The wars had been over for several months now and it was time to commence the rebuilding.

Truman looked up at the distinguished-looking man who still looked a little ill at ease in civilian clothes. However, he looked refreshed and healthy. A few weeks' paid vacation in Florida on the order of the president will do that.

"Please be seated, General Marshall, we have so much that needs to be accomplished and so little time."

Marshall did as requested. "I know, sir."

"Have you considered? Will you serve as my secretary of state?" Stettinius had resigned to return to the private sector. "To be frank, General, I had considered nominating Jim Byrnes, but he's been a little too controversial in the past. For this job we need a man of integrity, and that, sir, is you."

Marshall flushed slightly at the compliment. "I don't know if I deserve all that, but I will serve and I will do my best."

Truman could not help but be relieved. "Excellent."

"I do have some plans for the rebuilding of Europe and Asia, but they will be expensive."

"General, the price of peace cannot be as expensive as the cost of war. This time we must win that peace. What can you tell me now?"

"To begin with, Mr. President, we have been able to feed just about everyone in Europe and Japan. Nobody's getting fat, but there's food and people will survive. In Asia, however, there are parts of China where we cannot go because of the fighting between the Communists and the Nationalists."

"The Nationalists are losing, aren't they?"

"Yes, sir, they are."

"We may be backing the wrong horse in that war. What about Russia?"

"The situation in the Soviet Union is utter chaos. With Stalin confirmed dead—Beria shot him—there are little wars all over the place. The Baltic republics have proclaimed their independence, and Marshal Rokossovsky has suddenly remembered that he's Polish. He's leading a Polish army allied with the Czechs and Hungarians to defend those three countries, even though they sometimes hate each other, against Russia. There's a strong possibility the Ukraine will break away and join him. In the south of the Soviet Union, the republics of Armenia, Georgia, and Kazakhstan have, temporarily at least, put away their ethnic hatreds and are fighting a common enemy, Russia. That madman, Bazarian, is in charge in their war against Koniev's Russians."

Truman looked puzzled. "Bazarian? Isn't he the man who was shot by one of our boys and a couple of refugees? What's happening with them?"

"Well, sir, thanks to your decision to reconstitute the OSS, we have places for all three of them. They've shown a real knack for more than survival under adverse circumstances, so we're keeping them on. In return for their secrecy, they get real good government jobs."

"Speaking of secrecy," Truman muttered, "I wish we could have done something about that Burke and his wife and the book they've written."

"In hindsight, sir, it was definitely a mistake to discharge him so quickly. Of course, his wife's resignation from the State Department couldn't have been helped. On the other hand, he tells the story of his involvement in the war and the decision to use the first bomb fairly accurately. He was not a witness to the decision to drop the second on Koniev's army or the third on the Japanese at Hiroshima that finally did end the war. I don't think there'll be very many repercussions. Now that we have some additional atomic bombs, perhaps it will be good to keep reminding people."

"General, I'm not too sure anybody needs reminding. Thousands of people are still dying and much of the Weser River north to the ocean is polluted with radioactivity. The Germans are angry as hell, but that's tough shit as far as I'm concerned. After all, they're the ones who started the war, along with the Japs, that is. We are the world's only nuclear power and we should be able to keep it that way for the foreseeable future."

"I'm not concerned about the Germans' anger, Mr. President. We saved their country and they know it. Now that the war-crimes trials are about to start, I think they just want to distract public attention from that issue."

Truman agreed. Some of the big fish in the Nazi regime, like Goering and von Ribbentrop, were scheduled to go on trial. Doenitz and Speer, as leaders in the new German government, were exempt. This did not make Truman comfortable. At least they had gotten confirmation that Hitler and Goebbels were dead, and that Himmler had killed himself. Some others were missing, but they would be found sooner or later. Rumors had them heading for Argentina, but he'd have Marshall read the riot act to the Argentines. They'd cooperate or suffer the consequences.

They spoke of a few other things, like Churchill's replacement as prime minister by Clement Attlee. Attlee was angry that the bombs had been based in England. Too dangerous, he'd said. They should have been told. Screw him, Truman had replied, although more diplomatically.

As he left, Marshall turned. "At least the boys are coming home. We have that to be thankful for."

"Yes, we do," Truman said softly.

Alone for a moment, Truman speculated on his future. Once he had been terrified at the thought of being president. Now he realized he liked it and had thrived on it. The next election would be in 1948 and he would have to begin planning and campaigning for it if he was going to be able to continue in office. He liked Marshall's ideas and wanted desperately to see them implemented. He was especially intrigued by the plan to provide money for GIs to go to college. Slowing the return of millions of military personnel to the workforce would alleviate unemployment and possibly enable the nation to avoid another depression.

Some people told Harry Truman his political career had ended when the war did. Talk like that simply made him even more combative than he usually was. Hell, hadn't he won the war against Germany, Japan, and now Russia? He was confident he would win in '48 against whomever the Republicans sent against him, and now he damn well wanted to. He wanted to wipe away the stain of being what some called an accidental president. He had long ago decided he liked power and the opportunity to do something about his world.

But Marshall had been right about one thing. The boys were indeed coming home, and thank God.

THE EASY, ROLLING motion of the train was restful and allowed him to think. He had gotten on in Pittsburgh after a first train had taken him there from New York. Even though it had been jammed with passengers, his uniform and the fact that he had lost so much weight that he looked like a prison-camp refugee had prompted a middle-aged civilian to give him a seat. That he limped didn't hurt either. He was feeling a lot better, but he still needed rest and couldn't put weight on his leg for very long.

A couple of his fellow passengers wanted to talk about the war, but he rebuffed them politely. There was still just too much to think about. He had dreamed of this homecoming for so very long and now it was finally going to happen. But at what price? Sometimes the pain of all he had lost overwhelmed him. Not the physical pain—that was endurable and fading—but the inner pain and the memories of faces lost and voices never to be heard again.

Logan shifted his still aching leg into what he hoped would be a more comfortable position and tried to review what had happened to him. He would probably never remember the last few minutes in the bunker when, somehow, the one-armed Singer had dragged him through the collapsing ruin and then through the falling bombs to another shelter where a medic had given him first aid.

From there it was on to the field hospital where he spent the next several days in and out of delirium while doctors tried to save his shattered leg. They were successful. However, he would limp for a long while, and would probably always be able to predict rain, but the doctors said he would someday be able to walk normally, perhaps even run. He wanted to thank Singer, but Singer had been evacuated early and returned stateside. He'd gotten a letter that said Singer and his wife were together and that he and Marsha were going to start a family. Singer invited him to visit them in Boston, where Marsha had gone back to school. Jack wrote back and said sure, but in a while. Maybe a long while, since he would be finishing his own schooling as well, courtesy of a tuition payment plan developed by General Marshall.

How many friends had he lost? Bailey was dead, as were Dimitri and Crawford. Why them and not him? It would be a long time before he figured that out, if ever. The doctors and a chaplain told him it was normal to wonder about the luck of the draw and, no, he shouldn't feel guilty about being spared. He agreed. It was just luck that he was alive, and not divine intervention. He had a life to live and would live it without guilt. At least he could begin to purge his guilt when he got over his feeling of emptiness and pain.

Jack recalled General Bradley and General Miller visiting him in the Potsdam hospital and telling him everything was going to be okay. Later, he'd gotten a Silver Star directly from Eisenhower. He wasn't certain exactly what he had done except destroy that tank, but he accepted it. Singer got a Bronze Star for saving him.

The worst pain was the fact that Lis and Pauli had disappeared, which left him to deal with the reality that he'd made the wrong decision. America had won the battle and the war; thus, safety for them would have been in Potsdam and not on a small plane.

When he was finally shipped to England and was better able to communicate, he had tried to locate her, but to no avail. Some nice ladies at the Red Cross were helpful, but they had nothing on her or the boy. They tried to be kind and told him that there were many millions of unregistered people wandering all over Europe, and that she might yet be one of them. Or she might have gone to a refugee camp and the information had just not reached London. As yet, he was told, there was no central file of those now referred to as displaced persons.

On a hunch he had tried to find the correspondent, Ames. A sympathetic person at Reuters News Service had checked and found that Ames had never shown up either, which further devastated him.

Logan felt the train begin to slow. They were approaching Port Huron and, for him, home. Until the inner pain went away, it would be an empty home.

The train slowed to a stop. He put on his overcoat and, with his duffel bag over his shoulder, gingerly stepped out into the brittle cold of the early February day. There were crystals of ice in the air, and he felt them redden his cheeks. The train station was by the St. Clair River where it emptied into Lake Huron, and was probably colder than a lot of other places in the area. But it was also within walking distance of home.

The station was empty. What the hell? Hadn't they gotten his telegram? He hadn't expected a brass band, but it would have been nice for someone to have met him. He shrugged and started to walk.

"Hey, soldier."

The voice came from behind him and froze him. He stopped and paled. He couldn't breathe. He turned slowly. The hair was still dark, but it was clean and longer. The face was slightly fuller, but it was still the same face and the smile was the same one he'd recalled every night since Potsdam.

"Aren't you going to say hello?" she asked.

His voice came out a barely controlled whisper. "Lis?" The duffel bag dropped to the ground with an unheard thud. "How?" he asked as she came into his arms. "I couldn't find you, Lis. I tried so hard."

She smiled and hugged him tightly. Her eyes were glistening. In a rush she told him that Ames put down to refuel and crash-landed. He was badly injured, and she cared for him until he died.

"We stayed with some German civilians who were absolute saints. Finally, we were picked up by German soldiers who passed us through to the Allies."

She pulled back and smiled up at him. "Would you believe the first Allies I saw were Canadians? They flew us to Canada so fast you wouldn't believe it. Since then, I've been trying to find you. I located your family rather easily thanks to the note you gave me so long ago, and kept in contact with them, waiting for you to show up. They said you were wounded but on your way home and couldn't be reached. I moved in with them last week to wait for you. I've been sleeping on their couch ever since. They really are nice people."

He recalled his parents' house as being fairly cramped, and he laughed at the thought of Lis on the small couch. "Where's Pauli?"

"In Toronto. My relatives are going to adopt him. He's very happy. He's starting to forget the horrors."

"Good for him. Ah, Lis, where's my family?"

She released him and stood back, still holding his hands. "That was my idea. They're waiting at home with all the relatives and friends you ever had and half the food in the world. I said I wanted the chance to meet you alone at the station and see you first."

"Why?"

"Well, dear Jack, we had something very special and wonderful in Germany. I wanted to know if it was still special for you. I hope to God it is, but if it isn't, I'll understand and go away quietly. This way neither of us has to be hurt too much or be embarrassed."

He took her face in his hands. "Lis, I've thought about you every day and every night. I still can't believe this is real. No, you're not going anywhere without me. *Special* doesn't begin to describe how I feel about you. I love you."

He grabbed her again and held her tightly and listened to her say that she loved him as well. If it was a dream, he knew he didn't want to ever wake up.

A car drove by and the driver gleefully honked at the couple embracing in the cold. They didn't hear it. Nor did they see the dozens of people running down the road toward them.

ACKNOWLEDGMENTS

∎

This is my fifth alternate history novel, all published by Random House's Ballantine division, and I hope there will be many more. History has taken so many twists and turns that there is no lack of intriguing alternate history plots, only a lack of time to write them. My personal list of possible what-ifs is extensive and I suppose that is true of other writers of the genre. As they say: so many books, so little time.

I would like to thank my wife, Diane, my daughter, Maura, and all the other friends and family who have supported me and even made suggestions. I would also like to thank Ryan Doherty at Ballantine for his advice and patience, and for putting up with my sometimes warped sense of humor.

And finally, a word to my young grandsons, Quinn and Brennan. Sorry, but you're still way too young to read my books.

ROBERT CONROY is a semiretired business and economic history teacher living in suburban Detroit. This is his fifth alternate history novel.

S